P9-CQC-700

*He kissed as if he meant
to conquer her . . .*

Eliza could only stare back. He'd kissed her until her brain melted and her tongue turned to lead. Good heavens, she wished he'd do it again.

"Eliza—" He stopped and cleared his throat. "Miss Cross, that went further than I planned," he finally said, his voice very low and still rough with want.

His hands drifted to rest on her hips. He put his mouth next to her ear. "Should I apologize for what happened?"

The tiniest shake of her head.

His lips touched the sensitive skin behind her ear. "May I call on you?"

"Yes," she whispered.

Eliza gazed up at him, wondering if he could tell from looking at her that she was about to fall headlong in love . . .

Also by Caroline Linden

MY ONCE AND FUTURE DUKE

SIX DEGREES OF SCANDAL
LOVE IN THE TIME OF SCANDAL
ALL'S FAIR IN LOVE AND SCANDAL (novella)
IT TAKES A SCANDAL
LOVE AND OTHER SCANDALS

THE WAY TO A DUKE'S HEART
BLAME IT ON BATH
ONE NIGHT IN LONDON
I LOVE THE EARL (novella)

YOU ONLY LOVE ONCE
FOR YOUR ARMS ONLY
A VIEW TO A KISS

A RAKE'S GUIDE TO SEDUCTION
WHAT A ROGUE DESIRES
WHAT A GENTLEMAN WANTS

WHAT A WOMAN NEEDS

ATTENTION: ORGANIZATIONS AND CORPORATIONS
HarperCollins books may be purchased for educational, business, or sales promotional use. For information, please e-mail the Special Markets Department at SPsales@harpercollins.com.

An Earl Like You

⤙ THE WAGERS OF SIN ⤚

Caroline Linden

AVONBOOKS

An Imprint of HarperCollinsPublishers

This is a work of fiction. Names, characters, places, and incidents are products of the author's imagination or are used fictitiously and are not to be construed as real. Any resemblance to actual events, locales, organizations, or persons, living or dead, is entirely coincidental.

AN EARL LIKE YOU. Copyright © 2018 by P. F. Belsley. All rights reserved. Printed in the United States of America. No part of this book may be used or reproduced in any manner whatsoever without written permission except in the case of brief quotations embodied in critical articles and reviews. For information, address HarperCollins Publishers, 195 Broadway, New York, NY 10007.

First Avon Books mass market printing: September 2018

Print Edition ISBN: 978-0-06-267294-0
Digital Edition ISBN: 978-0-06-267295-7

Cover design by Guido Caroti
Cover illustration by Gregg Gulbronson
Cover photography by Michael Frost Photography

Avon, Avon & logo, and Avon Books & logo are registered trademarks of HarperCollins Publishers in the United States of America and other countries.

HarperCollins is a registered trademark of HarperCollins Publishers in the United States of America and other countries.

FIRST EDITION

18 19 20 21 22   QGM   10 9 8 7 6 5 4 3 2 1

If you purchased this book without a cover, you should be aware that this book is stolen property. It was reported as "unsold and destroyed" to the publisher, and neither the author nor the publisher has received any payment for this "stripped book."

To everyone who's ever felt plain, ordinary, and not special in any way. You are special, and uniquely wonderful.

Acknowledgments

Writing a book can seem like a lonely endeavor, an author hunched over her laptop typing away. In reality, it takes a whole crew of people to produce a book. My fervent thanks to Rebecca Smartis, who beta-read this manuscript and offered invaluable suggestions for improvement; to my incredible editor, Lyssa Keusch, who always makes my books better, and Priyanka Krishnan, her assistant editor; to Pam Jaffee and Caroline Perny, PR people extraordinaire (and my favorite brunch mates); to my friends Katharine Ashe and Maya Rodale and Eve Silver, for their insightful and trenchant comments on life and writing at very timely moments; and to my family—for walking the dog, ignoring the lax housekeeping, fetching the takeout, and being my bedrock of happiness and love when the book makes me want to tear out my hair.

An Earl Like You

Prologue

1817

I<small>F</small> H<small>UGH</small> D<small>EVERAUX'S</small> father had taught him anything, it was how to keep up a good face even when everything was going wrong.

Unfortunately Hugh did not realize this until his father was dead, and he discovered how very, very wrong things had gone.

It certainly shouldn't have been that way. Joshua Deveraux, sixth Earl of Hastings, seemed blessed from birth in every way. No adversity could shake his good humor or dull his ready wit, and as a result he was adored, even marveled at, by his somber, serious family. He grew into a legendary bon vivant, a striking contrast to his reserved father and grandfather. He had a way with people that won him praise and admiration from his peers and subordinates alike. Where his ancestors had viewed it as a sacred duty to marry an heiress and build the family fortunes, Joshua insisted on wedding a girl he loved, who had great beauty and charm but a small dowry. He even inherited his title and considerable estate while still young and very handsome, and was henceforth regarded as possibly the most fortunate man in Britain.

Hugh certainly grew up thinking so. Unlike other sons, he was raised at his father's knee, and there was no one he admired more. His mother was kind and loving, too, but his father was even more—clever, boisterous, energetic, and never angry. When Hugh got into scrapes and mishaps as a lad, his mother would reproach him with tears, but his father would thump him on the back and take him for a thrilling ride across the countryside. *No sense moping about what's done*, he'd say; *chin up and face forward.*

It was only when his father died that Hugh realized his father's good nature had concealed a few intractable flaws. Joshua had loved his wife and children deeply, but he'd never imposed the slightest economy or restraint on them. He raised his son to be master of a great estate, as he himself had been raised, but he never made Hugh privy to the books and accounts of that estate. And while everyone knew—in an indulgent, admiring sort of way—that the earl was far from miserly, no one suspected the truth until his death at the age of fifty-eight.

Bilious indigestion, declared the doctor over the deathbed.

Guilt, thought Hugh grimly, two days later.

Joshua, it turned out, had been unlike his careful, dutiful father and grandfather in nearly every way. Instead of building the family wealth, he had spent it—*all* of it. Nothing had been put aside for his daughters' dowries, and his wife's jointure was pathetically small. Not only had he omitted the most elementary steps to preserving his wealth, Joshua had been generous to every wastrel friend in need, spent prodigiously on art and horses and houses, wagered and lost extravagantly, and generally frittered away one of the largest fortunes in Britain. And no one had had any idea.

"The good news, my lord, is that the mortgages are quite reasonable," added the attorney, in what could only be called poor consolation.

Hugh's fingers had long since gone numb. They had curled into fists as Mr. Sawyer laid out his threadbare circumstances over the last hour. "So I own a grand estate, but haven't a farthing to maintain it."

Mr. Sawyer hesitated. "A very hard way of viewing it . . . but yes, rather true."

He eased his hands flat and spread them on the desk. A very fine desk, made by Chippendale for his grandfather, the fifth earl. Grandfather had believed in buying quality. Hugh had to breathe deeply to keep from cursing at some length. "How much of the estate is entailed?"

"Oh, all of it," replied the attorney. "Your father took care to renew the tails, as he should have done."

"Which means I cannot sell anything," Hugh said softly.

"Er . . . no," said Mr. Sawyer. He was quiet for a moment, then said with more optimism, "But your lordship is young and hale and, if I might say so, quite a handsome man. There are bound to be any number of heiresses—"

Hugh shoved away from the desk so hard his chair almost toppled over behind him. At the last second he caught it. Also by Chippendale. He couldn't afford to damage the chair; he might have to sell it to feed his mother and sisters. "In other words," he bit out, "I must do what my father didn't—retrench, practice every economy, and marry a girl with a fortune."

Mr. Sawyer coughed delicately. "It would be prudent, sir."

Hugh slashed one hand through the air. "Go."

The man blinked, then collected his papers. "Of course, my lord. I shall be available when you—"

"You're sacked. Don't come back."

The attorney blanched, but didn't argue. Hugh seethed as the man bowed out of the room. Sawyer must have known, for several years, that the late earl was spending far more than he could afford. Obviously he hadn't stopped it, but neither had he ever whispered a word of warning in Hugh's ear.

A thought struck him. Did his mother know? The countess was in deep mourning, her eyes still red from weeping every day. Hugh thought of his parents together, of his father laughing and teasing his mother, and realized this was the last thing he would have told her. However feckless he had been, the late earl had adored his wife and wouldn't have wanted to alarm her.

Which meant Hugh would have that happy task.

His shoulders slumped at the prospect. First she had lost the love of her life, and now he was about to take away her security and possibly her home. Because there was no way he could maintain all the Hastings properties on the funds he had left. The income from them couldn't come close; not only had his father been spending capital for years, he had done very little to make his lands productive. His estates were covered with acres of graceful lawns and perfectly maintained thickets, with ponds and temples and follies. Not farms or mines or anything that produced income.

When Hugh had asked about that, wondering why other estates were more constricted, Joshua had laughed. "Who wants to ride around fields of wheat? All those farms are so damned ugly. So many fields one may not ride across." Like an idiot, Hugh had accepted this answer and even felt appreciation for it the next time he took a rousing ride through those wide-open fields and woods.

Obviously all that would have to change, but it would take time and capital, two things he was suddenly quite short of.

A tap at the door started him out of his thoughts. His sister Edith slipped inside. "Are you done?" she asked. "I saw Mr. Sawyer leave."

He exhaled. "Yes, he's gone." *And may the devil take him.*

Edith came across the room and touched his hand. "Was he very dreadful?"

Hugh's mouth twisted wryly. "Aren't all lawyers?"

She laughed, but quieted almost immediately. "I wish Papa hadn't died."

"I know." Hugh put his arm around his sister and kissed the top of her head. Edith was beautiful and petite, like their mother, and far too young to be burdened with this. His father had protected his wife and daughters from every unpleasantness, and in that much, Hugh wanted to emulate his father, at least for a while.

Of course, if his father hadn't died, what would they have done? Hugh closed his eyes as the answer became apparent. The estate would have been mortgaged even more heavily and bled to the bone. Another five or ten years and Hugh might have inherited a far more desperate circumstance than he faced now—and with every likelihood that he wouldn't have had any more warning.

"Mama has been weeping in front of Papa's portrait for an hour," Edith said softly. "Can we do something to divert her? Shall we go to Rosemere?"

Rosemere was the estate in Cornwall. It was quiet and beautifully idyllic, and it would be a wonderful place for the countess to recover from her heartache. It had been his father's favorite home, the one he had rebuilt—at tremendous expense—and renamed for Hugh's mother, a token of his great love for her. If his mother could be happy anywhere, it would be at Rosemere.

But it cost the earth to maintain all these houses. Sawyer had laid out the estate accounts in grim detail, and the expenses were crippling. Hugh realized the best thing to do was put the grandest properties into Holland covers until he could find tenants for them, and retreat to the most economical home.

Ironically, and unfortunately, that was the London house. His father hadn't liked London, so the Hastings house near St. James's Square was comparatively modest. It had been leased the last few years, but was empty at the moment. It would be dreadful to go to London in mourning, but his sisters were almost old enough for their debuts—assuming he could afford to launch them properly. If Edith and Henrietta made decent marriages, at least they would be settled and secure. It would be vital to conceal all hints of poverty, of course, further proof that he couldn't tell his family how badly off they were.

There were even more reasons London was ideal. Hugh had been raised as a gentleman, with no profession or even much education of anything practical. But he *was* good at one thing, something his father had approved of as very aristocratic, something he could do without attracting any notice. London teemed with gaming establishments and gambling men. If he cut his expenses as much as possible and enjoyed modest luck at the tables, he could keep them afloat until he contracted marriage to an heiress.

Because that really was his only option. Everything was entailed, and auctioning off every stick of furniture and every portrait on the walls would only be a temporary windfall. He had to find a bride, as wealthy as possible, and the best place to do that . . .

He hugged Edith a little tighter. "Not Rosemere. I was thinking of London."

Chapter 1

1819
Greenwich

ELIZABETH CROSS HAD grown up as the lady of the house.

Her mother died when she was three, giving birth to the baby brother Eliza had begged for. A week after Susannah Cross died, so did that tiny boy, whom Eliza had called Flopsy. When she was older she learned his proper name had been Frederick, after her grandfather, but at the time she cried for Flopsy and for Mama, and gave her second favorite toy to be buried with them. And from then on, it was just Eliza and Papa.

Her papa was a very busy man, but Eliza was the center of his world. He wanted her to have the best of everything and was determined that she would grow up knowing important things, things her mother would have taught her. "You should be a real lady, like your mother," he would insist, even though Mrs. Cross had only been a baronet's daughter and therefore not a born lady.

As a child Eliza constantly worried that she was

falling short, but when she would anxiously inquire if she were becoming more like a lady, Papa would reply that she was doing splendidly, and he must do better to find someone who could teach her what she needed to know.

Eliza tried her best to learn, first from her governess, then from her teachers at Mrs. Upton's Academy for Young Ladies, then from the companion hired to help launch her into society. By the time she was nineteen, she was confident that she could hold her own with any duchess when it came to serving tea, arranging flowers or planning a menu, or choosing the most stylish gown.

But she was equally as confident that she would always be considered a nouveau riche upstart by the London society her father was so determined to impress. Edward Cross had made his considerable fortune speculating in shares of hemp and iron and lead, all desperately needed by the British Navy during the wars. No matter how elegantly she dressed or how superbly she danced, nothing would ever erase the fact that her dowry was due to trade. She was an heiress—and quite a rich one at that—but not remotely a lady.

To draw a horde of aristocratic suitors, the sort who could elevate her to the social status her father craved, a girl needed three things: beauty, connections, and money. Eliza knew she was no beauty, and she had no noble connections. And really, she thought that if she could only have one of those three things, money was certainly the best. Even if she never married or attended a single society ball, she would still have a safe home, enough to eat, and means to provide for her dog.

The dog was more important to her than the home and food. Willy was a puppy when she found him walking home from the village. He'd been just a tiny ball of straggly black-and-white fur, hiding under a forsythia bush, but he crept right out when Eliza went down on her knees and reached out her hand. He arched into her hand as she petted his head, and her heart melted into a little puddle of love. She carried him home in her arms, considering all manner of grand names for him.

Papa was not especially pleased to see the puppy. "A mutt," he said when Eliza showed him.

"He's a baby," she said. "And so sweet." The little tail thumped against her side like a heartbeat. He snuggled in the crook of her arms as if he were home. Eliza kissed his head and smiled.

Papa grunted. "What if someone comes looking for him?"

"No one will. He was waiting for me." Without waiting for his answer, she walked out and by the time dinner was served, the puppy had been washed, fed, and provided with a plush sleeping basket in Eliza's own room. There were disadvantages to being an only child, responsible for the household, but there were also distinct advantages, namely that Eliza tended to get whatever she wanted. No one said a word about getting rid of Willy from then on.

And Eliza found herself very content with her life. Papa was a restless sort, always out and about either on business or manly pursuits. He was still a relatively young man, very fit and hale, and Eliza suspected he kept a mistress, a widowed lady who lived in Portland Place in London. But that left her free to do as she pleased. Every fortnight she went into London to shop and take tea with her two dearest friends, Lady Georgiana Lucas and Sophie Campbell, whom she'd known since they met as girls at Mrs. Upton's Academy. She took long walks with Willy and visited the lending library in Greenwich. She helped out at the church, visiting the parishioners with her friend Belinda Reeve, the vicar's wife, and she could spend many happy hours pottering about her garden.

The only sore spot was the fact that she remained unmarried, without a suitor in sight. While Eliza was coming to accept, deep down, that she would end up as one of those rich old ladies with a pack of dogs—she hoped to be quite an eccentric—her father was not nearly so sanguine about the prospect.

"I thought lap dogs were something only married ladies had," said Papa at breakfast.

"Really?" Willy was lying obediently at Eliza's feet. He was a very well-behaved dog, as long as there was the chance of something tasty to eat. Eliza liked to reward good behavior. She slipped him a bit of bacon. "He didn't ask if I were married before jumping into my arms and coming home with me, so I doubt that's true."

"A lady ought to be out dancing with gentlemen, not feeding her breakfast to a dog."

Eliza rolled her eyes and fed Willy another small bite of bacon. "Yet more proof that I am not a lady."

"But you could be. You should be." Papa's brows lowered as he chewed, looking like a man working furiously at a problem. "If you would only—"

"Papa." She put down her cup and fixed a severe look on him. "Stop."

He grunted, but let the subject drop. Willy, energized by the bacon, jumped up and began sniffing around the floor under the breakfast table.

"I thought we agreed the little beast would stay in the garden," said Papa.

"It's raining." But Eliza pointed at the basket in the corner. Willy's ears sank, and he gave her a tragically sad look. Eliza kept pointing and finally Willy heaved a sigh and trotted to his basket. He settled his head on the edge and continued to watch her with alert brown eyes.

"Dogs don't mind a trifling spot of rain. He'd go right out if I tossed a bit of kidney out the door." Papa speared a piece on his fork and cocked his head. Willy's ears went up.

"Papa." Eliza frowned. "Don't tease him."

"I'm not teasing. I'd really throw it." Papa ate the kidney and put down his fork.

Eliza gave him a stern glance and changed the subject. "Sophie asked me to tea with her and Georgiana the day after tomorrow," she said. She had tea regularly with her friends, but always reminded her father. "And Mrs. Reeve sent her regrets that she and Mr. Reeve cannot dine with us tomorrow after all."

"Good news on both counts," said Papa with pleasure.

"Mrs. Reeve is a very kind lady." Eliza noticed her father's cup was almost empty, and she poured more coffee for him, adding a drop of cream, as he liked it. "If you would simply make a donation to the church, Mr. Reeve would cease asking." Mr. Reeve was the vicar, and not as gentle-mannered as his wife.

"When Mr. Reeve holds his sermons to less than an hour, I'll give him money."

"I don't think he'd take that well."

"I don't think a church needs gold chandeliers and marble altars. We'll see who's more determined to get his way." Edward Cross drained his second cup of coffee. "I'm meeting Southbridge and Grenville today. I'll be out late."

"Don't lose too much," she returned. She knew Sir David Southbridge and Robert Grenville were not only business partners of Papa's but gambling mates, as well. They never wagered against each other, but all three were ruthless competitors, in business and at cards. When Papa arrived home after late nights with them, usually much the worse for drink, he'd tell her stories about Grenville wagering thousands of pounds at the tables, or Southbridge's steely nerve in risking shares of his trading company on a horse.

"Lose!" Her father looked affronted. "I'll not be ordered about by a girl who waits hand and foot on a ragged mongrel."

"Now, Papa," she remonstrated, "you're looking much less ragged since you let Jackson trim your hair."

"Impudence!" he grumbled. "Why the Good Lord gave me a clever girl, I'm sure I don't know."

She beamed at him. "Who else would put up with you like I do?"

He gave her a narrow glance. "Ought to be putting up with a husband."

"I don't think that would go well," she replied. "I couldn't put up with any of the fortune hunters and idiots who called on me."

He made a face as he pushed back from the table and got to his feet. "There's no need for you to marry a clever man! You've got enough brains for both of you."

"And more than enough fortune. I know." Eliza folded her hands and assumed a dreamy expression. "Surely there's some viscount or baronet out there, titled and handsome but dull-witted and utterly penniless, who might be willing to have me."

A smile tugged at his lips. "That's not what I meant." She wrinkled her nose and finally he laughed. "I love you, Lilibeth," he said, calling her by her childhood nickname as he dropped a kiss on the top of her head.

"I love you, too, Papa, even though you long to be rid of me." But she said it with a fond smile.

Papa snorted. "Rid of you! As if I'm wrong to want my girl settled in a home of her own. Serves me right, eh?" he said to Willy, who barked in reply. "She runs circles around me with my own words."

"I just want you to know I'm happy," she protested. "Even as a spinster. If I never meet a handsome, charming, dull-witted, impoverished baronet, I shall still be happy, with you and Willy and my friends."

"Supposing he weren't an idiot," Papa said. "Would you have him then?"

She rolled her eyes again. He was in rare form this morning.

"You say you're happy, but won't you be jealous when your friends marry and have families? I hear Lady Georgiana is finally getting Sterling to the altar next spring. What if she no longer has time for your teas and shopping trips when she's got a babe or two on her knee?"

Eliza buttered her muffin. She had thought about that. Georgiana had been engaged to marry Viscount Sterling for two years now. The wedding hadn't happened because her brother, the Earl of Wakefield, was surly and reclusive, and had argued with Sterling over the marriage settlements for two years. Frankly it had begun to seem that Georgiana would be engaged forever, but of course that wasn't true. Eventually she would be Lady Sterling, with Sterling's heir in her arms. "I shall be very happy for her," she said in answer to her father's wheedling question. "She's been in love with Lord Sterling forever."

"And you should be in love, too! Your mother would say so if she were here."

"Mama would not want me to marry someone simply to be married," she returned. "I hope you don't, either."

He exhaled loudly. "Of course not. But I do want you to leave your mind open. There's bound to be at least one decent chap with a title who would see you for the diamond you are."

Eliza took a bite of her muffin. She thought that mythical man would have to look very closely at her to determine that, and none of the titled gentlemen she met looked twice at her. Nor did any of the common gentlemen. If she let herself dwell on it, it would be quite lowering, really; even with a large dowry, an elegant wardrobe, and every accomplishment a lady could have, Eliza rarely warranted more than a passing glance from a man of any standing. She knew she was plain and quiet, but she'd seen Lady Sarah Willingham, daughter of the Duke of Jarros, attract a few suitors despite being shy and having a squint.

"Perhaps someone will, someday," she said, choosing to placate her father.

He nodded in satisfaction. "Someone will. The only question is whether he'll take the dog, too."

"If he won't take Willy, I won't take him," she said at once. "I would never speak to anyone who didn't like Willy."

"Damned mongrel," grunted Papa.

But Eliza saw the shilling-sized piece of bacon he stole from the platter and flicked at her dog. Willy caught it in midair and swallowed it in one bite. His tail wagging, he barked in thanks. Papa was already out the door, shrugging into his coat as he strode down the corridor without a backward glance.

Eliza glanced at her pet in reproach as she finished her muffin. "You're horribly spoiled."

Willy yipped in happy agreement.

"For that, you can go into the garden by yourself." She rose from the table. "James, would you let him out?"

"Yes, miss." The footman stepped forward and snapped his fingers at Willy, whose ears drooped as he realized Eliza wasn't coming. She made a shooing motion, and the dog followed James.

She wondered when Papa would accept that she wasn't the sort of girl gentlemen flocked to. In his eyes she was lovely, but Eliza knew he was the only one who saw her that way. Plain girls had made splashes in society, but usually by virtue of being vivacious and witty. Eliza tended to grow mute and hesitant in the presence of elegant strangers, and any wit she had vanished from her brain if one of them actually spoke to her. Undoubtedly Papa hoped her enormous dowry would outweigh her shyness, but Eliza would rather be that eccentric old lady with a house full of dogs than marry a husband who only wanted her money.

So Papa could dream, but Eliza was far less certain. Perhaps some day she would meet an affable country squire who didn't need a beautiful, charming wife, but preferred a quiet girl content to play with her dog and tend her garden. And if not, she would just remain as she was.

Chapter 2

HUGH DEVERAUX WAS having a very good night.

It was about time. His luck had been lackluster for the last fortnight. Perhaps the last month. He hadn't lost a vast sum of money, but neither had he won one. And despite playing ruthlessly and keeping his head clear, he hadn't been able to make a sustained run of wins. Up one night, then down almost as much the next.

For the last year and a half, his London plan had worked reasonably well. Thanks to his luck at the card tables he'd been able to make the most pressing debt payments, open the town house, even provide some new gowns for his mother and sisters. Unfortunately, now he needed more than that. Edith was old enough to make her debut, and she needed a dowry.

At first he'd hoped he could give her land. He'd had his solicitors comb through every word of every deed, and they all said he couldn't transfer property to either of the girls on her marriage. He could take out additional mortgages on the properties for the money, but that would leave him in even more desperate straits. He'd sold some artwork his father had bought, but everything he tried to get rid of set off a night of tears for his mother, who remembered when and how every item had been acquired, and deeply mourned the loss of each memento of her husband. She was sentimental and emotionally fragile; she could assure him she understood his intentions entirely at breakfast, and be prostrate in bed by dinner after the painting or statue was carted away to the auction house.

Hugh had long since realized that his family would be no help to him. The move to town had been hard on the countess, leaving his father's grave and coming to the drab London house Joshua had despised so much. She accepted Hugh's explanation, that it was to give Edith her Season and find a husband, but grief clung to her. His sisters were no better. Edith fretted about their inability to entertain properly, and Henrietta begged for her own new wardrobe, chafing at the sight of Edith's stylish gowns. Hugh was beginning to think it would be easier to let himself be sent to the Fleet.

That would be surrender, though, and he refused to surrender. His father had left him a mess, but he was determined to claw his way out. All he needed, after all, was a reliable bit of luck.

His favorite gaming establishment had become the Vega Club, right in the heart of London. It was well kept and one needn't fear being knifed on the way home. The owner was a hard but fair man, and he insisted on only two vows from his members: that they not tell gossip about the club, and that they pay their losses promptly.

Hugh might have gnashed his teeth a time or two about the last one, but he wholeheartedly appreciated the first. Before he'd joined the Vega Club, tales of his wagering—often wildly exaggerated—had reached his mother's ears and set her all aflutter with worries that he was becoming wild and irresponsible.

His father had been dead for a year and a half, and Hugh still hadn't told her how badly off they were.

If his luck held like this for a few nights in a row, though, he might not have to.

He was up by almost nine thousand pounds. Tonight he'd got into a table with some gentlemen and a few Cits, men of large fortune and no name. Hugh liked playing with that sort of fellow. They were pleased to sit down with an earl, and when they lost to him, they didn't dare try to wriggle out of it. In addition, they were all in fine spirits tonight. One man kept calling for wine, and Hugh was fairly certain all three of them were three sheets to the wind.

Some might think it unsporting to play with a bunch of drunks, but Hugh knew better. They hadn't been drunk when they invited him to join their table, and he hadn't been the one to order the claret. None of them were green striplings, and since Hugh had heard their fortunes ranged from two hundred thousand pounds to well over half a million, he presumed they could afford to drink themselves stupid and lose a few thousand pounds. In fact, he was counting on it.

They had begun by playing simple five card loo. As long as one took a single trick, one didn't lose. Hugh was good at remembering that point and bowing out at once if his hand was unpromising. He took some ribbing for this, but good-naturedly laughed it off. More than once he'd seen a young man—or, at Vega's, a woman—heckled into playing too rashly, only to panic when he lost. Hugh was not at Vega's to lose.

But after a while, five card loo, even for rich stakes, grew too tame for some of them. "We're going in circles," complained Robert Grenville, shuffling his cards. "No limit, chaps."

"Unlimited!" William Harker, youngest son of Viscount Ellery, turned pale. He glanced nervously from side to side before pushing back his chair. "That's too high for me."

Grenville and another fellow, George Alderton, laughed. "Go on, then! Come back when you've grown a bit." Harker was thirty if he were a day. His mouth thinned, but he got up, collected his markers, and left. Hugh admired that. A man had to know his limits.

As for himself, though . . . The stack of markers in front of him was comfortingly large. Over eight thousand eight hundred pounds, in carved ivory counters. He could double or triple it in unlimited loo. This was Edith's dowry, sitting right in front of him.

Hugh stayed in the game.

Alderton, deep in his cups, missed taking a

trick and had to pay the amount of the pot, which opened at a thousand pounds and quickly rose over three. Hugh accepted his share—almost eight hundred pounds—with a carefree wink and a ribald comment about Alderton, making them all shout with laughter. Another round and then another, when no one missed a trick. The pot reached eight thousand pounds, and Hugh reminded himself to be careful. He folded his next hand, a lackluster set of cards without trumps.

And then . . . it happened. He didn't quite know how. The hand dealt him was solid; respectably high cards, two in the trump suit. He should have been guaranteed at least one trick. But one by one, each trick went to other players. Even his queen of trumps fell to the king. The hand ended, Grenville had taken it, and Hugh had nothing.

His heart made a strange echoing thud against his ribs. He'd lost. For a moment the room went dark and eerily quiet. He'd made a mistake, and cost himself everything he'd won tonight.

Alderton slapped the table. "A miss at last! Damn, I thought we'd never get him to stumble, chaps!"

Grenville sloshed more wine into his glass and raised it. "A toast to Hastings," he said slyly. "And to his coin, which we'll be glad to take."

Somehow a smile came to Hugh's face. *Chin up and face forward.* He shook his head as he pushed nearly his entire stack of counters toward the center of the table. Edith's dowry, gone. "I should have had more of Alderton's claret," he said lightly. "Damned sobriety tripped me up."

Grenville hiccupped with laughter, and Alderton tossed the bottle at him. Hugh caught it and made himself take a drink. The wine tasted like bile on his tongue. Tonight was ruined, but Hugh needed to be able to play with these men again, tomorrow or the night after. No one else could afford to lose the kind of money he needed to win. So he bowed and said farewell before walking away with the bottle still in his hand.

Damn. Damn it *all*. He wanted to throw the bloody bottle through a window. What had he done wrong? He wandered through the club as his mind replayed the last ruinous hand, trying to see where he'd erred, but there was nothing else he could have done. Someone else had held a card that beat every single one of his. God bloody damn it.

He let out his breath, careful not to display any sign of the furious turmoil inside him. All he'd needed was one more win. If it had been Grenville who lost, Grenville who held the queen instead of the king, there would be over thirteen thousand pounds in Hugh's pocket at this moment, more than enough for Edith's dowry. Instead he had markers worth barely twelve hundred, only two hundred more than he'd begun the night with and exponentially fewer than he needed.

"A hard loss," said a voice behind him.

Hugh realized he'd been standing in the doorway of the main salon. He turned so he wasn't blocking the way. "Your pardon, sir."

"Quite all right." The other man didn't stride through. He stayed where he was, watching

Hugh with an expression of interested sympathy. "Grenville's a cunning bastard."

"Is he?" Hugh managed a slight smile. "Very impressive, how he can be cunning and thoroughly foxed at the same time."

"There's the cunning—he doesn't drink as much as it looks like." The fellow nodded at the bottle Hugh still clutched. "Fancy a decent glass?"

"It's the only thing I've won tonight." He held it up and peered into it. "I might keep it."

"As a fond memento of happy times?" His new companion took it from him and deposited it on the tray of a passing waiter. "George Alderton drinks horse piss. Join me for a proper drink, won't you?" He waved one hand at the armchairs across the room, but there was an air of command to it.

Hugh straightened his shoulders, his guard up. "Forgive me, sir. I haven't the pleasure of your acquaintance."

"Cross," said the fellow. "Edward Cross at your service, Lord Hastings."

Hugh gave a bow in reply. Cross had something to say to him, had sought him out. That rarely boded well in his current circumstances.

Cross held out one arm again, a slight smile on his face. "Let's have a drink."

Chin up. Hugh nodded once and led the way. This salon was removed from the gaming tables, where patrons could order a meal or simply sink into an armchair to recover from a particularly taxing round of hazard. Like the rest of Vega's, it looked more like a gentleman's club than a gaming hell. Tonight it was mostly empty, perhaps because it was well past three in the morning.

Cross took the seat beside Hugh's and told a loitering waiter to bring a bottle of French port and two glasses. Hugh stretched out his legs and folded his hands over his stomach, waiting to hear what Cross wanted from him.

Did he owe the man money? He was reasonably certain not. The name was not familiar.

Had Cross heard of his difficulties and spied an opportunity? Hugh didn't know what it could be. He'd received two offers for the entailed Rosemere estate from men like Cross, and both times he'd had to decline. Rather unfortunately, to Hugh's mind. The offers had been very generous.

"I saw your last game," said Cross when the port was poured and the waiter had gone again.

Hugh rotated his glass. It was a very fine port. His father would have purchased several casks of it on the spot. "That's poor entertainment, when Vega offers so much more."

"Oh?" Cross gave his barely-there smile again. "I'd never sit down opposite Grenville or Alderton, but I do like to gloat a little when they lose."

God. The last thing he wanted to hear was gloating. Hugh drank, the wine flowing warmly down his throat. "I regret not providing an opportunity for you to do so."

Cross made a sound that might have been a chuckle. "You play well."

Not well enough, not tonight. Hugh conjured his sardonic grin again. "I thought you said you were watching."

"I was," replied Cross, not put off. "Losing to Grenville . . . Many men have done that. You, though." He cocked his head, watching him contemplatively. "You kept your head and played well."

"Only to lose in the end." Hugh regarded his port. "When I play well, I don't lose."

"Is that right?" murmured Cross. He refilled both glasses, even though Hugh's was hardly touched. "You took it with grace."

"Losing?" Hugh's smile felt painful. He had the odd feeling Cross was impressed. That didn't fit, somehow; the man looked competitive, the sort who would hate losing. There was a fair amount of gray shot through his dark hair, but otherwise he looked to be in the prime of life, lean and fit, his face tanned. He was clearly another Cit, but wore his wealth easily, just like his well-tailored jacket.

"Yes, losing," said Cross. "Not every man knows how to face it."

"A gentleman loses the way he wins: graciously, ever mindful of his dignity and his honor." His father had said those words, more than once. Hugh tasted the acid sting of betrayal again as he said them now.

"Most fellows can't, gentleman or not. I suppose that says something about their dignity, or perhaps their honor."

Or perhaps it was due to the fact that losing was awful, a sharp stab to the gut that could turn into a festering wound if it weren't salved by winning. Perhaps it meant nothing to Cross to see twelve thousand pounds slip through his fingers, but Hugh felt it like a condemned man watching his execution date draw near as hope of clemency dwindled.

There was only so long he could get by this way. Perhaps he ought to give up the tables for a while and dedicate himself to finding a wealthy bride. He'd hoped to see at least Edith settled before he did that. Henrietta could wait another year, but Edith had a suitor, the oldest son of Viscount Livingston. He sent her flowers and came to call twice a week; Edith blushed and smiled every time he was in view. Hugh lived in daily fear that the young man would come to him and ask for Edith, because then he would have to reveal the extent of his father's mismanagement. Joshua had used to tell his girls he would see them both duchesses, implying they would each have a large dowry. Hugh didn't want to tell them the money had never been put aside, and had instead been spent on building and furnishing the new wing at Rosemere, tying it up where he could not get it.

"It must be said that winning is vastly more enjoyable than losing," he finally replied to Cross's comment. "It is easier to remember one's dignity and honor when in good spirits."

"True, true. But there's an element of risk in damn near everything. Every enterprise has a risk of failure—and loss."

Hugh inclined his head. Did Cross have a point?

"You're a rare fellow," said the man then,

causing Hugh a start of surprise. He turned his head and saw that Cross was studying him intently.

"In what way?" he asked, suddenly alert and cautious.

Cross just smiled. "I like a man who can keep his balance."

For a split second, Hugh thought the man must know—there was something very canny about his words. It made his pulse stutter and skip, because Hugh had done his damnedest to hide his circumstances from everyone. Only his solicitors knew the full extent, and Hugh had maintained a pose of aristocratic indifference to debt in front of them. He knew he wasn't the only nobleman in London who owed more than his life was worth, but showing any sign of worry or alarm would only alert the wolves to come feed upon him.

So Cross couldn't possibly know. His heart settled back into a normal rhythm, though the damage was done. He'd had far too much experience of losing tonight, and was sick of talking about it. Whatever Cross wanted, he was taking too long to come to the point. Hugh drained his glass and set it on the table between them. "Thank you for the port, sir, but I must be getting home."

"It was a pleasure, my lord." Cross rose and bowed as he got up to leave. "Perhaps we'll meet again."

Hugh smiled briefly. "Perhaps." He made a mental note never to sit down at a table with Cross. "Good night."

Chapter 3

〰️❧〰️

IF SOMEONE HAD warned Eliza that something momentous was about to happen in her life, she would have made sure to put on a nicer dress.

Instead she wore a faded muslin, three years old, with a kerchief over her hair. Willy had got into something smelly and dirty, and he needed a bath. Willy hated the bath. When he caught sight of Eliza pulling out the large copper tub in the scullery, he wedged himself under a cabinet in the butler's pantry and had to be dragged out by his back paws. Eliza carried him, his tail curled all the way under his belly, to the tub full of warm water.

"If you would stay out of the kitchen scrap pile, you wouldn't have to get a bath," Eliza scolded him as she scrubbed the matted fur under his chin. Whatever Willy had rolled in was sticky as well as smelly, and her nose wrinkled as the maid poured buckets of clean water over him. Willy's ears were down flat on his head, and he wriggled in her grip as she held him under the rinse water.

"Open the door, Louisa," said Eliza, trying to

get a grip on her wet, wriggly dog. "I'm going to put him straight into the garden to dry."

The scullery maid swept open the door leading into the walled kitchen garden. Eliza gauged the difference, and heaved Willy out of the tub, clutching him against her chest. He wasn't very heavy, but he was all muscle, and when he was wet he might as well have been an otter.

Sure enough, he started twisting with renewed vigor, and managed to rake one paw across the underside of her chin. "Ouch! Willy—stop!" She tried to hold him tighter, but he was thrashing wildly now, slipping through her hands. "Willy— Willy, no, bad dog!"

The dog hit the floor running. He raced under the sink and sent buckets clattering out into the narrow scullery. Louisa, the silly girl, shrieked and cowered out of his way, accidentally knocking the garden door closed. Willy skidded on wet paws and slammed into the closed door so hard he rebounded and rolled over backward. Eliza gasped in concern, but Willy was back on his feet and running again. The poor dog. He was scared and perhaps hurt. She ran to open the door so he could get into the garden, where he loved to be.

"What's this noise?" Cook threw open the door from the kitchen. "Louisa, what be you doing?"

"No," cried Eliza as Willy shot past Cook's feet, making her shriek. Willy could get into so much trouble in the kitchen, especially when he was being chased. Willy adored being chased.

Cook fell back as Eliza ran by her. "Bar the door," she shouted to a startled footman. But his arms were full of dishes, and she threw up her hands as Willy jumped against the swinging door and escaped the kitchen.

Eliza yanked the kerchief from her head. "Bring the towel, Louisa," she called as she picked up her skirt and ran after the dog. Papa would be so annoyed. She hoped he was still out, or safely closed up in his study.

But as she rushed into the spacious entry hall, barely a step behind Willy, a dreadful sight met her eyes. Not Papa, but much worse: a visitor, and one she'd never met before. He was just handing his hat to the butler, and he looked up in astonishment as Willy hurtled toward him, yapping happily. Willy loved people, especially new people. He would jump on them and lick their hands, and he had been known to nip a dangling pocket watch or loose handkerchief off an unsuspecting victim. Unfortunately his teeth were rather sharp, and he also tended to leave little holes in whatever clothing he caught.

"Willy!" She lunged toward her dog. Papa would be furious if Willy stole the guest's handkerchief or ripped his coat. "Sit!"

The wicked animal bounded out of her reach, his tail wagging. He paused long enough to give a hard shake. Eliza flushed in mortification as the gentleman leapt backward to avoid the spray of water. "Willy, sit," she said firmly, advancing on the dog. From the corner of her eye she saw Louisa, the scullery maid, hovering in the doorway with a towel. Perhaps, if she were very lucky, the gentleman would think she was also a maid.

Willy cocked his head, watching her. Eliza advanced on him without looking away. *Stay there*, she silently commanded the dog. She didn't dare look at the visitor.

"If I may, Miss Cross," began the butler just as she got within an arm's length of her pet. At his voice, Willy jumped sideways, gave another bark, and took off toward the visitor at a run.

Eliza let out a horrified noise and threw herself forward. She managed to intercept Willy, but the dog pulled her off balance and onto her knees, dragging her under the large round table that stood in the center of the rotunda hall before she got a good grip on him. The dog wriggled, but she clamped her arms around him until he gave up the fight and began furiously licking her face.

"Are you all right?" asked a voice.

Eliza dodged Willy's tongue and looked up to see the gentleman visitor bending down to regard her with a mixture of caution and alarm. Abruptly the indignity of her position flooded in on her, and she felt her face turn red. "Yes, perfectly," she said, crawling from under the table, still clutching the wet dog.

His brow quirked ever so slightly, doubting her assurance, but he extended one hand. "How fortunate."

She had no choice but to let him help her up. He lifted her easily back to her feet, despite Willy's struggles. He had already removed his gloves, and his palm seemed to leave an impression of tingling warmth on hers. She cringed to think of the traces of soapy bathwater her hand must have left on his. "Thank you, sir." Breathless, she swiped at her hair, cringing as the loose lock flopped wetly against her ear. "Please pardon Willy, he's very . . . energetic. But friendly!"

The visitor's eyes moved from her to Willy, who arched his neck in a renewed attempt to reach him. Eliza knew Willy only intended a welcoming lick, but it might look rather like he meant to bite. The gentleman straightened his shoulders, subtly drawing away as she wrestled the dog back into place.

"I'm relieved to hear it," he said. His voice was really lovely, rich and smooth and unmistakably upper class, with the sort of diction that had been honed from birth. It fit with the rest of him, tall and well-dressed and impossibly handsome. His dark hair was combed back, but curled around his ears and collar, hinting at what he might look like when he was at ease, at home. His jaw was sculpted, and though he wasn't smiling now, there were little lines around his mouth that hinted he did smile, a lot.

But it was his eyes that made her acutely aware of how disheveled and dirty she was, clutching her dog to her soaked apron. His eyes were kind, and curious, and faintly amused; she just knew that still-quirked brow meant he was laughing inside at the chaotic welcome she'd given him.

And so, unprepared and embarrassed, Eliza did what she usually did when confronted by a handsome man. Her tongue froze to the roof of her mouth and her face burned red, and she heard herself giggle nervously. She should introduce herself. She should apologize. She should say something witty, or at least polite, and instead she just stared at him, more awkward by the moment.

"Eliza." Papa's voice was sharp. "What is going on?"

Oh dear. She jerked her gaze away from the mystery gentleman. Papa stood at the top of the stairs, surveying the scene with displeasure. "Willy got away from me after his bath."

Papa's lips thinned and he glared at the dog. Willy's tail thumped against Eliza's hip, and he yipped in delight at the sight of Papa, who fed him bacon. "Lord Hastings, my daughter Elizabeth. Eliza, this is the Earl of Hastings."

An *earl*. Mortified, Eliza made a clumsy curtsy. "A pleasure to make your acquaintance, my lord," she murmured.

"Miss Cross." The visitor bowed. The light of humor in his eyes was gone now.

"I'd better put Willy in the garden," she said. "Please excuse me, sir." She started to curtsy again, almost lost her hold on Willy, and settled for walking very quickly out the back of the hall. Louisa, hiding behind the door, popped out as she approached, the towel in her outstretched hands. Eliza glared at her, irrationally annoyed at the girl. It wasn't Louisa's fault the dog loved to be chased, nor was it Louisa's fault Cook had opened the door at the wrong moment. It was Willy's fault, and as a result she'd met a handsome, good-humored gentleman . . . while dressed like a servant and smelling of wet dog.

Just my luck, she thought, letting Louisa bundle Willy into the towel. And on top of that indignity, Papa would be angry with her for letting Willy loose in the house. "Bad dog," she whispered to her pet as she went back to the kitchen. Willy's ears drooped, but the moment she set him down in the garden, he gave a bark and a joyful leap, and was off chasing a bird.

"Sorry, miss," said Louisa hesitantly. "I didn't know he'd run like that."

Eliza mustered a wry smile. "In the future, keep the door closed, and don't be alarmed if he races around before going out. He won't hurt you."

The girl smiled nervously and curtsied. "No, ma'am."

Suddenly Eliza understood. Louisa was young, only fourteen or so, and Eliza had been just the same at that age. "Are you frightened of dogs, Louisa?"

Her eyes grew wide. "No, miss," she said in a very small voice. "Not—not much, anyway."

Eliza gave her an encouraging smile. "Don't worry. Can we try to help you over it, with Willy?"

Blushing, the girl nodded. Cook's voice rang out then from the kitchen, calling Louisa sharply to come wash some pots, and Louisa ran off with a hasty curtsy. Eliza took off her sodden apron and hung it on a peg behind the door. She put away the tin of soap and the copper tub; someone else had already emptied and rinsed it.

When Willy came back to the door and barked to come in, she gave him a rough toweling until his short fur stood up all over, giving him a wild and fluffy look. She couldn't help laughing. "You're still a bad dog," she told him, and he licked her face as if to apologize for it.

She took him to her room via the servants' stair, both to spare the carpet on the main staircase and to avoid any chance of meeting Papa or his guest. If she ever met the Earl of Hastings again, Eliza would much rather be clean, dry, and prepared for the encounter. She should have a clever comment ready about their first meeting.

I apologize for not falling at your feet this time, my lord, she imagined herself telling him with an artless laugh.

No, that would remind him too vividly of her graceless sprawl on the floor.

Willy sends his regards, my lord, and begs me to assure you he has much better manners than he displayed the other day, she could say ruefully, casting all the blame onto the dog.

Or: *Shall we begin again, my lord, and forget the time my dog charged at you?* She batted her eyelashes at her reflection, pretending the handsome Lord Hastings was the one smiling back at her, or even not smiling but watching her with that little quirk to his eyebrow hinting at deep, private amusement over their first, disastrous meeting. He might find it charming, and remark that she was far prettier without an ugly apron on; she would bow her head and smile in acknowledgment of the gallantry. Then he might ask her for a dance, or at least fetch her a lemonade, and from then on they would be . . . friendly. *Yes, Hastings came to dine last night*, she imagined telling her friends casually, as if such a thing happened all the time.

Such a thing had never happened. Such a thing probably never *would* happen. And she was both silly and naive to think Lord Hastings might find her charming.

"Ugh!" Eliza made a face at herself in the mirror. "I should hope I never see the man again," she said to Willy. "He surely thinks I'm half mad, thanks to you." The dog yawned, then trotted to his basket in the corner and curled up in it, tired from his race through the hall and then his romp in the garden. Eliza shook her head even as her heart melted a little. She rang for her maid to help her change out of her wet dress, and tried to dismiss handsome earls from her mind.

"I MUST APOLOGIZE FOR the dog," said Cross as he closed the door of his study. "My daughter has a tender heart."

Hugh nodded once in acknowledgement. "An admirable trait in a woman."

Cross paused, giving him a sharp look. "Yes." He went around his desk. "Won't you sit down, Lord Hastings?"

Hugh took a very comfortable armchair. Nothing elegant by Chippendale in here; it was large, easy furniture, upholstered in the softest leather. Everything in the house that he'd seen had been that way—no slavish deference to fashion, but a refined comfort in materials of the highest quality. If he'd had any doubts about Cross's wealth, they were gone now.

It had been a fortnight or more since their odd conversation at the Vega Club. Hugh hadn't thought much about it after that night, and he hadn't seen Cross again except from across the room. Hugh had not expected to speak to the man again in his life, but it seemed Cross had other ideas. What he didn't know was why.

His host offered him a drink, which Hugh declined, and finally took his own seat. "To what do I owe the pleasure, my lord?"

"I received a letter from Sir Richard Nesbit," said Hugh. "As a courtesy, informing me that he'd sold some debt markers he held from my father."

"Very accommodating of Nesbit."

Hugh inclined his head, even though he thought Sir Richard was a very dodgy fellow. "Why did you buy them?"

Cross leaned back in his chair. "I believed the investment was promising."

"Oh?" Hugh raised one eyebrow. "What investment?" The markers Nesbit held had been from a horse race five years ago. Joshua had wagered three thousand pounds on a colt who finished last in every heat. Hugh considered the debt invalid, but Nesbit still held the signed note—until Cross bought it, apparently at full value.

"You, my lord," Cross said easily, a smile on his face. "You are your father's son, are you not?"

Hugh ground his teeth together behind his austere expression. "Nesbit had no legal claim.

It was a debt of honor of my father's, and he's dead."

Cross waved one hand. "Ah. Then Nesbit got the better of me."

"Why?" repeated Hugh, his voice soft and even.

The other man smiled, a dry twist of his lips. "Do you know how I made my fortune, Lord Hastings?" Hugh stiffened. Cross went on without waiting for a response. "Speculation. A damned risky business, but rewarding."

"Speculators, as I understand, buy when they see a chance of profit," said Hugh. "The longer the odds, the greater the profit. The odds of profit from Nesbit's markers are very long indeed." *Nil, to be precise.*

Cross shrugged. "Then I've lost. Speculators are accustomed to that, too."

"I would accept that as a rational, if very stupid, explanation if it were the only instance." Hugh shifted his weight, trying to keep his anger in check—anger and fear. "Since it struck me as a strange thing to do—speculating so wildly on a debt you know will never be paid—I spoke to my solicitor. He assured me I have no more obligation to discharge the debt to you than I had to Sir Richard, but he also mentioned a few curious documents he'd received of late. You've bought more of my loans."

Cross dipped his head in acknowledgment.

"To what purpose?" Hugh's composure was slipping. Fury tightened his voice. "Spare me any rubbish about investments and odds. You have systematically bought up a very large portion of my debt. No one does that on a whim. Why?"

"Calling it an investment was not rubbish."

"If you own it, you must know how large it is," Hugh said in icy tones. "How unlikely it is ever to be repaid in full."

It had stunned him, when his solicitor mentioned that the bulk of his debts were now held by Edward Cross. He hadn't even connected the name to the man for a moment. To the best of his knowledge, he and Cross had had no other contact than the single strained conversation at the Vega Club. Why would a man buy up a perfect stranger's debt? It brought back every sense of unease Hugh had felt that night.

It was unsettling enough that he finally had to come ask. Cross hadn't contacted him, hadn't spoken to him, hadn't done anything to collect on the very large sum Hugh now owed him. Who the devil was this man? By his reckoning, Cross had paid off over eighty thousand pounds of mortgages, loans, tradesmen's bills, even debts of honor racked up by Hugh's father. There was no chance it had been done out of generosity or altruism.

"If you won't explain why, at least assure me you will hold to the repayment terms I already agreed to," Hugh demanded when the man only gave a maddening shrug instead of answering him.

"Repay it as you're able, my lord. I can afford to wait." Cross twisted in his chair as the sound of barking drifted through the open window behind his desk. "Do you like dogs, Lord Hastings?"

Hugh's eyes narrowed. "Yes." He rose from his chair. "If you won't explain your actions and do not intend to make unreasonable demands, I shan't impose on you further. My solicitor will see that payments are directed to you."

"Stay a moment, Hastings," said Cross absently. He seemed to be listening to the dog instead, his gaze fixed on the window. "All dogs? Even mongrels like the one my daughter has?"

Hugh wanted to leave, but didn't. It galled him that someone had this hold over him. "I like any good-natured dog. I'm not fond of lapdogs who bite."

"Good, good," murmured Cross. Finally he looked at Hugh again, and got to his feet. "I thank you for your visit, sir."

Thin-lipped, Hugh glared, but finally made a stiff bow.

"Perhaps you'll dine with us some night," added Cross. "My daughter and I would be honored to have you join us."

The cool but polite refusal was on the tip of Hugh's tongue. He really wanted nothing to do with Cross or his daughter, but the desire to *know* was like a splinter, sharp and festering. "Perhaps."

"Would tomorrow evening suit you?" Cross smiled faintly at his expression. "I've no wish to detain you today, my lord, but there are . . . opportunities we could discuss."

"Opportunities." Here it was, thought Hugh grimly. Whatever Cross wanted from him. His name on some venture? His influence with other aristocrats? He had precious little Cross could want, but he did have friends and was well-regarded in town. The Hastings title was an old and venerated one.

Cross waved his hand. "Nothing criminal! They could be very much to your benefit. I didn't mean to give offense—quite the opposite. Come to dinner and we'll speak of it then." His distant air had vanished, and the tone of command again permeated his otherwise pleasant invitation.

His jaw tight, Hugh nodded. What choice did he have?

Cross owned him.

Chapter 4

Eliza paced the carpet in the drawing room, deeply worried.

Papa had invited the Earl of Hastings to dine. "Why?" she'd blurted out in horror when he told her at dinner the previous day.

"We might have business together, His Lordship and I." Papa hadn't noticed her dismay. "I want to make a good impression, so wear something fetching." And he'd winked—*winked*, as if he hadn't seen with his own eyes how unattractive and awkward she'd been when the earl called.

Once Eliza got over her shock, she rushed to begin planning. The ordinary menu was discarded, and a better, more impressive one planned. All the maids were dispatched to clean the dining room and drawing room from top to bottom. She went through her entire wardrobe in search of a decent dress. Somehow that seemed vitally important, if she hoped to supplant the first dreadful impression the earl must have formed of her. Willy, against his will, had been shut up in her room, and the staff was forbidden to let him out no matter how much he barked.

But if she was confident that the dinner, the house, and even her dress were beyond reproach this time, there was still the question of what she would say to the man. Anxiously she wiped at an imaginary smudge on the clock on the mantel. She still had not thought of a witty comment to make, let alone enough comments to form a conversation. As bad as it was to suspect the earl thought her mad after a few minutes in her company, she was very afraid he would think she was an idiot after an entire evening.

The door opened. "The Earl of Hastings," said Roberts, the butler.

Eliza squeezed her hands together one more time in a final prayer for poise, and turned to face her guest.

The force of how handsome he was hit her like a blast of heat from the kitchen ovens. Tonight his hair was tousled into romantic curls, and his black evening clothes made his eyes even darker. He strode in with easy grace and made an elegant bow. "Good evening, Miss Cross."

"Lord Hastings." Her face felt hot as she curtsied. "Won't you be seated?" She perched on the edge of a chair to avoid crumpling her skirt.

He glanced from side to side as he sat on the sofa. "I am on guard this time, if any dogs are to join us."

Eliza blushed and gave a nervous laugh. "Oh no! Willy has been safely locked away. I do apologize for the way he behaved yesterday."

Lord Hastings smiled. There was a deep dimple in his cheek, and all those little lines around his eyes crinkled. Eliza's heart fluttered. "I daresay he behaved much as any boy would after a good scrubbing in the bath."

"Oh?" Flustered, she wet her lips. "I wouldn't know. I am an only child, sir."

"When I was a boy," he said, his smile lingering, "I might have fled a bath or two myself. Not generally once it was complete," he added as she smiled involuntarily, "but with no less fervor." He paused. "He's a pup still?"

"I think he's about a year old." Lord Hastings raised an eyebrow in question, and she explained. "I found him under a bush last summer. He was a tiny thing then, but he's grown a great deal . . ." She cleared her throat. "Our head groom, who is very knowledgeable about dogs, thinks he must be a year old."

"I never argue with my head groom," replied the earl at once. "Wiser men are hard to find in Britain."

Eliza laughed again, but less nervously this time.

"I hope he is faring well, after leading you on such a chase."

"Very well," she said. It was easier to talk about Willy than anything like politics or society gossip, and Lord Hastings was making it very easy. Eliza loved her dog and instinctively warmed to the earl for showing interest in him. "Willy is very fond of chasing birds in the garden. His utter lack of success in catching any only seems to redouble his determination to try, and he often ends up in the mud." She wrinkled her nose. "Although sometimes I think he likes being in the mud, since it looks like he's rolled in it from head to toe."

The earl laughed. A shiver went up Eliza's spine. Heavens, he had a wonderful laugh, and even more wonderfully, she had inspired it. "No wonder he needed bathing."

"Yes. Although for a dog who likes mud and mud puddles as much as he does, Willy hates getting bathed. His tail goes down and he looks at me as if I've just sentenced him to the block."

His eyes were still crinkled up in a faint smile. "I trust he forgives you soon after."

"Yes, well . . . I might—I might have given him a bit of ham afterward in apology." Lord Hastings laughed again at her hesitant confession, and Eliza's smile grew wider. "The way to Willy's heart is to feed him. Even Papa—" She paused; where was Papa? It was unlike him to keep a guest waiting.

"Is he a favorite of your father?" prompted the earl after a moment.

Eliza blushed a little. "Papa will never admit it, but I think he's very fond of Willy. He accidentally gave Willy his name—it's short for 'will he ever stop barking?'"

"No," said Hastings in open amusement.

"Oh yes! He said it every time Willy was playing in the garden—chasing birds, you know—and I hadn't thought of a better name for him. I began calling him Willy to tease Papa, but then it just . . . stuck." She made a helpless gesture with one hand as the earl grinned, his dimple catching her eye again. What a handsome man he was. And so kind and charming, too. She'd sat here talking to him all this time and not felt stupid or tongue-tied once. "I think Papa's quite fond of Willy, but he refuses to admit it."

"It's very much his loss," declared Lord Hastings. "Dogs are often better company than people."

"Yes, indeed!" Eliza beamed at him in delight. "Very much so."

He smiled at her again, so warmly Eliza thought she must be dreaming. Never had she met a gentleman so friendly and informal. She hoped he did a great deal of business with her father and came to dine regularly. For a moment some of her fanciful imaginings didn't seem so ridiculous.

The door opened and Papa strode in. "Good evening, Hastings. Apologies for my tardiness." He bowed.

The earl, who had risen at his entrance, returned the greeting. His face was wiped clean of expression and humor. "Mr. Cross."

Papa folded his hands behind his back, looking quite pleased with himself. "Eliza, my dear, you've met our guest, so there's no need for further introductions."

"Yes, Papa." She edged toward the door. "I'll tell Roberts we're ready."

Papa waved one hand. "Nonsense. I know you've got it plotted down to the minute, and the footmen are standing ready to lift the covers as we speak. Shall we?" He swept out his hand.

"Miss Cross?" The Earl of Hastings offered his

arm to her. Eliza jolted in alarm; she had not expected to touch him. But Papa had already turned and walked out of the room. Gingerly she put her fingertips on his forearm, unable to stop the tiny shiver that went through her as his muscle flexed.

The dinner passed like a dream. Lord Hastings was much more formal with Papa than he had been when it was just the two of them, talking about dogs, but Eliza had expected that. She knew her father had a certain reputation for being hard and ruthless in business, and he'd said Lord Hastings came on business. Most people who did business with Papa acted with reserve. They didn't know her father had a soft and loving heart, but she suspected she might be the only person who saw that side of Papa regularly.

There was no talk of business, though. Instead Papa seemed determined to bring up every difficult topic under the sun. He quizzed Lord Hastings about the prospect of parliamentary reform. He asked the earl for his thoughts on Catholic suffrage. Next came the Corn Laws, and Eliza began to fear her father would give offense. When Papa began pressing the earl to say clearly whether or not he supported the laws, Eliza had enough. She'd listened in silence, but it was clear to her their visitor was not enjoying himself. His dark eyes were flat and unsmiling, and his answers grew shorter and more clipped. She wondered why her father was hounding his guest, as if he were judging the earl instead of trying to court his business investment.

"Enough of that, Papa," she said in light reproach. "I wonder if Lord Hastings has seen the new production of *Lionel and Clarissa* at the Theatre Royal."

The smile Lord Hastings gave almost bowled her over. It was warm and relieved and filled with gratitude. Apparently he had not enjoyed the political conversation any more than she had. "I have not, Miss Cross, but my mother and sisters assure me it is marvelous. They particularly enjoyed the melodrama accompanying it."

"Did they?" She smiled in surprise. "Papa, may we see it? If Lady Hastings and her daughters have been, it cannot be improper."

"Perhaps." Papa leaned back and gestured for more wine. "Would your friend Lady Georgiana Lucas accompany us?"

Eliza gave him a warning glance under her eyelashes. He was prone to mentioning Georgiana, sister of the Earl of Wakefield, when he wished to impress someone. "She might, if you take a box and Lady Sidlow gives her permission." Countess Sidlow was Georgiana's starchy chaperone in London, and she was not fond of theater. Georgiana was not usually permitted to go. "Will you take us?"

Papa chuckled. "You know I can't refuse you, my dear."

She beamed at him before turning back to the earl. "How old are your sisters, Lord Hastings?"

"About your age, Miss Cross," he said. "Edith is the elder, and Henrietta the younger. Edith is in her first Season this year, and Henrietta is eagerly anticipating her own next year."

That meant the Hastings girls were a few years younger than Eliza, who was three years past her Season, even after persuading her father to let her wait until she was nineteen. "How exciting for her. Is Lady Edith enjoying it?"

"Very much. She is especially pleased by her court gown." He said it with a wry lilt to his voice, which also made Eliza smile.

"Any new gown is worth a moment of delight, let alone one that fine." She had seen Georgiana's magnificent court gown, though never had one of her own. Not even Papa could get her presented at court, much to his irritation and Eliza's relief.

"Ladies and their shopping!" Papa shook his head. "I'll never see the fascination with silk and lace."

"Fortunately that age of fashion is over for gentlemen," Eliza said pertly. "Although you would look very handsome, Papa, in a long wig, with a velvet coat dripping in gold lace, and of course the heels worthy of Charles II."

Lord Hastings made a faint sound that might have been a smothered laugh. Papa raised one brow at her, his mouth twitching. "Fortunate indeed. Keep your laces and ribbons and all those other fripperies."

"I will, thank you."

"They are far more suited to ladies," said Lord Hastings. He raised his glass to her. "Every lady of my acquaintance does far better justice to lace and silk than any man ever could. Particularly you, Miss Cross."

Her heart gave another sigh. She knew it wasn't

true, but he was very gallant to say so. "Thank you, sir."

By the time dinner was cleared away and Eliza excused herself to leave the gentlemen to their brandy and their business discussion, she felt flushed and tipsy. She went to the drawing room and opened one of the tall windows that overlooked her garden. The soft scent of roses drifted up to her as she leaned out into the cool air.

Lord Hastings had to be the most handsome, charming, delightful man in all of London. After the first few moments she hadn't felt awkward or shy with him, and not once had she stammered herself into embarrassed silence. She hadn't even giggled, which was astonishing to her. For a moment she let herself imagine he might come to dinner regularly. Might compliment her regularly. Might stop by their box at the theater to pay his respects. Might smile at her in that way he had that suggested he found her interesting and charming . . .

Then she laughed a little at herself for spinning daydreams again. "Silly," she whispered to the silent roses. "But at least it's a lovely dream."

Chapter 5

Hᴜɢʜ sᴛɪʟʟ ᴡᴀsɴ'ᴛ sure why he'd come.

It was a long trip to Greenwich, and he had no idea what Cross wanted to discuss. But it had kept him awake all night, thinking about why Cross might have bought his mortgages and other debts, and so here he was.

The one bright spot had been Miss Cross. Whatever her father was up to, Hugh was certain she had no part of it. She was shy for one thing, with a pretty pink blush whenever he teased her about the dog. Hugh probably wouldn't have noticed her if she hadn't burst into his life looking like a half-drowned scullery maid in pursuit of a dog, but he could tell her heart was warm, and she seemed without guile or calculation.

Unlike her father.

When the door closed behind her, as she left him and Edward Cross to the brandy the servants rushed to serve, he dismissed Eliza Cross from his mind and focused on her father. "Well?" he drawled.

Cross's posture relaxed. He took a healthy sip

of his brandy and lounged back in his seat. "How was your dinner, sir?"

"Excellent." Hugh could feel the frost on his own words. "To what do I owe this invitation?"

Cross shrugged, and motioned for the servants to leave. "A desire to become acquainted."

Hugh counted to ten to keep his temper from boiling over. "Mr. Cross," he said, biting off each word, "we are not peers. We have little in common. There is no reason for us to become acquainted except for the fact that you now own most of the debts I owe."

"Thanks to your father," Cross interjected.

Hugh clenched his teeth. "Yes. That is the way of inheritance."

"Not mine," said Cross baldly. "My father left me nothing, for good or for ill."

"How kind of him." Hugh stared stonily at the man. "What do you want from me?"

"How much have you won at Vega's?"

He jerked at the invasive question. "That is hardly your concern—"

"That's your income, isn't it?" Cross nodded as Hugh seethed in impotent silence. "I thought about it for several days. I've watched plenty of aristocrats play deep at Vega's, but you don't fit their pattern. You play as if it doesn't matter whether you win or lose ten thousand pounds, but we both know that's not true—you need to win." He paused, his eyes piercing. "Don't you? You need it to stay afloat, to pay your creditors just enough to hold them at bay. I mean no affront," he added as Hugh made a choked growl. "I'm not a gentleman, remember. I see nothing wrong with needing to earn an income of some sort, rather than have it simply flow to you by divine right."

"What," repeated Hugh, "do you want?"

"Part of what made me successful was my eye for need, and surplus." Cross looked rather pleased with himself. "When one party has a need, find someone who has a corresponding surplus. Connect the two, and everyone is better off."

Hugh breathed in and out, letting his eyelids drop closed. He was helpless, trapped here while Cross rambled on about his philosophy of life and success.

"You," his host went on, "have a need. A rather crushing one. Now, some gents in your shoes might marry a duke's daughter with a plump dowry or a wealthy widow—but you haven't. Haven't even courted one, unless the gossips have missed it." Cross shrugged. "There are only a few reasons why a man in your straits wouldn't do that. I heard no rumor hinting that you have any unnatural desires, which likely means that you haven't found a woman with enough fortune to put you back in clover."

This was a circle of hell, Hugh decided. Who the devil was this man who thought he could pry into the most intimate details of a stranger's life?

"There now." Cross's voice grew almost genial. "You look so grim, Hastings! I presumed you knew what gossip said about you. It took no effort at all to hear it."

Hugh had spent the last year and a half acting a

part: the role of an earl with rather empty pockets but rich in land and consequence. Society from bottom to top understood that character very well, accepted it and embraced it. He was still invited to the most elite *ton* parties, and no tradesman had refused him credit. On one hand, it was reassuring to hear that he'd been successful, but on the other hand . . .

"I wonder why you cared to hear anything at all of me," he said to Cross. "A perfect stranger."

The other man grinned. "Do you? Come, lad, I heard you were clever. Good with cards, a careful gambler, never lose your temper or your good humor. Always a gentleman! I admire that." He shifted in his chair, leaning forward as he reached for the brandy. Hugh hadn't touched his, but Cross's glass was empty. "But neither am I afraid to lay my cards on the table. You have a need—a desperate need for money, and quite a lot of it from what I understand. Your sister Lady Edith is being courted by Livingston's heir, isn't she?"

"Yes." The word felt like the confession of a sin.

Cross nodded. "And she's got no dowry, has she?"

Hugh jolted in his seat. How the bloody hell could Cross know that? "What?"

"Richard Nesbit knew your father well," was all Cross replied. He went on with his prosecution of Hugh's failings. "Neither has your other sister, I expect. She'll be making her debut soon, won't she? That's not one but two dowries you'll need."

Feeling as if his limbs were made of wood,

Hugh rose. "Pray excuse me, Cross," he said coldly. "I must be going."

"I have a surplus," said Cross. "Of the very things you lack. Sit down, Hastings," he added when Hugh didn't move. "Not only a surplus of funds, but of a daughter without a husband."

For a moment Hugh could only stand in bemusement. Then a disbelieving laugh erupted from his throat as Cross's meaning sank in. "Are you mad? You think—you think I should marry your daughter?"

"I'd like it above all else," said the man bluntly. "Whether she'd like it is another question, but if you married her, your troubles would be over."

Hugh just stared at him. What a deranged idea. Yes—the man must be quietly deranged. There was no other explanation.

"I'll forgive the mortgages and debts outright," Cross said, his voice no longer casual and relaxed. "Elizabeth has a dowry of fifty thousand pounds, and she'll inherit the rest when I die. Almost half a million pounds as of now." A predatory smile glinted across his face for a moment. "I'm not done yet, of course. It might be twice that when I shuffle off my mortal cloak."

"Does she know about this lunatic plan?" Hugh finally found his voice.

"No, nor will she." Cross's expression hardened. "At the first word you breathe to her about this conversation, my offer is irrevocably withdrawn. I'll call the debts as strictly and as promptly as the law permits, and Hastings—I won't hesitate to set the bailiffs on you."

Hugh's lungs felt squeezed in a vise. "Very well. I won't speak to her." *Ever again*, he hoped. God spare him the sight of another Cross, even one as pleasant as Elizabeth Cross.

"The thing is, my daughter wants to make a love match." Cross poured himself more brandy. "If you were to court Eliza, whether or not she accepts you would be entirely up to her. She deserves to be adored, pursued, ardently courted, and she'll not settle for less."

Hugh laughed harshly. "You want me to play a lovesick swain, but with no guarantee the lady would even have me. What are the odds, Cross? Since this is a gamble, I need to know my chance of success."

"I've no bloody idea," said Cross, unruffled. "She smiled at you very easily, though, and I know my girl—she could fall for a gent like you."

Hugh rested his knuckles on the table and let his head hang. He was trapped in a nightmare. If he'd thought his father's mess couldn't be any worse, Fate had just served him a mighty comeuppance. "How, may I ask, did you choose me for this scheme?"

"You lost well." Cross grinned at Hugh's furious glare. "You seem to be a decent chap. I kept my ears open, and, well, what I heard boded well."

"You heard I was desperate," he bit out.

"And just as desperate to hide it." Cross slapped one hand down on the table, making Hugh look up and meet his gaze. "I'm a fair man, Hastings. If you make a good show of courting

Eliza and she turns you down, that's it—I'll not ask anything else of you. Pay the debts as you have been, and we'll have no more reason to speak."

Hugh closed his eyes. That was small mercy. But as much as he wanted to walk out of this room and let Cross stew in his own plots, he had to think rationally, even ruthlessly. Cross held his debts, but Hugh knew some of them were worthless, personal debts of honor signed by his father that he had no obligation to pay. Even so, Cross could make life unbearable for him if he so chose.

However.

Cross wanted something very dear from him. He wanted Hugh to marry his daughter and presumably give him a noble grandson. He even wanted Hugh to make the girl fall in love with him. Although he'd been putting it off, Hugh knew that marrying an heiress of his own class wouldn't have required such a thing; marriages were arranged for power and influence all the time. There would not need to be any pretense of love with an aristocratic girl, who would understand exactly what bargain she was making from the beginning.

Slowly Hugh resumed his seat. If Cross could throw down a gauntlet, he felt at liberty to make some demands of his own. "You ask a great deal," he said evenly. All those evenings of winning and losing without breaking his equable demeanor came to his aid now. "Those are high stakes indeed—the rest of my life, till death shall us part, my name, my title, my heirs, even my affection. Assuming the lady consents, which she may well not."

There was always that option, he supposed—court the girl but in such a manner that she would gently refuse him when the moment came. But that would be leaving money on the table, something Hugh had learned not to do. "Of course, if I dedicate myself to winning her, society will notice. Other unmarried ladies will presume my affections are engaged, and turn their attention to other gentlemen. If Miss Cross should refuse me, I would find myself still in debt, having lost the better part of a Season I might have spent contracting marriage to another." He arched a brow as Cross leaned back in his chair, thin-lipped.

"What will you gain, you mean? If she refuses you?"

"Precisely," said Hugh with a hard edge to his tone. "My time has value, Cross, to say nothing of the effort of courting a woman."

Cross gave him an appraising look, as if he were rethinking his evaluation of Hugh as an adversary. "What do you want?"

"Ten thousand." That would be Edith's dowry. By God, he had to get something out of this.

Cross's eyes were shrewd. "A high price for a month of your time."

Hugh shrugged, his card player's mask in place again. "I'm the seventh Earl of Hastings, the tenth Viscount Dayne and Baron Carlisle. My title was granted by King Henry V. You could have made this offer to any man in London, but you chose me. Yes, I place a high value on my time." *If you're going to buy an earl for your son-in-law, you'd best be prepared to pay the price for one,* he thought savagely.

To his surprise, Cross nodded after a moment. "Done."

"And I'll not make a debt payment while I'm courting her," Hugh pressed. "If you intend to forgive the entire debt in the event I'm successful, there's little point. Besides . . ." He smiled thinly. "I need funds to wage a proper courtship."

Cross's face grew stony. "That's quite a lot of flowers, Hastings."

"Those are my terms." He picked up his brandy glass at last and raised it. "Are we agreed?"

The other man didn't move for a moment. Hugh held his pose, his expression calm, waiting.

"Done." Cross raised his glass, and they drank, Hugh with a sense of disbelief. "One more thing," Cross said as Hugh pushed back his chair. "You have to take the dog."

Compared to having a bride foisted on him, a dog was nothing. Hugh jerked his head in agreement.

They walked to the drawing room in silence. Hugh's nerves still vibrated like plucked strings; what had he done? When they went in and found Miss Cross seated at the pianoforte, he studied her with new eyes. Did she really not know about this mad scheme of her father's? It would greatly affect how he chose to proceed.

She looked up from her music at their entrance. For a second, alarm flickered in her soft green eyes, but she rose to her feet and made a curtsy. "Have you concluded your business?"

Her voice was pleasing, not shrill or strident. Hugh bowed his head, newly attuned to every little thing about her. "We have, Miss Cross," he said before the other man could answer. "I hope we've not kept you waiting."

That pretty pink blush crept up her cheeks again. "No, not at all." She looked at her father. "Would you like me to play for you, Papa?"

"By all means, my dear," was Cross's hearty reply.

Hugh avoided meeting the man's gaze as he took a seat where he could see her face. She spread out her music and sat down, running her fingers over the keys. With one more slightly nervous smile at him, she began to play. She had a lovely singing voice. Most well-bred young ladies could play, but few could sing, and Miss Cross could.

Eliza, he reminded himself. Perhaps his future wife, the mother of his children, the woman who would share his bed and his house. She loved her dog, she sang beautifully, and she liked the theater. Other than that he knew nothing about her. Could he do this?

She wasn't a typical beauty. Her face was round and her hair was an ordinary shade of light brown. A string of pearls circled her neck, and Hugh was sure her pale green silk gown had cost as much as Edith's court gown, but it suited her. Some women had no sense of style and bought the latest fashion whether it made them ugly or exquisite. With two sisters and a mother in his house, Hugh knew enough of ladies' clothing to see that this lady chose well. When she reached to turn the page, he got up and went to stand beside her to turn the next one. Her voice wobbled a bit as he did so, but she played on.

Her skin was lovely. He spied a few freckles on her nose, but her shoulders and bosom were as pale as cream. Her bosom . . . Hugh reached for the next page and stole a quick glance downward. Plump and tempting, now that he looked at it. Her hands were graceful on the keys, and his mind wandered involuntarily into thoughts of what they would feel like on him. What it would be like to kiss her. What she would be like in bed. Would she be shy? Frightened? He found himself hoping not, even though he hadn't even decided to court her yet.

Was half a million pounds worth it? Could he convince the girl he was mad with passion for her? Hugh thought he probably could. Could he carry it through into wedding her? Could he face the rest of his life with her, always wondering when Edward Cross would whisper more threats and demands in his ear?

Her hands went still. Hugh stared at the nape of her neck, at the honey-colored wisps curling against her pale skin. Could he chance it? Did he have a choice?

"Bravo," called Cross from his seat. "What did you think, Hastings?"

He had to clear his throat. "Lovely. You've a splendid voice, Miss Cross."

She twisted to look up at him, her eyes shining with delight. "Thank you, sir."

Hugh smiled on instinct. That look . . . She wasn't a beauty, nor even very pretty. London society would call her plain. But when she gazed at a man that way, with her heart in her eyes, she was not ordinary.

She sang another, and by then Hugh had had enough. He took his leave, blaming the long trip back to London. Miss Cross gave another graceful curtsy and wished him a safe journey. Edward Cross bowed and simply said, "Until later, my lord."

The cool night air felt like an Arctic chill on his face as he walked down the long gravel path to the dock. Cross's house, a splendid mansion of pale Portland Stone, sat in a lordly position above the Thames on the western edge of Greenwich. He'd sent his private yacht to fetch Hugh, and the pilot was waiting for him as he reached the river. Hugh settled into the plush seating at the prow of the boat and watched London glide past in the last glow of twilight. It would be dark soon, the time of night he usually set out in pursuit of winning.

If he married Eliza Cross, he wouldn't have to do that ever again.

Hugh let out his breath. Taking Cross's word that she had no idea what her father was suggesting, he tried to consider the girl on her own merits. Would he have considered courting her in the absence of her father's manipulation?

Absolutely not, because he'd never heard of her—never even met her.

Would he have considered her as his bride if he'd met her some innocuous way, at a ball or a Venetian breakfast?

Almost certainly not.

Would he have considered her as his bride if he'd met her innocently, and discovered she came with a vast fortune?

Perhaps.

And there was the rub.

Hugh had accepted the fact that he must marry for duty. Most of his ancestors had, save his father, and the Hastings estates had prospered under their hands. Only Joshua, strong-willed, passionate Joshua, had married simply for love, and he'd nearly been the ruin of three hundred years' accumulation of wealth and power. Truth be told, Hugh thought it was safer not to marry for love, because he needed the money so much more.

So, was there any reason Eliza Cross shouldn't be the heiress he courted?

If Cross had offered a straightforward arranged marriage, this would be so much simpler. Hugh had friends who had wed that way; it was a business transaction, arranged by the families and approved by the lawyers. A man only had to find his bride appealing enough to bed her until she bore an heir, and then both were free to live their own lives. Perhaps this would turn out that way.

Even as the thought crossed his mind, he suspected deep down that she would not want that. And it was unfair to trick her into agreeing to it, no matter what her father thought.

Well. That was Cross's doing, not his. Hugh had bargained a fair compensation. There was no reason not to court the girl for a bit and see how things went. If she saw through him and refused, he'd still have gained Edith's dowry. But if somehow a spark caught between them, if she fell for him as her father foresaw, if he felt enough affinity to be content with her as his wife . . .

Hugh had risked longer odds.

Chapter 6

ＥLIZA WAITED FOR her father to say something about the Earl of Hastings the next morning, but he seemed to have forgotten all about the man. He was in an exceptionally good mood, teasing her about the toys she'd fetched from the nursery for Willy.

"Those were put away for my grandchildren," he said as she tossed a wooden ball across the garden. Willy tore after it, his ears flat back as he bounded over a low stone wall.

"You know," remarked Eliza, "Willy is probably much better behaved than a small child would be. He goes to his basket and sits quietly when told to."

Papa scoffed. "He chews the table legs!"

"He hasn't done that in months." Eliza forbore mentioning that Willy had shredded an old bonnet she'd carelessly left out just the other day. "Besides, these toys for your grandchildren were actually *my* toys, and as such I decided to use them again." Willy trotted back, ball in his teeth, and Eliza knelt to praise him. "Good boy, Willy."

"Your mother packed them away when you grew too big for them," Papa complained. "She told me they were for our grandchildren, and now the mutt will chew them to pieces."

"You'll have to buy new toys, then, if you ever have grandchildren." Eliza heaved the ball and Willy raced off again. "What a terrible pity for you."

Papa barked with laughter. "I take that as a promise you'll give me grandchildren! You're my only hope, Lilibeth; I'd like a pair of boys to dandle on my knee, and a little girl to spoil outrageously."

Eliza rolled her eyes. "No one can promise to have children, let alone how many boys and how many girls."

"Nevertheless I want some of each, and I'm counting on you." He winked at her.

Willy brought the ball back, his tongue flopping out of his mouth in joy at the game, and Eliza threw it once more, as hard as she could. Willy liked to run, and the grounds were expansive. "It would be easier to get some dogs. Then you can choose what breed, what sex, even what color."

"We have enough dogs already—more than enough." Papa ignored her scowl at the slight to Willy.

Eliza was used to her father's persistent talk of her marrying, but this talk of grandchildren was new—and depressing. It was one thing to accept that she would be an eccentric old lady with a pack of dogs for company, and another to remember that meant she would never be a mother. Eliza loved children. Belinda Reeve, the vicar's wife, had two small daughters, who delighted and charmed Eliza every time they met. No matter how much she told herself she could spoil Georgiana's future children, or Sophie's, they wouldn't be *her* children. They wouldn't crawl onto her lap and put their little arms around her neck; they wouldn't call her Mama and tell her they loved her with sweet childish lisps.

Like her friends, Eliza was an only child—Georgiana's brother was twenty years her elder and didn't count. The three of them had promised they would be godmothers to each other's children, but Eliza was sure she was the only one of the three who would never have to make that request. Georgiana would be Lady Sterling soon, and Sophie was far too beautiful to remain unwed, even though she had no money and had been disowned by her grandfather. Where Eliza would have been devastated to be on her own, though, Sophie had a plan. Sophie was a survivor, and since she'd been able to take care of herself so far—rather well—Eliza was sure Sophie would find a husband once she decided she wanted one.

That would leave Eliza, alone and unwed, knitting lace caps for her friends' babies and never for her own.

"What did you think of Lord Hastings?" Papa asked, scattering her morose thoughts.

Eliza flushed. "Very charming." Willy dropped the ball at her feet, and she stooped to retrieve it, grateful to hide her face. "Has he decided to do business with you?" Papa never would have invited him if he hadn't wanted to partner with the earl.

"I believe so," said Papa thoughtfully. "He's no fool, that one."

She smiled. "Then he must have decided! Who would pass on a chance to learn from the great Edward Cross?"

Papa did not, as expected, laugh at her teasing or scoff at it. He stared off across the grass as Willy raced after the ball yet again. "Well, we shall see. I suppose if he comes back, I'll have my answer."

She started. "He's coming back?" While it wasn't uncommon for Papa to have business partners over for dinner, he usually went into London to see them. Even his friends like Mr. Grenville rarely came all the way to Greenwich.

"Perhaps." Papa slanted a curious look at her. "Does that bother you?"

"Why would it?" She waved one hand in front of her burning face. "Of course not. My, it's warm out."

"He seemed very taken by your singing last night," Papa went on.

Stricken by a sudden suspicion, Eliza shot a wary look at him. But Papa was watching Willy, whose eye had been caught by some robins. The birds were scratching for worms, but flew away in a chorus of squawks when Willy bounded toward them. "I like a man who has a good ear," added Papa absently, squinting at the robins fluttering above her dog's frantic leaping.

Thank goodness. For a moment she'd had the terrible thought Papa was hinting that she try to flirt with Lord Hastings. All that talk of grandchildren . . .

"What sort of business are you planning with him?" she asked instead. Her father was involved in a variety of things, and if Lord Hastings would be expected again at their home, Eliza needed something intelligent to say to him.

"What?" Papa frowned, then waved one hand. "Nothing exciting—don't trouble your head about it, my dear. It may well come to nothing. But I should be on my way. Grenville wants to persuade me to invest in his latest scheme."

"Oh no. Not again."

"Something about balloon travel," Papa went on with a nod. "Some chap he knows thinks he's sorted out how to pilot the silly things from Norwich to Amsterdam without crashing into the sea. Grenville envisions turning it into a courier service to the Continent."

Eliza laughed. "I can see you're taken by the prospect. Mr. Grenville has a way of talking you into the worst ideas."

"He's a bloody charlatan," said Papa fondly, of one of his dearest friends. "I'll be back for dinner."

"I'm taking tea with Sophie and Georgiana today," she reminded him.

"An excellent diversion. Remember me to both of them." Papa kissed her cheek and left, probably not to return until the small hours of the morning. Thank goodness he hadn't noticed her expression when she'd thought he was implying

Lord Hastings might admire her. That was too ridiculous even for Papa to suggest.

HUGH TRIED TO PUSH Edward Cross's mad proposal from his mind for several days, until one of his worst fears came to pass. Reginald Benwick, eldest son and heir of Lord Livingston, called on him and asked for Edith's hand.

The moment Mr. Benwick was announced, Hugh's mind began to race. Damn it. He'd made a little progress since the disastrous evening when twelve thousand pounds slipped through his fingers, but not enough. He could give Edith at most five thousand, and that would leave him scraping for pennies to feed his mother and sister.

"My lord," said Mr. Benwick when he had been shown in, "I have come to treasure your sister Lady Edith very dearly. She is a wonderful, sweet-natured, beautiful lady, and I would like to make her my wife."

"Have you spoken to her?" Perhaps Edith would save him and string the boy along for a few more days . . .

But no. Benwick nodded, fairly glowing with satisfaction. "I have, and she has consented. I would like your blessing."

Hugh smiled. "If she's given you her blessing, mine counts but little! I am happy to give it. May you share a long life together in contentment and joy."

"Thank you, sir." The young man jumped out of his seat. "May I go to her now? She's been waiting very anxiously for the results of our interview."

He raised one brow. "Has she? Ought I put you through some sort of test of valor? I've never done this before, you know."

Benwick grinned. "Neither have I! And I am vastly relieved to have it out of the way." He paused. "My father said I should tell you his solicitors will call upon yours, when it is agreeable."

To write the marriage contract. To spell out the transfer of Edith's dowry, which she did not have. Hugh waved one hand carelessly. "There's plenty of time for the lawyers. If I know my mother and sister, they'll need to begin shopping at once if they're to assemble a grand enough trousseau by the end of the year."

"The end of the year?" Benwick blinked. "I had hoped to marry her sooner, my lord—certainly before the end of the year."

Hugh laughed even as his small hope that he could put this off for a few more months capsized and sank. "I never interfere between a woman and her modiste. It's up to you to urge them on, my good man. But I suspect Edith will be an eager bride."

His visitor laughed, too, relief coloring his face. "Oh I do hope so! Even a month will seem an eternity." He stopped, looking abashed. "But I should go to Lady Edith—my Edith," he repeated more tenderly. "I want to tell her right away. Thank you, my lord." He bowed and hurried out the door.

Hugh let out a shuddering breath and hung his head. He was out of time. And he couldn't bear to see his sister disappointed now. Somehow he had to scrape together a reasonable dowry. For a moment Edward Cross's voice echoed in his mind: *my daughter has a dowry of fifty thousand pounds . . . she'll inherit half a million more . . .*

A tap at the door made him jump. His mother, Rose, peeked in, her face wreathed in joy. "I saw young Mr. Benwick leave," she began, then stopped. The pleased smile slid from her face. "Darling, what's wrong?"

He heaved a sigh and made his expression even more tragic. If he told her the truth, she would be inconsolable, and incapable of keeping it from his sisters. He had lied to her for a year and a half, and now it was impossible to stop. "He's going to take her away, Mother. Who shall tease me about my waistcoats from now on?"

She smiled again and closed the door. "Henrietta might try, if you ask her."

"No, no." He propped his chin in one hand. "I shall have to suffer the agony of not knowing if a blue silk embroidered with red elephants suits me."

"Edith tells me they wish to be married soon. She will need a trousseau."

Hugh thought of all that she'd spent at the modiste already. What else could Edith possibly need? "Oh? Of course," he said, pretending ignorance. "I thought we could let her take her pillow, and her hairbrush . . . perhaps that chair she favors in the drawing room . . ."

"Darling," said his mother in reproach.

"I'm teasing, of course." He came around his desk to take her hand. "I hope she truly cares for him."

She gripped his hand in both of hers. "She

does. Your father would be so pleased. He used to say he looked forward to giving her to a man who could love her as much as he loved me—" She choked off, but waved it aside when he offered a handkerchief. "He'd be so pleased," she repeated in a steadier voice. "A future viscountess. Do you think you can arrange the settlements quickly?"

"Er." Hugh busied himself with replacing the handkerchief, buying a moment. "We'll see how miserly Livingston plans to be."

"Oh no!" His mother blinked in dismay. "If he is, then you must be doubly generous with her. Edith deserves her happiness."

Somehow he managed to smile. "She does."

He had been standing at the crossroads for a week, waiting, hoping, praying something would happen to spare him the choice he had to make. Now he saw there was nothing and no one coming to help him. One way lay telling the truth, tearing the veil from his mother's and sisters' eyes and letting them see how penniless they were. He would have to explain the depth of his father's mismanagement and deception. He would have to tell Edith that he had no dowry to give her, and that he must tell Lord Livingston even if it caused the viscount to withdraw his consent for the marriage.

The other way lay in sacrificing himself. It would be easier at first, though there was a chance he could end up regretting it for the rest of his life. Still, he'd known, deep down, that it would probably come to this; the only surprising part was the girl. He thought of Eliza Cross's pink-cheeked smile as she spoke of her dog, and the gratitude in her eyes when he turned the pages of her music. She wasn't scheming to manipulate him. She seemed to be a perfectly lovely girl. She had a fortune he desperately needed.

He took a deep breath. "Edith might not be the only one reciting vows soon."

"But Henrietta isn't even out—" His mother's mouth dropped open. "You don't mean . . . ?" she whispered in amazement.

He managed a rueful smile as he held up his hands. "Perhaps. Perhaps not. I've met a young lady, is what I ought to have said."

"Who?"

"No, no, I'll not say a word until I know if she returns my regard." He wasn't sure if he wanted Miss Cross to fall for him or not. If she didn't, he'd still get a dowry for his sister. But either way, he intended to court her.

There really wasn't much of a choice.

Chapter 7

ᏬᎦᏍᏏᎦᏯ

Eliza had just dug up another pernicious weed from her garden, clearing a space for the young rosebushes that were finally ready to be planted, when the butler came to find her. "Lord Hastings has come to call, ma'am."

"What?"

Roberts blinked at her dismayed exclamation. "I informed him that Mr. Cross is not at home, and His Lordship then inquired if you were."

Eliza looked around, her heart sinking. Once again, she was wearing an old dress, dirty and crumpled from gardening. Her hair was tied up in a severe knot and flattened beneath her ancient straw hat, and her arms were streaked with grime and little bits of the weed she'd been hacking out of the rose bed. Lord Hastings had a terrible knack for catching her at her worst.

The butler's question was waiting. Slowly she climbed to her feet. Papa liked the earl; he hoped their business venture came to fruition. He would be disappointed if Eliza hid in the potting shed and sent Lord Hastings back to London instead of receiving him in her father's stead like a proper lady. She would have to do this.

"Beg His Lordship's pardon," she told Roberts, "and tell him I will be with him soon. Offer him something to drink. Tell Martha to prepare tea—a full tea, not just a few cakes—and send for Mary to attend me at once." She pulled off her gardening gloves and swiped the hat from her head. "And put Willy in the kitchen garden," she added, catching sight of the dog. He was sleeping under the bench by the fountain now, but he'd spring to life the moment she started toward the house.

Roberts nodded, and Eliza picked up her skirts and ran.

It took over a quarter of an hour to reach her room, frantically scrub the dirt from her face and arms, change her dress, locate proper slippers, and have her maid, Mary, brush out her hair. Eliza closed her eyes in despair as Mary fussed over it, and finally told the girl to wind it up into a simple chignon. She flew back down the stairs, slowing to a walk outside the drawing room even as her pulse still raced. She told herself it was the exertion and not the prospect of facing a handsome man, but when the footman opened the door and she walked in to see Lord Hastings rising to greet her, her heart gave a leap that had nothing to do with her mad dash down the stairs.

"I'm so sorry, my lord, for keeping you waiting," she said breathlessly, making her curtsy. "My father is not at home and I did not expect visitors."

He smiled. Today his dark hair was tousled

into loose curls, and his dimple appeared with devastating effect. "It's my own fault, Miss Cross, for not sending word to your father first. You're very kind to receive me."

"Nonsense." She caught herself before the nervous giggle could break free. "It's quiet out here in Greenwich. Visitors are always welcome."

Bless the heavens, Roberts tapped at the door and brought in the tray she had ordered. Eliza busied herself serving. Lord Hastings accepted a small plate of sandwiches and a cup of tea with just a splash of milk and a tiny bit of sugar, which made her heart take another silly leap. She took her tea exactly the same way. *Which means exactly nothing*, she told herself.

"Do you like Greenwich?" he asked politely.

Eliza's eyes went wide. "Greenwich? Yes. Oh." She bit her lip, remembering. "I said it's quiet. It is very quiet, much more so than London. My good friend Georgiana Lucas lives right in Cavendish Square, and she tells me it's noisy at all hours."

"It is," he agreed with a faint smile. "Is she the sister of the Earl of Wakefield?"

"Yes." Too late Eliza realized she ought to have called her friend Lady Georgiana. "Are you acquainted with her?"

"No, but I hear of her. My sisters think she is one of the most elegant ladies in London, and more than once they have come home from a walk in the park near fainting with rapture over the dress Lady Georgiana wore."

Eliza laughed. "They are correct! Lady Georgiana has exquisite taste."

Again his eyes crinkled in that almost-smile. "I must say the same of you, Miss Cross, if you've had the decorating of this house."

This time she blushed with pleasure. House decorating was, she felt, one of her few talents. Papa had thrown up his hands and said she could do whatever she liked to any room but his study, and so Eliza had indulged her every fancy. The drawing room was her favorite, in soft yellow with crisp draperies of ivory silk. The furniture was light but comfortable, upholstered in striped damask, and all the lamps and ornaments were crystal. The tall windows looked out over the lawn spreading down to the river, and on sunny days the entire room glowed.

"I have," she acknowledged, trying to smother the bubbling delight inside her. "My mother died when I was a child, and my father would cover the walls with oak paneling and hang velvet draperies everywhere, if it were left to him." She wrinkled her nose. "Very manly, but also very dark."

"He was wise to give it into your hands."

"Thank you, my lord." She could feel herself blushing hotter under his approval, and took a quick sip of tea to hide it. "Are your sisters both out?"

"No. Henrietta won't be out until next Season, but our mother has allowed her to attend some events. She said it's unfair for one sister to go to balls and soirees and expect the other sister to sit quietly at home." He gave a rueful grin. "But I must say, Henrietta is *avidly* anticipating her own debut."

Eliza smiled wistfully. "Your mother sounds very wise. Your sisters are fortunate to have her."

He regarded her with compassion. "We all are. She's a loving mother."

She swallowed a burst of envy. "I never had a sister, either, though I often wished for one."

Lord Hastings's mouth quirked. "I cannot say I am sorry I have sisters, though they can be vexing at times. They may not be as pleased to have a brother."

"Oh no, I'm sure they are!"

He laughed and she blushed.

Eliza had dreaded her Season, and only had one because Papa insisted. He took a house in the middle of London, hired a very proper companion, and wrangled a list of invitations. Eliza soon realized that the companion had only accepted the post because Papa offered her an indecent amount of money, and the invitations were to second tier events or hosted by people who owed Papa a favor. Despite her father's best efforts, nothing could pry her way into the most elite parties, and Eliza was vastly relieved when it ended.

Lady Henrietta, of course, would face no such barrier, which was probably why she was eager for her debut. Perhaps having a sister would have made her Season more enjoyable, Eliza thought. "I hope Lady Henrietta has a wonderful time next year," she told the earl.

"I'm sure she shall. Do you enjoy the Season's events, as well?"

Her mouth opened, but no words came out. Oh dear. How to answer without looking like a recluse or a hopeless wallflower? "I enjoy the theater," she said carefully. "Not so much balls." She waved one hand with a wry smile. "I found balls and parties very overwhelming when I came out into society, and now I prefer more intimate gatherings of friends."

"Those are always the best society," he agreed with a smile.

"I also like a quiet evening at home," she added. "Reading or playing the pianoforte. Especially if Papa is home. He's often out late, and it's a special evening when he is home."

"Er—yes. I'm sure." He inclined his head.

Eliza fiddled with her cup; they were running out of polite topics of conversation. What should she say?

"Have you decided to go into business with my father?" she blurted out.

His brows rose, and he paused, holding his teacup in midair. "I beg your pardon?"

Mortified, Eliza tried to smile. "He said you had not decided, when you came to dinner. Forgive me for prying—"

"No," he said, staring at her. "Of course you must wonder."

Her hands were shaking. She set down her cup and twisted her fingers together. "If you have decided, I only wanted to assure you that Papa's not nearly as harsh as he sometimes seems. He's very . . . very competitive, I suppose, and he likes to win. But that serves him well in his investments, and his investors are usually quite pleased."

A thin line appeared between his brows. He also set down his cup and pushed the plate of sandwiches aside. "Does he speak to you of all his business affairs?"

Too late Eliza remembered what Mrs. Burney, her one-time companion, had tried to drill into her head. The aristocracy thought it was vulgar to discuss money, and as she was a female, no one cared about her opinions of it anyway. Her face felt like it was on fire. "No," she murmured. "I—I only wondered . . ."

"Did you?" He sat back, studying her with an odd expression. "I confess, it's been a difficult decision to reach. Your father is a demanding man."

"Oh no—well, yes," she amended. "When it comes to business he is. To me he is the kindest, most loving parent I could imagine."

One corner of his mouth lifted, but it looked more bitter than amused. "I have not seen that side of him."

"It's true!" Anxious to make up for introducing this disastrous topic, Eliza moved to the front of her chair. "He's very generous to anyone in need. My friends from school were always welcome here, and he's almost as fond of them as if they were his own daughters, which is lovely because Sophie is an orphan, and Georgiana nearly is. He would do anything to keep them from harm."

"And he would do anything for you."

"Well, yes. He's a very affectionate father . . ." She trailed off hesitantly. The earl's eyes were dark and opaque, his face set in hard lines. She hazarded a weak smile. "To me he is wonderful, but I suppose most daughters think so of their fathers."

Some of the tension faded from Lord Hastings. "Every lady deserves a father who would do anything for her."

Her smile brightened. "Yes. Very much."

"This proposal he put to me—" Lord Hastings stopped and looked sharply at her. "He didn't explain it to you?"

"Oh no, I've no idea," she said quickly. "Sometimes he tells me, if he thinks it's a silly idea. One friend of his has a plan to travel to Amsterdam by balloon. Papa thinks they'll crash into the North Sea instead. Generally he assures me the things he does are far too dull to talk about and would put me to sleep. Trading shares of grain, and things like it."

"Right." Hastings regarded her in silence for a moment. "I suppose there's no harm in telling you that I have decided to do business with Mr. Cross. Even if he doesn't discuss things with you, you would sort it out soon enough. We'll probably see more of each other, as your father and I work together." His smile this time was a little crooked. "Now you're forewarned."

Eliza flushed a painful shade of red at how unprepared she'd been thus far. "How wonderful," she said. "I'm sure Papa will be quite pleased to hear it." The clock chimed the hour, making her jump. "Would you like to leave a message for him? I expect him home after dinner."

"If you would pass on my agreement to his proposal, I would be very grateful." He looked at his teacup, then drained it. "Thank you, Miss Cross. I must return to London."

Oh thank heavens the visit was over. Eliza leapt to her feet. "I certainly will tell him, my lord. And I do apologize again that he was not here to see you himself."

"No, no." He also rose, and suddenly smiled at her, so beautifully dazzling she almost swayed on her feet. "It was an unexpected pleasure to see you instead, and I cannot bring myself to regret his absence."

Flattering empty words, and yet Eliza felt her insides go up in flames like dry kindling touched with a taper. She walked out with him and managed to make a polite farewell, watching as he swung into the saddle of a handsome roan gelding. He tipped his hat to her, then rode off. Eliza exhaled, watching until he disappeared through the gates at the Deptford Road.

We'll see more of each other, echoed his words in her mind. *It was an unexpected pleasure to see you.*

Eliza knew very well he had not meant them in any romantic way. He couldn't possibly, being a charming, sophisticated aristocrat who was almost too handsome to be real. But still, he'd said those words, to *her*, without any prompting or prodding, and there was a very happy little smile on her lips when she went back into the house.

Chapter 8

Hugh spent some time thinking about how to proceed. It did not appear Miss Cross went out in society much, which was both for the better and for the worse. On one hand, it wouldn't put his courtship of her right in front of the *ton*'s face, perhaps sparing him any rude gossip for a while. But on the other hand, it would be far less convenient. He couldn't simply plot to attend the same events she did, because she didn't attend many. He would have to seek her out in Greenwich, which meant he'd have to come up with multiple excuses to go there. He sent a terse note to Cross pointing this out and telling the man it would be considerably easier if he would take a box at the Theatre Royal and escort his daughter regularly.

Cross replied that he had already done so, and expected to see Hugh there the next night.

Hugh did not tell his mother and sisters he planned to attend the theater. He had been avoiding them lately. All three spoke daily of the wedding plans, the trousseau, what Edith would need in her new household. Edith was aglow with happiness, and every sentence out of her mouth managed to mention Benwick in some way, reminding Hugh every bloody day of how urgently he needed to act. Henrietta, a generous and loyal sister, happily played along with Edith's adoration. Rose was bursting with pride at having her eldest daughter engaged, and in a true love match; she had long openly wished her children would have the sort of marriage she'd had. Hugh found it hard to keep quiet when she said things like that.

In time, of course, they would have to know about Miss Cross. He hoped they would like her, and she them.

Hugh had deliberately gone to Greenwich when Cross was away, hoping to meet her again. Now that the choice was made, he wanted a fresh view of her. It was a vast relief to see that she was as he had thought the first time he met her, somewhat shy but kind and decent. He wasn't sure what he thought of her looks yet. The first time he'd set eyes on her had not been promising, but even a beauty would have looked wretched in that dingy apron, smelling of wet dog. She'd been exquisitely dressed and even pretty when he dined at Greenwich, but then looked as if she'd been cleaning with the servants again when he called.

He told himself it didn't really matter what she looked like, but it would be harder to persuade everyone he'd fallen in love with her if she went about looking like a scullery maid half the time. His mother had been a noted beauty in her youth, and his sisters took pride in appearing at their best, even for an afternoon at home. They would wonder in amazement if he claimed to fall in love with a girl who dressed like a shopkeeper's assistant.

Hugh bought a ticket in the pit for the evening performance, and made his way through the throngs. It didn't take long to spy Mr. Cross and his daughter; the man had taken the largest, most prominent box, one usually taken by a duke or royal personage. Miss Cross sat at the front of it, leaning forward in obvious delight. Her father appeared quite pleased with himself, sitting with his arms folded as he nodded to everyone who glanced his way. Hugh wondered if he knew people were staring at him because they were scandalized, not because they were admiring, then decided it was probably all the same to Cross.

He went up at the first interval. The door to the box stood open, but no one went in. The father and daughter looked rather lonely in the spacious box, sitting at the front with their heads together. Hugh cleared his throat and tapped on the door. Miss Cross looked up, and her lips parted at the sight of him.

"Good evening, Miss Cross." He bowed. "Sir."

"Lord Hastings." She rose and curtsied, her cheeks pink.

"Am I intruding?"

"No, no, come right in." Cross was watching, one arm propped on the rail, his eyes shrewd.

Hugh ignored him and strolled toward the daughter, his future wife. "Are you enjoying the opera?" It was some melodramatic production called *Devil's Bridge*. Hugh hadn't registered a word of it.

She brightened. "Oh yes, very much! Are you, sir?"

He couldn't help but smile at the enthusiasm in her voice. She hadn't exaggerated her fondness for theater. "I am. My sister saw this opera last week, and I've heard about nothing since but Miss Kelly's performance." That was marginally a lie. Edith *had* seen the show, with Benwick and his parents, but she hadn't cared for it, and the only words she'd said about the soprano star had been dismissive.

Miss Cross smiled. "Yes, Miss Kelly has excellent intonation."

"Is your family here as well?" asked Edward Cross.

Hugh managed to smile as if it were no matter. As if he would bring his family and publicly introduce them to the man who had arrogated to himself Hugh's choice of bride. "No. I have been enjoying the show from the pit."

"Down there?" exclaimed Miss Cross. "Is it as boisterous as it looks? I don't know how anyone could hear the singers."

"It is a bit boisterous," he admitted with a grin and a wink. "But I was too late to secure a seat in the stalls."

"Poor planning," said Edward Cross, shaking his finger. "I hope it's not your habit."

There was a warning in that. Hugh looked right at the man. "Normally I plan quite carefully.

There are times, though, when circumstances change rather abruptly and one must adjust plans to suit them."

Cross gave his faint smile. "How fortunate that you are so agile in your thinking."

"One must be," returned Hugh, "given the manipulations of Fate."

"I don't know about the manipulations of Fate," said Miss Cross, sounding determinedly pleasant. Hugh realized his exchange with her father had turned tense very quickly. "But you are very welcome to join us in our box, sir. It's quite large and comfortable."

He affected surprise. "Are you certain? Is no one else joining you?"

"No." She gave her father an exasperated glance. "Speaking of poor planning, Papa did not tell me he had taken a box until this morning, and there wasn't time to invite anyone."

"And so I have had you to myself," the man answered, unrepentant.

She threw up her hands, but with a smile. "Lord Hastings, I hope you will join us."

"Thank you, Miss Cross. I would be delighted." He turned to her father, hating the man for the satisfied expression he wore. Cross had schemed to keep other guests from the box, just as he'd schemed for Hugh to find them here. "I wonder if I might have a word, sir?"

Cross got up and followed him to the rear of the box. Miss Cross resumed her seat and rested her hands on the rail, leaning forward to study the crowd. Hugh couldn't help noticing the smooth curve of her neck and shoulders, bare except for a string of flawless pearls. Her pink gown was exactly right for an unmarried young lady, but made of finest silk and lace. She had excellent taste, he admitted. Many women with Cross's vast fortune at their disposal wouldn't be able to resist every expensive adornment in London.

"Well done, Hastings," said Cross in a low voice. "I understand you called on her the other day."

Hugh's mouth tightened. "No, sir, I called upon *you*. You were out. It would be improper for me to call upon a young lady alone."

"Right." Cross looked amused. "The rules of your game."

God save him. Hugh breathed deeply. "The rules of society, yes. Would you want the *ton* to think your daughter is a loose woman, given how determined you are to see her made part of it?" Without waiting for an answer, he asked the real question. "What is the nature of our fictitious business relationship? Your daughter asked and I will have to tell her something at some point."

Cross's eyes had narrowed at the reproof. Now he looked contemptuous. "You have an estate in Cornwall. Quite a large one, too. Tell her you suspect there's a vein of ore beneath your land. I made a pretty fortune off tin and copper from Cornish mines."

Hugh stiffened in fury at the thought of Cross digging mines in the grounds of Rosemere, the estate his father had rebuilt and renamed in honor of his mother. He'd rather be sent to the Fleet than allow that.

But no, it did not matter what excuse he gave. Cross wasn't going to dig up Rosemere, and Miss Cross would never have to know. "As you say."

"Ride out to call as often as you want." Cross's eyes gleamed in the dim box. "I'm usually away from home before dinner."

When he could see Miss Cross alone. Hugh jerked his head in acknowledgment.

Cross nodded once, then turned back to his daughter. "Eliza, would you like some lemonade or ratafia?"

"Thank you, Papa, please." She turned her head to smile at him, and in that moment she looked rather lovely. With her face lit by affection and happiness, she wasn't actually plain, Hugh realized. Her face was unremarkable, true, but there was a brightness and an animation to her tonight, some spark that made her arresting.

Cross left without asking if Hugh wanted any wine, and he went to take the seat beside her. "Thank you for inviting me to join you."

The pulse throbbed nervously at the base of her throat, but her smile was warm and steady. "Of course. Usually Papa gives me leave to invite friends when he takes a box."

Hugh let his voice drop. "I take it as an honor to be invited, then."

The corners of her mouth quivered, and she blinked as if startled. "Oh—well—" Color suddenly roared up her face. "That is, I did not mean to presume, my lord—"

"I know." He made the smallest touch on her gloved hand. "I could see the offer was made only out of kindness. Although . . . I would count it an honor to be called your friend."

Her eyes were perfectly round. They were not green, he realized; more of a hazel, with some gold and brown mixed in. Her lashes were long, thick and dark, and she looked almost shocked, staring at him.

Hugh sat back in his chair. "How does Willy fare?"

Her shoulders eased. "Perfectly well. He chased a duck into the river the other day and required another bath." Hugh made a face and she smiled. "I spoke to all the staff, and now the doors stay firmly closed when Willy is in his bath, so he can't run wild in the house again."

"You said you found him." Talking about the dog put her at ease. It seemed the safest topic for now.

"I did." Her face brightened, and she turned in her chair to face him. "Under a bush near Kew. William—that's our head groom—believes he's half spaniel, half pointer, and that he was the result of an illicit liaison between some gentleman's hunting dog and his lady's lapdog."

Hugh laughed. "I'm sure it happens all the time."

She regaled him with a few more anecdotes about Willy. Her demeanor completely changed when she talked about the dog, Hugh realized. Instead of blushing and shy, she grew animated and droll. She made him laugh with the story of Willy meeting a new calf at the market, and he was surprised when the lights went down again for the farce to begin. Edward Cross slipped into the box as the orchestra began to play, handing his daughter a glass of lemonade.

Hugh paid no more attention to the farce than he had to the opera. He took every opportunity to study the young woman sitting beside him. She didn't hide her amusement at the production on stage, laughing at the pranks of the fool and clapping one hand to her mouth when the hero fell to his knee and proclaimed his love for the fainting maiden. Hugh sensed it was all genuine, as genuine as her nerves and her devotion to Willy and even her welcoming words to him this evening. Eliza Cross was not a liar.

Her father, though, would put Machiavelli to shame.

When it was over, he bade them farewell. While Miss Cross was adjusting her shawl, he leaned close to Mr. Cross. "I shall call on Thursday next at two o'clock," he murmured. "Tell her you expect to be home by then, but delay half an hour."

Cross nodded once.

"And for God's sake, let her invite her friends as usual the next time you come to the theater," Hugh added. "She'll become suspicious if we keep meeting this way, and a woman's heart is influenced by her friends' approval."

Cross gave him a sharp look, but Hugh ignored it and walked away, into the crowd of people leaving the theater.

He was considering the evening, and realizing

with some surprise that it had been more enjoyable than expected, when someone slung an arm around his shoulders. "Hastings," exclaimed a voice in his ear. "As I live and breathe, man! What are you doing here?"

He laughed and shrugged off his friend's hold. Robert Fairfield, younger brother of the Duke of Raleigh, punched him in the shoulder, grinning broadly. "Fancy seeing you here. I didn't know you liked opera."

Fairfield made a face. "Not much. My mother's in town. She thinks I ought to get married or some ridiculous thing, and she's dragged me 'round to balls and theater and I don't know what else. It's a bloody miracle I haven't succumbed to an intense affliction of stupendous boredom."

"You, married? That *is* ridiculous," agreed Hugh.

"Right!" His friend grinned. "But you, apparently not. Got your eye on Double Cross's daughter?"

Hugh paused on the brink of denying it. He couldn't confirm it, not yet, but he did need to start planting seeds. "Double Cross? You mean Edward Cross?"

"That's the one. Stole a promising investment right from under Raleigh."

"Stole?" repeated Hugh slowly. "How?"

"Well—*stole.*" Fairfield made a face. "My brother was in a lather over being denied it. Blamed Cross. Something about canal bonds, I don't know. All I was told is, Cross fights dirty and we should all hate his guts."

His muscles eased. He already knew Cross

played dirty, and it wasn't wrong to say he hated the man, either. "I'll keep an eye on my investment, then."

"And your back," warned Fairfield. "Before you know it, Cross will have swindled you right out of your trousers and your braces, and leave you holding your small clothes up with both hands." Then he grinned slyly. "Of course, if you think to win his daughter, that would steal a march on him . . ."

"Miss Cross seems a lovely girl, I must tell you," he said, deliberately ignoring the rest. "My sisters would call her sweet. Not like her father at all."

"No?" His friend looked thoughtful, then shrugged it off. "Are you headed for Vega's tonight?"

Of course he was. If by some miracle the gods of luck smiled on him, he might yet win enough to give Edith a proper dowry. Of course, Cross would still own him, and Hugh didn't think all the luck in the world would enable him to win enough to pay that debt. "I'll see you there," he told Fairfield, who raised one hand in farewell and ambled off with some other young bucks.

Well, he'd known all along it would attract notice. If merely entering a box caught Fairfield's attention, Hugh should assume half of London would know about it by tomorrow. He would have to think of what to tell his mother and sisters.

Chapter 9

ELIZA WAS HAVING a hard time keeping herself from thinking of Lord Hastings.

She had never had this problem with any of Papa's other partners. It was probably because most of them were neither handsome nor charming, while the earl was both, but it was more than that. Mr. Grenville had used to bring her sweets when she was a girl, and Sir David had used to tell her she looked like her mother, but it was clear they didn't have any interest in her. The earl actually spoke to her, asking about Willy and complimenting her voice. At times he seemed more interested in her than in her father, which was rare. Papa was a larger than life personality, with a booming laugh and a brash, bold way. She told herself that couldn't possibly be the case, and no doubt the earl was simply being polite. Georgiana had often told her true gentlemen, like her fiancé Viscount Sterling and surely the Earl of Hastings, had exquisite manners.

But goodness, she took far too much pleasure in the man's polite attention.

When she wasn't daydreaming about the earl, Eliza had more to worry about. Her friend Sophie had landed in a spot of scandal. Sophie, who supported herself by gambling at the Vega Club, had made a shockingly large wager with the Duke of Ware, who was known to be adamantly opposed to wagering. Georgiana had teased Sophie about the duke's rakish young brother, Lord Philip, whom Georgiana believed—or more likely, hoped—to be madly in love with Sophie, but Sophie laughed and called him more trouble than he was worth. Eliza didn't think Sophie, who had watched out for herself since she was orphaned at the age of twelve, would lose her head over Lord Philip or his brother, but her concerned letters had gone unanswered, which was very unlike Sophie. When she turned to her father for help, he promised to find out what he could, but then reported that Sophie had not been out in London as usual; he thought she might be ill. Eliza was becoming worried.

She went to her garden to think, as was her habit, pacing the gravel paths and cutting flowers while she pondered what to do to help Sophie. Miss Jane Harby was getting married tomorrow, and since Jane's sister Mary was Eliza's personal maid, Eliza had offered to supply flowers. Mary had just taken in the first basket of freshly cut lilac and columbines when Eliza looked up from neatly raked beds to see Lord Hastings making his way out to her.

She almost dropped her shears. Willy, who had been sunning himself on a patch of grass, leapt up and bounded toward the earl, who gave him a pat on the head. He was here again. At least this time she was presentable. She curtsied as he drew near, her heart hammering.

"I hope you'll pardon me, Miss Cross," he said, his eyes crinkling in that way that made Eliza willing to forgive him anything on the spot. "Your butler agreed I might walk out to join you as it's such a fine day."

"Of course, sir," she said. "I suppose Papa has been delayed? He did tell me he would be home early today." He'd made a special point of telling her so this morning at breakfast. He hadn't said why, but he must have been expecting the earl.

"We had an appointment for two o'clock," confirmed the gentleman in question. "Do you mind if I wait and hope he arrives soon?"

She smiled, all worries about Sophie fading for the moment. "Certainly."

He fell in step beside her. Willy barked and sniffed around their feet before trotting off to investigate the rosebushes. "I feel as though I have imposed on you a great deal lately, Miss Cross. I must apologize."

"Not at all!" Her face felt hot, remembering how she'd daydreamed about him. "Of all Papa's partners, you are by far the most charming and least imposing."

He laughed. "You're very kind. Is there a steady stream of them through your drawing room? Men discussing steam engines and balloons and other investments?"

"Not a steady stream, no." She glanced up at

him. "Are you investing in railway steam engines? Papa thinks they're death machines, liable to explode."

"I happen to agree with him," said the earl with a wink. "If they can stop them exploding, though, that would be a different matter."

"Yes, not killing everyone nearby would be a great improvement," she said somberly.

Hastings laughed again. Eliza's heart seemed to dance around her chest at the sound. "There may be ore on my Cornish property," he said. "Your father has offered his expertise." He made a slight grimace. "I know nothing about ore."

"Neither do I. But I have heard Cornwall is beautiful."

"It is—at least, the small part of it I own." Real pride warmed his voice. "Have you never been to Cornwall?"

"I would like to go," she said frankly. "Papa has been, many times. He always tells me he visits the dirty disagreeable places and I wouldn't like it."

He made a soft *tsk*. "Then you must never go with him. I could show you the most beautiful spot on earth—Rosemere House. It sits above Plymouth Sound near Saltash. My father rebuilt the house, but there are the remains of a Norman keep on the grounds. You can see the sea from the house, and there is a reflecting pool in the garden that looks like a map of the celestial sky on clear nights."

"How lovely!"

"It's the most peaceful place on earth," the earl went on. "The name, Rosemere, is for my mother—a Rose by the sea." He glanced around.

"Although I do believe the gardens are a trifle more ordinary than yours, Miss Cross. You would surely work wonders if you were given free rein there."

She warmed with pleasure. "Thank you, sir. I'm sure they are splendid—I plant what I like to see when I look out the windows. There's no art to it, only my personal whim."

He stopped. Eliza looked up in surprise. "Never say there's no art to it," he told her. Goodness, his eyes were dark and mesmerizing. "I know peace and beauty when I see it, and there is more in this garden than anywhere else I've ever been."

She knew it was flattery, she knew it wasn't true, but she still felt a small explosion of joy in her chest that he would say it. "That's because the irises are in bloom," she tried to say, but he shook his head.

"I don't mean the irises."

But he couldn't mean *her*. Flustered, Eliza caught sight of Mary coming back with the empty basket. "Do you mind if I continue cutting flowers, my lord? A girl from the village is getting married tomorrow and I promised to send some to the church."

"By all means. Is she a friend?"

"No, she is sister to my maid, Mary. She's to marry a shipwright from Deptford." Eliza took the basket from Mary and sent the girl off. There was no reason for that except that she wanted to have Lord Hastings to herself.

"How very generous of you to send the flowers," he said as they strolled the paths.

"Generous!" She laughed, flipping one hand in dismissal. "Not at all. I have plenty, and no wedding should be without flowers. Jane was here this morning to choose the ones for her bouquet. These will only be on the altar." She knelt down to cut some lilies and added them to her basket. And when Lord Hastings offered to hold the basket as she cut some irises and more lilies, she couldn't keep a silly smile from her face.

"Thank you for carrying that," she said after a while. They had continued talking as she cut, and she'd lost track of everything. The basket was now bursting with greenery and she reached to take it from him.

"It was my pleasure, Miss Cross." He held it out, waiting patiently as she pushed her shawl out of the way and pulled off her gardening gloves. Eliza reached for the basket, but it was heavier than expected, and she almost dropped it. With a quick motion Lord Hastings righted it before the flowers could spill out, and in the process stepped very close to her.

"Sorry," she said breathlessly as she hefted the basket in both hands.

He didn't let go. Eliza looked up and her breath caught in her throat. He was looking at her, and his expression made her heart start to pound and her hands start to shake.

"Miss Cross," he began. "I hope you don't think me presumptuous, but . . . I am rather glad your father was delayed today."

She couldn't blink. She couldn't move. He

reached out and drew her shawl lightly over her shoulder from where it had drooped.

"Do you?" he asked softly.

"What?" Her voice sounded faint and dazed.

Hastings's mouth curved, and his eyes crinkled, almost teasingly. "Think me presumptuous," he whispered. "You can tell me."

"No!" It burst out of her like a shout, but she had only enough breath for a whisper.

Something shifted in his eyes before he lowered his lashes. He took her hand in his and raised it. Eliza quaked inside as his lips brushed slowly, softly, over her knuckles. His hands, still gloved, were so large and strong around her limp fingers. His eyes flashed up for a moment, as if gauging her reaction, and then he turned her hand over and touched his lips to her wrist.

Eliza thought she might have whimpered out loud. She must have dozed off in the sun and was having another dream about him, one in which he looked at her with those obsidian-dark eyes and gave her the slow smile that made her stomach jump and leap, but no—this felt real. The handle of the flower basket was digging into her palm, her heart was pounding so hard she could almost hear it, and he was so close she could see the beginnings of stubble on his jaw, right near his beautiful mouth—

"Good day, Lord Hastings!"

Papa's voice broke the spell. Eliza startled so badly the basket tipped and dropped half the flowers onto the path. Lord Hastings released her hand. Willy gave a happy bark and ran to meet Papa.

"I would apologize for keeping you waiting, sir, but I've been home this quarter hour or more." Papa reached them and gave Eliza a fond smile.

"Have you been? Good Lord." The earl smiled disarmingly. "I scarcely noticed the time passing. Miss Cross was kind enough to entertain me in the meantime."

Papa chuckled. "I cannot fault you for forgetting me, then. She's far better company than I!"

Hastings gave Eliza a warm glance. "I cannot disagree."

Oh dear. She felt dazed and light-headed at the way he was looking at her. "It's always a pleasure to see Lord Hastings. I don't mind entertaining him in the slightest, unlike some of your partners, Papa."

Her father gave a bark of laughter. "I don't doubt it! Well, Hastings, shall we go inside? Down to the drudgery, eh?"

The earl gave Eliza another look, and she smiled back helplessly. He did not look enthused at the prospect. "Good day, Lord Hastings. Thank you for carrying the basket."

"It was my pleasure, Miss Cross." He bowed, and followed Papa into the house.

Eliza watched until they disappeared, then gave a little moan. She knelt and began gathering the flowers before Willy could trample them. Flowers for a wedding, in the church where she'd sat every Sunday since she was a child. Where a girl in love would pledge herself to a handsome fellow who looked at her with deep, dark eyes and smiled a crinkly little smile meant only for her. A bridegroom who looked very much like the Earl of Hastings in her mind.

There would be no stopping her imagination now.

Chapter 10

HUGH COULD FEEL the two separate strands of his life begin to converge.

One of them, the one where he had agreed to court Eliza Cross, was going more smoothly than expected. He still harbored a deep and abiding resentment of Edward Cross, but he felt more and more drawn to Eliza. Her father calculated everything down to the inch, and connived to have that inch measured in his favor, while Eliza cut flowers from her own garden so a maid's sister would have a beautiful wedding. Her father schemed to have his daughter married to an aristocrat, while Eliza brought home a mutt she'd found under a bush. She was warm, generous, and honest, with a quiet but droll sense of humor, and he found himself looking forward to seeing her.

He could hardly believe she was Cross's natural daughter. The more time Hugh spent with her, the less resemblance he could see. Perhaps Cross had found *her* on the side of the road, and they were no relation at all. It gave Hugh some dark amusement to think so.

The other sphere of his life was not so easy to manage. As expected, people had noticed when he spent the evening in the Crosses' box at the Theatre Royal; within a day his mother had heard it, and soon drew him aside. "I hear you were at the theater the other night."

"I was. Edith recommended the opera, and I thought I would see what the fuss was."

His mother's brows rose. "Edith thought it was dreadful."

"Did she?" Hugh frowned. "I must have become confused and wandered into the wrong production . . ."

"And right into Edward Cross's box?" She gave him a reproving look. "He's not your usual companion, dear."

Hugh felt no obligation to speak highly of the man. "Not at all. But he believes there may be ore at Rosemere and he's mad to find out." He made a distasteful expression. "Nothing will come of it, I'm sure."

"Rosemere!" His mother's eyes went wide, and she pressed one hand to her throat. "You wouldn't really let that man dig up the grounds of Rosemere, would you? It's bad enough we must let it out to tenants when we might be there ourselves, where your father and I were always so happy—" She stopped, her lip quivering.

Hugh reminded himself that if things went well with Eliza Cross, if he did indeed end up married to her, Rosemere would never be in danger again, either from tenants or speculators looking for ore in the fields. His mother would be able to spend the rest of her life there, mourning and venerating his father, who had put Hugh in this impossible position, and he would never need to spoil her memory of him.

But for now, he had to keep up the pretense. "I'm sure nothing will come of it," he repeated with a wave of one hand. "Don't trouble yourself, Mother."

Her eyes shone with gratitude. "Of course not. I should have known better, dear, forgive me—I know you would never do something so abhorrent, not only to me, but to the very honor of Hastings. Rosemere is your birthright."

Rosemere was mortgaged to the eaves of its mansard slate roof. The elegant new wing, with its splendid plasterwork and silk-upholstered furnishings and crystal chandeliers, had been built with Edith's dowry. The landscaping must have cost Henrietta's dowry, and the two hundred acres his father had bought five years ago, to provide privacy and an unimpeded view of the sound from the house, would have funded a widow's dower for his mother. Rosemere hardly felt like Hugh's at all.

For a split second he thought of what Eliza might do with the property. Her garden was a riot of color, from the roses sprawling over every arbor and fence to the irises and lilies raising their regal heads above the humbler grasses and ferns. Hugh liked it. Rosemere, for all its beauty, had neat, bounded gardens that might have been out-side a Tudor kitchen, where one felt constrained and restricted, not at ease.

"I am determined to be a good steward of Rosemere," he told his mother.

She smiled in relief. "I know, dear. So like your father." She went up on her toes to kiss his cheek, and Hugh closed his eyes at the rush of resent-ment in his chest. He was tired of hearing how like his father he was, particularly from people who couldn't know how wrong they were.

That thought made it easier to say what he must. "I must confess another motive in joining Cross the other night. His daughter was with him, and she invited me."

"His daughter?" The countess raised her chin, a flash of apprehension in her eyes. "You can't mean . . ."

"Mother." He took her hand. "It was a surprise to me, but she's nothing like her father. I think you would like her a great deal, if you met her."

"The daughter of the man who wants to dig up my beloved Rosemere? You think I should receive her?"

He ignored her shocked tone. "Don't you trust my judgment?" He gave a crooked grin. "It's im-proved a great deal since I assured you Robert Fairfield was a modest fellow, and wouldn't lead me into any trouble at school."

Her face softened. "You were both boys! Boys are full of high spirits, and any woman who thinks her child won't get into trouble doesn't de-serve to have a son. Besides, I know his mother."

"I don't recall you being so understanding when we set fire to the tutor's laundry," he said with a laugh. "But you can trust me on this."

Still smiling, she sighed and touched his arm. "I will. But I hope you consider carefully what it would mean to bring a girl like that into our circle."

"Good heavens, I didn't mean to suggest we adopt her," he said in mock indignation. "I only said I think you would like her, if you ever happen to meet her."

"And I know very well what that means," she retorted. "I said much the same thing to my parents when I first met your father."

He reeled back as if struck. "Good gracious, Mother. Do you mean to suggest I've met the woman of my dreams, and am just too thick-headed to realize it yet?"

"The daughter of a common speculator would be a very odd choice," she pointed out. "I hope you aren't being swayed by a passing interest."

On the contrary; he had a deep and abiding interest in saving his estate. He kissed his mother's cheek. "You know me better than that. I'm off to Tattersall's and won't be home until late." He still spent his days as if he hadn't a care in the world, about money or anything else.

She bade him farewell and left, her expression clear. Hugh knew it meant she believed he would never do something so shocking or crass as to court a Cit's daughter. He could only hope she would be swayed by Miss Cross's obvious kindness and warmth when the time came for him to tell his mother he meant not only to court her, but to marry her.

THE FLOWERS CAUGHT ELIZA off guard. It was a small posy, wrapped in silk ribbon, but with a note that threatened to topple her world off its axis. *These are nothing to the beauty in your own garden, but they made me think of you. Your servant, Hastings.*

She read it approximately fifteen times before believing it was real. The posy she put into a vase herself and set on the windowsill by the pianoforte, where she could see them as she practiced. But her fingers seemed to have lost any sense of the keys, and she finally closed the cover.

The card taunted her, lying next to her music. She picked it up and read it again. The Earl of Hastings had sent her flowers. And there was little to explain it, except the remote, incredible, virtually impossible chance that he was flirting with her.

Eliza had received flowers before. During her Season, Papa had taken a house right in the center of London to make it easier for her to attend balls and soirees and take drives in the park with gentlemen. And gentlemen had come— they asked her to dance, and to walk, and to drive. Some sent her flowers. But it never took long for Eliza to realize that each and every one of them was there because of her dowry. The man who proposed to her the second time they met. The baronet who called her his dear Emily. The dashing army captain who sent a sonnet in praise of her fine dark eyes, having never noticed her eyes were green. Even one of Papa's associates, thankfully one of the younger ones, had called on her—although he quickly admitted he thought they made a good match because of how well he got on with Papa.

Once Eliza started turning aside the fortune hunters, she stopped receiving many callers. Her suspicions made her even more reticent and shy about talking to any man who approached her at a ball, and soon they stopped doing that, as well. Eliza almost fainted with relief when the Season ended and they went back to Greenwich.

Lord Hastings was different from those callers, though. He was an earl, which meant that if he wanted to marry an heiress, he could have found a duke's daughter and been welcomed. He had seen her at her worst, soaking wet and smelly, and had not recoiled in disgust. He even had a way of charming her out of the horrifying nervous giggle that seemed to escape her lips any time a handsome man spoke to her . . . and yet he was the most attractive man she'd ever set eyes on, let alone spoken to.

What could he possibly mean by sending her flowers?

She mentioned it to her father that evening. "Lord Hastings sent me a posy of flowers today," she said over the fish course, as casually as she could manage.

Papa's fork paused in midair. "Did he? Were they pretty?"

"Yes."

"Did you like them?"

"Of course!"

"What's the trouble, then?" Papa speared another bite of fish and watched her as he ate.

Eliza frowned. "There is no trouble, Papa. I was only surprised."

"I thought you liked the fellow."

Her mouth opened, then closed. She did like the earl, a great deal. Eliza snatched up her glass and took a healthy drink. "He's very charming. Exquisite manners."

"Is that all?" He leaned forward, his eyes keen on her. "If you don't like him . . ."

"No!" She pursed her lips. "I like him very much, Papa. He's charming and amusing but I am astonished he would send me flowers."

Finally, Papa smiled, his small, knowing smile. "Are you? I'm not."

Eliza tensed in sudden suspicion. "Why not?"

"How could he keep from admiring you? You're the finest girl in Britain, a man would have to be an idiot not to feel like sending you flowers."

"Papa." She rolled her eyes. "Stop. You know as well as I that it's ridiculous—"

"No, I do not know that," he returned. "He's a fine fellow, I grant you, but why shouldn't he admire you?"

She put down her glass. "We are not talking about admiration, and you know it. We are talking about why a man like him—an earl—would send me flowers."

"Listen to me, Lilibeth." He pointed his fork at her, suddenly very serious. "Never think a title makes one man any better than the others. What did he do to deserve it? Nothing; he was born to a man who inherited the position. Take away the coronet and arrogance, and an earl is just a man like any other."

"Not quite," she retorted. "He might marry the daughter of another earl, or a duke, or anybody he chooses—"

"The Duke of Exeter wed a commoner," said her father, unmoved.

"Marry—!" Eliza shook her head. She'd been afraid her father would get this idea, and yet it felt almost reassuring. After a day of wondering what that posy could mean, just hearing Papa say it out loud made clear how ridiculous the thought was. The tightness in her chest eased. "Lord Hastings is not going to marry me."

He shrugged. "Nothing says he couldn't."

"I'm sorry I mentioned it," she said in exasperation. "It was a simple posy. He might have sent posies to a dozen other girls."

"If I had to wager on it, I'd say no." Papa gave her a sly look. "We'll wait and see, eh?"

Chapter 11

❦

Hugh took his time walking up the steps. Once he went into the ballroom and danced with Eliza Cross in front of all London, it would be much harder to retreat.

The host of this ball was his old friend Viscount Thayne. He had known the viscount since they were lads at Eton, but more importantly Thayne owed him a favor. Tonight it was being repaid: Thayne had told his wife to send an invitation to the Crosses.

The posy had been well received. Eliza thanked him profusely the next time he called in Greenwich, ostensibly on Mr. Cross but in reality on her. He wondered if she had grown suspicious that he always seemed too early or too late to catch her father at home, but if so she never showed it. By now Hugh was convinced she really didn't know what her father was scheming, and it made him at once both relieved and angry. It was a relief to believe that she was as she seemed, but the more he liked her, the less fair it seemed that she was being fooled. And Hugh wasn't such an ogre that he didn't care for her feelings.

On the contrary, he was coming to like her very much. Unlike many society girls, Eliza didn't act as if any gentleman nearby was obliged to amuse her. She expressed such delight in a simple posy, he couldn't help wondering what she would say if he presented her with a real gift. She seemed utterly content to spend time in her garden with her dog, and didn't evince the slightest boredom at living in Greenwich, away from the whirl of society. He told himself it must be easy, with Cross's vast fortune at her disposal; she needn't fret about a dark and drab drawing room, as Edith did, or moan about her lack of new gowns, as Henrietta did. But somehow he knew it wasn't just the money. Eliza wasn't the type to complain. Instead she gave every appearance of being content with her life and taking joy in small pleasures.

Tonight he would see how she carried herself in society. If she would be his wife, she would have to attend and host events like this one. He'd seen how nervous she was when he first visited Greenwich; would she be the same tonight, in a room full of elegant strangers? It would change nothing about his circumstances, but he found himself hoping very strongly that she would be poised and composed. Everyone would suspect he had married her for her money, but if she were a total failure among the *ton*, they would know it for certain.

He reached the ballroom and found it crowded and stuffy. Lady Thayne wasn't satisfied unless her parties were described as absolute crushes, so she tended to invite too many people. Hugh wandered through the crowd, greeting acquaintances at every turn, including several friends of his mother's. He hadn't told her he was coming tonight, and she would scold him tomorrow. But he kept going until he caught sight of the Crosses.

For a moment he looked right past her. His mind had fixed on her as a plain girl, but when he saw Edward Cross, it gave him a bit of a start to realize the lady beside him was Eliza. Tonight she looked . . . rather splendid, to be truthful. Her honey-colored hair wasn't pulled into braids and twists like other girls', but held in a soft roll at the back of her head. Her gown was deep midnight blue, making her skin look as lustrous as the pearls around her neck. As he watched, she turned her head to smile at her father, and sapphires glittered at her ears.

He strolled toward them. "Good heavens, Mr. Cross," he said, affecting surprise as he reached them. "And Miss Cross! Good evening to you both."

Eliza curtsied beautifully. "Lord Hastings! What a delight to see you."

"See, I told you," said her father warmly. "Eliza worried we wouldn't know anyone! She didn't want to come."

She gave him a look of veiled reproach. "Papa."

"I'm very glad you did." Hugh smiled at her. She beamed back, and he felt an odd sensation in his chest. Tonight she was far from plain.

They talked of nothing for another few minutes, until the musicians began tuning their instruments and couples began forming on the floor for the dance. "Miss Cross, would you honor me with this dance?"

She blushed, just a little, the pink coming into her cheeks. With barely a flutter of her eyelashes, she gave him her hand. "Of course, my lord."

Hugh could feel Cross's satisfied gaze upon his back. He ignored it. It was a country dance, an energetic reel that left no time for talking. She danced well, another relief. Hugh returned her to her father and excused himself to bide his time. He found a spot near the terrace doors and a glass of wine to occupy his hands.

"I detect a marked partiality," drawled Robert Fairfield beside him. "First the theater, now Thayne's drawing room."

"Do you?" Hugh sipped his wine. "What do you make of it?"

His friend laughed. "Nothing! Just warning you that I've seen that expression on a man's face before, and I know what it means."

Hugh stiffened. "What are you blathering about?"

"You can't take your eyes off the Cross girl." Fairfield shook his head. "I hope I'm in time to make the first wager on when your wedding day will be."

"What are the odds of that?" Hugh played along.

"I daresay I could get whatever odds I wanted at the moment. Tomorrow, not as easily." His companion hesitated, then leaned closer. "An odd choice but a clever one. London's forgotten about her but she's quite an heiress, isn't she?"

Hugh just looked at him. Fairfield's smile grew. He clapped Hugh's shoulder. "Well done, mate."

"Shut it," returned Hugh. Fairfield walked off, his laugh drifting back.

That clinched the matter, he supposed. Fairfield was likely joking about wagering on his marriage, but after Hugh danced with her a second time, plenty of others would notice. Especially the lady herself.

With that in mind, he made his way over to Eliza Cross again and requested the next dance.

ELIZA HAD TRIED VERY hard not to watch Lord Hastings, or at least not to watch *only* Lord Hastings. Her eyes seemed unable to avoid him, though, no matter how innocently she tried to keep her gaze on the other guests and dancers.

Papa had been pleased as anything to receive this invitation. When she asked if he knew Lord Thayne, he waved one hand and said they'd met. Eliza knew from past experience that meant he'd played piquet or some other game at the Vega Club with the viscount. She suspected the invitation might have arrived to pay some debt Thayne owed her father; Papa was good at getting what he wanted from people, and he often said he didn't need more money.

But while Papa was delighted, Eliza viewed it with trepidation, remembering her lonely Season at balls like this. The appearance of Lord Hastings, and his greeting to them, was a great surprise and a tremendous relief, that there was at least one person she knew who would stop and speak to her.

And then he asked her to dance. A simple country dance, but just clasping his hands threw fuel on her smoldering imagination. Did his eyes linger on her? Did he hold her hand a second longer than necessary? Did she imagine a little extra warmth and attention in the way he drew her hand around his arm?

Yes. Yes, she surely did imagine all that, but it filled her with such a glow of happiness she didn't care.

Papa fairly blazed with satisfaction when the earl had returned her to his side and left them. For once Eliza didn't feel like scolding him about it. The two of them were content to stand at the side of the room, admiring the other guests and savoring private thoughts. Eliza thought this time she and her father might even be sharing the same daydream.

And then Lord Hastings came back, and asked her to dance with him again.

She hadn't danced since their last. This time she almost forgot to breathe, because it was a waltz.

It was the first time he had touched more than her hand or her arm. He led her out and set his hand on her back. She gave him a nervous smile as the musicians began; he grinned and eased her closer, until her breasts brushed his chest and she could feel his thigh against hers.

Lightning could strike her on the way home, Eliza decided, and she would die a happy girl.

"You dance wonderfully," Hastings told her as they glided around the floor.

"Thank you, sir." Eliza had diligently practiced

for hours at school, with the dancing master and then with her friends. So far she'd had precious little experience with handsome, eligible gentlemen. "I might say the same to you."

He laughed. "I take it with extra gratitude, as this ballroom is so crowded I'm not sure I haven't stepped on five people's toes."

"Not mine," said Eliza lightly. She wouldn't have noticed even if he had.

"Lady Thayne is fond of a packed ballroom, but I cannot share her enthusiasm." He made a faint grimace as another couple swooped very near them. The earl adjusted his hold on her, shortened his step, and swung her gracefully around the couple. Eliza's chest constricted at the easy way he pulled her against him for the maneuver.

"I confess, a little more space would be wise, if she wishes to permit dancing." Someone bumped her from behind, and Hastings gave the fellow a thunderous scowl.

"This is ridiculous. Would you like to step out onto the terrace?"

It was possible lightning had already struck her. Eliza felt every thump of her heart like a thunderclap inside her skin. Somehow she managed to nod, and without breaking step Lord Hastings turned her neatly around the blue velvet draperies and through the French windows standing open to the terrace.

It was much cooler on the terrace, and there were no guests outside, probably due to a light mist of rain. Lord Hastings took her hand and led her to the shelter of a magnificent wisteria, grown up the wall and a nearby column. He leaned against the column, putting his back to the rain, and folded his arms. "Better?"

She smiled. "Very much. Thank you."

There was enough light from the French windows for her to see his smile, including the dimple. "You look beautiful tonight."

Unwillingly, Eliza felt a prickle of despair, a certainty that he didn't mean it. It was one thing for fortune hunters to pay her empty compliments, but she couldn't bear to hear it from him. "I know I'm not beautiful, sir."

His brows went up. "Why would you say that?"

She pursed her lips in exasperation. Why did he have to say something foolish and spoil the moment? "I never have been. Please don't say things you don't mean."

For a second he was taken aback. "I beg your pardon."

Eliza sighed. "I'm not beautiful. I like beautiful clothes, and Papa insists on buying me beautiful jewelry"—she touched the pearls at her neck— "but I find myself doubting the eyesight or the sincerity of anyone who tells me *I* am beautiful."

It took him a moment to reply to that. Eliza's stomach felt sour. Was Lord Hastings to be just like the other idiots who courted her? What a terrible pity . . .

He cleared his throat. "I did not actually accuse you of *being* beautiful. I said you *looked* beautiful tonight. A subtle but significant difference."

"Yes, the gown," she started to say.

He stepped closer. "Is my eyesight failing? Let

me make a closer study." He took another step, until she had to tilt back her head to look at him. "Hold still," he said, amusement softening his tone. He touched her chin.

Eliza froze.

Gently the earl tipped her face from side to side, his dark eyes intent upon her. "A few freckles," he said thoughtfully. "But I find those charming." His thumb brushed along her cheekbone and Eliza's hands fisted in the folds of her skirt. "Your lashes are very long," he murmured. "And your eyes . . . Your eyes are lovely. Like the fields of Rosemere under a summer sky, when the grasses are tall and verdant, and golden finches swoop in and out." He fingered a wisp of hair that had fallen loose at her temple. "Your hair is the color of honey, and soft—like a favorite linen shirt that's been washed a hundred times. Your lips . . ." He paused, his thumb lingering at the corner of her mouth, and Eliza almost whimpered aloud. "I want to kiss you," he said, almost inaudibly.

The breath whooshed from her lungs, and she nodded. A faint smile curved his mouth and then he bent his head. Eliza stood rigid as his lips touched hers, softer than a breath of air and gone almost as quickly as one. He lifted his head and looked at her. "Have you ever been kissed before?"

She flushed scarlet and had to wet her lips before she could speak. "Not *well* kissed . . ."

His shoulders shook. "Miss Cross, you leave me speechless." He cupped her jaw in his hand as his other hand came to the small of her back and pulled her against him. "I'll try to do better," he whispered against her mouth, and then he kissed her again.

If she had expected another soft touch of his lips against her, she was quickly proven wrong. This time his mouth settled on hers with intent, firm and insistent. When she gasped at the difference, his tongue slid between her parted lips and teased her until she moaned. He kissed as if he meant to conquer her, and Eliza was all too happy to surrender. His hands moved over her, gripping her waist, sliding up her shoulders to hold the nape of her neck as his mouth traveled over her eyelids and down her jaw. She whimpered as his teeth grazed her earlobe, setting her earring swaying, and she almost melted when his hand brushed her breast. It was an accident, she thought wildly, because they were pressed so close together—somehow her hands had got around his chest, beneath his jacket—but then he did it again.

He muttered something profane and tore off his glove, and then it was his bare hand on her breast, his palm cupping her, his fingers teasing along the edge of her bodice until—oh heavens—his thumb went right over her nipple. Eliza's start of shock turned into a shiver of ecstasy as he stroked the hard little nub again. He pulled her hard against him, until his hips met hers and she felt his unmistakable arousal. His mouth was hot and wet against her neck, and dimly Eliza thought that if he asked, she would tear off her dress and give herself to him right here on Lady Thayne's terrace, in the rain, ten feet away from a ballroom full of people. *This* was what it meant to want someone with a burning passion. Thank all the saints in heaven she'd got a chance to feel it once in her life . . .

He released her abruptly, clamping his hands on her elbows as she stumbled forward. He looked a little wild, with his hair mussed and his eyes burning. He quivered with every breath, and Eliza could only stare back. He'd kissed her until her brain melted and her tongue turned to lead. Good heavens, she wished he'd do it again.

"Eliza—" He stopped and cleared his throat. "Miss Cross." A thin line appeared between his brows, as if something confused him. "That went further than I planned," he finally said, his voice very low and still rough with want.

She could barely give her head a helpless shake, and raise one hand in some futile gesture of forgiveness. A shudder went through him, and he let go of her. He half turned away, scrubbing his bare hand over his face. After a moment he faced her again, but there was something wild and unsettled in his expression. "I should return you to the ballroom. Your father will wonder where you've gone."

Papa. Oh *Lord*. Eliza gripped her hands together. Papa would surely know from one glimpse of her face what had happened. She thought he would be pleased—elated, actually—but she didn't want to hear him point out that he was right and wasn't she glad for it. This kiss, this devastating, exhilarating, wonderful kiss still felt too fresh and alive on her lips. Papa's gloating might sour it; he would be thinking of a wedding and grandchildren while she just wanted to revel in the knowledge that the Earl of Hastings found her attractive. He wanted to kiss her. He even wanted to make love to her.

Eliza supposed some fellow might have felt that way about her before, but this was the first time it was a man she wanted to kiss back. A man she wished would fall in love with her, and even make love to her until she expired of bliss.

Hastings bent and retrieved his glove. Eliza smoothed her hair with trembling hands, remembering how he'd torn off that glove to touch her. His gaze fixed on her chest as he rose, and she realized, with mortification, that her dress was askew. She turned her back, but his arms came around her.

"Let me." His hands steady again, he ran his palms up her bodice to smooth her gown back into place. He took his time, his cheek against her temple, and Eliza tried not to shake like a leaf when his fingers brushed her nipple one last time before his hands drifted to rest on her hips.

He put his mouth next to her ear. "Should I apologize for what happened?"

The tiniest shake of her head.

His lips touched the sensitive skin behind her ear. "May I call on you—just you, not your father?"

Her heart was about to stop. She would faint and slide right through his arms to land in a senseless heap on the ground. "Yes," she whispered.

"Thank you." Gently he turned her around. Eliza gazed up at him, wondering if he could tell from looking at her that she was about to fall headlong in love with him. A small smile touched his lips, bemused but reassuring. "Until then, my dear." He raised her hand and kissed it before very properly offering his arm. "We should return, before your father comes to call me out."

A shaky laugh burst out of her. If only he knew how desperately Papa longed for her to have a suitor. "I would persuade him against it, my lord."

He laughed. "I hope I could do that on my own, but I will never refuse your support." He took her back into the ballroom, which now seemed incredibly loud and hot and crowded. Eliza whisked open her fan and waved it furiously, trying to dispel the blush she could still feel on her face.

The Earl of Hastings had kissed her. Had put his hands on her like a lover would. Had held her against himself as if he wanted to devour her. And then he asked to call on her. There was a chorus of joy thundering in her head, and she barely heard the earl's words of farewell.

Papa had disappeared, but she soon caught sight of him, at the back of the room, deep in conversation with Mr. Grenville. Eliza made her way to his side, and he gave her a distracted nod. Mr. Grenville looked at her and flashed a knowing smirk, as if he knew what had happened. Eliza blushed all over again. Mr. Grenville was a rogue, and she prayed he wouldn't say anything to Papa.

She stood quietly beside her father for some time, smiling blindly at the dancers and utterly uncaring of the fact that no one else asked her to dance. Every moment of her waltz, and then that kiss, spooled through her mind as if they were still happening, over and over again.

"I've had enough. Shall we go?" Papa's voice made her jump.

"Oh! If you want to, Papa." They went through the crowd and sent for the carriage. Eliza didn't catch even the smallest glimpse of Lord Hastings.

"Did you enjoy the evening?" Papa asked when they were cocooned in the dark coach, heading home.

Eliza smiled to herself. "Yes, Papa. Very much."

HUGH DRIFTED THROUGH THE ballroom, speaking to friends and acquaintances without remembering a word of what he'd said. Some commented with surprise on his choice of partner. He'd meant to make a statement, to Eliza and to society, and by God, he'd done it.

The thing was, he really hadn't meant to do more than kiss her chastely. Just enough to declare his intentions and gauge her reaction. Instead he'd ended up almost ravishing her against the side of the house outside a ballroom filled with people. What was wrong with him?

She'd made him laugh, of course, saying she'd never been well kissed. A charming joke from a spinster. So he'd kissed her again, and somehow between the sensual little moans she made and the way her fingers dug into his shirt as if she wanted to tear it off, he'd gone a bit mad. He'd had her breast in his hand, for Christ's sake.

The memory made a fine sweat break out on

the back of his neck. Plump and firm with a thoroughly aroused nipple. He wanted to taste it. He wanted to strip her bare and lay her down and taste every inch of her, but especially those round tempting breasts. So much for fearing a shy, paralyzed virgin; she might be innocent, but Eliza had pressed against him and kissed him back until he completely forgot that he was pursuing her because of her father's manipulations.

That thought cooled his blood somewhat. Edward Cross wanted him to court and marry his daughter, did he? Hugh smiled grimly. Cross was about to get exactly what he wanted.

And so was he. Not only Cross's money, but Eliza herself.

Chapter 12

$\iff$

HE WENT IN search of his mother the next morning and found her in her private sitting room, with Edith beside her.

"Good morning, darling." Rose tilted her head to receive his kiss on her cheek. "You're up early."

"I might say the same about you." He regarded his sister with concern. "Is this healthy? I believed ladies avoided the morning sun for fear it would render them hopelessly unfashionable."

Edith rolled her eyes and laughed. "We weren't out late last night like you were, silly."

Hugh had gone to Vega's last night after leaving Thayne's house, more out of habit than anything. Naturally his luck had returned and he walked out nearly three thousand pounds richer, now that he was within reach of almost twenty times that much. "As if I've got much choice! I hear nothing but shopping and ribbons and what Lady So-and-So wore to the ball last night." He gave a mock shudder. "There's too much talk of lace within these walls. It's more than my brain can bear."

Edith threw a pillow at him. "Your male brain is weak indeed!"

Hugh caught the pillow and grinned. "I've come to have a word with Mother, minx. I cannot handle speaking to two females at once, with my weak male brain."

"Very well, I'll go." Edith collected her embroidery and rose. "Before I leave, I have a question for you, Hugh. Reggie has tried to call on you twice and you've been out both times. When shall I tell him you'll be home so he can come again?"

Hugh had been deliberately avoiding Reginald Benwick. The young man had sent him two messages as well, pressing for a quick negotiation of the marriage settlements. He was unhappy with the Hastings solicitor, who was thankfully following orders to be as slow and unresponsive as possible. Hugh planned to put Benwick off for at least another fortnight.

"Reggie? Oh yes, young Benwick. I'll see him at some point. I've been busy of late, Edith."

Her brow creased in frustration. "But, Hugh—"

"Soon," he said firmly. "Don't pester."

Edith turned to her mother for support, but Rose simply looked toward the door. "Your brother answered you, Edith."

His sister's eyes flashed with hurt, but she ducked her head. "Yes, Mama. It's so hard to be patient, though."

"Of course it is, when you're in love," said their mother affectionately. "You must endure." Edith nodded and left, closing the door behind her. "Is there a reason you're not anxious to settle things with Benwick?" his mother asked.

"I've not had time," said Hugh in a voice that warned her not to pursue it. "I'll deal with him soon enough. I need a favor, Mother."

She was not pleased with his answer about Benwick, but her face softened at the request. "Of course, darling, anything."

"Invite Elizabeth Cross to tea."

"Who?" She inhaled sharply. "No—not Edward Cross's daughter? You can't be serious!"

"That's the one, and I am perfectly serious." He met her shocked gaze evenly. "Please."

She jumped to her feet, wringing her hands. "No. No! You cannot mean it. I wondered, when you spoke so warmly of her the other day, but, Hugh—I warned you about getting attached unwisely—"

"Mother, I try not to impose on you often. I am asking this now, and I expect you to do it." Hugh didn't often exercise his authority as head of the family, but this time he had to. "Send the invitation today."

Her mouth set mutinously. "I am not pleased."

"Thank you, Mother." He got up. "I do think you'll like her. She's a lovely girl, warm and kindhearted."

"I don't like this," she warned him.

"Be gracious to her," he said. "For me." *For all of us*, he added in his mind.

She frowned but threw up one hand. "Very well."

He got proof that she'd done it the next morning. Edith was pacing in the hall when he went down to set out for a morning ride. At his approach she ran forward and seized his arm. "Tell me it's a lark!" He frowned and she squeezed tighter. "Eliza Cross. It's a joke, isn't it? You lost a wager, or—or—"

He walked into the morning room, his sister still clinging to him, and closed the door. "It's not a joke, or a lark. What have you got against Miss Cross?"

"Besides the fact that she's nobody, a plain little mouse who wouldn't warrant a second look without an enormous dowry?" Edith's face turned hard. "Her father is the greatest scoundrel in Britain, and you want Mama to serve her tea."

"She is not her father."

"Reggie is appalled. He could barely speak of anything the rest of the evening last night at Lady Brewster's soiree, even though I assured him I don't want anything to do with her."

Hugh let out his breath. He didn't have patience for this, but resisted the urge to say that Benwick should mind his own affairs. Benwick was part of the reason Hugh was doing this in the first place, Benwick who expected a handsome dowry from him for Edith. "Calm yourself, Edith. It's only tea."

She stared at him. "It's not," she said in a low voice. "You've never asked Mama to invite another young lady to tea. You sat in her box at the theater. I could laugh that off, but then you danced with her—*twice*. Everyone was speaking of it last night, everyone!"

"Don't exaggerate."

At his tone, tears filled her eyes. "Please don't, Hugh," she begged. "Please! I—I won't sit with her!"

"I only asked Mother to do that."

"Neither will Henrietta!"

"If Henrietta doesn't want tea, she doesn't have to join Mother, either."

Edith wrung her hands, obviously searching for some argument that would dissuade him. "Her father is awful. Appalling! I can't believe you would pursue a connection with someone like him."

Hugh might agree on all counts, but Edith's vehemence was surprising. "What do you know of her father?"

"Lord Livingston despises him. Reggie wouldn't tell me why, but he assured me it was terrible. Now will you see reason?"

He might have known it wouldn't be smooth sailing, with Eliza warmly welcomed to his family. "Livingston may despise him, but I've not invited Mr. Cross—only Miss Cross. It's not like you to be so cold to someone you've never met."

Edith's chest heaved. "And it's not like you to be so—so bullheaded! And stupid! What can you possibly see in her?"

Much more than he'd expected to see. For a moment the memory of Eliza's delighted smile, of her breathy moans, of the feel of her breast under his palm, filled his head. It was surprising that that was what came to his mind first, instead of the vast fortune Cross was promising him, but he couldn't tell his sister any one of those reasons.

Thank the blessed Lord, he didn't have to tell her anything at all.

"That's enough, Edith." He turned on his heel and walked from the room. She ran after him, still babbling, but Hugh put up one hand to stop her. *"Enough,* Edith," he repeated quietly but firmly. He took his hat and gloves from the butler, and left her staring after him in furious despair.

ELIZA WALKED UP THE steps of Hastings House, sedate and polite on the outside but bubbling with excitement on the inside.

The invitation from Lady Hastings had caught her completely off guard. She had hoped the earl himself would call in Greenwich again, but a note from his mother came instead, on thick hot-pressed paper with the Hastings seal in blood-red wax. Eliza had taken it to her father, speechless with disbelief.

"Eliza!" He'd looked at her with such astonished delight. "The Countess of Hastings?"

"She's invited me to take tea with her."

"Well, of course you must go!" Beaming, he'd kissed both her cheeks. "What an honor—for Lady Hastings, of course, and I hope you have a pleasant time, as well." It made her laugh at the time, but now she felt the prickle of nervous perspiration on her neck. What if she said the wrong thing? What if she spilled tea all over herself? What if—?

"Miss Cross." Lord Hastings's voice was a welcome interruption to her thoughts. He came across the hall and bowed before offering his arm. "Eliza," he said, much more softly. "It's a pleasure to see you again."

"Thank you, sir. I'm delighted to be invited."

He smiled as he led her up the stairs. "My mother is eager to make your acquaintance."

Eliza didn't dare think too hard what that meant, because they were at the drawing room door all too soon and she needed to concentrate on her manners. The countess stood in front of the tall windows facing St. James's Square, the table already spread with a delicate tea service. She was a petite, beautiful woman, and she smiled graciously when the earl presented Eliza.

The visit passed like a dream. The countess was formal but kind, and Lord Hastings kept the conversation flowing. The topics were as banal as any social call, but Eliza left feeling overwhelmed by the experience. In spite of her nerves she'd not giggled once, and the earl even laughed at something she said.

Lord Hastings escorted her out of the drawing room when the visit was over, after Lady Hastings had thanked her very beautifully for calling. "It's over," he whispered to her as they went down the wide stairs.

Eliza exhaled and gave a shaky smile. "It was wonderful."

"Yes," he said in amusement, "but I could see you were nervous. Mother liked you."

"Did she?" Eliza didn't even know why she longed so desperately for that to be true. "I hope so."

"I would not say it if I didn't believe it."

They had reached the bottom of the stairs, where the butler waited, expressionless and facing away from them. With a finger to his lips, the earl took her hand and whisked her into a small morning room. Quietly he closed the door.

"What—?" she began, but he put his hands on her hips, propelling her backward until she hit the side table. With one motion he lifted her onto it, took her face in his hands and kissed her. Eliza sighed and threw her arms around his neck to kiss him back.

"I've thought of that since Thayne's ball," he whispered. "I thought of you . . . and this . . ." He kissed her again, his hand resting beside her knees. Eliza's legs widened on instinct as she strained closer to him, searching for that closeness they'd had on the terrace. He growled and ran one palm over her skirt, a light touch that made her quiver with anticipation. "Just like this, yes," he breathed, easing her knee aside until he pressed forward, his hips between her thighs.

Eliza might be a virgin but she was not ignorant. Without a mother to instruct her, she had listened intently to any bit of knowledge about men and women, boldly asking her married friends for more information when necessary. She had begun to think it would never be necessary, for her, but for the first time in years, she was very grateful for the knowledge. She gripped his jacket for balance and raised her gaze to the earl's. "That's very bold, sir."

"Is it?" His dark eyes gleamed. His hands slid around her hips. "Should I stop?"

Eliza swallowed. "No."

His mouth curved, a sensual, dangerous expression. "I suspect I should, my dear Eliza." But his hand kept moving, up her back. "If I don't stop soon . . . I won't want to stop at all." He cupped her jaw in both hands, lifting her face as if for his kiss. It felt like her bones were trembling. "If I don't stop now, I'll want to drive you mad, until you beg me not to stop." Eliza shuddered. She already didn't want him to stop, even though she couldn't speak—couldn't think—"I dream of driving you mad with pleasure," he breathed, his breath hot on her neck as he nuzzled her ear.

Kiss me, she thought wildly.

He did not. Slowly he withdrew his hands, and even more slowly he lifted her down from the table and set her back on her feet. Then he did kiss her once more, tenderly and sweetly. She could only look at him, flushed and flustered and still throbbing with desire. The wry smile faded from his lips, and his brow creased for a moment.

"I'm a beast," he said thickly. "You should slap my face."

Mutely she shook her head. Never. Not when she wanted him so badly. Not when she was falling harder for him every day.

Hastings took a deep breath. "Your carriage is waiting. I wish . . ."

"What?" she whispered. She still couldn't believe this was real. Surely at any moment he would shake his head and step back with a look of distaste that he'd been kissing the plain, awkward girl with no connections.

At her question he grimaced, and reached out to smooth a wisp of hair back from her temple. "I wish I had more time with you. Come, my dear."

She walked out with her hand on his arm, her heart pounding. *More time with you.* He handed her into the waiting carriage, and gave a little bow as the footman closed the door. He stood on the steps watching as the carriage drove off. Eliza kept her eyes on him until they rounded the corner, and then she fell against the velvet-covered seat, wrapped her arms around herself, and gave a giddy laugh of joy.

She was helplessly, irrevocably in love.

HUGH LINGERED DOWNSTAIRS A few minutes after the carriage vanished around the corner. He'd wanted to kiss her again, to see if it had been real at Thayne's ball, and now he felt even more off balance. She kissed with longing and joy, and it had been very difficult to keep his hands off her.

When his blood had cooled, he went back upstairs and found his mother standing at the window, gazing out. He doubted she was watching Eliza leave, but he strongly suspected she had noticed how long it took Eliza to reach the carriage.

"Thank you, Mother." He closed the doors behind him.

She stood stiff with anger. "I wish I understood."

He ignored that. If all went according to plan, she would never know. "What did you think of her?"

"She is as you said—warm, sweet, a bit shy. Not a beauty but very elegantly turned out." She made this admission reluctantly. "You say she can dance and sing. I suppose that is something."

"Her garden is a place of wonder," he offered. "She'll transform Rosemere if given the chance."

His mother turned to him, disapproval stamped in every line of her expression. "And that's why you've chosen a common swindler's daughter?"

Not for the first time Hugh had to swallow his irritation. "She is not her father," he repeated.

"Edith is very upset," his mother went on. "Benwick put a flea in her ear about Edward Cross, and she refused to be here today. You know Henrietta always follows Edith's lead. I hope you realize what you're doing, forcing this girl upon your family."

He'd had about enough of Edith's tearful bleating about Benwick. "Is this how you would react if I paid court to one of Thayne's sisters?"

"Of course not! We know them!"

"And in time you'll know Eliza. Put some effort into it, Mother. I assure you she's eager to secure your regard."

Her face set and tears glinted in her eyes. "I wish your father were here to talk some sense into you."

Hugh also wished his father were here, to spare him the trouble of righting their ship. But then, Joshua was the one who had almost capsized it. He doubted his father would be any help at all to either of them.

"How soon do you expect to do this?" she asked when he said nothing.

"Within the fortnight, I hope."

His mother flinched. "So soon!"

He had no choice. When he thought only of Eliza, he felt rather content with the marriage; Lord knew he was ready to take her to bed, and he thought they would get on amiably as man and wife. But the demands of his family and the smug smile of Edward Cross made him want to snarl and rage. It made him think too clearly and harshly about how he had been manipulated into courting her at all . . .

Once again he swallowed that anger and did what he had to do. "As soon as I can manage it."

Chapter 13

Now, FINALLY, THERE was no reason to argue with Papa when he hinted at the earl's interest. Eliza didn't even want to. It was no trial to relate every detail—well, almost every detail—of her visit to St. James's Square. Her father did not need to know that Lord Hastings had kissed her and touched her and made her think wicked, wanton thoughts. Mrs. Upton, her very proper schoolmistress, would be appalled that Eliza had allowed such liberties.

Papa, though, was delighted. He listened with a fond smile as she recounted Lady Hastings's beauty, her kindness, the excellence of the tea served. "I told you he admired you," he teased. "Admit it—I was right."

Eliza laughed. "With pleasure. I—I like him very much, Papa."

He leaned forward. "Very much? The way you like strawberries in cream? Or that mongrel mutt?"

"More than strawberries, but less than Willy." Papa scowled, and she wrinkled her nose at him and laughed. "It's not the same thing, and you know it. I love Willy."

"What about Hastings?" Papa raised one brow. "Could you love him?"

Eliza bit her lip. She thought the answer was yes. But she'd only known him a few weeks, unlike Willy. And he was not a dog, whose heart could be won by food and kindness, and who would return her love forever. Lord Hastings had never said he loved her, or even cared for her. He'd asked to call on her, and he'd kissed her. He'd said he wanted to make her mad with pleasure. Eliza hadn't missed the omission, but then . . . she'd never told him her feelings, either.

"I believe so," she murmured in response to her father's question.

His face eased. "Good. The man did hint the other day that he had something more important than business to discuss with me."

Oh goodness. That could only mean . . .

"He wants to marry me?" she squeaked out.

Papa's mouth quirked. "I'm afraid so, Lilibeth. Shall I send the blighter on his way, broken-hearted and rejected?"

"No!"

He chuckled. "Then I must give him my blessing?"

Her fingers shook. "Yes," she said softly. "If he asks."

"He will, love," said Papa with quiet confidence. "He will."

And in spite of herself, Eliza began to believe it. She told her friends. Sophie was entirely sup-

portive, assuring her that Lord Hastings was the
fortunate one and asking Eliza to recount every
detail of the acquaintance. It even turned out Sophie had fallen in love herself, with the Duke of
Ware. Their wager had indeed been scandalous,
far more than Papa had told Eliza, but it had led
to the happy result that Sophie lost her heart even
though she worried that the duke wouldn't marry
her. Not only was she supporting herself at the
gaming tables, she had no family connections to
speak of.

Still flushed with joy at her own unexpected
romance, Eliza urged her to tell the duke everything. Who could not love Sophie, with her brave,
witty manner and her indomitable spirit? And if
he loved her, the duke would cast aside any obsta-
cle to marry her, Eliza was sure of it. Why, Lord
Hastings had overlooked the very real difference
between his station and hers. It gave Eliza goose
bumps to think that she would be a countess, and
Sophie a duchess.

Georgiana took it even better. When Eliza
stepped down from the coach to meet her for a
walk in the park, her friend rushed forward despite Lady Sidlow's call of disapproval. She towed
Eliza through the gates of St. James's Park. "You
must tell me all," she commanded, tucking her
arm around Eliza's. "Do not leave out anything!"

Eliza laughed. They turned into the Mall. Lady
Sidlow's carriage followed at a slight distance;
Lady Sidlow did not like to walk, but Georgiana
declared she would go mad if she didn't get some
exercise. The compromise was that she was per-

mitted to meet a friend three times a week and make as many circuits of the park as she liked. Eliza knew she was not the friend Lady Sidlow wanted most for Georgiana, but the countess had forbidden Georgiana to see Sophie after that scandalous wager, and Georgiana declared her other friends, members of the *ton*, weren't energetic enough.

"There isn't much to tell," she replied modestly.

Georgiana hooted in disbelief. "Not much! You write a trifling short note saying the Earl of Hastings *might* be about to propose marriage to you. I *might* have fallen over in astonishment. You've never mentioned his name! And earls do not propose marriage on whims—this I know. So tell me everything!"

Eliza blushed. "Do you know him?"

"Not to speak to, but I've seen him. He's absolutely lovely, in a very manly way, of course. I am slightly acquainted with his sisters and his mother."

"I met his mother." Eliza couldn't hold back a smile as Georgiana gasped and squeezed her arm in delight. "She was so gracious, Georgiana. Lord Hastings said she liked me."

"Of course she did! Who could not?" Georgiana laughed. "But tell me about him—I know plenty about the countess. How did you meet him?"

Eliza could feel the silly, happy smile forming on her face. "He had business with Papa. He came to call." The memory of their first encounter made her squirm a little.

"Was it love at first sight?" Georgiana demanded.

"Er . . . no," admitted Eliza. "I had been giving Willy a bath and he got loose. I met Lord Hastings by falling in a heap at his feet, trying to keep Willy from licking him to death."

Georgiana's peal of laughter drew a rebuke from Lady Sidlow.

"But he came to dinner the next night and I managed to be presentable," Eliza went on. "He complimented my singing," she added with a shy, guilty smile.

"And well should he. Your voice is beautiful. But, Eliza, this is all very ordinary! Tell me how he won your heart!"

"Well, he . . ." Eliza blinked as she thought. Hastings hadn't *done* anything particularly dashing, like rescue her from a runaway horse or save her from a lecherous dance partner. "He sent me flowers. And he danced with me twice."

Georgiana's brows lowered doubtfully.

Eliza flushed. "He kissed me," she whispered. "More than once."

Her friend brightened. "And was it lovely?"

"Divine," she said on a sigh of pure joy. "Everything a kiss should be and more."

"More?" Georgiana giggled. "It's a good thing he's about to speak to your papa, then."

Eliza agreed.

"So it's a case of mad passion." Georgiana beamed at her. "I can tell you've fallen in love with him."

Again Eliza nodded, aware that she was smiling like an idiot.

"Is it a secret? May I tell Lady Sidlow?" Georgiana cast a look over her shoulder at her chaperone. Countess Sidlow was a cousin of her mother who had agreed to sponsor Georgiana through her debut, but Georgiana wasn't very fond of her. The countess was strict and proper, and she regularly forbade Georgiana from doing things she deemed immodest or too exciting. "Not because I long to confide in her, but because she spends all her time telling me which young lady every unmarried man in town is after." Georgiana rolled her eyes. "She said the other day she thought Catherine Thayne would be a good match for Lord Hastings, and I would dearly love to tell her he found someone far better."

"Oh no." She put her hand on Georgiana's arm. "Please don't say anything to anyone, not yet. What if I've been mistaken? It would be mortifying if he stops coming to call, and everything turns out to have been my imagination."

Georgiana snorted. "I daresay it's not! You're the least likely person to imagine a gentleman's interest, so if *you* think he's about to propose, I expect he's already got the license in his pocket."

"Georgiana!" Eliza gasped.

Her friend grinned. "I won't say anything. But I *shall* begin planning which dress to wear to your wedding."

Hugh took his time approaching the Cross house.

It wasn't to give himself time to consider and reconsider. That time had already passed. He'd skipped the Vega Club and gone to an opera last night, alone, where he let the surge and swell of the music roll over him. What would have happened if he'd decided to pursue a wealthy bride first, before settling his sisters? He would be married now, to a girl of his own class. It would probably have been a marriage of convenience, as well; his bride, to say nothing of her father, would know exactly who had the upper hand. He hadn't pursued a society bride precisely because he wasn't eager for that.

Instead he was going to marry Eliza Cross, daughter of a manipulative Cit who had made an obscene fortune speculating in raw materials during the war. And she thought it was a love match.

That was the point that kept him from sleep last night. It wasn't as if Eliza was the same as her father, calculating and brazen. Eliza was . . . well, aside from her parentage, she was lovely. Genuine, warm, and kind. At first Hugh had been sure Edward Cross would tell her, or at least hint at, what he'd done, and he'd kept a wary eye out for any signs that Eliza knew her father was coercing him.

The fact that he'd seen none was both good and bad. Good, in that Hugh didn't want to marry a scheming liar. If her nerves had been staged, if her delight at his courtship was planned, it would have driven a permanent wedge into their marriage. He was enormously relieved Eliza was exactly as she appeared to be.

But deep down, Hugh knew it was very bad that she didn't know. That made *him* a liar, a cheat, and a manipulator, just as bad as her father. The more he knew Eliza, the more he liked her. It was entirely her father's doing, but he didn't doubt that she would be horribly hurt if she ever discovered the truth.

The butler, by now accustomed to him, didn't bat an eye when he asked to see Miss Cross, not Mr. Cross. Hugh took it as a good sign that he wasn't even made to wait, but was shown straight into the bright drawing room.

Eliza was having tea with another woman. A small girl sat on the sofa between them, and another even smaller girl sat on Eliza's lap. In the moment between the opening of the door and the butler's announcement of his arrival, Hugh caught a glimpse of her, laughing with pure joy as the little girl tried to feed her a biscuit.

"The Earl of Hastings, ma'am," said the butler.

Eliza blushed. Her companion gasped aloud, reaching at once for the child on Eliza's lap. Both women rose and curtsied, although the child on the sofa merely looked at him with big brown eyes. Hugh winked at her as he bowed. "Forgive me for interrupting a tea party."

"Not at all," said Eliza, her face a pretty pink. There was a spot of jam on her bodice, right near her breast, and she brushed some crumbs from her skirt. She looked at her friend. "Mrs. Reeve, may I present the Earl of Hastings? He is a business partner of my father's. My lord, Mrs. Reeve, who is our vicar's wife, and her two daughters, Cassandra and Jane."

"An honor, ma'am," said Hugh. The woman

murmured something polite, even as her gaze sharpened and grew curious.

"We were having tea to celebrate Miss Cassandra Reeve's fifth birthday," Eliza said. The pulse in her throat beat rapidly, but otherwise she was composed.

"A very happy occasion indeed. A happy birthday to you, Miss Reeve." Belatedly he noticed the small, child-sized posies of flowers on the table, the beautifully decorated tea cakes, and the handsome new doll sitting on a cloud of silver paper at the end of the sofa. Eliza had planned a party for her friend's child.

"Thank you, my lord." Mrs. Reeve dropped another curtsy. "We must go, Eliz—Miss Cross. Thank you." She nudged the little girl in her arms, who repeated, "Thank you, Miss Cross," in a wispy little voice. "Come, Cassandra."

The child slid off the sofa and looked up at Eliza before flinging her arms around Eliza's knees. "Thank you, Miss Cross," she said.

Eliza's face softened and she rested her hand on the girl's head. "You are quite welcome, Cassandra."

Cassandra collected her doll and the flowers, Mrs. Reeve collected her children, and they left. Hugh turned to Eliza as they were left alone. "I hope I didn't frighten them away."

"Oh no! Not at all." She was so fetchingly flustered, still trying to brush away the crumbs unobtrusively. "I did not expect you . . ."

He grinned. "Next time I shall send word ahead, to avoid disrupting any more parties."

"It was only a small one," she said with a smile. "Have you come to see Papa? I'm afraid he's away from home."

Hugh drew a deep breath. "No. I've come to see you. Does that displease you?" he asked at her startled expression.

"No!" She crossed the room and yanked the bell rope. "Let me send for a fresh tea tray . . ."

"Will you walk in the garden with me instead?" Suddenly he wanted to be out of Cross's house, away from anything that would make him think of the man who had maneuvered him into this spot. The garden was Eliza's, where she planted what she loved and felt at ease.

She cast one look of despair at the chaos of the tea tray, then mustered a bright smile. "Of course."

They walked out into the sunshine. Hugh offered his arm, and she took it at once. That was a good start. He wasn't really in doubt that she would accept him, but nothing could be left to chance. Willy bounded up to join them after a few minutes, and Hugh could feel the tension drain out of the woman beside him. She went down on her knees to stroke the dog's ears.

He also knelt. Willy licked his hand and then flopped onto his back, presenting his belly. Hugh obligingly gave him a good scratch, until Willy's back leg was maniacally twitching in midair.

Eliza laughed. "You have a way with him, my lord."

"He's a good dog." Hugh peeled off his gloves and stuffed them into his pocket. Willy leapt to his feet, and Hugh cuffed him lightly from side to side, finishing with a few long strokes down the animal's back. Willy circled his feet several times, gave a happy *woof*, and bolted off after something rustling in the lilies.

"He likes you," said Eliza warmly, and Hugh remembered Cross telling him he would have to take the dog, too.

He grinned. "I hope he's not the only one." Her eyes grew round, and she quickly turned to watch the dog, now sniffing along the edge of the walk. Hugh captured her hand in his. "Eliza. Am I making you nervous?"

She smiled nervously, not quite meeting his eyes. "No. Are you trying to?"

Hugh laughed. "On the contrary." He tucked her hand around his arm and started walking. "I've been very pleased to make your acquaintance."

"And I yours." She was breathless. Good.

"My mother was, as well." That wasn't quite true. His mother had cornered him just this morning and tried to persuade him against this. Hugh had assured her he knew what he was doing.

But it had the desired effect; Eliza flushed with delight. "It was my honor to meet her."

They skirted the fountain in the center of the garden. Hugh spied a small building of white stone, tucked around the corner down the hill. He nodded toward it. "What is that?"

"It is the folly, my lord. It's very peaceful, with a view of the garden."

"Very good." He turned his steps there. She said her father was away from home, but Hugh couldn't shake the feeling that Edward Cross was watching over his shoulder, prodding him onward. The farther he could get from that man, the better. Let him have privacy for this moment with Eliza.

Chapter 14

⤞⥈⤝

THE FOLLY WAS a small temple, with a pair of sofas and small tables arranged in the middle. There were also draperies, tied back out of the way. It had a splendid view of the gardens, with the house looming above on the hill. It was perfect. Hugh released Eliza's hand and began untying the draperies.

"You looked quite fetching with the little girl on your lap."

"Oh!" She turned red and brushed at the jam stain on her bodice again. "They're darling girls."

He gave her a warm smile. "They are, but you'd be even more fetching with your own child in your arms. You should have children of your own."

"Oh—I—I hope to, some day . . ."

He undid the knot on the last drape; when he closed it, they were cocooned alone in this little temple.

Eliza stood in the center, looking uncertain. Hugh started toward her. "Miss Cross. Eliza." He took her trembling hands in his. "You're still nervous."

"Well." She looked up at him through her eyelashes. "Now you are making me a bit nervous, yes."

"Don't be." He brushed his thumb over her cheek, letting his fingers trail around her jaw. Her lashes fluttered, and her head tipped slightly into his palm. "I don't want to," he whispered, edging closer. "I don't try to."

"I—I know." She wet her lips, and Hugh felt an unexpected stab of desire. This was his future wife—the bride he'd been coerced into courting—and by God he wanted her naked under him. It was a good omen.

"What makes you uneasy?" He moved even closer, gliding his hand along the side of her waist. She sucked in a breath but made no protest.

"You," she whispered. "You're—you're very handsome, my lord . . . Far too elegant for a girl like me."

"Really?" He could feel her quick, shallow breaths against his skin. "That seems unfair."

"Unfair?" Her hands hovered a moment, then rested lightly on his chest. Her head fell back, all but begging him to kiss her. "How so?"

Hugh threaded his fingers into her hair, holding her in place. When her eyes were glazed with passion and her lips were parted in want, she was mesmerizing. "Deciding I'm too much of anything for you. Don't you know I want to kiss you again?"

"Do," she begged at once, and he did. He covered her mouth with his and tasted her, deeply and thoroughly. She made sensual little sounds, pressing unabashedly against him, until he lifted his head and rested his forehead against hers.

"Eliza." His breath rasped in his throat. Again it caught him off guard how much he wanted her. "I should do this properly . . ." He set her away from him and went down on one knee. "My dear Eliza, would you do me the honor of becoming my wife?"

Her face was pale, her eyes bright, her smile ecstatic. "Yes, Lord Hastings, I will."

He came back to his feet and caught her in his arms, swinging her off her feet. Eliza gasped and then laughed, her arms around his neck. He pressed another kiss on her lips: exuberant but also relieved.

He wanted her. Every nerve in his body was urging him to kiss her again. And a small, cold, calculating part of his brain whispered that seducing her right now would seal the bargain. Cross couldn't object, couldn't wriggle loose, couldn't change his mind or impose any other conditions once she might be carrying his child.

He let her feet come back to the ground and cupped her face in one hand; she looked up at him with adoration in her eyes. Hugh stifled the twinge of his conscience. He meant to be a good husband, faithful and kind. That was all he had to offer anyone. Love was too reckless to premise a marriage on. But passion . . . passion could keep them both satisfied for a long, long time.

Starting now.

His hand came up to her bodice. "This has been tempting me since I arrived." He drew his finger across the splotch of jam and felt her nipple hardened under his touch.

Her face flamed. "I should have changed—"

"No, I like it," he whispered, and bent down. Slowly he licked the fabric, swirling his tongue over the strawberry-soaked cloth.

Eliza had long since decided the entire afternoon was a dream. Not only had he come to see her, he went down on one knee and proposed, like the most romantic suitor imaginable. And now he was kissing her, touching her as he'd done before when she nearly lost her mind from wanting him.

But this time . . . he was her betrothed husband. There was no way Papa would refuse his suit, which meant they would be married soon. Eliza was head over heels in love, and when his lips touched her breast, every sensible, restrained thought in her head went up in smoke.

With a sudden motion, he swept her up in his arms and carried her to the chaise. Eliza hid her face against his shoulder, embarrassed by how sharply her body throbbed in want, but he set her down gently against a pile of pillows as he laid her back.

"My darling," he whispered, his lips on her throat. "Soon to be my wife." Eliza shuddered at that word, *wife*. Hastings's hand tugged at the back of her dress—undoing the buttons, she realized with thrilled disbelief. He wanted her. He eased the front of her bodice down, and Eliza yanked her arms free of the sleeves, suddenly desperate for his touch, his kiss, his mouth on her everywhere. His teeth flashed in a roguish grin, and he tugged the dress farther down, then her shift. His expression grew taut and fierce as he looked at her. "Mine," he said quietly. "Mine, to have and to hold." He cupped one hand reverently around her breast.

Eliza made a stifled choking noise. Hastings laughed under his breath and lowered his head. His tongue was soft and hot, and she arched off the chaise when it traced her bared nipple.

"Better than jam," he whispered, peering up at her through the dark curls falling forward across his brow. Eliza trembled, that this beautiful, wonderful man wanted her, and without a word she clasped his head to her bosom. His hands closed on her ribs and his weight came to rest on her, and then he began to suckle.

She bucked in astonishment, but he held her, helpless beneath the pull of his mouth. Tears wet her lashes and still he tasted her, first one side, then the other, until her breasts felt tender and swollen, sensitive to the slightest touch.

"Eliza," he breathed, catching her nipple between his teeth for a moment. "I want you so desperately. I think I've gone mad for you . . ." Her legs had fallen apart when she sprawled backward on the chaise, and now she felt, with a shock, his hand come to rest between her thighs, right where she felt the most insistent ache of all. "I want to drive you mad for me." Slowly his fingers stirred, pressing between her legs. Eliza gulped for air. "Do you want me, too, darling?"

Back and forth his hand went, making her shake with each pass.

"Shouldn't you—don't you—my father," she panted, trying to make sense.

"He gave me his blessing already," Hastings whispered, his tongue flicking over her breast again. "Yours is the only desire that matters now . . ." Somehow his hand had got under her skirt, gliding over her knee and pausing to tug loose her garter.

A great buzzing filled her head. Never had she felt such a deep, desperate craving for someone. It seemed as though she might die without his touch. When his hand slipped up her thigh, she widened her legs without thought. When his fingers brushed the curls that covered her there, her back arched and she pressed into his touch. And when she felt the satisfied hiss of his breath against her bare bosom, she only gripped his head tighter to herself and stopped thinking of anything but him.

Her skirts were bunched at her waist now. He stroked his palm between her legs, making her flinch. "So soft," he said, sounding enthralled. "And so wet . . . you want me, don't you?"

He wanted to make love to her. Eliza had almost given up hope of being the object of any man's desire, let alone a man as wonderful as this one. "Yes," she gasped. "I do want you. Please."

"I warned you the other day . . ." His finger stroked delicately through the curls on her mound, lower and lower until he paused. "If you ever begged me, I would take you and make you mine. Here. Like this." Ever so slowly, he pressed that finger inside her.

Eliza's thoughts scattered. He was inside her. Not the male part of him, but he could feel how wet she had grown, just from listening to him say he wanted her. She had asked a lot of questions; the fact that her body was wet and slick meant she was ready for a man, hungry for a man. Belinda Reeve had told her women could feel that way for the wrong man, but this—this was *Hastings*, who was going to marry her. Hastings, who was everything she'd ever dreamed of. Hastings, with whom she'd fallen madly in love. "Yes," she managed to say, "I'm yours."

He raised his eyes to hers. "Yes?"

Somehow she nodded. "Yes. *Please*."

His mouth curved in a languid, wicked smile. His finger stroked deeper. Eliza writhed against the storm he built inside her. At some point he moved, sliding between her knees, now spread wide in wanton abandon. He nipped at her mouth. "They say this might hurt."

Her heart nearly burst with love at this tender concern. She put her hands on his jaw and smiled. "I don't care, my love."

His eyes flashed. He rose above her, and she felt him pressing against that aching center of herself. He flexed his spine and pushed hard. Eliza gave a startled squeak, jolted out of her daze of passion by the pain. "Shh," he murmured soothingly and pushed again, until she thought she might be torn apart.

He inhaled deeply, his hands tightening on her. He opened his eyes, dark and hot with passion, and said, "That's the worst."

"Is it all?" The throbbing was one hundred times worse, and no longer pleasant. She tried to move away, and he said something profane under his breath, holding her in place.

"Not nearly." He pulled back and pushed forward again. Eliza mewed in discomfort, but he kissed her and she forgot it. Again he moved, back and forth, until her hips moved against his on instinct. It still stung and ached, but oh— not really pain, not quite pleasure—she twisted against him, clinging to his shoulders, trying to take satisfaction from the very obvious thrill he felt. His face was dark, almost savage; his eyes glowed like coals. He hiked her knees around his waist, sliding deeper into her in the process.

"How beautiful you are," he whispered raggedly. "Here." He pulled back and pushed forward again.

"How?" She felt feverish and stupid, unable to sort out his meaning.

He bared his teeth in a hungry grin, then took her hand and sucked her fingers into his mouth. He slowed and stopped moving, then placed her hand, her fingers laced with his, under her bunched-up skirt, right on the place where their bodies joined. "Touch," he said, his voice almost unrecognizable. "Feel how perfectly we fit together." He shoved up her skirt and pushed himself upright to watch as she tentatively swirled her fingers around.

Good heavens. He felt enormous, buried inside her. Eliza's hand began to tremble as her fingers slid around his thickness. Enormous, but . . . good. He pulled back and thrust deep again, sliding between her fingers until they were wet with the proof of their desire for each other.

"Eliza." The word was almost a command, harsh and urgent. He was holding himself stiffly above her.

Gingerly she touched herself, on the tiny pulse throbbing right above where he entered her. A jolt of sensation rocked her, and it felt as if all her muscles tightened. Hastings growled, his hips jerking. Eliza circled her finger again, watching his face all the while. Every time she felt a quickening in her belly, he seemed to swell even larger within her, and the tension in his face grew tauter. His arms were trembling beside her, but he did not move, letting her explore.

Eventually, though, his hips surged against hers. Eliza felt wild; she spread her legs wider and gripped her skirts in one hand. Hastings added his fingers to hers, stroking her firmly as he moved inside her. He bent his head and caught her nipple between his teeth, just sharply enough to make her writhe and cry out. Her muscles hurt; her bones were melting. She gazed in dumb adoration at the earl, her love, her lover, her husband-to-be, and then—

Everything went still, and dark, and white-hot with pleasure. A second later her senses roared back, ten times keener than before, and she felt the tears run down her face as she reached for Hastings. He thrust hard into her, his face dark and fierce, once more before he exhaled in a gust. Eyes closed and breathing hard, he rested his forehead on her bare bosom.

Her heart was pounding a thousand times a minute. Scarcely able to believe it was real, she rested one hand on his hair. The dark curls were damp. With a sense of incredulity, she realized what she'd done; she was his, and he was hers. Consummating the marriage before the wedding made it binding.

A silly smile formed on her lips. Hastings lifted his head, gorgeously rumpled, and his mouth quirked with satisfaction. "My lady," he said, his lips brushing hers.

"My lord," she said, still shocked it was so.

"Hugh." He kissed her harder. "My name is Hugh."

She knew that, of course. She'd looked it up after the first day he walked with her in the garden. "Hugh," she repeated tenderly.

His smile was intimate and knowing. "I shall speak to your father immediately about setting a date for the wedding."

Eliza flushed from head to toe. He must have guessed what was going through her mind, for he pressed one finger to her lips. "Only about the wedding," he said firmly. "Not a word about this."

She beamed at him in gratitude. He levered

himself upright and Eliza felt cold without his body atop hers, inside hers. He fished out a handkerchief and pressed it gently between her legs. She blushed scarlet when he took it away spotted with blood.

"Let me clean it," she said, reaching for it as she shoved down her skirts.

He only winked and folded it into his pocket. "Proof that you're mine and mine alone." As before he helped fix the top of her dress, taking every chance to touch her breasts. Eliza wondered in a daze how soon they could be married, and he could make love to her yet again.

He tucked his shirt back in and buttoned his trousers, almost entirely as he was before except for his charmingly rumpled hair. Eliza dared to reach out and smooth some of the wayward curls down, and he let her. A thrill of happiness shot through her; as his wife, she would be able to touch him whenever she liked.

"Shall we go back?" He offered his arm.

Eliza didn't want to. For one thing, she knew she looked a fright, with her dress crumpled and her hair mussed, to say nothing of the glowing smile on her face. Her belly throbbed with every move she made. Instead of going back to the house, she wanted to stay here, in this sheltered little world where it was just the two of them. Hugh might hold her and kiss her and make love to her again, and this time she would be ready for it . . .

"Eliza?" He was waiting, watching her quizzically.

She blushed and told herself not to be a ninny. She put her hand on his arm very properly, as if she hadn't just given herself to him on a chaise in the folly, and let him lead her back to the house. After all, they would have years and years to make love to each other, and be in love, and live happily ever after.

Chapter 15

❦

Hᴜɢʜ ᴡᴀsᴛᴇᴅ ɴᴏ time sending word to Edward Cross that his suit had been accepted, and he wished to set a date for the wedding. Now that the deed was done, there was no reason for delay.

He also asked Cross to advance him ten thousand pounds of Eliza's dowry. Benwick had grown annoying, and it was time to settle things with him. Edith had refused to speak to him since the day Eliza came to tea, and Hugh hoped that a happy engagement of her own would soften her feelings toward her future sister-in-law.

The first part of the plan went smoothly. Cross responded at once, suggesting a date less than a fortnight hence for the wedding and saying that his solicitors would forward the funds at once. He closed the note with an insouciant wish for Lady Edith's happiness. Hugh scowled at that. He was tired of Cross interfering in his life, and felt an overwhelming urge to keep his mother and sisters away from the man.

The last step was telling his family. His mother

knew as soon as he came into the room; he could tell by her face. His sisters looked at him in surprise, since he didn't usually join them for breakfast.

"Hugh!" Henrietta jumped up and dashed across the room to give him a hug. "What a surprise!"

"Good morning to you, too," he said with a laugh. "Why so surprised? Never be astonished by a man wanting breakfast, Hen. Even the best of brothers must eat sometimes." He took his seat as his mother poured a cup of coffee and a footman set a plate in front of him. "Good morning, Mother."

His mother's smile was a little strained. "Good morning, dear."

"Good morning, Edith," he said pointedly to his other sister, whose attention had returned to her breakfast.

"Good morning, Lord Hastings," she said coolly, her attention on her eggs.

"Edith," murmured their mother.

Henrietta glanced at her sister's set face, then turned to Hugh, determinedly cheerful. "When will Edith's wedding be, Hugh? I long to have a new gown for it, but Mother says there may be no need this Season. That cannot be right—Mr. Benwick is so eager to marry her, surely you won't make them wait until next year."

"As it happens," Hugh told her, "I have just sent a message to Mr. Benwick this morning, arranging an appointment with the solicitors." Edith's head jerked up, and she gave him a wide-eyed look. "As to new gowns, I have no opinion on that, but if you can have one made quickly—" He stopped because Edith had leapt from her chair with a shriek of delight and run to throw her arms around his neck.

"Thank you, Hugh, thank you!" She kissed his cheek. "I will write to Reggie immediately. Mother, shall we have the wedding here? Or is there time to get St. George's?"

The countess took a sip of her tea. "You may send an inquiry to the church. I suppose it depends on what Mr. Benwick wants."

Edith laughed. "Reggie will want whatever is sooner! Oh, if only you'd told me earlier, Hugh— thank you!"

"What choice did I have?" he exclaimed in mock indignation. "All I've seen are sour looks and sad faces around here. It's enough to make a man flee the house . . ."

"Silly!" She resumed her seat, still beaming. "All you had to do was see Reggie so that we might set a date. You have only yourself to blame, for being so slow about it."

"Yes, yes, I understand we men are slow about everything." He picked up his coffee. "Perhaps when I am married, my wife will keep me on time."

"The poor girl," teased Henrietta. "Who would accept that challenge?" Edith laughed, obviously thinking they spoke in jest. The countess gave Hugh a speaking look and reached for her teacup.

"It may come as a shock to you, but I believe I've

found someone willing to take it on." He raised his brows as Henrietta's and Edith's mouths dropped open in identical shock. "Try not to faint in amazement."

"Who?" demanded Henrietta. "Is it Catherine Thayne?"

"Fanny Martin," guessed Edith.

"Mrs. MacMurray? Tell us, Hugh!" demanded Henrietta eagerly.

"Elizabeth Cross."

The room fell silent. Edith gaped at him in horror. Confusion flashed across Henrietta's face before recognition made her sit back, wide-eyed and mute.

His mother bestirred herself. "Has she accepted you?"

"She has." He spoke heartily, trying to convey pleasure with the news. No one moved. He held out his hands. "Come, has no one a word of congratulations?"

"Congratulations, Hugh," murmured Henrietta, with a hesitant look at her sister.

"No," said Edith suddenly. "I shan't say a word in praise of such madness. How could you do this?"

"I went down on one knee, and she said yes." He hardened his heart to the mutiny in her face.

She turned to their mother in appeal. "Surely you can't approve?"

The countess didn't look at Hugh. "It is your brother's choice to make, Edith. We must be gracious and kind to his wife."

Hugh's mouth firmed. He knew "gracious and kind" was not what Eliza wanted. She hoped to gain a mother and sisters, as well. But he left any reproof unspoken; there would be time for his family to accept Eliza. Once they saw how warm and genuine she was, he was sure they would.

Not that it mattered. In ten days' time, Eliza—and her dowry—would be his, before God and the law.

THE NEXT TWO WEEKS passed in a blaze of joy for Eliza.

It wasn't entirely on her own behalf. As Eliza had hoped, Sophie had confessed all to her duke, and in return the duke had persuaded her to marry him. Their wedding was small but lovely, and not even Georgiana's avid whispers of some last-minute scandal at the Vega Club could make Eliza stop smiling. She hoped she would be as radiantly happy as Sophie on her own wedding day, even if she could not be as beautiful.

And then it was *her* wedding day. She had wanted it to be small and intimate, and it was. The sun shone in a flawless blue sky, and Willy wore a yellow bow around his neck. Mary curled her hair into the most fashionable cluster of ringlets and set a wreath of barely opened yellow rosebuds on top of it. Eliza hardly recognized the girl in the mirror; today she was pretty.

Her father was waiting to walk her down the stairs. She saw him wipe away a tear when she stepped out of her room, and he kissed her cheek with unusual gentleness. "More beautiful than your mother," he said gruffly. "May you be as happy with Hastings as I was with her."

"Thank you, Papa," she whispered. "For everything."

Mr. Reeve married them in the drawing room, with Belinda standing happily beside him, and Cassandra and Jane holding matching bouquets at her side. Papa had finally made the donation he wanted, and the vicar was beaming ear to ear as he said the words that made her Hugh's wife. Eliza could hardly look away from her bridegroom. His hair had been slicked back and he wore a green jacket that reminded her of her garden, mossy and vibrant. He repeated his vows in a clear, firm voice, while Eliza could barely whisper hers, but then he put a gold ring on her finger and they were wed.

"Eliza!" Georgiana enveloped her in a hug when it was over. "I wish you every joy in the world."

"As do I," said Sophie, now the Duchess of Ware. "I've never seen you look happier."

"I've never been happier," she said honestly. "Not just for me"—Georgiana raised her brows, her eyes sparkling—"but for all of us." She clasped her friends' hands. "Never did I imagine . . ."

Georgiana laughed. "I did! I told you years ago you would find someone who adored you."

"And who didn't care about your deplorable lack of skill at sums," put in Sophie, making them all laugh.

"I don't know about that," said Eliza, flushed with love. "Hastings hasn't asked me about sums yet . . ."

"No, I wager he's thinking of something else entirely when he looks at you," murmured Sophie, watching Hugh. He stood across the room, speaking to his mother and sisters.

Eliza's mood dimmed a fraction at the sight. Lady Hastings—now the dowager countess—had given her a gracious smile and welcomed her to the family, but with genteel reserve. Lady Edith and Lady Henrietta had been no more than polite. Lady Edith in fact was almost cold, and Lady Henrietta had tried to avoid looking at her at all. Eliza had never had siblings, and she didn't remember her mother. She had hoped her sisters-in-law would be like true sisters, but it was clear they didn't feel the same.

"Yes, as a married lady now, you must learn to recognize what it means when a gentleman looks at you that way." Georgiana darted a wary glance over her shoulder, but Lady Sidlow, her chaperone, was speaking to Sophie's husband. The duke was regarding Lady Sidlow with ducal hauteur, but Eliza had noticed he always looked that way until Sophie crossed his vision. Then his blue eyes grew hot and his mouth softened, and she would swear he was imagining doing wicked things with his wife.

"You mean the way His Grace looks at Sophie?" As they were watching, Ware glanced their way, and the searing look he gave Sophie made them all blush.

"Yes," murmured Sophie, pink-faced. "That way."

"I know," Eliza whispered. "I know about all that. I never thought I would *need* to know, but—"

"My Lady Hastings." Hugh's voice behind her made her jump. She turned to see him bow. "May I take you in to our wedding breakfast?"

She blushed. "Yes." Her friends waved her on, Sophie returning to her duke and Georgiana heading toward the Hastings girls with a determined expression. Eliza couldn't help but notice that their faces grew markedly more welcoming at her approach.

"Why so grim?" Hugh took her chin in his hand and studied her face. "Regrets already?"

She laughed in embarrassment. "No! More that I feel suddenly overwhelmed—no longer simple Miss Cross, but the Countess of Hastings, who sounds so much grander."

He grinned. "Does she? And yet I plan to take her to bed and make her sigh and moan in ecstasy tonight, which sounds much finer than being grand."

"Stop!" Scarlet-faced, she squeezed his arm. No one was near enough to hear, but it still gave her a shocked thrill when he said such things to her.

"Then don't look at me like that." His voice dropped, and his eyes wandered over her. Eliza felt lovely in her peach silk gown with white lace, but when Hugh looked at her that way, she wanted to tear it off. "It makes me want to steal you away, back to the folly, and leave everyone else to the cold meats."

"We couldn't possibly," she whispered back, even though she would have preferred it. Lady Edith was watching her with something very close to dislike.

Hugh sighed. "Later, then." He raised her hand and kissed her knuckles, right where her new ring shone.

"Yes," she said happily. "Later."

They left Greenwich several hours later. Papa had arranged for the yacht to take them back into the heart of London, where Hugh's driver would meet them. Sophie and the duke departed in their carriage. Since their wedding a few days earlier they had been at the duke's country house in Chiswick, and Sophie murmured to her that they might never go back to London. Georgiana had wanted to go on the yacht, too, but Lady Sidlow firmly denied it. The carriage was good enough, she declared, and Georgiana bade Eliza farewell in a flurry of hugs and promises that she would call on her as soon as possible.

"After all, Lady Sidlow cannot fault me for visiting the Countess of Hastings!" she whispered in glee. Her chaperone was insufferably proud, to Georgiana's disgust.

Eliza laughed and waved good-bye. Hugh waited behind her, but when she turned, he cocked one brow. "May I take you home now, ma'am?"

"Of course." Eliza blushed as Roberts brought her cloak and bonnet. It wasn't for the last time, but it suddenly felt like it. On impulse, she seized the older man's hand. "Good-bye, Roberts. Look after Papa, would you?"

The butler, who had been in their household for as long as she could remember, smiled. "I will, madam."

Papa walked with them down to the dock. Mary, her maid, had left for London earlier with Eliza's baggage to make everything ready at her new home. The dowager countess and her daughters were already aboard the yacht, and Hugh stood waiting to hand her onto the deck.

Eliza threw her arms around her father. "I can't believe I'm leaving," she said on a little gasping sob. "Good-bye, Papa."

"There." He smoothed her hair. "No tears! You've made me so happy, Lilibeth. A noble husband for my beautiful girl—your mother would be so proud and delighted. You tell me if Hastings doesn't make you happy," he teased with mock severity. "Remind him I want several grandchildren, and that I don't like to wait . . ."

With a watery laugh, she kissed him good-bye and let him hand her over the rail into Hugh's arms. They stood on the deck together and waved until Papa was out of sight. Only then did she lean into her bridegroom's side and sigh.

"You may visit him whenever you want," he told her.

"I know. It just seems so strange to leave him." Her eyes felt sticky at the thought of Papa alone in the big house every day. She knew that was silly; he would surely spend most of his time in London, playing cards with Mr. Grenville and visiting the widow in Portland Place. He had always said nothing would make him happier than to see her wed, and he must have many reasons for it.

"You'll get used to it," Hugh assured her. "Let me see to my mother. She isn't fond of boats." He went forward to where his mother and sisters sat, leaving her to her thoughts.

Chapter 16

W‍HEN THEY DISEMBARKED at Whitehall Stairs, a carriage was waiting for the ladies and a horse for Hugh. He helped her up the step and winked. "Almost home," he said with a grin.

Eliza smiled, but a nervous flutter started in her chest. Home. She barely remembered the Hastings house near St. James's Square. She'd been so nervous about meeting his mother, nothing much about it had registered, but now it was her home. She tried to pay more attention as they drove.

The house was not as large as she remembered. Only five windows wide, it was smaller than its neighbor and built of old red brick. Eliza had thought it looked charming and quaint the first time she visited, but now it looked a bit dingy, as well.

Well. There was nothing wrong with dirt. It could all be scrubbed away, and now that she was mistress of the house, it would be her responsibility to see it done.

Lady Edith and Lady Henrietta barely stopped to leave their bonnets and cloaks in the hall before heading right up the stairs. Lady Hastings murmured something about writing letters before excusing herself into the small morning room where Hugh had kissed her. Eliza knew it was rude, but she didn't know why. Perhaps they were feeling a little melancholy at the thought of Hugh being married, or were exhausted after the wedding. Eliza hoped they would warm to her in time, and she resolved to be as cheerful and understanding as possible to that end. Fortunately Hugh stepped up and put her at ease, presenting her to Wilkins, the butler, and Mrs. Greene, the housekeeper.

"Would you like to see your room now?" he whispered in her ear. "You must be tired."

Eliza blushed at the tone in his voice. "Yes, thank you," she said, even though she wasn't much tired. He gave her a sly look that promised no sleep at all, and they turned toward the stairs.

A frantic scrabbling stopped her on the second step. "Willy!" she cried in delight. Her dog had been sent on ahead with Mary, and he came racing around the corner with a harried footman in chase. Eliza fell to her knees and hugged Willy, who still wore his yellow bow, now rather bedraggled. He went wild, licking her face and ears until she laughed aloud.

"What—?" Lady Hastings stood in the doorway, one hand on her bosom. "What is this?"

Eliza got back to her feet—a difficult endeavor with Willy still trying to nip the lace on her dress. "This is Willy, ma'am."

She turned to her son in dismay. "A dog?"

"Willy is a dog, Mother, but a well-behaved one." Willy, naturally, chose that moment to leap and steal the handkerchief from Hugh's pocket. Eliza cringed at the sound of ripping cloth. Lady Hastings looked appalled. Hugh merely laughed and pushed the dog back to the floor. "A mostly well-behaved dog."

"I don't—" The dowager stopped. She glanced at Eliza and sighed. "Never mind."

"Don't worry," Eliza hastened to say. "He's happiest in the garden. I'll make sure he doesn't disturb anyone."

"How thoughtful of you," said the dowager, "but there is no garden. Wilkins will have to assign someone to walk him."

Eliza intended to walk him herself, but her mother-in-law's expression kept her quiet. It was clear Lady Hastings did not like dogs. She bobbed a curtsy. "Yes, ma'am."

"Thank you, dear." The dowager turned and went back into the morning room. Eliza gripped a handful of fur at Willy's neck to keep him from running after the woman.

"Come," urged Hugh, his hand at her back. "Let's go upstairs."

Eliza said nothing until they were alone in the master bedchamber. It was smaller than her room at home and she was surprised how dark it was. The furnishings were dark wood with blood-red upholstery, the carpets were an indeterminate shade of brown, and even the walls were covered in dreary papers. It was hideous.

But Hugh was here, and when he closed the

door and took her in his arms, the rest faded away. Eliza rested her cheek against his chest and felt at peace for the first time all day.

"A bit much, is it?" he asked.

She nodded. "I fear your mother and sisters don't like me." It just slipped out before she could stop it.

"What? No, they're merely reserved," he said. "Perhaps nervous, as well. It's not every day a new lady of the house arrives. Be yourself, and my mother will come to love you."

"What about Edith and Henrietta?" she dared to ask.

He huffed. "Edith has been upset with me for some time. She'll get over her temper fit, and Henrietta always follows her. Besides, Edith is engaged herself. Now that the tedium of my wedding is over, she can embrace the thrill of her own, and that will raise both my sisters' spirits."

"Tedium!"

He laughed. "Wasn't it? All that talking and nonsense, keeping me from this." He cupped her face and kissed her. Willy whined, and Hugh raised his head. "Willy, basket," he said in a tone of authority. To Eliza's shock, her dog cocked his head, then trotted over to the familiar basket by the hearth and settled down. "Good dog," Hugh told him before sweeping Eliza into his arms.

He'd got her dress and petticoats off and had her twisting in his arms, wearing only her chemise as he kissed his way up and down her body, when a knock sounded at the door. Hugh growled, but when it came a second time he called out, "Yes?"

Her hair over her face, her heart pounding and her skin tingling from his kisses, Eliza didn't hear what the intruder said. But Hugh muttered a curse and rolled to his feet. He'd only lost his jacket and shoes, and when he opened the door he stood to block Eliza's view—or rather, to block the visitor's view of her. After a brief exchange, Hugh closed the door again, a letter in his hand. He broke the seal and read it, a scowl deepening on his face. When he finished reading he went to the window and stared out, tapping the letter against his thigh.

Eliza slid from the bed. "What is it?" she asked.

"Nothing."

His curt tone stopped her cold. She bit her lip, and got her dressing gown, thoughtfully laid out by Mary. She wrapped it around herself and went to stand beside him. "Is it very bad news?"

Hugh said nothing. His face was hard, and he looked to be deep in thought. Eliza simply waited. It must be something very shocking or alarming, but until she knew, it was best not to say anything.

"I have to go out," he said abruptly.

Now? Her heart sank at the thought that they would not get to resume their very pleasant activities on the bed. "Is there anything I can do?" she ventured.

He glanced at her, and she took a step backward at his expression. It was bitter, almost angry—but it changed as soon as his eyes met hers. A rueful smile touched his lips. "You can wait for me, just like this, Lady Hastings. The thought of it will bring me hurrying back as quickly as I can."

"Oh." She smiled in relief. "If you wish . . ."

"I do wish." He pulled her to him and gave her one more searing kiss. "This is my wedding night, you know."

"It's not night yet," she said breathlessly.

"And I regret losing even one hour of it to anyone else." He retrieved his jacket from the floor, and put on his shoes. "You might take a nap while you can."

Eliza was blushing with happiness when he left. It was still daylight, so she rang for Mary to help her dress again. She might as well see her new home, and the obliging housekeeper gave her a tour from the cellars to the servants' rooms under the eaves.

Hugh didn't come home, not when the dinner hour arrived and Mary told her the other ladies had ordered trays in their rooms. Eliza supposed they had planned to give the newlywed couple some time alone, so she also requested a dinner tray. She took Willy for a walk with a footman half attending, half directing her through the square nearby. Willy bitterly resented being kept on a lead, and Eliza was relieved to return home and send him to the kitchen for his dinner.

But Hugh did not come back, even as the streetlamps were lit and she watched a dozen carriages come and go at houses nearby, marveling at how bright and busy London was compared to Greenwich.

And he still hadn't come back when she found herself yawning and dozing off in her chair. With a sigh, she called for Mary again and got ready for bed. Willy gave her a sad look, so she patted the mattress beside her. With a single leap he was on the bed, circling several times before curling into a furry lump beside her. Eliza stroked his head and smiled, but somewhat sadly. She had not expected to spend her wedding night with Willy.

HUGH WAS READY TO smash in Reginald Benwick's handsome face.

He had been on the verge of making love to his bride, savoring one of the most unexpectedly wonderful aspects of his situation, when the young man's note arrived. Virtually steaming with outrage and arrogance, it demanded to know if it was true that Hugh meant to marry Edward Cross's daughter. If so, Benwick wrote, it would severely damage his inclination to tie himself to Hugh's family, and he demanded Hugh call on him at once to explain the matter.

Edith had refused to speak to him for almost a week now. She had gone to the wedding only because their mother required it. Hugh knew that if he didn't act immediately, her fury would be twice as terrible. He could live with that, but he could not ask Eliza to do the same. He'd seen the cold way Edith looked at his bride, and it pushed his patience to the end. Edith was being a child, but the best way to improve the situation was to mollify her and speed up the engagement to Benwick. Once Edith was a married lady herself, she would forget her sulks over Hugh's marriage.

So he left his wife, ravishingly mussed and mostly undressed, and went to Curzon Street. Benwick was waiting for him with his father, Viscount Livingston. And both of them erupted in fury when Hugh informed them that he had married Eliza Cross that morning.

"Intolerable," raged the viscount, face purple. "I thought you had some discernment! What would your father say?"

"I expect he would congratulate me," said Hugh evenly.

"Not for wedding the daughter of that scoundrel—no, not for all the money in the world." Livingston was a tall fellow, with a paunchy belly and a mane of graying hair. His son stood behind his chair, his nose in the air, as if Hugh had also taken on the reek of whatever tainted Edward Cross. "That was it, wasn't it?" pressed Livingston. "The money?"

"That is none of your concern." Hugh was keeping his temper, but only just. "I fail to see how it involves you." He transferred his attention to Benwick. "Is this your doing?"

"I never approved of your interest in that woman," was his prissy reply.

"How fortunate you want to marry my sister, then, and not me," returned Hugh. "I daresay you and Edith shan't have to see my wife more than once or twice a year."

Livingston snarled. "They'll be relations! That—

that gutter-born wench shall bear the Hastings heir, and how, sir, how shall my son avoid it then? He will be expected to recognize the brat!"

Hugh came to his feet. "Livingston, watch yourself," he said coldly. "Confine your remarks to the marriage settlements or we shall have to speak only through our attorneys."

"Bugger the settlements," declared Livingston. "And the attorneys."

Hugh blinked. "What?" Just a few days ago he'd sent word to his solicitor to draw up a settlement, with ten thousand pounds to Edith. Cross had kept his word and the money was sitting in Hugh's bank, ready to deliver to Benwick.

Livingston's eyes gleamed. "That man cheated me out of twenty thousand pounds. Cross is a viper—if you don't know it yet, you will. Take this as a well-meant warning, Hastings. Find a way to annul the marriage. Send her back before it's too late."

"Send her—" Hugh stared incredulously. "I *married* her. I cannot send her back."

Livingston waved one hand. "Find a way. I'd plead fraud if I were you. If you think Cross didn't defraud you, that only means you haven't realized how just yet. Repudiate her and send her back. I'll not have my son and heir associated with that man in any way."

The viscount's meaning began to sink in. Hugh turned to Benwick, looking for an ally this time. "Benwick, this is madness. You told me you love Edith. She loves you! Surely you aren't going to be so fastidious as to spoil that."

Benwick didn't look happy, but he nodded resolutely. "I cannot marry a woman with such connections."

Hugh was stunned. Shocked. Horrified. "You're breaking the engagement," he said in disbelief. "You're jilting my sister."

Benwick flinched at the word, but his father nodded, his face fiery with spite. "He can't jilt her. You never signed a settlement—wouldn't even discuss one! There's no engagement to break."

Still staring at Benwick, Hugh clenched his jaw. "You're jilting my sister," he repeated. "Over *my* marriage."

The young man hesitated. His father growled. Benwick swallowed and said firmly, "I must."

Hugh left. He walked in a daze, shaken to the core by the meeting. What was he to tell Edith? No—he couldn't even think of it. Her heart would be broken. Her despair would be terrible. She would hate him forever.

Surely Benwick would reconsider. Livingston would relent, once his temper cooled. Surely on the morrow they would remember the ten thousand pound dowry; the attorney had been quite clear about the terms of the settlement Hugh was offering. Surely . . .

What if they didn't?

He should take Eliza into society at once, so everyone could see how unlike her father she was. Perhaps her friends would help her acquire a little confidence and polish, even throw a ball for her. Nothing improved a woman's status like a glittering ball in the home of a sponsoring member of the *haut ton*. A ball given by the Duchess of Ware would surely lend Eliza some panache . . . But then Hugh remembered that the duchess had been a regular at the Vega Club until very recently. She was hardly part of the *ton* herself yet. And Lady Georgiana was an unmarried lady still, incapable of steering society's opinion.

He couldn't bear to go home. At Piccadilly he turned east, and found himself walking up the steps of the Vega Club. It was as good a place as any to ponder his troubles. Hugh rarely drank, but tonight he found a seat in the back of the salon and ordered a bottle of wine. Tonight was a good night to get drunk.

By the time he staggered home, the moon was high in the sky. Hugh groped in his pockets for his latchkey, but it wasn't there; he had not planned to stay out late. He knocked at the door, and blessedly his mother had set a footman to wait for him as usual.

"Shall I send for Mr. Bernard?" asked the servant as he bolted the door.

Hugh waved one hand. "No." There was no need to wake his valet. He trudged up the stairs, yanking at his neckcloth. Eliza must be sound asleep by now—not that he could tell her what had happened. He peeled off his clothes in the narrow dressing room and quietly let himself into the bedroom.

The curtains were open, and the glow of the streetlamp outside fell across the bed. At his entrance, Willy raised his head from the bed—from Hugh's pillow, actually. Hugh's mouth twisted.

"Willy, basket," he ordered quietly. The dog regarded him for a moment, then stretched out to take up half the bed. The blankets rustled, and Eliza's arm flopped across Willy's neck. The dog heaved a sigh and thrashed his tail once, as if to say *she has me—you're not wanted*.

He gazed at his sleeping wife. She was an innocent party in all this—perhaps the only one. Her father might be a poisonous spider, corrupting all he caught in his web, but Eliza was not. Hugh couldn't undo the marriage. In truth, he didn't want to. Not only for the vast fortune she'd brought him, but because he was coming to care for her a great deal. She would be horrified and humiliated if she discovered that Edith's engagement was in danger because of her. No one deserved that. He'd seen the overtures Eliza had made to his mother and sisters; she wanted them to like her. And he had promised her they would . . . in time.

If Benwick followed through and jilted Edith, though, he thought it was possible they would despise Eliza. Hugh didn't know how he would prevent any of it.

But he was not getting pushed out of his own bed by a dog. "Basket," he repeated, pointing. This time Willy slunk off the bed and went to his basket. Hugh eased between the covers, wondering how his attempts to save his family had all gone so horribly wrong.

Chapter 17

ᗺᑎ

ELIZA AWOKE TO someone kissing her neck.

Today, though, it was not Willy.

"Good morning," Hugh murmured, his hands skating up and down her arms. "I can tell you're awake, Lady Hastings."

She tried to stifle her laugh. "How can you tell that?"

"Because I've been making free of your body for some time now, learning every little thing that makes you twitch and sigh and moan." His hand settled around her breast, his thumb stroking roughly over her nipple. "As your husband, I ought to know these things."

That explained why her heart was already racing and her skin felt hot. Eliza stretched and realized with a shock that her nightgown was up over her hips—and even more, that her husband was naked. No sooner did she move her legs than his slid between them, his own strong and hairy and so much bigger than hers. It was startling, and arousing, and so shocking, she said the first thing that came into her head. "Where's Willy?"

His chest shook with silent laughter. "He whined to go out some time ago. Bernard took him to the kitchen."

"Oh." Eliza wished she weren't such an idiot, to mention the dog when her husband was making love to her. "Thank you."

"I had to throw him off the bed last night." His hand slid down her belly, right between her thighs. Her pulse went wild. He *was* making free with her body, and she was feverishly anxious for him to do it faster and harder. "I don't want to begin our married life by making rules, but that is one: the dog sleeps in his bed, and I sleep in mine." He nipped at the skin below her ear. "With my wife."

"If you insist . . ." His fingers probed boldly between her thighs and Eliza parted her legs in invitation.

"I do." He groaned, his mouth open against her neck, as he pushed one, then two fingers inside her. "*My* wife," he repeated, with a strange emphasis. Eliza sensed something was off, but he spread her legs with both hands and tormented her until she couldn't think, let alone speak.

She was almost ready to explode, begging him in a voice she didn't even recognize, when Hugh finally turned her over. His face dark, he moved above her and thrust home with such force her body spasmed and she gave a little cry of release. He curled one arm behind her head, his muscle as hard as iron, and began moving, driving hard and deep. Eliza thought she would faint—she couldn't breathe, she couldn't see anything but him, and he was riding her so furiously she had to curl her legs around his hips. He growled at that, kissing her until she saw stars, and finished with a shout, his head thrown back.

"My wife," he rasped. "Forever."

Eliza spread her hands on his bare chest, heaving and damp with sweat. Her heart was so full of love it ached. She pressed her lips to his skin. "And you're mine, forever," she whispered tenderly.

They stayed like that for several minutes. Eliza marveled at the weight of him; this gorgeous man was her husband. *Hers.* He delighted in her body and found her appealing. She ran her hands down his muscled back, still in disbelief that she could touch him. He stirred enough to settle one hand around her breast, and she shivered at the intimacy of it. They were married. There might be a child—or four—to bind them together. It was everything she had ever wanted.

"I love you," she said softly.

"Good," he muttered. Eliza gave a gasp of embarrassed laughter, and Hugh went up on his elbows, a heavy-lidded, satisfied expression on his face. "What shall you do today?"

She noticed he didn't respond to her declaration, but let it go. Such things were difficult for men to say, and Hugh had amply demonstrated his affections. "When was this house last decorated?"

He looked blank. "Decorated? I've no idea."

Eliza nodded. The house was dark and outdated. It was older and smaller than Papa's house, and it didn't have the advantage of being on a hill above the river in full sunlight, but there was no reason it must keep to the styles of fifty years ago. "I plan to speak to your mother. She's a very elegant lady, and I wonder if perhaps she doesn't have time, or perhaps interest, in decorating. Because the drawing room is dismal, and this room would send anyone into a melancholy."

"Ah." Hugh rolled off her and stared at the ceiling, his fingers idly plucking at her hair, which was in a wild tangle across the pillows. "My father wasn't fond of London, so we rarely visited before this Season. The house has been for let these past several years, and it surely needs a fresh touch."

"Yes!" Eagerly she scooted closer, resting her cheek on his shoulder. "Then your mother won't take offense if I invite her to refurbish it with me?"

His fingers paused. "I hope she wouldn't. You are mistress of the house now, Eliza."

Eliza knew better than that. "But I don't want to insult her. I—I don't remember my mother at all, and I would like to endear myself to yours."

Hugh eased his arm from under her and sat up, swinging his feet to the floor. "She won't object if you refurbish the house." He rose and put on his dressing gown. Eliza sat up, clutching the linens to her chest in speechless dismay. "I have some matters to attend to today, but I'll return for dinner."

"Of course," she murmured, but he was already striding toward the dressing room. The door closed behind him, and she wondered what she'd said wrong.

HUGH WASHED AND DRESSED, then sent Bernard to fetch Willy from the kitchen for Eliza. His mother didn't like dogs and Edith was frightened of them, but Eliza deserved to have her pet with her.

In part of his brain he knew he ought to stay home and help smooth his bride's way with his family, and Eliza had handed him the perfect way to do it. When they reached London, his mother had openly longed to throw out the dusty draperies in the drawing room and buy new furniture. Hugh had resisted because he could not pay for new draperies or furniture, but now there was plenty of money to spend on the house. His mother should be delighted to have a daughter-in-law who not only wanted to refurbish, but had both funds and taste to do so. All he had to do was present Eliza's plan to his mother in the right way, and both women would be happily occupied.

But his overriding goal today, the thing he had to do before anything else, was patch up the rift with Livingston and Benwick. He would have to keep his temper, of course, and not react to any slights Benwick might utter about Eliza. If Edith weren't desperately in love with the fellow, he wouldn't bother, but of all the things Hugh had done to protect and care for his sisters, this might be the most important. For Edith, he could hold his tongue.

His equanimity took a blow when he went down the stairs and saw Edward Cross. The man had just come in—the butler still held his hat and coat—and when he saw Hugh on the stairs he smirked. There was no way to stop the instinctive surge of animosity.

"Good morning, Lord Hastings," Cross said with a wide smile.

"Mr. Cross." Hugh bowed his head. "I did not expect you."

Cross raised one brow. "No? But we're family now."

The last thread of his patience snapped. "Come, then," he said coldly. He turned on his heel and strode toward his study.

"No need to be irate," said Cross when the door was closed. "I've brought you a wedding gift." He took a packet from his pocket and held it out.

Hugh knew what it was even before he opened it. Promissory notes, mortgages, and bills, all annotated with *Paid in full*. The sight of his father's signature sent a bolt of fury and anguish through him that almost rivaled the one he'd felt at the sight of Edward Cross. "Thank you," he said woodenly.

"As we agreed." Cross gave his faint smile. "I've already called upon my solicitors and instructed them to pay Eliza's remaining dowry funds."

It was exactly as agreed; they had both honored the bargain struck little more than a month ago. In just a few words yesterday, he'd gone from nearly bankrupt and deeply in debt to wealthy and prosperous, with the expectation of enormous riches to come. His debts were paid and his accounts would soon swell by another forty thousand pounds. And yet Hugh felt hollow, as if he'd won a Pyrrhic victory.

Slowly he folded the documents and put them in a drawer. He faced his father-in-law and willed away his anger. "Mr. Cross," he said, "you may call upon Eliza any time you like. You are welcome here as long as she will receive you."

"How generous," remarked the man, still smiling.

"Our business, however, is concluded. Since our first discussion, I have been repeatedly and constantly reminded that you are not an easy man, and you have enemies."

"Every man has enemies. I daresay there's some who resent your place and power in the world." Cross folded his arms.

Hugh breathed evenly, holding his temper in check. "What happened between you and Viscount Livingston?"

Cross looked mildly surprised. "Nothing of import. We had some business in mining shares."

"He claims you cheated him."

"Does he?" Cross lifted one shoulder. "He's an ass. He thought any investment he made would triple. As it turned out, he was wrong."

Hugh also thought Livingston was an ass, but it had been too much to hope Cross might confess to some misdeed Hugh could persuade him to rectify. "You don't seem concerned to be called a swindler."

"Not by the likes of Livingston," said Cross with cold disdain.

The likes of Livingston, who would—hopefully—be Edith's father-in-law. If, that is, Hugh could convince him to overlook the fact that Edward Cross was *his* father-in-law. "The 'likes of Livingston' form the society I live in," he said. "I am not so cavalier about their good opinions."

Cross eyed him for a moment. "There's nothing I could do to earn Livingston's good opinion. If he'd profited from our association, he would have still thought me a common, vulgar man, not fit to join his society. But then, perhaps that's what you thought, too, my lord."

"I confess I never thought of you at all before you barged into my life and forced me to."

Cross smirked. "And it's not come out too badly for you."

Hugh hated the fact that Cross was right. "I certainly hope it turns out well, since my side of the bargain is for the rest of my life."

The other man's smirk disappeared. "What are you saying?"

Right. The man was not subtle, so Hugh shouldn't be, either. "I would prefer not to see you often—if ever."

Cross seemed bitterly amused by that. His mouth twisted, although his eyes were hard. "Ah. I may visit Eliza only."

Hugh inclined his head. "It would be best if you sent word before calling."

"So the rest of you can clear out and not be soiled by my visit?" Cross chuckled. "How shall you explain that to your wife?"

"I don't plan to," said Hugh. "I shall simply

arrange to be elsewhere, so that you and she may converse at leisure, without interruption." And more importantly, he could divert his mother and sisters. They were civil to Eliza but regarded Mr. Cross as just short of villainous. If Benwick jilted Edith because of Cross, there would be civil war in his house.

Cross's mouth tightened. "What about the children?"

Hugh quelled the instinctive refusal. "We'll address that if it becomes necessary."

"When," said Cross. "I expect to see my grandchildren."

Hugh hesitated, then nodded. He expected to have an heir, hopefully several. Eliza would be a loving mother. But he'd be damned if Cross had any sway over his children. The man could see them and play with them, but no more.

For a moment they stood in silent combat, glaring at each other. Finally Cross relented; his curious smile returned, and he made an elaborate bow. "As you wish, my lord."

"Mr. Cross." Hugh paused, choosing his words carefully. "I do not wish for us to be enemies. Eliza is my wife now, which makes us family. I pledged before God to protect and honor her yesterday, and I will keep that vow. But I resent your interference in my affairs and your manipulation of my actions, and I cannot bring myself to regard you as a friend."

"No," the other man agreed. "I understand. I didn't bargain for a friend, I bargained for a good husband for my daughter. As long as you are that, we have no quarrel. I'll spare you my presence, if you wish, and not darken your name to Eliza." Hugh nodded once in acknowledgment. "But Hastings . . . If you are *not* a good husband, remember that well—I am not your friend, and there is no length I wouldn't go to for my daughter." Cross delivered his parting shot without any expression at all. He bowed once more, and left.

Chapter 18

Eliza's campaign to win over her new mother-in-law and sisters-in-law did not get off to a good start.

Not wanting to seem proud or aloof, she got up and went downstairs to breakfast. Outside the room, she could hear the murmur of conversation, even laughter. She pressed her trembling hands against her skirt, lifted her chin, and walked in with a bright smile. "Good morning."

Aside from a spoon dropped by Henrietta, the room fell silent. Lady Hastings looked astonished, Henrietta anxious, and Edith jumped up and went to the sideboard, turning her back to Eliza.

"I hope I'm not intruding," Eliza added, trying and failing to keep the hesitation from her voice.

"Not at all, my dear. Of course you are welcome." The dowager looked at the servant. "Geoffrey, prepare a plate for Lady Hastings."

Eliza stifled the urge to say she would get her own plate. She took the empty seat next to her mother-in-law. "What lovely china," she said when the footman brought her plate. "Thank you, Geoffrey."

Silence settled over the room. Eliza tried to study her new family, hoping to find some way to win them over. She wasn't sure why they were so restrained; she'd heard them laughing and talking with each other before she came in, and Hugh spoke of his sisters with easy affection. It could simply be the presence of a stranger in their house, at their table, but they didn't seem that formal.

She thought she had the best chance with the dowager, who had been gracious and kind, if reserved, to her so far. The older woman was still lovely and dressed in the height of fashion. The silver streaks in her blond hair were only visible up close, and she was slim and dainty, the perfect lady. Henrietta, the younger sister, had Hugh's dark eyes and hair, but Edith, fair and blue-eyed like her mother, was the beauty of the family.

"I wish to apologize for Willy," she said. "I don't want him to inconvenience anyone."

The dowager smiled briefly. "How considerate of you. No one warned me, so he startled me."

"He is a good dog," Eliza quickly added. "He's used to playing in the gardens at my father's house, but he is also trained to behave indoors."

Silverware clattered on china. Eliza looked up to see Edith staring at her, pale-faced. "You brought the dog?"

"Really?" chimed in Henrietta with a great deal more enthusiasm.

"Yes." Eliza smiled at the girl, pleased to have elicited anything positive.

Edith shot a look of dismay at her mother before lowering her gaze to her plate. Henrietta's delighted expression faltered, and she too looked away. Eliza didn't know what to say, and so she sat and sipped her tea, cowed into silence.

After breakfast she took Willy for a long walk. It wasn't the same as being in Greenwich, but Green Park was close by, and they took a meandering path through it. Eliza realized she would be able to walk regularly with Georgiana now, and her heart felt lighter until she returned to the house.

Just walking into it lowered her spirits. The house faced the open square, in view of trees and grass and sun, but it seemed perpetually in shadow. The front rooms were dark and drab. Eliza reminded herself not to be spoiled as she handed over her cloak and took Willy into the morning room. She would invite Georgiana to call, as soon as possible. Seeing a friend would help immeasurably.

She wrote the note and went to have it sent. The house was very quiet. "Where is Lady Hastings?" she asked the butler.

"She has gone out with Lady Edith, ma'am," Wilkins replied.

"I see." At a loss, Eliza drifted back to the morning room. Willy looked up and woofed at her. Eliza sank to the floor and the dog crawled into her lap, resting his head on her arm. She smiled and scratched his ears. "Good boy," she told him. "What would I do without you?"

A tap on the door made her look up. Henrietta peered around it. "Is this your dog?"

Eliza scrambled up from the floor. "Yes! Come in, he's very friendly. Willy, sit," she told the dog firmly.

Tail wagging, Willy sat at her feet. Henrietta came in, a nervous smile on her face. "What should I do?"

"Just hold out your hand and let him sniff it." Eliza held her breath as her sister-in-law came closer, her gaze fixed on Willy. Tentatively Henrietta put out her hand, and Willy, thank the blessed Lord, stayed quietly on the floor. He sniffed Henrietta's offered hand and licked her fingers, then sat back and looked at her hopefully.

"He's very gentle," said Henrietta in astonished delight.

"You're doing precisely the right thing." Eliza beamed in relief. "Would you like to pet him?"

"Oh—yes."

"Willy, down," ordered Eliza. The dog dropped onto his belly, but his dark eyes stayed on Henrietta. "Go ahead," she encouraged.

Henrietta sank onto the sofa and patted the dog's head, then stroked her fingers into the ruff of fur around his neck. "He's very soft."

"He particularly likes it when you scratch behind his left ear."

The girl did so, a surprised smile spreading over her face as Willy rolled over and gave a gusty sigh of obvious pleasure.

"Do you like dogs?" Eliza ventured. She took the chair next to the sofa.

Still petting Willy, Henrietta laughed. "I think so. We've never had dogs. Mama doesn't like them, and Edith is frightened of them." She dug her fingers into Willy's fur, and he responded by stretching out across her feet.

"I hope no one will be afraid of Willy," said Eliza. "He's very friendly." She tried not to let any apprehension color her voice. She would hate to have to choose between her dog and her mother- and sister-in-law.

"Oh, he is." All the hesitation had vanished from Henrietta's voice, replaced by wondering delight.

"Why is Edith frightened of dogs?" It wouldn't explain Edith's animosity toward her, but Eliza was desperate to understand her.

Henrietta grimaced. "A large dog knocked her down and bit her when she was a child. After that she would scream with fear whenever a dog came near her, which made our mother very anxious, so our father banned all dogs from the estate. The hunting hounds were kept at a neighbor's."

"How frightening." Eliza was sympathetic. "Willy isn't large enough to knock her down. I hope she'll warm to him."

Henrietta rolled her eyes. "Edith doesn't change her mind easily. She already doesn't like—" She stopped abruptly, and Eliza had a terrible fear the girl had been about to say *you*. Edith's attitude was too cold to be simple reserve.

"I'm so pleased you came to get to know him." Eliza leaned down and ran her fingers through Willy's black-and-white fur, scratching on his belly where he liked it. "He'll be your friend forever if you feed him a bit of ham."

"Will he?" Henrietta grinned. "I'll try it."

"Would you like to walk him with me later? We discovered Green Park this morning, and Willy was thrilled."

Henrietta bit her lip. She put her hand back in her lap. "Perhaps."

That was too far to push matters. Eliza jumped to her feet. "Would you like to see him do tricks?"

As hoped, the girl brightened. "Oh yes! Please."

After ringing for some cheese, one of Willy's favorite treats, Eliza put him through all of his tricks. He stood up on his back legs, he rolled over, he found and fetched Eliza's handkerchief after she hid it under a cushion. She even had him leap over the sofa and crawl back under it, which made Henrietta clap her hands in delight. Willy came and rested his head on the girl's knee, his tongue lolling out, and at Eliza's prompting she fed him a bit of cheese.

"Hugh says you will make your debut next year." Eliza was groping for a safe topic of discussion.

To Eliza's relief, Henrietta smiled and nodded eagerly. "I'm *so* looking forward to it. Edith has told me many tales of the balls and parties she's gone to. She's promised to be my sponsor next Season, in addition to Mama. I've begun dreaming of my court gown, which Hugh tells me is a sign I shall trip on my train or do something else humiliating."

"No," declared Eliza. "I'm sure you won't."

Henrietta giggled. "I hope not! He can be a terrible tease. After he said that I told him I would make him practice everything with me."

"And I understand your sister is to be married soon," Eliza dared to say. "How wonderful for her." Perhaps she could help plan Edith's wedding and share in that excitement.

Something changed in Henrietta's face, as if she had remembered something unpleasant. "Yes." She cleared her throat. "I should go reply to my friend Cecily's letter. She's at home in Cornwall."

"Does she live near Rosemere?"

"Yes." Henrietta looked at Willy, who was lying on the floor gnawing at a stick he'd somehow brought in. "Thank you for letting me pet him."

"Of course, any time," she said, but Henrietta was already on her feet, slipping out the door. Eliza gave Willy a helpless look. He rolled over and offered his belly. "What did I do?" she murmured, obligingly rubbing his stomach. She would have to ask Hugh and hope he could tell her.

With a sigh she glanced around the morning room. It was small, the walls faded pewter, the floor scuffed under a dark rug. The furniture needed new upholstery and the decorations were almost nonexistent. The least she could do was make a plan to improve it. She went to get her notebook, where she sketched ideas, and set to work.

Chapter 19

HUGH MANAGED TO find Reginald Benwick at his club and all but forced him into a private room. He swallowed his pride and apologized for offending Lord Livingston, but pointed out that he could not undo his marriage. He asked what he could do to make amends, given that he could not and would not repudiate his wife.

"But that is the problem," Benwick argued. "*She* is the problem."

"She is not her father," said Hugh, for what felt like the hundredth time. "What has my choice of wife got to do with your feelings for Edith?"

Benwick looked away. "You know it's not that simple, Hastings."

"Right." His opinion of the young man had dropped a great deal, but overnight he remembered that Benwick must still be dependent on his father. It was Livingston's ire that drove his son, but with the right touch, Benwick would calm down and remember how eager he'd been to marry Edith. With the right inducement, he would stop talking about jilting her. "I understand. It has struck me recently that ten thousand pounds, while it was what my father wished for her, is a modest dowry for the daughter of the Earl of Hastings. Another three or four thousand would be more appropriate to her status."

Benwick hesitated. A slight frown touched his brow.

"Whoever marries my sister will be a fortunate man," Hugh pressed. "She's beautiful, charming, intelligent, and accomplished. You know that. She's also got a loving heart, and will be a devoted and loyal wife."

The frown deepened into a scowl. "Cross is a thief."

He wanted to throttle the boy. "No one wants to marry Cross. But think how you'll feel to see Edith on some other fellow's arm, or dancing with him. How it will ache to picture her smiling up at another man, knowing she'll bear his children instead of yours."

Benwick squeezed his eyes closed. Hugh felt a surge of hope; he was wavering. "I shall hate it," he said thickly. "Nevertheless . . . Nevertheless, I cannot force my father into a connection with Edward Cross." He gazed defiantly at Hugh. "He nearly ruined my father—did you know that, Hastings? It caused great difficulty for my family."

"We all make unwise investments from time to time," Hugh tried to argue, but Benwick shook his head, his resolve back in place.

"It was more than unwise. Cross maneuvered to get my father's money invested, then cheated him out of it. He should be in prison, not watching his daughter wed an earl." He almost spat the last. "You've let a viper into your home, sir. I care very deeply for Lady Edith, but my father is adamant. If I must choose between her or my family, I will side with my family every time."

"Why must you choose?" Hugh raised his brows. "You're a man, not a boy. You know they have no objection to Edith herself. Surely you deserve to choose your own bride."

Temper flashed in Benwick's face. "Thanks to Cross, my marriage is important to my family as well as to me. I promised my father half of Edith's—my bride's—dowry funds, to pay his debts." His eyes turned speculative. "I suppose if you were willing to make good on Cross's swindle, I could consider it . . ."

"I beg your pardon?" Hugh was thunderstruck.

"Cross cheated my father out of twenty thousand pounds. I want it back."

Hugh leaned back and folded his arms, outwardly calm but cursing and raging inside. For all his whining about swindlers, Benwick was apparently no better. Still . . . Edith loved him. Gritting his teeth, Hugh nodded. "I can make her dowry twenty thousand."

"No, the half I owe to my father is twenty," Benwick retorted. "For forty thousand, I shall overlook your unfortunate connection."

Hugh came upright in offended outrage. "You can't be serious."

Benwick raised his chin, his cheeks mottled red but his hands trembling. "Perfectly."

He couldn't do that. It would leave him with

only ten thousand pounds, and Henrietta making her debut next year. He couldn't possibly give one sister forty thousand and the other sister only ten, and leave himself, his wife, and his mother with nothing.

He glared at Benwick in disgust. "So all your talk of affection for my sister was worthless. You should have mentioned sooner that you only viewed her as a potential fortune. I would have shown you the door immediately and saved us both a great deal of trouble."

"I do care for Edith!" Now Benwick's entire face was red. "How dare you, sir!"

"If you love her, it can't be much," said Hugh coldly. "You veer from adoration and eagerness to declaring you would jilt her, and now proclaim that you would choose your family over her every time. But for the princely sum of forty thousand pounds, you'll take her. That isn't love, Mr. Benwick, that is haggling like a fishwife."

"You don't understand. You don't have to choose between following your heart and loyalty to your family!" retorted the young man. "I *do* love her—I *would* marry her, even in spite of your noxious connections. But my father is insistent, and he'll not be placated until Cross's crime is made right again."

Hugh came within a heartbeat of punching him in the face. His hand was in a fist, his weight shifted. One solid punch, right to Reggie Benwick's perfectly straight nose, would make him feel vastly better. The stupid little coxcomb had no idea what he was talking about. "Loyalty to your family requires you to try extortion? Loyalty to your family requires you to hurt a sweet and loving girl?" Benwick flinched. Hugh gave him a scornful look. "If you come to your senses and wish to have a serious negotiation, you know where to find me. Until then . . . Good day, Mr. Benwick." He brushed by the other man and left without waiting for a reply.

But on the street the reality sank in. Edith was going to be jilted. Hugh hoped the boy would have the grace—or shame—to do it gently and privately, but based on Benwick's behavior today, it seemed unlikely. He pressed a fist against his forehead. He had to warn her. Even though it would make her hate him.

He put it off as long as possible, but eventually he made his way back home. He wished he could whisk Eliza off to their room and have dinner with only her, then make love to her for the rest of the night. He wished Edith would get swept off her feet by another young man this very night and forget Benwick. Perhaps they should all decamp to Rosemere and shake the dust of London from their feet forever. There were sure to be a few decent gentlemen in Cornwall who would be content with a bride who had ten thousand pounds. He only needed two, one for each sister.

He stepped into the hall and found chaos. Willy was barking while Eliza, on her knees, held him back. Edith cowered on the stairs, clutching the bannister, her face white with terror.

"Willy," he commanded. "Quiet." The dog stopped barking at his voice, and Eliza took advantage to scoop him into her arms. With an expression of abject apology she hurried to the back of the hall and disappeared toward the kitchen.

Hugh crossed the hall and took Edith into his arms. She was shaking like a leaf. "Shh," he whispered.

"He made so much noise." Her teeth chattered so hard he could barely make out her words. "Why did she have to bring a dog?"

"I should have warned you," he told her, stroking her back. He'd had so much else to worry about, it never crossed his mind to mention Willy to his family. They barely tolerated mention of Eliza.

"Oh, Hugh." She looked at him with tears trembling in her eyes. "Can't she take him back to Greenwich? Just until I marry Reggie and leave this house?"

God damn Reginald Benwick. "We'll think of something to keep the dog away from you." He glanced at his other sister, who had just come running down the stairs, pale and wide-eyed. "Is Mother in?"

Henrietta nodded, and rushed back up to fetch her. Edith ran to her mother, and Hugh closed his eyes as his sister's shoulders shuddered with silent sobs. After a few moments the dowager smoothed back Edith's hair and made a gentle shushing sound. "What happened, dearest?"

Edith looked at Hugh with red eyes. "I called on Lady Harlow and Millicent," she said, naming a neighbor across the square and her daughter, one of Edith's good friends. "I came into the house and took off my bonnet and that—that dog attacked me!"

"Attacked!"

Hugh pinched his nose at his mother's horrified exclamation. "What did he do, Edith?"

"He ran into the hall and jumped on me," she said, her voice trembling. "He seized my reticule and tried to rip it from my arm. He tried to bite me."

"He wasn't trying to bite you," said Eliza. Hugh looked up to see her standing at the back of the hall, pale but composed. "He would never bite anyone."

Edith's eyes filled with tears. "He did! He bit at my clothes and he barked like a hound from hell!"

"Did he bite you?" Hugh interrupted. If the dog had bitten someone, he would have to go, no matter how dearly Eliza loved him.

"He tried!"

"I am so sorry," said Eliza softly. She looked as if she would cry.

"Of course, dear," said Rose, embracing Edith a little tighter. "Edith was bitten by a dog when she was young. Your dog may not have harmed her, but she was very frightened."

"Eliza and I will find a way to keep the dog away, Edith," said Hugh. "Are you really not hurt?"

She gave him a look of betrayal, but shook her head. Their mother led Edith upstairs, Henrietta following in cowed silence. Hugh looked at his wife, and held out one hand.

She came to him without a word. He pulled her

into the morning room and shut the door before wrapping his arms around her. She shuddered and clutched at his jacket, and he realized she'd been frightened, too.

"Willy was *not* trying to bite her," she repeated, her voice muffled against his chest. "Her reticule teased him." She stepped back and showed him Edith's reticule, a frivolous little work of blue brocade with fringe along the bottom and a charm dangling from the drawstring. Some of the fringe had been torn off by Willy's eager teeth.

"That doesn't justify it."

Eliza's mouth opened in indignation. "Of course not! He was a very bad dog! I only meant to prove that he wasn't trying to bite her and he didn't attack her! He only wanted this." She shook the reticule.

Hugh sighed. "I know." He dropped onto the sofa and propped his elbows on his knees. She stood stiffly for a moment, hands in fists about the reticule, but then came and sat beside him. She put her arms around his neck. He turned his head to rest his cheek against her plump bosom and heaved a silent moan of pleasure as her fingers combed gently through his hair.

"What happened today?" she murmured. "You're upset."

Without opening his eyes, he smiled. "How can you tell that?"

She laughed, sounding embarrassed. "I just can. I'm so sorry Willy made things worse. I didn't realize the door was unlatched, and he got out unexpectedly."

"I should have warned Edith, and explained to you that Willy should be kept away from her."

"I wasn't letting him run wild. Henrietta told me a large dog bit Edith when she was a child."

He sighed again in pleasure. She was digging her fingertips into the tight muscles at the back of his neck, and it felt divine. "She told you that?"

"Mmm-hmm. She came in to meet Willy earlier. Henrietta likes dogs, she's simply never been around one. She saw how well-behaved Willy can be."

"He must be even better behaved when my mother and Edith are about."

"Why does your mother dislike dogs?" she asked softly. He felt her lips press lightly against his temple.

Hugh leaned his head back and regarded her. There was so much concern and compassion in her face. "Because of what happened to Edith. The dog who bit her left a scar on her leg—not a large one, but my mother was terrified Edith would get an infection. It took a long time to heal."

"And that's why your father banished all dogs from the estate," Eliza murmured. "What parent would not?"

He was mildly surprised. "Henrietta told you that, too?"

She nodded. "I cannot bear to banish Willy entirely, but there is a boy who works in Papa's stables, the son of our head groom. He's very good with dogs, especially Willy. If I wrote to Papa and asked him, I feel certain he would let Angus come to us and keep Willy occupied and out of everyone's way. If you approve," she finished a bit uncertainly.

Hugh's eyebrows went up. "I do approve. That is a very clever thought, Lady Hastings."

Her answering smile beamed with happiness. "I want very much to endear myself to your sisters. Not even Willy shall get in the way. And when Edith is married, Angus can return to Greenwich, if we no longer need him."

It was like a bucket of ice water in his face. Hugh gathered her close, lowering his face to her bosom. This dress gave a splendid view of her breasts, and he pressed a kiss there, right over her heart. He had spent far too much time today thinking about Edith's marriage, failing before it began, and not enough time thinking about his own marriage, which was turning out to suit him better and better each day.

"Enough about all that," he said. "Have you spent any time today thinking of ways to keep your husband occupied?"

"Hmm." She arched her back as he ran his tongue over her skin. "I worked on a plan of refurbishment for this room. I hope to show it to your mother soon."

Hugh made a murmur of agreement. Eliza could refurbish the entire house if it made peace with his mother. He slid one hand up to cover her breast. "Perhaps you could *start* thinking of your husband?"

Her hands were tangled in his hair. She moved to straddle him, giving him better access to her bosom. "I think of him all day long," she said breathlessly. "I have to distract myself with up-holstery and drapery fabrics to keep from pining away without him."

Hugh gave a guttural laugh. It was surprising how much he wanted her, how intoxicating it was that she was in his lap, rocking back and forth without any inhibition whatsoever.

"Have you thought of me?" she whispered, her hands soft and teasing on his neck.

"Yes." At the moment, she was all he could think of. "Rather longingly."

"Let me satisfy your longings, then." Her hand slid down his chest and tugged at the buttons of his trousers.

Hugh sucked in his breath. "Lady Hastings," he managed to say. "Where did you learn this behavior?"

She blushed. "Sophie told me. Do you like it?"

For answer he pushed up her skirts and made love to her right there on the sofa, holding her astride his lap and showing her how to ride him. It was hard and fast and over too soon, but as she shuddered in his arms, Hugh clasped her to his chest and had just one thought:

What a damned stroke of luck that he'd married her.

Chapter 20

❧❧❧❧

Eliza went down to breakfast full of determination.

As before, she heard voices in the breakfast room. As before, she went in with a smile on her face. "Good morning," she said, this time without hesitation. She belonged here now. She was the Countess of Hastings, even if it still made her head spin to think so, and in the few days since her wedding, she had remembered something Sophie once told her: *everyone else will believe your pose if you do.*

Today she thought she understood the animosity in Edith's face. Henrietta gave her a tentative smile, which was progress, and Lady Hastings bowed her head. "Good morning, dear."

Eliza took her seat at the foot of the table and turned directly to Edith. "I want to apologize again for my dog," she said earnestly. "He wasn't trying to bite you, only to grab your reticule. That is not an excuse," she added as Edith's expression turned hostile. "It was wrong of him, and I only say it to assure you that he is not a danger to anyone. Only to reticules with intriguing little things dangling off them."

Henrietta stifled a smile, and Eliza's spirits soared. "I also want you to know I plan to keep Willy well out of your way," she told Edith.

"How?" the girl asked stiffly. "Are you sending him back to Greenwich?"

"No, I've asked my father to send Angus, a boy from the stables there who is good with Willy. It will be his job to look after the dog." She looked at the dowager. "I've spoken to Cook, Mrs. Greene, and Wilkins about it. Willy will still sleep in my chamber, and Angus will sleep in the old nursery, where he can fetch him easily and without disturbing anyone."

The older woman glanced at Edith, her brows raised. Edith lowered her gaze to her plate and murmured, "Thank you."

"Of course," cried Eliza in relief. "We are sisters now, Edith."

Somehow that was the wrong thing to say. Edith's spine stiffened, and she gave the barest nod without meeting Eliza's gaze.

She swallowed a burst of frustration. She wanted so much to be cordial, if not friendly, with Edith and had no idea what she was doing wrong. She would have to be patient, it seemed.

"Lady Hastings." She turned to her mother-in-law. "Hugh told me this house hasn't been decorated in quite a while."

The other woman's face froze. "No," she murmured.

"He told me there were tenants the last few

years, when your family didn't come to London."
Eliza kept her voice calm and sympathetic. The
last thing she wanted to do was offend the dowager. "I expect the house suffered some wear in
that time."

"Oh yes," said Henrietta. "Mama was just
speaking of replacing the carpet in the drawing
room. It looks like someone spilled hot ash on it!"

"Hastings has not given his approval for new
carpets," said her mother with a warning look at
her daughter.

Eliza was ready for this. She already knew his
answer; she had asked Hugh again last night if
she could buy new carpets and draperies. *Whatever you like*, he'd said. "Perhaps if we appeal to
him together?" she suggested with a hopeful
smile.

The countess's smile was brief. "Perhaps."

She spread jam on her toast. "I confess, decorating was one of my favorite things at home. I
changed every room of the house except my father's study, where I was forbidden to interfere."

"Oh?" For the first time Lady Hastings showed
some curiosity. "Then you planned the color
scheme in the drawing room where you wed?"

"I chose everything in that room, ma'am."

"Everything?" Henrietta echoed in amazement. "It's a beautiful room!"

"Thank you. My mother died when I was
three," Eliza explained. "Whenever I wanted to
decorate a room, my father allowed me free rein."

"And the dining room?" Lady Hastings leaned
forward.

"I did that, as well."

The older woman sat back, contemplating her for a minute. "What did you think for our drawing room, dear?"

Eliza's heart soared. "It's not a very bright room, so I thought pale green, or perhaps yellow. But I saw the most beautiful purple brocade in Percival's warehouse, and it would make magnificent draperies. They would look very striking with celery-green walls."

The countess's expression sharpened into intense interest. "Violet or lavender?"

"Neither. Amethyst." Eliza sipped her tea, trying not to look too eager. "I made some sketches in my notebook. Perhaps I could show you?"

Lady Hastings hesitated only a moment. "Yes, dear. I would like to see them."

That was a second victory.

The third came later. Lady Hastings had gone out to a dress fitting, and Edith had disappeared. Eliza tapped on Henrietta's door, holding her breath.

"Henrietta, I desperately need your help," she said when the girl opened the door. "May I come in?"

Slowly Henrietta let her into the room, her eyes flitting down the hall as if afraid someone would see her speaking to Eliza. She had a bad feeling the girl was checking for Edith. "What is it?"

"I feel dreadful about this." Eliza showed her Edith's reticule, the one Willy had stolen the previous day. She'd sewn the fringe back on, but his teeth had torn a small hole that could only be patched, marring the brocade. "I would like to get Edith a gift to replace it, but I don't know her taste. Would you come with me to Bond Street in search of something?"

Henrietta perked right up. "Today?"

"Yes." Eliza smiled in encouragement. "I would like to give it to her at dinner tonight."

"Well—yes. For Edith," she added quickly, lest Eliza think it was her own desire to go shopping in Bond Street.

They set out a short time later, with Mary trailing behind. Henrietta became quite talkative once they were away from the house. She confided that they had not visited the shops as much as she would have liked. "Edith needs a trousseau, of course, but otherwise Mama has been hesitant. I suspect Hugh scolded her about spending too much money."

Eliza knew her father had provided an enormous dowry, which Hugh would have by now. Still, she didn't want to make a point of that. "Oh goodness, I don't think Hugh should pay for this. It is my gift to Edith, to atone for my naughty dog. I shall spend my pin money on it." She hardly ever spent all that Papa gave her, and still had plenty.

They went into several shops, looking at gloves, bonnets, handkerchiefs, reticules, even parasols without finding anything that suited Eliza's critical eye. She wanted something not simply lovely, as Henrietta called several bonnets and one parasol, but something special. And finally, in a tiny shop at the end of the street, she found an exquisite fan, with sticks of carved ivory covered by lace and the palest pink silk. Tiny sequins sparkled along the sticks, and it snapped shut with an engraved silver clasp.

Henrietta inhaled in longing. "It's beautiful!"

"And perfect for Edith, who is so fair." Eliza opened it to study how delicate it was. "Do you think she would like it?"

Henrietta's gaze lingered covetously on the fan. "Very much."

"Wonderful." Eliza fluttered it in front of her face with a grin. "Shall we?"

Her sister-in-law nodded eagerly, and Eliza asked the shopkeeper to wrap it.

"To which account, madam?" the woman asked.

"The Earl of Hastings," said Henrietta before Eliza could speak. "This is my sister, the Countess of Hastings."

The shopkeeper's eyes widened. "Of course, my lady."

Eliza was torn between wanting to argue with Henrietta, when she had intended to pay for the fan from her pin money, and wanting to throw her arms around her. *My sister.* That meant more to her than anything else.

Henrietta leaned close. "Let Hugh pay the bill," she whispered with an impish grin. "Besides, no one pays in coin, Eliza."

Of course. Eliza wasn't used to having accounts at all the shops in London. The shopkeeper brought back the fan, neatly wrapped, and they went out into the sunshine. "Thank you for your advice, Henrietta. I do hope Edith will like it."

"It's exactly her taste! She adores delicate, lovely things . . ." Henrietta stopped speaking as a gentleman stepped out of a shop directly in front of them. In the act of putting his hat on his head, he didn't see them at first. "Mr. Benwick," said Henrietta in surprise.

He looked up. He was a well-dressed, handsome young man, with wavy brown hair and dark eyes. At the sight of Henrietta he paused, but when he saw Eliza he froze. Henrietta made a smothered noise, one hand going to her mouth. For a moment they all seemed frozen in place—Henrietta in shock, Eliza in uncertainty, and Mr. Benwick staring at them both in increasing hauteur.

"Good day, Mr. Benwick," said Henrietta hesitantly. "May I present my sister-in-law, Lady Hastings. Eliza, this is Mr. Reginald Benwick."

Edith's fiancé. Eliza smiled and dropped a curtsy. "How do you do, sir?"

He opened his mouth, glanced at Henrietta again, and then turned on his heel and walked away without a word. Eliza's stomach plummeted. That could not be good. When she looked at Henrietta's face, she feared the girl would faint. Henrietta was gazing fixedly at his departing figure, her lips parted and her hands in fists.

"Henrietta." Eliza touched her arm. "Henrietta. Let's not stand on the street staring." Henrietta didn't move, so Eliza looped her arm securely around the girl's waist and towed her onward, ignoring any curious glances. "Come," she whispered. "*Come*, Henrietta."

When they reached the house, Henrietta ran up the stairs with a mumbled excuse. Eliza looked at Mary, who shrugged.

Fortunately Hugh was at home. She found him in his study, working at his ledgers. At her entrance, he glanced up. "Come in, my dear."

She closed the door. "Henrietta and I have just returned home from shopping in Bond Street."

He chuckled, still writing. "One of her favorite activities!"

"I wanted to get a gift for Edith, after Willy tore her reticule."

"Did you find one?" Hugh turned the page and made more notes.

"Yes, an ivory fan." Eliza frowned. "Then something very strange happened. Isn't Edith betrothed to Mr. Reginald Benwick?"

Hugh's laughter cut off abruptly. His head came up. "Why?"

"We met him in the street. Henrietta said his name and when he turned to look at us . . ." Eliza bit her lip. It hadn't been when Mr. Benwick looked at Henrietta, it had happened when he looked at *her*.

"What did he do?" Hugh shot out of his chair and came around the desk, scowling. "What did he say to you?"

She flushed. "Nothing. Not a word. He—he turned and walked away without even a nod or a bow."

Hugh's mouth flattened, and for a moment he looked almost dangerously angry. Eliza had never seen him look that way, but the expression was gone in an instant. He plowed his hands into his hair and walked away, across the room to the window. "The little wretch," he said, sounding no more than irked. "How ill-mannered of him."

"Is there trouble with him and Edith?"

"Edith has done nothing to cause it. Benwick is being difficult."

Eliza nibbled her lip. The man gave them the cut direct, which was far beyond being a bit difficult. "Difficult about what?"

Hugh didn't answer for a moment. Eliza wondered why, but his handsome face gave away nothing. "It's a complicated and disagreeable story," he finally said, dropping into the worn leather armchair. "His father is kicking up a fuss, and Benwick has taken his side."

"About the marriage settlements?" Eliza had asked her father about her own marriage settlements after Hugh proposed. She hadn't wanted them to drag on and delay the wedding, not after Hugh made love to her in the folly; she'd been prepared to plead with her father to be reasonable, even lenient. But Papa had laughed and said Hastings was so eager, there were no disagreements at all. The documents had been drawn up and signed within a week.

"In a way."

Eliza came to sit in the chair beside his. "Hugh, what is going on? With Edith, and with Henrietta, and now with Mr. Benwick. It almost seems like . . ." She twisted her hands together. "I cannot help but notice that every time I come into the room, everyone grows quiet."

He frowned. "You were just shopping with Henrietta. Did she refuse to speak to you all the way to Bond Street?"

"No, but Edith will hardly say a word to me!"

"The dog," he reminded her.

Eliza flipped one hand impatiently. "It's more than Willy, Hugh! Why would Mr. Benwick give me the cut direct?"

He rested his elbows on his knees and scrubbed his hands over his face. "Don't mention a word of this to Edith."

Eliza shook her head. "Of course not."

"Benwick wants more money," he said in a low voice. "A great deal more. I feel it would be unfair to give my sisters unequal dowries, which makes Benwick's demand unreasonable."

"But didn't your father put aside their dowries?"

Hugh still didn't meet her gaze. "Not as much as Benwick wants. He's being . . . difficult."

Oh dear. Eliza sank back on the sofa. No wonder. "Was that what sent you out of the house on our wedding night?" she asked softly.

"Yes." He cocked his head to look at her. "Edith loves him. He told me he loves her. I'm trying to strike a fair compromise, but I admit—I'm not sure he deserves her anymore."

"Not at all," Eliza murmured. A burst of love for her husband filled her chest. Hugh had been so eager to wed her, he hadn't argued with Papa at all. And now he was trying to save Edith's betrothal as well, even in the face of outrageous demands that belied any affection Mr. Benwick claimed to have for Edith. She reached for his hand. "You're a magnificent brother."

He flinched. "Edith won't think so if Benwick jilts her."

"No! Surely he wouldn't do that!" Eliza was aghast.

"I don't know, Eliza. But please—say nothing to anyone. Especially not to Edith. If all my efforts with Benwick fail, I shall tell her myself."

"Of course not," she murmured. He smiled, a little grimly, and squeezed her hand. She was pleased he had confided in her, even such unsettling news.

But she couldn't shake the feeling that he still wasn't telling her everything.

HUGH WAS BEING A coward and he knew it.

Not only because he hadn't told anyone about Benwick's demands. After some thought, he'd instructed his solicitor to contact the Livingston solicitor and inquire if they wished to proceed, with Edith's dowry at fourteen thousand. He'd set a deadline as well, making it clear that his permission would not be renewed at a later date. If Benwick did care for her, that might shake the boy back to his senses.

Perhaps Benwick had merely been taking a gamble, asking for forty thousand. He had to know it was not only offensive but utterly mad to demand that much. The only girls with dowries that size were daughters of merchants who'd made obscene amounts of money in trade and were now keen to buy their way into the aristocracy. Girls like Eliza, whom Benwick disdained.

But if this failed, Hugh swore to himself, he would break the news to Edith, as gently as possible, and then to everyone else. Since Benwick had displayed no courage and even less affection, Hugh had already begun composing his speech. He just wanted to be able to say he'd done everything he possibly could, so Edith wouldn't pine away for the fellow.

He hoped he would never have to say anything about the other secret he was keeping. Eliza had noticed Edith's animosity, and now Benwick had given her the cut direct in the middle of Bond Street. The trouble was, he didn't know what to tell his wife. He had no qualms about calling Livingston and Benwick snobbish and rude, but Edith was a harder case to explain. And if Eliza ever discovered that Benwick jilted Edith because of her . . . Even worse, if she ever discovered why Hugh had married her . . .

He didn't even want to think about it.

There was one thing he did know, and that was the importance of presenting Eliza to the *ton* before Livingston had a chance to blacken her name. He searched through the post stacked on one side of his desk—he'd pensioned off his father's secretary and not hired a new one, thanks to his impoverished state—and unearthed several invitations. He took them to his mother with instructions to accept them all, thinking it was better for her to do it this time. Once she was known to London hostesses, it would be Eliza's task.

"So many," Rose exclaimed in surprise.

"If you don't wish to attend, I will take her alone."

She studied the pile of invitations. "No. I shall go." She touched the topmost one. "I wouldn't want anyone to think I'm ashamed of your bride."

"I hope you are not," said Hugh after a moment of astonishment.

His mother set the letters aside. "She was a great surprise to me, and I still suspect you've not been completely forthcoming about your motives, but it is not my place to pry. You are entitled to choose your own wife."

That was the most tepid approval he'd ever heard. "Thank you, Mother."

She looked up at his dry tone. "No, no—you mistake me. She's a lovely girl—well, not a beauty, but thoughtful and kind and warm. When you declared your interest, I worried. Not because of Eliza herself, since I did not know her, but because she was not part of our circle and society is not always welcoming to outsiders."

She hadn't been very welcoming, but Hugh was grateful for any improvement in her feelings. "What has changed your mind?" he asked instead.

His mother sat in silence for a moment. "I cannot name any one thing. She's . . . She's not what I expected."

I could say the same, Hugh thought, with a mixture of relief and pleasure. Eliza was far better than he had hoped she would be. She had a warm sensitivity to the feelings of others. She was thoughtful and sincere. And she was far more seductive than he would have ever guessed the first time he met her.

When Hugh considered the society ladies he knew, the women he might have married without Edward Cross's interference in his life, he couldn't name a single one who appealed to him more than Eliza did. Catherine Thayne, whom his mother had hoped he would marry, was a beauty, but a chatterbox who spoke mostly of herself and her friends. He couldn't picture her rushing out to buy a new fan for Edith in apology for anything. Hugh had known Catherine since she was a child, as her brother was his good friend, and she'd always had the arrogance of a spoiled, beautiful girl.

But Eliza . . . Every day it seemed he learned or noticed something appealing about her. He looked forward to seeing her when he came home. He wanted to make love to her every night—and she wanted him to. She might blush at the things he coaxed her to do, but she came to their bed with enthusiasm and passion. He liked simply talking to her, which he had not expected. Eliza was a wonderful listener, caring and thoughtful, with clever ideas and a knack for making him laugh even when he didn't mean to.

And that was why, if Hugh were honest with himself, he felt like such a craven coward. He was lying to his wife, and he suspected she knew it. At times he considered just telling her everything, about her father and Edith and even Benwick. It would be like lancing a boil, he told himself, painful and messy but necessary, and once lanced it would eventually disappear. But every time, he dismissed the idea because of how much it would hurt Eliza to hear about her father's conniving scheme and Benwick's snobbery and even Edith's disdain.

The deeper, darker truth was that Hugh feared his own actions would hurt her the most. Lancing the boil might prove mortal.

He didn't want to hurt his wife, and he damned sure didn't want to risk losing her. Not when he thought he might be falling in love with her.

So he added one more facet to the bargain he'd made with the devil: keep the truth from Eliza at all costs, for her sake and for his own. With any luck, her innate kindness would win over Edith, as he could already see happening with Henrietta and his mother. Less likely but still possible, Benwick would either come to his senses or be enough of a gentleman to keep his mouth shut. And if Hugh had any luck at all left in his life, everything would continue on its current promising track, with Eliza none the wiser that it had all begun so sordidly.

Chapter 21

Eliza BEGAN TO have hope that her new family was warming to her.

Edith had accepted the ivory fan with quiet thanks. Eliza caught the puzzled glance she gave her mother, just as she saw the approving nod the dowager gave in reply. When she brought out her notebooks of sketches and color ideas for the drawing room, the dowager invited her to her own private sitting room, where they shared tea and the dowager quizzed her—delicately and politely—about her upbringing. When Eliza mentioned Mrs. Upton's Academy, her mother-in-law smiled in surprised delight; she knew of it, and what she knew was flattering. The dowager herself suggested they visit the drapery shop together to see the amethyst brocade that would look so lovely in the drawing room, then gave her a true smile, genuine and warm, and called her by name for the first time. It was a wonderful moment, even if it did indicate how cool her initial welcome had been.

Eliza had heard enough from Georgiana to

know the matrons of the *ton* spent a great deal of time deciding which lady should marry which gentleman, quite independently of any desire of the parties involved. After much thought, she decided that the dowager had probably pictured her son married to someone else, someone like Millicent Harlow or Catherine Thayne, whom they met in Oxford Street one afternoon on a visit to an upholsterer. They were both beautiful, vivacious ladies, elegantly dressed and longtime friends of the family. They were quite knowledgeable about all the society people and events that Eliza knew nothing of, and she could see why the dowager countess would want one of them as her daughter-in-law.

She also made great strides with Henrietta, although only when Edith was not present. Henrietta came to play with Willy, and even went with Eliza to walk him in St. James's Park once, where she threw sticks for him to chase and laughed at the way he tried to creep up on a flock of pigeons. When it came to Willy, or fashion, or even music—Henrietta played the pianoforte very well—they had plenty of conversation, easy and open. Henrietta told her stories of Hugh as a young man, to Eliza's delight.

But whenever she mentioned Edith or anything to do with her, Henrietta either changed the subject or pretended not to hear. Eliza had no desire to make Henrietta choose between them, but Edith's antipathy remained as strong as ever, and it was bothering her.

"I've no idea why, but I think Edith despises

me," she told Georgiana on one of their walks in the park, which they took twice a week now.

"I hate to say something uncharitable about your sister-in-law, but she's a bit of a snob." Georgiana gave her a sympathetic look. "I fear the Livingston connection only reinforced it."

"Oh." Eliza frowned. She still hadn't received a good explanation for Mr. Benwick's rudeness in Bond Street. "Are they a very old family?"

Georgiana scoffed. "Not at all! Not older than the Hastings family, at any rate, and Lord Livingston is only a viscount—your husband outranks him, regardless of how old his family is."

"Then perhaps they are offended by my origins," she said slowly. Papa's father had been a laborer, working his way up to foreman building canals. Papa had begun there as well before he received a small inheritance from an uncle, and began speculating. Her mother had been the daughter of a baronet, but she was an only child. When Eliza's grandparents died, the title went to a distant cousin Eliza had never met or heard from.

"They certainly wouldn't be impressed by them," said Georgiana frankly. "I think Mr. Benwick came to town to look for a well-born wife, the higher the better. His father is very demanding. He must have been quite pleased his son won Edith Deveraux."

Eliza thought that didn't reflect well on Edith, if she had decided to hate Eliza only because her fiancé's father disapproved of her. Of course, who knew what Mr. Benwick had told her? And if she'd fallen in love with the man, it would be hard for her to ignore his feelings. "What is Mr. Benwick's reputation?" she asked instead.

"Oh, he's very handsome and a marvelous dancer." Georgiana waved one hand carelessly. "Not as handsome as Sterling, of course," she added, speaking of her own fiancé. "He's not especially witty, but quite amiable. He's liked well enough around town, and several young ladies were extremely downcast when he proposed to Lady Edith. What did you think of him?"

Eliza hesitated so long Georgiana stopped walking. "Eliza," she said, shocked. "Don't tell me you've not met him. He's supposed to marry your sister-in-law in two months!"

"Truly? That soon? I didn't know they had chosen a date . . ." Mindful of Hugh confiding that Benwick was kicking up over the settlements, Eliza began to wish she hadn't said anything.

"When she accepted him, he told everyone they would be wed by the end of the Season." Georgiana's gaze narrowed on her. "You didn't answer my question."

Now she didn't want to tell anyone. Perhaps it had been a momentary fit of pique, or he'd felt unwell, or . . . something, any sort of reason other than he hated the sight of her. "Well . . . well, not really. I saw him on Bond Street once."

Georgiana raised her brows expectantly. Eliza flushed, not wanting to lie. "It was a chance meeting, not a proper introduction."

"Was he rude?" Her friend's expression was

amused and puzzled at the same time. "Did it not go well?"

"Never mind," said Eliza, pink-faced.

"Eliza," said Georgiana sternly.

"He turned his back and walked away without a word." She lowered her gaze as she said it, feeling the sting all over again. "Henrietta was very shocked, but she wouldn't explain—I don't think she knows why!"

"That cretin!" Lady Sidlow, sitting in her carriage nearby, glanced up in displeasure at Georgiana's outburst. "He gave you the cut?" Georgiana demanded in a harsh whisper. "Of all the rude, churlish things to do! I'm going to find out why."

"No!" She seized her friend's arm. "Please don't say anything about it—"

"I won't mention you at all, but I will not stand by and do nothing." Her eyes alight with militant fervor, Georgiana linked their arms and started walking briskly, towing Eliza along with her. No amount of protest or demand got Georgiana to recant her desire to do something—some unspecified thing Eliza feared would make things even worse with Edith.

"Honestly, Eliza," said Georgiana at last. "Something should be said! If you can't hold up your head in front of the *ton* and stare down their whispers and slights, they'll be merciless. You must demonstrate that you have power as well, and that you will not be meek in the face of blatant rudeness."

Eliza stopped, breathless and flushed after Georgiana's energetic pace. "This is why I was a dismal failure in my Season. I feel quite powerless when they whisper and stare at me."

Her friend scoffed. "You are the Countess of Hastings. Your husband married you because he adores you, not because it was arranged for political or monetary advantage like so many *ton* marriages. Dozens of women in London want desperately to be in your shoes."

"But what should I do?" Eliza asked uncertainly. Jealousy was not the foundation of friendship, and she would rather have friends than be envied from afar.

Georgiana smiled. "Fortunately, everything you already do well. Dress beautifully. Let Hastings gaze lovingly at you. Be charitable to the unfortunate and kind to the wallflowers."

She rolled her eyes. "That is not what makes one admired, Georgiana. Society likes someone with a good wit, especially when it's used on others. They like dash, extravagance, and style, all of which I lack."

"Well—they do," the other girl conceded. "But they also admire elegant women of poise and character. The Duchess of Exeter!"

Eliza did not know the Duchess of Exeter. If not for Sophie, she wouldn't have ever met a duchess in her life. During her ill-begotten Season, she had stood on the fringes of every crowd, watching but never speaking to elegant people like duchesses and countesses. It still amazed her that she was one of those countesses now, and she had no idea how to act.

"I'll be discreet," Georgiana promised when

Eliza just stared at her doubtfully. "Or you could ask Hastings. He would hate to see you snubbed."

She mustered a smile. "An excellent thought."

Eliza returned home feeling more unsettled than when she'd left. She wished she could ask Hugh—or rather, she wished she could believe what he'd said when she asked him the first time. Edith had been cool to her even before Willy attacked her reticule, but Hugh avoided her direct question about it, instead telling her about Mr. Benwick. As much as she appreciated that, it didn't explain everything about his sister's behavior.

She did not want to make her husband choose between her and his family. She knew he cared for her, but he had loved his mother and sisters his entire life. She had seen the easy camaraderie between them, at least when she wasn't part of the group. No matter how much she told herself that this was natural, that it would take time for her to become part of the family, it was hard to see Hugh make Edith smile and laugh, when the girl only had chilly politeness for Eliza.

And when she'd told him she loved him, he hadn't replied in kind. He'd said plenty of other lovely things to her, but Eliza couldn't recall a single time he expressed affection for her. He called her darling and told her he wanted her, but that was not the same as loving her.

She went up the stairs, drawing off her gloves. Workmen had arrived before she left with Georgiana to begin painting the drawing room, so she headed there to see how work progressed.

"Don't do that!" said the dowager sharply.

Eliza paused just outside the open door, only to realize the command had not been to her. In the drawing room, just out of sight, the dowager continued instructing the servants who must have been removing the artwork from the walls. "Over there with that one," her voice floated into the corridor. "And the mirror, as well."

She peeked around the door, smiling at the scene. The draperies were down, and servants were packing things from the cabinet and mantel into straw-filled crates. She was about to go in when another voice stopped her.

"But why hasn't he come, Mama?"

Eliza went still. There was such hurt, such bewilderment in Edith's tone—such heartbreak. She had to be speaking of Mr. Benwick.

"I don't know, my dear," said her mother gently. They must have been standing near the door, for Eliza could hear her perfectly. "Perhaps his family has required his time."

"Perhaps," Edith said, in the tone of someone who thought it was rubbish but didn't want to say so. "But surely he could say that. His note is so—so terse! As if I were any acquaintance instead of his betrothed!"

The dowager sighed. Eliza could just picture her embracing her daughter, stroking her hair in comfort, as she'd done when Willy ran at Edith. "Men are curious creatures," the dowager said. "A horse race in Richmond, a boxing match on the heath . . . I've learned these things might distract a gentleman so violently he forgets all his ordinary habits."

"Reggie's not like that," protested Edith. "It's been over a week, Mama! You—you don't think it's because of . . . well . . . ?"

Her mother laughed. "He's a man, Edith. No matter how deeply in love, he feels the lure of masculine pursuits, I assure you. Don't you remember last month when he and his fellows went to Brighton for a week? He left you no word, and you were sure it meant he didn't care for you, but then he came back, more devoted than ever."

"Yes, that's true," said Edith slowly.

Eliza felt horrible. She wanted to warn the dowager that there might be more to it this time, that Mr. Benwick was being less than devoted in his demands. It tore at her heart to hear Edith so upset and perplexed because the man she loved—the man she believed loved her—was being cold and distant. After all, if Mr. Benwick had changed his mind about the marriage, he ought to be man enough to come and break the news gently to Edith. He even ought to let her slap his face and call him rude names.

But she had promised Hugh not to say a word. She squeezed her eyes closed and reminded herself of that as Edith slowly began to cheer up, persuading herself that, yes, her mother must be right, that Mr. Benwick would surely come to call soon. For the first time Eliza didn't feel upset that Mr. Benwick had walked away from her in Bond Street, as now she had no trouble hating him on Edith's behalf.

"Why are you lurking in the corridor?" murmured Hugh near her ear.

Eliza jumped, but managed not to shriek. She whirled on him. "You startled me!"

He winked at her. "Happily, I hope. Have the workmen driven everyone out?" He spoke in a normal tone this time, and reached for the door.

"Oh, wait," whispered Eliza urgently, but it was too late. He swung the door open. His mother and sister were indeed arm in arm, but quickly broke apart. Edith turned her head away and took a stealthy swipe at her eyes, which made Eliza's heart constrict.

"How are things progressing in here?" Hugh asked, hands on hips as he took in the dismantling of the room.

"Very well, dear," the dowager replied.

"It's quite a dirty job," Hugh remarked. "I don't see how we can receive callers for a while." Edith looked at him in horror, as if he had just forbidden visitors. "Clearly we shall have to go out more. Have you got a dress for a ball, Edith?"

Reluctant interest sparkled in her eyes. "Yes."

"I accepted some invitations," he remarked. "I hope you'll deign to accompany me—unless you prefer the dust, of course."

His sister's face lit up. "Oh yes, Hugh! As if anyone could prefer the dust!" She hurried to him and threw her arms around him. "Who did you accept?"

Laughing, Hugh kissed her temple. "Lady Gorenson, for her musicale in two nights, and Lady Montgomery's ball."

"Delightful." The dowager smiled fondly at the pair of them.

"Hugh . . ." Edith plucked at his waistcoat button, smoothing it flat. "Have you heard from Reggie?"

Eliza saw the change in his face—it was slight but telling. Edith, still fiddling with the button, did not. "Not recently," he said, sounding completely unperturbed. "I told my solicitor to write to Livingston's, and solicitors never do anything quickly." He had to move for the workmen carrying out the sofa, and glanced at Eliza, still lingering at the door. "Come, tell me what your plans are for the room, my dear," he said. "Now that we're irrevocably committed to refurbishment."

She stepped slowly into the room. Edith turned pale at the sight of her, but only dropped her gaze to the floor. "Green walls," Eliza said, feeling again like the unwelcome intruder in a happy family. "Deep purple draperies and upholstery."

"It will be lovely," interjected the dowager, giving Eliza a fond smile. "I've wanted to decorate this room since we came to town."

Hugh chuckled. "I'm sure it will be the most splendid drawing room in London. We might even have to hold a soiree in it."

Edith's head came up and she stared in amazement. The dowager hid hers better, but Eliza would have wagered she was no less surprised. "If you wish, of course we shall." She looked at her daughter. "Edith, your fitting with Madame de Louvier is in less than an hour. We must go soon."

"Yes, Mama." Without a glance at Eliza, Edith followed her mother from the room.

The workmen must have still been securing the sofa in the cart outside, destined for the upholsterer's shop. She and her husband were alone.

"My mother is in alt." Hugh tugged her into his arms and into a loose imitation of a waltz in the empty room. "She's wanted new drapes forever."

"Why didn't you let her buy them? She has excellent taste."

He flicked one hand. "There was so much else to do—Edith's debut, paying calls, renewing acquaintances . . ."

"Was it the cost?" she persisted. The number of small inconsistencies and veiled looks had grown until she couldn't ignore them all. During their several trips to warehouses and drapers' shops, Eliza discerned that the dowager had been eager to redecorate but Hugh had repeatedly refused. Then suddenly he gave Eliza carte blanche to do as she liked to the whole house, without any comment on the expense.

Eliza suspected it was her own dowry funds she was spending, which did not bother her. But she didn't like that her mother-in-law seemed unaware that there might not have been other funds. Having been mistress of a household for years, Eliza wondered if the dowager really could not know, but Georgiana had told her many society ladies not only didn't speak of money, they didn't care about spending their way deep into debt.

Her husband only seemed amused. "Worried about the accounts already?"

She flushed. "No! I wondered why you didn't

tell your mother there was no money for carpets before we married."

That wiped the humor from his face. He stopped dancing and let her go, then strode past her and closed the door. "I preferred not to," he said in a low voice. "Does that satisfy you?" She hesitated, and he gave her a coaxing smile. "It occurred to me that my wife, if I were so fortunate to find one, might like to have a say in decorating her new home. And as it turned out, I was correct, to everyone's benefit."

"Well . . ." She wrung her hands. That made sense and yet . . . why couldn't he tell his mother that? "I don't like deceiving people."

"Deception!" He scoffed in disdain, but stopped when he saw her frown. "It was not deception so much as omission. My father sheltered her from all concerns, and then she was heartbroken at his death. Planning Edith's debut and now her trousseau has brought her joy and helped her get over her grief. I should have squashed that with nattering concerns about how many pounds spent on upholstery?"

"No, but . . ." Eliza squeezed her eyes shut for a moment, then plunged onward. "I also think you should tell Edith about Mr. Benwick immediately."

Hugh's face dropped all expression. "What?"

"I overheard just a tiny bit of conversation," she explained. "Edith is worried and upset that he's not come to visit lately. Has he told you he wishes to proceed with the settlements?"

He didn't have to answer. His expression

turned hard and cold, as she had rarely seen him. Eliza felt a prickle of unease but pressed on.

"Then tell her, before she makes a fool of herself," she urged. "She still loves him and has no idea he's about to desert her. She might say or do something humiliating. You must tell her, Hugh."

He pinched the bridge of his nose and sighed.

"If you don't tell her, she'll feel horribly betrayed and upset when she discovers not only Mr. Benwick's change of heart, but that you knew about it and didn't warn her," Eliza added softly.

With a muttered curse, he turned and paced away from her, swinging around in front of the windows. "Why are you so upset about this?"

Eliza fluttered one hand in helplessness. "Do you think I'm wrong? You know your sister better than I do."

He glared at her, but did not argue.

She crossed the room to him. "She can survive the loss of Mr. Benwick. You will always be her brother, though, and you don't want her memory of this time to be that you lied to her."

A visible shudder went through him. "No."

"So you'll tell her? Even a hint that it may happen?" She stepped closer and put her hand on his arm. "I know it will be difficult . . ."

He flinched away from her touch. Eliza froze, but Hugh turned and pulled her into his arms, resting his cheek atop her head. "It will be awful," he said with a heavy sigh. "But of course I'll do it. I have to. I planned to all along, you know. But I dread it."

She snaked her arms around his waist. Her

heart felt full. "No one likes to be deceived," she said. "Edith will be glad you told her, eventually."

He said nothing for a long moment. "If she doesn't, it would be no more than I deserve."

"No!" She looked up at him. "She'll forgive you."

His eyes were dark and brooding. "Will she? Would you?"

"Of course!" she cried. "As long as you were honest with me, I would always forgive you."

He smiled, but it was grim. "I hope you're right about that."

Chapter 22

❧❧❧

Hᴜɢʜ ꜰᴇʟᴛ ʜɪᴍꜱᴇʟꜰ sinking through the levels of hell.

His solicitor had heard nothing from the Livingston solicitors. It had been a slim hope, but now even it was gone, as his deadline arrived and passed. He'd been bracing himself for the nightmare of telling Edith, and then Eliza had to pour salt on the wound by speaking of honesty.

Damn Edward Cross. Now Hugh began to wish Cross *had* told his daughter all about his plan to share an earl for her; then there wouldn't be a lie infecting his conscience, eating away at him every day.

He found Edith in the library with Henrietta. They were decorating bonnets, talking and laughing and holding up their creations for approval from each other. He watched them for a moment, Henrietta dark and impish, Edith fair and graceful. They were so happy in this moment. He was glad for that, after their father's death and the move to London and the upheaval of his marriage. If only he wasn't about to spoil it.

Henrietta looked up. "Hugh! Are you spying on us?"

Edith laughed. "As ever! Although how anyone could be unnoticed with that hideous waistcoat is beyond me."

Hugh smoothed one hand down his front. "I thought the green was very fashionable." Edith made a face at him. "I wonder what you're doing wrong, to fear being spied upon, Henrietta."

"New bonnets! Look, isn't it darling?" Henrietta held up her creation.

"As a hedgehog," Hugh agreed, earning a gasp and a wrinkled nose from his sister. "Hen . . . May I have a word with Edith?"

"Uh-oh," murmured Henrietta merrily. "Thank goodness I'm not the one in trouble!"

Edith frowned as Henrietta gathered her things and left. Hugh closed the door and took Henrietta's chair beside his sister. "I'm not in trouble, am I?" she asked warily.

"Should you be?"

She flushed. "I've done my best to be civil to Eliza."

Hugh raised one brow. "It sounds as though you've not been successful."

"I don't like that dog!" burst out his sister in a low, tense voice.

"Is that all?" he asked.

She yanked on a ribbon in her lap. "Reggie says her father is despicable."

Hugh breathed deeply. "About Reggie . . . Edith, I'm afraid he's being difficult."

Her face went white. "Difficult? How?"

The rest of the conversation went as Hugh had feared. Edith first refused to believe it, then angrily accused him of being tightfisted. Only when Hugh told her Benwick's demand did she fall back in her seat, shocked and silent.

"He said he wouldn't marry me for less than forty thousand pounds?" she asked in a small voice.

Hugh nodded once.

"But—but—" Her chest was heaving. "But he *loves* me! He said so! Hugh, he declared it in front of others . . ."

"I don't think he meant it," said Hugh. "Not really."

Edith shook her head, at first slowly, then harder. "No. No, no, no. He did mean it, he just—he just—" She sucked in her breath. "It's because of *her*, isn't it?"

Hugh lied without hesitation or compunction. "It's because of his father. Livingston wants money—he required Benwick to promise him half of your dowry funds. I told Benwick to stand on his own feet and think of you, and he said he would choose his family over you every time. That's how much he cares for you, Edith."

"But he *hates*—" she began.

"Do not say a word against Eliza," Hugh cut in to warn her. "She is my wife. Reginald Benwick can despise her all he wants, but if that caused him to break your betrothal, he's not worthy of you anyway."

She stared at him, tears shining in her blue eyes. "I've been jilted? *Jilted?*"

"I expect that's why he hasn't called," said Hugh quietly. "He hasn't got the decency or the courage to tell you himself."

"He might change his mind . . ."

He sighed. "Would you still want him after this?"

For answer she jumped up and ran. He heard a choked sob as she wrestled with the door, then she was gone. He looked at the half-finished bonnet she'd left on the chair. The raspberry-pink ribbons were so cheerfully innocent, it made him want to pitch the thing into the fire.

He lurched out of his chair and went to find his mother. She was supervising the painting of the drawing room, but he drew her aside and told her what had happened. Horrified, she declared she must go to Edith at once, and hurried out.

Hugh watched the workmen patching holes and scrapes in the plaster walls, preparing to cover them with fresh green color. Chosen by Eliza, funded by Eliza, and planned by Eliza to win his mother's approval and affection. For the first time Hugh felt a perverse—and wholly irrational—surge of anger at her. She was too good for all of them. They couldn't seem to do anything right. He married to give his sister a dowry, and she got jilted because of his marriage. His mother venerated his father, never once questioning him about anything, and Joshua left them all in bankrupt ignorance. Edith turned her back on Eliza to please Benwick, and still got her heart broken. And Eliza . . . All she did was think of others and give freely of herself and her time, from cutting flowers for a servant's wedding to giving Hugh her heart when he didn't deserve it.

Where was she?

The butler told him she had gone out with the dog. Hugh put on his hat and coat and went after her, feeling even worse because she had to leave the house to enjoy Willy's company. He crossed Pall Mall and went into St. James's Park, finally catching sight of her near the canal. Willy ran around her, his black-and-white tail streaming behind him like a flag, and Angus, the boy from her father's stable, chased after him.

Something very odd filled his chest at the sight of his wife. She stooped to pick up a ball, and her skirts wrapped around her legs and hips enticingly. She stood and drew back her arm, and the curve of her bosom was outlined in glorious silhouette as she flung the ball for the dog to chase. His hands flexed at the memory of those curves against him, of her soft skin under his lips, of the way her eyes widened in amazement every time she reached climax in his arms.

She was the wife he hadn't wanted. She was the girl he'd been blackmailed into marrying. He had been forced to court her and seduce her, winning her love by pretending an affection he hadn't felt, and now the joke was on him. Now he was the one seduced, just by watching her throw the ball across the park for Willy. Now he was the one losing his heart and feeling the weight of his deception like a cross upon his back.

She didn't see him until he had almost reached

her. "Oh!" Her smile was bright and delighted, lighting up her face. "I didn't expect to see you here."

He kept walking, his gaze fixed on her. Damn Edward Cross. Hugh deserved a society heiress who would give him his heir and then take a stream of lovers. Someone who wouldn't tempt him to think wicked thoughts about her and feel unworthy of her in the same moment.

Her face changed. "What is wrong?" Willy ran up with the ball, tail wagging furiously, and she motioned Angus to come get him. "Hugh, what is it?" she asked anxiously as he reached her side.

"I told Edith."

Eliza's expression melted with sympathy. "The poor dear. How did she . . . ?"

"Not well."

"Oh dear." She bit her lip. "Think how much worse it would have been for her to hear it from someone else, though."

He had. But Hugh felt the surge of anger again, even though there was no one to focus it on. Eliza had been right to press him to tell Edith, and he'd been wrong to put it off. He was no better than his father, trying to protect his mother and sisters from everything unpleasant, and as a result the news came as a sudden blow to Edith. Yet another thing he'd done wrong. "I hope that's the end of it."

"Georgiana would say she ought to go out and flirt with other gentlemen. Nothing diverts a girl's mind like an attentive new suitor."

Hugh looked at her sharply. Eliza wore a hopeful little smile; she'd been teasing. It dropped away when she saw his face. "I'm sorry," she said at once. "I didn't mean to make light—"

"No, no. You've no need to apologize." Willy ran back with the ball, dropping it at his mistress's feet despite Angus's shouts for him to come. Hugh bent and scooped up the ball, flinging it as hard as he could. Willy took off with a joyful bark. The ball landed in the canal. Across the grass, Angus gave a whoop and followed Willy, who plunged into the water and sent ducks squawking out of the way.

Hugh laughed. "He'll need a bath now."

Eliza didn't reply. He looked at her; she was watching him somberly, her green eyes shadowed.

"What's the matter?"

"Was I wrong?" she asked quietly. "About Edith?"

He scowled. "No."

"Do you resent me urging you to speak to her?"

Damn it all, he did—utterly without reason or justification. "No."

She didn't believe him. She was too insightful for him, too. And suddenly Hugh wished he could begin anew with her. *No more lies*, he reminded himself. "Yes. I did resent it," he admitted harshly. "Not because I thought you were wrong but because I knew you were right. I didn't want to break my sister's heart. I kept hoping Benwick would come to his senses and be reasonable—and spare me the hard task of telling her. I would have even been cowardly content for *him* to tell Edith that he no longer wanted to marry her."

"Because you love her." Eliza reached for him. "Of course you don't want to hurt her."

"I wanted to protect her, as my father would have done." Hugh gave a humorless laugh at that irony. He put his hands on his hips, subtly evading her touch. "Instead I made it worse."

"No! *Mr. Benwick* made it horrible," she said firmly. "He's the villain here, proposing marriage and telling her he loved her and then changing his mind. You were very fair and patient with him, but he's the one who broke Edith's heart, not you."

"Eliza." He took a deep breath and took her hand, threading his fingers through hers. She had said she would forgive him if he were honest, after all. "Part of Benwick's change of heart involved you. He—or rather, his father despises your father. They had an unfortunate business dealing at some point, I gather."

All the color drained from her face. She stepped back and tugged, but Hugh refused to let her go. "That's why Edith hates me," she whispered.

"Most likely," he agreed. "Which is no good reflection on her. I thought she would realize it when she knew you. I thought Benwick cared for her enough to rebuff his father. I thought . . ." He fell silent, realizing how inane his excuses sounded. "I didn't want to hurt you," he said. *I wanted to protect you, too.*

"Hugh," she said in agony. "How could you not tell me that? I would have spoken to her . . ."

"And said what?" Again he resisted her attempt to pull free. "Livingston is being irrational.

Benwick is choosing his father over Edith. That puts the lie to his claim to love her, and if this is the way he treats her, it's far better that she learn it now, before she's his wife and bound to him forever. If anything, Edith should be relieved."

"Of course she won't be!" Eliza protested. "Not when her heart is broken . . ."

"Her love was wasted on him." *Just as yours has been wasted on me so far.*

She looked at him in reproach, but stopped arguing. "The poor girl," she said softly. "How it must have hurt her."

Hugh expelled his breath. Even after what he'd told her, even after the way Edith had treated her, she felt sympathy and kindness for his sister. His sense that she was too good for him roared back. "Even if he came to me on his knees, I wouldn't let him marry her now. He's proven himself inconstant and callous and my sister deserves better." *As do you*, he silently promised his wife. "And now I am done speaking and thinking of Reginald Benwick. Do you have a dress for the theater?"

She blinked. "Yes, but—but Edith—"

"Edith will recover. You told me so," he reminded her. "Tonight I would like to take my wife to the theater, if she'll go with me."

A fine blush colored her cheeks. "Of course."

He grinned and raised her hand for an impulsive kiss. He watched her face as he grazed his lips across her knuckles; her own lips parted and her eyes softened and warmed. She was in love with him. Hugh's conscience twinged painfully.

He should tell her the whole truth now and throw himself on her mercy. At this point he deserved a storm of tears and recriminations—followed, he hoped, by forgiveness.

But Willy ran up and dropped the ball on her skirt, and she jumped back with an exclamation, pulling free of Hugh's grip. He watched as she scolded the dog and made him sit before handing the ball to Angus and sending the two of them off again.

By the time she turned back to him his resolve had weakened. *When I have become worthy of her,* he promised himself, *then I can tell her. Once I've atoned for the lies I told her in the beginning. Once I've sorted out what I really feel for her, it will all be much easier to explain.*

And so he said nothing.

Chapter 23

Eliza MADE SEVERAL excuses for the fact that Hugh hadn't told her the truth. It wasn't an outright lie, merely an omission. He didn't want her to be hurt, she reminded herself; his reluctance had been real. If Mr. Benwick's dislike was entirely because of Papa, there was nothing Eliza could do about it anyway.

But while she could understand Edith choosing to side with the man she intended to marry—the man she believed loved her—Eliza couldn't deny a sharp little pain that Edith had done so with such vigor. She had very willingly and quickly turned a cold shoulder to her brother's bride even though she adored Hugh and he adored her. Georgiana had called Edith a snob, and Eliza felt horrible for thinking it must be a little bit true.

She was trying to be kind and understanding to her sister-in-law, and this unquestionably stung. It would be obnoxious to repay Edith in kind, but Eliza couldn't help taking some of Georgiana's advice. She would hold up her head and be strong, and not let any slight cow her. She was a countess now, Hugh's countess—incredible thought—and she must rise to the demands of her position.

However, there was one thing she could do that didn't require any fortitude or bravery on her part. "Papa, did you have any business dealings with Lord Livingston?" she asked her father when he came for his weekly visit. It was safe to do so, because everyone else was away from home by a stroke of luck.

"Livingston!" Her father looked surprised. "Why do you want to know about him?"

"So you did." She sipped her tea, watching him over the rim of the cup. "What went wrong?"

His mouth quirked. "I never said I knew the man."

"You didn't deny it," she pointed out. "I know you, Papa. What did you do that he didn't like?"

"Did Hastings put you up to this?"

"No, why would he?" she asked, startled. But then she realized. "He spoke to you about Livingston, too, didn't he?" Hugh would have tried everything to save his sister's engagement.

Her father waved one hand. "Once. I told him it was nothing significant and he let it go."

"It was not insignificant," she told him. "Lord Livingston's son was engaged to marry Lady Edith."

"I know."

"Lord Livingston is holding a grudge against you."

"Idiot," muttered her father.

"Papa!"

"What else can I say?" Scowling, he put down his cup of coffee. "Livingston bought shares in a tin mine—one of Grenville's schemes." She just looked at him in reproach. He sighed. "The tin mine closed a year later. Livingston probably lost his stake. Is that what you want to hear?"

"I want to hear the truth. Were they your shares?"

"I didn't make him buy them," said Papa. "He came to me. Quite insistent he was, too, and offered me a premium for them. Was I supposed to refuse?"

Eliza's eyes narrowed. "So Mr. Grenville persuaded you to buy into one of his cork-brained schemes, and then Lord Livingston offered you an easy way to make a profit."

Papa looked exasperated. "That's the way business works, Lilibeth."

She frowned. She could see why Livingston might be unhappy, but it didn't sound as though her father had cheated him. Was the viscount simply being vindictive? "What happened to the mine?"

He drummed his fingers on the arm of the sofa for a moment. "I don't know why you're troubling your head about this. Investments go bad from time to time. It's not unlike gambling, you know, and sometimes you lose. Anyone who doesn't understand that should put his money in the four percents and leave it there. And before you accuse me of misleading Lord Livingston," he added, wagging one finger at her, "I told him I thought it was a dodgy deal. Grenville thought he'd discovered a new way of extracting ore from old mines, but it only pulled up small amounts. Livingston brushed my warning aside. He wanted to take the chance that it would pay off magnificently, and I let him. That's all."

Eliza hesitated. "He was angry enough about it to end his son's engagement . . ."

Papa raised his eyebrows. "And the young man agreed to that? Not a very devoted suitor."

"No," she murmured.

"I understand things are different with nobility—sons kept under their fathers' thumbs and all that—but calling off an advantageous marriage for spite is idiocy," Papa went on.

Eliza cleared her throat. "He offered to marry her after all for a larger settlement."

Papa snorted in disgust. "Poor negotiation. You fix the price before you extend the offer."

"But now poor Edith's heart is broken," Eliza said softly. "She loves him."

"Then I am very sorry for her," he replied more kindly. "But a man should keep his word. If he's the sort who does not, she's better off without him."

Eliza agreed, but she couldn't see why Lord Livingston felt so cheated by her father that he would spoil his son's marriage to an eligible young lady. "It seems irrational . . ."

"Which is why I haven't wasted much thought on Lord Livingston, and refuse to do so now." Papa held out his cup, and Eliza obligingly poured him more coffee. "When shall I have a grandchild to bounce on my knee?"

Eliza blushed bright red. "Papa!"

He winked. "Patience isn't my strength." He paused, growing more serious. "Are you happy, Lilibeth? Is Hastings a good husband?"

"Yes." Her mouth curved. "Very happy. If only this hadn't happened to Lady Edith . . . She—she's blamed me for her broken engagement."

Pique flashed across his face. "That seems very undeserved. Are Lady Henrietta and her mother kind and welcoming?"

"Yes," she said slowly. "At least, I think they're warming to me."

"But not initially?" His expression was grim.

"I suspect Lady Hastings had someone else in mind for Hugh to marry," she confessed. "But she's been gracious, and I believe she's taking to me. We're redecorating the drawing room together. And Henrietta . . . She followed her sister's lead initially, but she's a lovely girl. She's becoming quite fond of Willy."

"And Hastings?" her father pressed again. "Is he good to you?"

"Yes, Papa." She gave him a warning look. "Don't go browbeating him."

"Why would I do that?" Papa acted surprised. "What does he need browbeating for?"

"Nothing." Eliza meant to solve any lingering problems in her marriage herself. "It's not your place."

He regarded her with fond concern. "It's my place to see that you're happy. If Hastings doesn't do right by you—"

"He has," she said firmly. Telling Papa her

worries would do no good, and only put him on edge. "Don't you dare do anything, Papa."

"You act as if I'm not trustworthy." He put on a wounded expression she knew was all art.

"I'm acting as if I know you," she said firmly, but with a laugh. "I know you like to interfere, but your help is not wanted in this case."

"If you need help . . ." he began.

"No!" She set down her teacup with a clink. "I do not need help. If I do, I will ask for it."

A smile broke out on his face. "That's my girl. Well, as long as Hastings is making you happy, I shall keep to myself."

HUGH ALMOST HELD HIS breath the first evening they went out, but he needn't have worried.

Not only did Eliza look her best, in a deep peacock-green dress that made her eyes glow, she seemed to have tapped some vein of poise and composure inside herself. He'd seen her shy and uncertain before, and feared she might retreat into it in the face of Livingston's spite. Instead she walked into the Gorensons' musicale with her head high, diamonds sparkling at her throat and ears, as if she were a princess royal.

It helped, no doubt, that her friend was there. Lady Georgiana linked her arm through Eliza's and led her around the room, introducing her to every prominent lady in attendance. Hugh let them go, but kept his eyes on her.

"How remarkable they would be such friends," remarked his mother beside him.

Hugh raised his brows. "Why?"

"Why—why, they're so . . ." She paused thoughtfully. "They are quite different. Lady Georgiana is so vivacious. Eliza is far quieter. I worried she was terribly shy when you invited her to tea."

Except she wasn't. Hugh knew she didn't hesitate to speak her mind when she felt strongly about something. She wasn't shy in bed, either. Perhaps she wasn't shy at all, but merely cautious in new situations. "Do you wish I'd married someone like Lady Georgiana?" he asked, and was surprised to feel something inside himself recoil at the thought. Lady Georgiana was beautiful and vivacious, as his mother said—much like Catherine Thayne and Fanny Martin, either of whom his mother would have been delighted to see as his bride. Once upon a time he'd thought he would marry someone like that, and only now did it strike him how exhausting that might have been.

His mother took her time replying. Finally he glanced at her, wondering if she were struggling with how to admit that, yes, she did wish that, but instead her face was surprised.

"Once I did," she said. "But now . . . Eliza was a wonderful choice. She's not at all what I expected your wife would be, but all for the better."

Now he was the one surprised. "Really."

She gave him a glance of reproach at his tone. "I was wrong earlier, when I tried to persuade you against courting her. And I was wrong not to welcome her more warmly." She smiled ruefully. "You chose better for yourself than I would have done, and I am so proud of you for it."

Hugh looked at his wife again. She was listening to Lady Clapham with a smile on her face. Lady Georgiana broke in with something that made all three laugh. Eliza's face was luminous with happiness. The *ton* might never call her beautiful, but Hugh realized that he rather thought she was. It was the way she smiled. The way her bosom rose and fell when she laughed. The way her eyes lit with an extra glow when she glanced up and caught him watching her, and their gazes connected for a small eternity. The rest of the room seemed to fade away around him, and Hugh found himself smiling at his own wife like a love-struck ninny. He bowed slightly at her, still smiling; she blushed, but then she winked at him, a roguish wink that made him want to sweep her into a private room where he could kiss her senseless and tease her about tempting him to do wicked things to her at a society musicale.

He wanted to laugh.

Yes, he had done remarkably well. Even if she hadn't been his choice at all in the beginning, there was no other woman in the world he wanted now. And on that thought, he headed across the room toward her.

ELIZA THOUGHT SHE MUST be tipsy, or daydreaming, or perhaps had suffered a whack on the head and was now enjoying a marvelous delusion.

The same society matrons who had never deigned to look in her direction during her futile Season were smiling right at her tonight as Georgiana towed her around the room. Georgiana, of course, knew and was known by everyone, and was clearly held in high regard by them all. Eliza had expected no less, but it was still dazzling to see the effects of Georgiana's determined charm—and, perhaps, her own new title—at close range.

Lady Clapham complimented her gown. Lady Reynolds invited her to tea. Someone else—Eliza lost track of who—admired her jewels. She could hardly keep straight all the names and faces of her new acquaintances.

After several minutes, Lady Sidlow summoned Georgiana away, leaving Eliza with Lady Gorenson. Their hostess was very cordial, presenting her to several more people, but Eliza was relieved to spot Hugh making his way through the crowd toward her, albeit slowly as he was stopped by every other person he passed. Society was exhausting, it turned out.

"Here is someone you should know," said Lady Gorenson gaily, breaking into her thoughts. "If you are not already acquainted with Mr. Benwick. I understand you may soon be very closely acquainted . . . ?" She gave Eliza a teasing smile.

Eliza turned around to see Reginald Benwick, staring at her with haughty determination in his face. He drew breath, obviously readying a cutting response. Eliza didn't give him the chance. "I believe you are mistaken, Lady Gorenson," she said, quietly but clearly. "I have no wish to make this gentleman's acquaintance." She turned and walked away, her head high.

Lady Gorenson scurried after her. "My goodness, Lady Hastings, I am astonished—I've heard rumors he is engaged to Lady Edith!"

Eliza stopped and put her hand on her hostess's arm. "I hope I may confide in you, ma'am." Lady Gorenson blinked, then nodded eagerly. Eliza glanced around, but they were in a relatively quiet corner, sheltered behind a large group of young ladies talking and laughing. "He did call upon Lady Edith, but he turned out to be very unsuitable, and Hastings has turned him aside."

The other woman's eyes looked ready to fall from her head. "No," she breathed. "But he's quite eligible . . ."

Eliza made a subtle noise of disagreement. Lady Gorenson sucked in her breath. "No!"

Lowering her voice even further, Eliza leaned close. "I understand his father's financial situation isn't entirely stable. He pursued Lady Edith only in hopes of gaining her dowry, it seems."

"She told people she was in love with him!" burst out Lady Gorenson in a whisper.

Eliza bit her lip. "He deceived her into thinking he loved her. And who could not? Edith is so lovely and so loyal. For that cruelty I can never forgive him, and I have no wish to make his acquaintance. My only solace is that Hastings realized it before anything had been settled, and now he's forbidden Mr. Benwick the house. But you must not tell anyone that," she added hastily, as if she hadn't meant to say it. "I don't want to cause a scene with Mr. Benwick or his family—as long as he can't hurt Edith any more than he has."

"Of course." Lady Gorenson goggled at her. "I'd no idea."

"You must understand why we don't speak of it," Eliza murmured in reply. "I'd rather no one know, for Edith's sake."

"Of course," said her hostess again. "I completely understand!"

Eliza smiled in gratitude and pressed her arm, then turned to go meet Hugh. Her knees were shaking, and she thought she'd better warn him about what she'd done. But she hadn't gone more then two steps before she came face-to-face with Edith, ashen-faced and wide-eyed.

She stopped cold, her heart sinking. *Oh no.* Edith had been in the group of girls behind her the whole time.

"You told Lady Gorenson that Mr. Benwick was practically a fortune hunter," said Edith, her voice barely audible.

She bit her lip and wondered what was the right thing to say. She always seemed to choose wrongly, when it came to Edith. "I couldn't bear to be politely introduced to him after what he did."

"Why?" Edith sounded genuinely bewildered.

Eliza looked at her, so young, so beautiful, so headstrong. "What he did is appalling," she said evenly.

"But . . . But I—" Edith gave a tiny shake of her head, her brows knit. "Why—?"

She lightly touched Edith's arm. "It does not matter what justification he gave. The way he treated you is unpardonable. I would think so no matter who the poor girl had been, and I cannot admire Mr. Benwick for being so rude and cruel."

Edith's mouth trembled. "No," she agreed. She hesitated, then added, very softly, "Thank you."

Without another word, Edith slipped back to the cluster of young ladies she'd been with before. Judging by the whispered conversation they struck up, and the furtive glances several girls gave Eliza, she guessed they were talking about her set-down of Mr. Benwick.

"Is something the matter?" murmured Hugh, his fingers grazing her waist in a casually affectionate touch that made her heart leap.

Eliza glanced at him. "No." She cleared her throat. "I may have suggested to Lady Gorenson that Mr. Benwick is an unprincipled fortune hunter and you've forbidden him the house."

"What?" He looked startled.

"And Edith overheard." Eliza dared a quick look at her sister-in-law. As she did so, Edith glanced up and met her eyes. To Eliza's surprise and cautious delight, Edith gave her a small nod before turning back to her friends. In spite of herself, she smiled—only to notice Hugh staring at her. She sobered. "I hope I didn't—"

"No," he said quietly. "I think you did exactly right. As of now, Mr. Benwick *is* barred from my house, so it's not even a lie."

She beamed at him gratefully. She hadn't truly expected that her actions would displease him, but it was enormously reassuring to hear him say it.

"I'd no idea Benwick would be here tonight."

He raised his head and looked across the room. "I should inform my mother and see if she wishes to leave."

"Don't you think," began Eliza hesitantly, "that we ought to stay?"

"Stay!" He frowned. "And give him the chance to be cruel to Edith in person?"

"No, to give Edith the chance to show everyone that she's not pining for him." She looked at Edith again. There was a smile on her face now, and she even wrinkled her nose and laughed at something her friend said.

Hugh continued to scowl. "I don't like it."

Eliza also wouldn't mind going home. The drawing room was crowded and hot, for all its elegance, and Georgiana, her only friend here, was off somewhere else. But something Georgiana had said, about holding up her head to prevent the gossips from being merciless, was very much in her mind tonight. She'd been doing that—not backing down, pretending she had the courage of an Amazon queen and the nerve of a circus performer—and it appeared to have worked. It seemed foolish to leave now and let that effort go unfulfilled. "If Edith walks out the instant Mr. Benwick appears, what will people think?" She could see him, too, standing at the side of the room sipping wine with a sulky expression. "I think it far better that he bear any shame or disapproval than Edith."

"Lady Hastings." Hugh tipped up her chin until she looked at him. "You are a remarkably insightful woman."

She blushed. "Oh, no . . ." She'd merely learned the hard way what happened when one was quiet and retiring and did nothing to counter vile rumors.

"You are," he insisted, his eyes dark and intent on her. "And if there weren't a hundred people watching, I might kiss you for it."

Her heart skipped, jumped, and soared. Whatever she'd had to endure—from Edith's animosity to the loss of Willy's company to being required to attend society events like this one—it was all worth it. Because of Hugh's love. He'd seen past her shy, plain person, right into the depths of her heart, and he loved her as she was. Eliza smiled at him, certain she looked like a lovesick idiot and not caring in the slightest. "Perhaps I was hasty, about wanting to stay for the rest of the musicale . . ."

He only laughed, low and sensual, as he drew her to his side and tucked her arm around his. "I shall make up for lost time tonight, Lady Hastings. You may depend on it."

Chapter 24

⚭

THE NEXT WEEK unfolded so splendidly that Hugh, without meaning to, fell prey to the seductive but treacherous belief that he would never have to tell Eliza the truth.

Her set-down of Benwick wasn't without repercussion. The day after the Gorenson musicale, the first whispers reached his ears. Benwick had stormed out of the musicale in a bad temper, and Hugh wasn't surprised to hear reports that Livingston was telling everyone at his club that Hugh, having only married for money, had got what he deserved with a rude, arrogant upstart for a wife.

He *was* surprised at the source of rebuttal. His mother was livid when she heard, and embarked at once on a tour of drawing rooms around London, assuring everyone that Eliza was the most delightful girl, that Hugh had seen her worth, and that Benwick was acting out of spite after his courtship of Edith was rejected. Edith had told her what Eliza said, and it sealed the dowager's loyalty to her daughter-in-law.

But the most surprising thing, the thing that

seemed to wipe away all the trouble and up-heaval his marriage had caused initially, was Edith's confession. She stopped him on his way out the door one day and asked for a word. He followed her into the morning room, hoping it wasn't something else about the dog. He'd hardly seen Willy, and he knew Eliza missed having her pet around.

"I want to apologize," said Edith when he had closed the door. She twisted her hands together. "For all the things I said about Eliza."

"Ah." Hugh resisted the urge to say anything else.

Edith bit her lip. "I thought it was important to be loyal to Reg—to Mr. Benwick. I believed his claims that her father was quite evil." She looked at the floor. "And I felt rather superior for think-ing so."

"Now, I presume, you don't."

She raised her head, and he was startled to see tears in her eyes. "No. Eliza defended me and lied to Lady Gorenson when she might have con-firmed that I'd been j-j-jilted." Hugh reached for her but she stepped back. "I was an idiot to listen to Reggie. And he was a liar, about her and many other things."

"He was."

She swiped at her eyes. "I'm very sorry. I wanted to tell you."

"I'm glad you did," Hugh said.

His sister took a deep breath. "You were very clever to marry her."

That caught him off guard. "You think so?"

Edith nodded. "I thought she wouldn't have any taste, but she has. I thought she would be crude and gauche, but she isn't." She glanced around the room with red-rimmed eyes. "And I suspect you gave Mama permission to decorate the house because she persuaded you, which has made Mama so happy."

"Thank you, Edith," he said quietly. "But perhaps you ought to say these kind words to Eliza."

Her smile wobbled. "I did tell her, right after breakfast. I wanted to tell you, too, since I was so beastly to you."

And Hugh felt a great weight lift off his chest. His mother loved Eliza. Henrietta adored her, and her dog. Now even Edith admitted she'd been wrong, and approved of Eliza. Again the feeling that he was going to get away with everything whispered through his mind, insidiously exculpatory, and he went to find his wife.

She was in the drawing room, a kerchief on her head and an apron over her dress. The walls had been painted a light green, the floor newly buffed and waxed, and she was directing servants who were hanging drapes of deep purple satin, gleaming richly in the newly brightened room. Hugh stood beside her and watched them angle the heavy rod into the hooks.

"What do you think?" she asked.

"I think you look quite fetching."

She blushed. "I meant about the drapes."

"Men don't think about draperies, they think

about undressing their wives." He savored the way the blush spread down her neck, toward the neckline of her dress. "Come with me."

"Where? Hugh!" she protested as he plucked the kerchief off her head.

"You've done quite enough." *For the house, for my family, for me.* "Let's run away for the day."

"Run away—where?"

"Anywhere," he said, but he had a particular place in mind. "We leave in half an hour." He paused on his way out of the room. "And bring Willy."

They drove out with Angus on the back of the carriage and Willy lodged between their feet. "But where are we going?" Eliza asked for the fourth time.

"Away from town." Away from gossiping matrons and broken engagements and the drawing room's new drapes. Away from every reminder of what he had done and the lies he had told. Again he thought to himself that he would begin anew with her, and not waste the clean escape he'd managed.

He drove north, around the bustle of Piccadilly and up Portland Street to the Islington Road. Eliza exclaimed at the expanse set aside to become Regent's Park but they passed it entirely. He didn't stop until they reached a hill rising above the future park, where he stopped the horses and set the brake. Willy leapt down with a joyful bark and shot off after a flock of sparrows pecking at the grass, sending them into the sky in a flurry of chirping.

Hugh jumped down and held out his arms. Eliza reached for his hand, but he pulled, catching her and holding her tight against him. And she smiled at him, so delightfully pleased, that he resolved to do it more often. "Primrose Hill," he said, sweeping out one hand. "With a stunning view of London, yet none of the unpleasantness."

"Why are we here?" She looked around, brows raised, endearingly puzzled.

"I cannot seem to get you to myself in town."

She blushed. "Did you want me to yourself?"

He did. It had never struck him that way, but— "Yes," he said honestly.

"Well." She cleared her throat. "You never said so before."

I never thought so before. "Today I did." He whistled sharply. Far across the grass, Willy raised his head, the breeze blowing his fur up around his head like a lion's mane. Hugh whistled again, and the dog came bounding back, a stick in his mouth. Hugh wrestled the stick away and flung it, causing Willy to bolt after it. "Shouldn't I be able to steal my wife away for a day?"

Her face turned pink. "Oh—yes, but—it seemed very sudden, and it's the middle of the day. It's not like—"

Not like you, she meant to say. He hadn't taken pains to spend time with her. He'd gone about his usual habits since their wedding, and simply taken their moments together for granted. It caused an avalanche of shame inside his chest.

"Perhaps not, but it felt right today."

Eliza had never heard that particular note in

his voice. It seemed to burrow into a tender spot on her heart, sending a warm happiness through her. He hadn't said any words of love, but more and more frequently they were implied. Perhaps that was all he would ever do. Georgiana had warned her that gentlemen of rank and title often didn't care to express deep feelings or emotions. Hugh had demonstrated such affection that she felt silly for wishing he might say three trifling words. Anyone could say those words, after all, while Hugh had *proven* he cared for her. Perhaps it wasn't even a thing aristocratic couples said to each other.

They threw the stick for Willy for quite a while, until his tongue was hanging out. Hugh could fling it a great distance, which pleased the dog to no end. Eliza sat on the grass and let him flop into her lap, happily tired out at last. Willy licked her face until she laughed and stood up to escape.

"Enough, Willy!" she said, wiping her face with a handkerchief. Having settled the horses while they played with the dog, Angus took off with Willy to explore a nearby wood.

"Hard to blame him, really," remarked Hugh, watching with his arms folded. "Maybe I'll do the same."

Eliza laughed. "You want to lick my face?"

"Perhaps I do," he said with a rakish grin. "Come here . . ." With a shriek, Eliza ran, but he caught her in just a few steps. "Mine," he said, swinging her off her feet. "All mine!" He kissed her hard on the mouth.

"Much better than licking," she said, her cheeks pink.

"Wasn't it?" Grinning, he did it again. "I'll do it even more after a bite to eat."

He produced a blanket and a hamper from the boot of the carriage, and spread the blanket on the grass. Eliza opened the hamper and discovered fresh strawberries, cold ham, sliced bread and chutney, and a bottle of champagne. "A feast," she exclaimed in surprise.

Hugh stretched out his legs and lounged on the blanket beside her. "Hardly more than tea."

She held out a strawberry, and he ate it from her fingers. "Except for the lack of tea, and cakes, and any sort of proper setting."

"That's why we ran away for the day—to escape propriety." He looked at her. "Do you mind?"

"No." She thought she would do almost anything he suggested, but didn't say it.

"Good. I . . ." A frown crossed his face, there for a heartbeat and then gone. "I wanted to spoil you." He reached for the champagne and opened it. "You've been working hard on the drawing room. You've quite won my mother's heart, you know."

"Have I?" She sat up straighter, beaming. "Oh, I do hope so. That is . . . I hope she thinks well of me."

Hugh poured a glass of the fizzing wine and handed it to her. Eliza took a tiny sip, marveling at the decadence. Champagne at midday! "Very well indeed. It took them by surprise when I began calling on you, but they've completely got over it." He gave her a rueful look. "I've been told many times it's my fault for knocking them off stride."

Eliza thought it was more than that. She sipped her champagne and traced a leaf that had fluttered onto the blanket beside her. "I suppose they hoped you would wed a lady."

"They likely expected it," he agreed, "although no one ever said so to me. If anything, my mother expressed hope that all her children would marry someone they could care for. She adored my father and wanted nothing less for her children."

There it was again, the suggestion that he loved her. Eliza tried to repress the wish that he would say it plainly. *Silly*, she scolded herself. Actions spoke more than words, and here he had stolen her away for a romantic picnic, just the two of them—plus Willy, who did not count—and she was disappointed. What a ninny she was. "My parents also loved each other," she said, pushing those thoughts aside. "I always hoped to find the same."

"Hmm." Hugh was watching her, his glass dangling from his fingertips. "Your mother died when you were a child?"

"Yes. Not quite four years old. She and my infant brother."

"It must have been lonely to grow up with only your father." He said it evenly, but Eliza could hardly forget what he'd said about her father.

"I never knew what it was like to have a mother, so I couldn't miss her. My father sent me away to school when I was eight, so I could learn all the things she would have taught me. And I met Sophie and Georgiana there, who became like sisters to me." She smiled wryly. "I was terribly excited to gain some real sisters when we married."

"Are they? Like real sisters."

Eliza took a deep breath. It certainly hadn't been smooth or easy, but . . . "Yes," she said firmly. "Henrietta is wonderful. And Edith was in an impossible situation. Mr. Benwick was dreadful to her, and I'm so happy she's got over him."

"You put him in his place," said Hugh with a grin. "Splendidly, too."

"I'm very pleased that worked," she confessed. "I feared it might backfire, and anger Edith or upset your mother . . ."

Hugh snorted. "Mother only wished she'd thought of it herself. And Edith . . ." He paused. "You showed Edith true grace and decency, and made her rightly ashamed of how she behaved."

"She did apologize to me." Edith had been almost tearful as she confessed how stupidly she'd believed Mr. Benwick's allegations. Eliza cared more for her promise that they would start anew, and get to know each other better. "Although I don't think she'll ever care for Willy the way Henrietta does."

Hugh smiled. "Probably not."

"I spoke to Papa, you know, to see what he'd done to Lord Livingston." Eliza hadn't told Hugh about that conversation, thinking it was better not to mention Papa unless absolutely necessary, but there was an air of frank intimacy between them today. She hadn't missed how Hugh never spoke of Papa, nor of the possible ore at Rosemere that had seemed so important before the wedding. It was hard not to wonder if the trouble with Lord Livingston had ruined Hugh's good opinion of Papa. Her new life would be absolutely perfect if her father and her new family could be reconciled, though. "He admitted he did business with Lord Livingston, but fairly and honestly."

Hugh's smile looked a little rigid. "It hardly matters now. I lost every trace of respect for Livingston, and wouldn't be surprised to discover he's a liar."

"I wish you and Papa were more cordial," she said without thinking.

"Your father and I understand each other completely," he said, which wasn't the same thing. "But I'm astonished he sent you away to school! He seems more protective than that."

She rolled her eyes and let him change the subject. "I'm glad he did. It was wonderful there, with other girls my age and all sorts of lessons. Mrs. Upton's is the finest academy for young ladies in Britain, and Mrs. Upton was so kind and encouraging. My father wanted me to be a true lady."

Hugh regarded her with a thoughtful gaze. "So he did."

Eliza flushed. "I never thought I would be a countess! That still defies belief."

"Does it?" He put down his glass and pulled her to lie beside him. "Are you unhappy as a countess?"

"No!"

"Why, then?" He propped himself up on one elbow above her. "Was it only your father's dream? What did *you* want?"

She blushed under his close study. "I—I didn't have a particular dream. To find someone kind and patient, who wouldn't mind Willy, I suppose. That was as much as I hoped for."

"Hmm." The sun behind his head obscured her view of his expression. "Instead you got me."

"What? Oh—Oh no," she exclaimed in alarm. "I didn't mean . . . You must know you're more than I ever dreamed of. I could not believe it when you asked to call on me—I thought it was a lark, or a mistake, or perhaps a sign you'd lost your wits. But I . . ." She laid one hand on his cheek. "I was happy beyond words," she finished softly.

For a moment he didn't move. "You always manage to unman me, Eliza."

"What do you mean?"

"You do," was all he said to her flustered query. "In the best way. Shall we eat?"

They ate ham and bread spread with chutney, a specialty of the cook. They nibbled on strawberries and finished the champagne. As if determined to lighten the mood, Hugh told stories of his youth, including some pranks he and his friends got up to at school. Eliza told him how Sophie and Georgiana had become like sisters to her at Mrs. Upton's Academy, including how Sophie had nearly been dismissed on her first day for trying to teach Eliza sums with a pack of cards.

When Angus came back, with Willy at his heels, Hugh got to his feet. "Shall we have a walk?" he asked Eliza. She nodded, and they left the boy plundering the remains of the picnic and the dog stretched out on the grass.

In the distance, far down the hill, London lay quiet and neat from this perspective. Eliza shaded her eyes and looked toward Greenwich, but the sun was too dazzling. Today everything was dazzling, and so far removed from her previous life she couldn't even remember what things looked like from Greenwich.

"Shall we turn into the wood?" Hugh suggested as she blotted her brow. "Is the sun too hot?"

"Yes, let's." Gratefully Eliza followed him into the shade of the copse. They walked until a narrow brook cut off their path, and then followed it upstream, the ground rising beneath their steps.

"You ought to have warned me to wear sturdy boots," said Eliza after a while, breathing hard as she climbed over a fallen beech, its upper branches now drowned in the rushing stream.

Hugh laughed. "Perhaps I like you flushed with exercise. Take off your pelisse."

"Oh, I'm not *that* warm," she began to say, but he stepped up behind her and put his hand on the small of her back.

"You will be," he whispered, his cheek against hers. His other arm came around her shoulders and tugged loose the ribbon of her bonnet.

She went up in flames every time he touched her. Eliza reached for the buttons. "What do you plan to do?"

He lifted the bonnet from her head, giving him better access to her bare neck. "What will you allow me?"

Anything. Everything. She thought he knew that, but it did give her a feeling of power that was wholly new and exhilarating. She turned out of his loose embrace and stepped away, peeling off her pelisse as she did. "It depends how you ask, I suppose . . ."

He followed, hanging her bonnet on a low branch of a convenient tree. He tossed the pelisse over it, and Eliza felt her nipples harden as his eyes fixed on her bosom. "Should I beg?" He fell to one knee. "Shall I worship at your feet?" His eyes gleaming, he took hold of her ankle.

Eliza blushed. "Worship seems unnecessary."

"Is it?" His hand slid upward. "Men worship all manner of things, most of them unworthy. Let me show you something that will cause you to sing alleluia."

"What?" Nervously Eliza glanced around. There wasn't another soul to be seen, but still— they were outdoors, where anyone might walk by and see him, on his knees before her, with his hand—now both his hands—under her skirt.

"Now, now—you'll have to trust me." Gently he pushed away her hands when she made a weak effort to shove down her skirts as he raised them above her garters. "Do you?"

"Yes, but—" She jumped as his palms glided up her thighs until his thumbs reached the slit of her drawers.

"Good." With a searing look, he pushed her skirts up even more and pressed his mouth to the spot where his fingers were. Eliza gave a loud wheeze, and he laughed softly as he nudged her legs apart—spread *her* apart—and kissed her again there.

She had no idea what he did, but it almost made her fall over. She slumped back against the tree, her arms behind her trying to hold on to the bark. Light, delicate, so teasingly soft and wet . . . she knew he was using his tongue on her and she should be mortified and yet she only let her knees fall apart so he could do more of it. By the time he got to his feet and gathered her close, she could barely stand.

"Put your arms around my neck," he whispered. Shaking, Eliza complied. He lifted her against him and then he was inside her. Eliza sucked in her breath. Hugh gripped her bottom with one hand and tilted her hips, pushing deeper.

"Don't let go," he growled. He shifted, setting one foot on a prominent root of the tree, and Eliza instinctively raised her knees around his waist. Now Hugh's breath hissed between his teeth, and she felt a wild euphoria that she could elicit such desire in him.

He moved slowly, one arm braced on the branch by her head and one hand under her hip, holding her, supporting her, moving her as he willed. Eliza clung to him, her every sense alive and taut—they were out of doors, with Angus and Willy nearby, but when Hugh looked at her with that heavy-lidded gaze, she thought she might combust if he didn't make love to her immediately, even against a tree in St. John's Wood. She grew weak when he touched her, but when he looked at her as if he couldn't wait to have her, Eliza was discovering she became a wanton, wicked woman without shame or modesty. And she reveled in it.

Her head fell back as her body began to tighten. Incoherently she urged him on, trying to move in time with his thrusts. Hugh groaned, his mouth coming down hard on hers. "Look at me," he commanded, his lips against hers. "Open your eyes, Eliza, and look at me . . ."

She forced up her eyelids, hardly able to breathe. His hair fell around his face in inky waves, his eyes smoldered like coals, his grip on her was almost painful, and she came with a great gasp of joy. A wild grin lit Hugh's face as he moved, harder and faster, and then broke. For a moment his full weight fell against her, pinning her to the tree so the bark bit into her shoulders and snagged her hair, but Eliza held him tight, bliss coursing through her veins. *I love you*, she thought fervently. *Even if you never say the same to me.*

"I love you," he whispered, his voice ragged.

Eliza jerked, thinking she must have spoken aloud. "What?"

"I love you," he repeated, beginning to smile. "Did you not hear me the first time?"

"No, I—" She stopped before she could say something stupid. Instead she threaded her hands into his hair and pulled his face to hers, kissing him hard, her mouth open, her heart bared. He kissed her back, his hands rough on her. "I love you, too," she told him shyly.

"That's why I wanted you to myself," he murmured.

"You have only ever to ask," she promised him with a little laugh, while her heart sang.

He touched her nose, his smile lingering. "I plan to more often."

And Eliza felt that she would never know more happiness than she did in that moment.

Chapter 25

❧❧❧

THE EVENING OF the Montgomery ball began splendidly, with no inkling of how badly it would end.

Eliza wore one of her new gowns, of deep burgundy silk. She had always liked rich colors and finally felt at liberty to wear them in public. Georgiana had enthusiastically encouraged her to order this style as well, even though it was lower cut than usual and featured an extravagant amount of beading on the bodice.

"Eliza!" gasped Henrietta when she went downstairs. "Your gown!"

Her steps slowed before she determinedly kept going. What was wrong with her gown? Oh dear—she would make them all late if she had to change . . . "Yes?" She pinned on a bright smile and hoped it didn't look anxious. "What about it?"

"It's magnificent!" Eyes wide, Henrietta circled her. "It sparkles when you move."

Eliza smoothed one hand down the bodice. Was sparkling a bad thing? Perhaps she hadn't grasped the intricacies of *ton* fashion. She glanced at Edith, who also looked startled. "Is it too much?"

"No, no," Edith replied in surprise. "I intend to copy it on my next gown, if Mama will allow it."

"Once she sees how beautiful it looks on Eliza, I'm sure she will." Henrietta looked up. Like her sister, she wore a lovely dress, in a shade of pastel pink Georgiana had once termed "virginal blush." "Mama, have you seen Eliza's gown?"

"Oh my, no," said the dowager as she emerged from the morning room. Like her daughters, she regarded Eliza with fascination. "It's marvelous."

Eliza blushed with delight under their admiration. "Thank you. I didn't want to be an embarrassment to anyone tonight."

"Goodness." The dowager laughed lightly. "You outshine us all, my dear!"

She knew that was not true. The dowager was still a beautiful woman, and her sage gown suited her fair coloring. Henrietta's pink dress set off her dark hair, and Edith was as beautiful as an angel in her white gown, her golden curls fashionably arranged and a coral bracelet around her wrist. And—to her surprise—the ivory fan Eliza had given her.

Startled, she met Edith's eyes. The younger girl blushed, but obligingly spread open the fan. "How does it suit me? I've been waiting for a chance to carry it."

Edith had accepted the gift with quiet thanks, but never used it. Eliza realized she had unconsciously been looking for it every time her sister-in-law went out, and to see it on her wrist tonight made her heart soar. It felt like proof that she was truly part of the family.

"It complements your gown perfectly," Eliza told her. Edith's smile was grateful.

She barely heard the footsteps on the stairs behind her before Hugh appeared at her side. "I apologize for keeping you waiting," he said, still tugging on his gloves. "I'll be the envy of every man there, arriving with four lovely ladies." Then he turned to face Eliza.

Never before had she seen that expression on a man's face when he looked at her—a startled amazement that rapidly gave way to something hot and lustful. She blushed under it, but not from shame.

"Come, girls," said the dowager behind her. "The carriage."

Eliza barely heard them bustle out, the butler and footman in attendance. Hugh reached for her hand and pressed his lips to her wrist. "My Lady Hastings," he murmured, "you'll cause a riot tonight."

Instead of giggling nervously and protesting, she arched her brows. "Do you think so? Oh dear. I only wanted to catch one man's eye."

"Fortunate fellow." His hand slid around her waist, urging her toward him. "What did you plan to do with him, once he was thoroughly bewitched?"

"Dance with him. Perhaps go in to supper with him. Cause a small scandal by watching him all night." She touched his cravat, straightening the pearl pin stuck through it. "Then take him home with me and make love to him until he can't stand."

Sophie had told her it wasn't wrong to say lustful, wicked things to her husband. Sophie's advice was once again proven absolutely right when Hugh inhaled unevenly and lowered his head until his lips brushed her ear. "Temptress," he whispered. "Precisely what I hoped you'd say, and now the thought of it shall torment me all night long." The smell of him swamped her senses; his hand on her back slid down to linger a moment on her bottom. "I suppose we cannot beg off the ball and go directly to the lovemaking."

She smiled even though her heart was pounding, and her body had reacted to his touch. It ought to be a crime, the way he could reduce her to a wanton creature just by looking at her with hot, dark eyes. "Your mother and sisters are waiting," she said breathlessly.

"Which has nothing to do with my question." Slowly he released her. "I shall hold you to that promise . . . to dance with me."

Flushed, she beamed at him. "I never break my word."

THE MONTGOMERYS HAD TAKEN a set of large public assembly rooms for their ball, as it was to celebrate the betrothal of their daughter to the Duke of Warnford's heir. The glittering elite of London society were in attendance, and Eliza felt dazed, as if the very air had become gilded, too fine for her to breathe. Georgiana was to attend, although Eliza didn't see her. She would have to keep looking, since she did not want to spend this evening like a wallflower.

But to her amazement, gentleman after gentleman solicited dances. They were all friends of Hugh's, so she accepted—and found herself promised to dance with two earls, one viscount, the brother of a duke, and the heir to a marquess. One after another, they swept her away from her husband, although Eliza finally realized he was not dancing, aside from one set with each of his sisters.

"With whom should I dance?" he replied when she asked him during supper. "The only woman I want to partner has promised every set."

She gasped. "You encouraged me to do it! They are your friends!"

"I was wrong," Hugh said. "Encroaching beasts, all of them. I might call out Fairfield for the way he looked at you."

Never had a man looked at her in any lascivious way, including Lord Robert Fairfield. Hugh was being silly. Still, it sent a shower of sparks through her that he would say it. "I hope you won't," she told him. "He asked me to save him a dance later in the evening."

Her husband looked annoyed. "He can be disappointed. I want you." He whispered the last, intense and urgent.

Eliza flushed hot from head to toe. "Hugh!"

"I want to make you say my name all night long," he breathed, as proper as anything except for the wicked things he was saying as they walked back into the ballroom. "I want to make you moan it, and scream it, and beg me to—"

"Stop!" Scarlet-faced, she poked him with her fan.

"You won't say that once I get you into bed," he went on in that wicked black velvet tone.

Eliza knew. Even when he shocked her, she never wanted him to stop adoring her, wanting her, loving her. But now she would have to smile and dance with someone else while thinking about all the delicious ways Hugh would make love to her when they got home. "I'll never make it through the next dance," she said in a suffocated voice.

"How fortunate your next partner is me." He sent a speaking look at the approaching Lord Carrington, to whom she had promised the first dance after supper, and his friend obligingly spun on his heel and walked away.

Eliza gaped even as her heart leapt. "What are you doing?"

"It's quite simple." He stopped, trapping her hand with his own, on his arm. "I've discovered I don't like to share my wife."

"It's only a dance," she said.

He pulled her to him as the musicians began tuning their instruments. The next dance was to be a waltz. "It's not merely a dance," he said, suddenly serious. "It's a chance to hold you close, to feel you move in my arms. A chance for all of London to behold my good fortune in being your husband. A chance to make you smile, because you love to dance. I wouldn't want to miss a moment of that."

It was not possible to love someone more than she loved him at that moment. "No," she whispered, gazing into his dark eyes. She didn't want to miss a moment with him, either.

The music began. Hugh took her hand and held her indecently close as they danced. Eliza felt as light as a feather, as if she floated above the floor in his arms. Hugh's attention never wavered from her, and the knowing little smile on his face made it seem as though the two of them were alone in the room. They might as well have been; Eliza barely registered the guests around her.

"Do you know," she said shyly, "the first time you danced with me was the moment I began to fall in love with you?"

"Was it?" Interest lit his face. "At Thayne's ball."

She nodded. "No one else asked me to dance that night." Oh dear—that made her sound rather pathetic. "Papa and I didn't know anyone there," she hastily added. "It was beautiful, but I expected to stand at the side of the room all night until you appeared."

His jaw tightened. "You should never spend all night at the side of the room."

"I didn't mind." She smiled at him. "In truth, I didn't really want to dance with anyone else."

A vaguely satisfied expression crossed his face. "No?"

"I danced with enough gentlemen during my Season to know why they wanted to dance with me. I would have rather stood at the side of the room." Once it would have been mortifying to admit to anyone that men only danced with her because they were after her father's fortune. Now it seemed as though those awkward dances and balls had been the hour before the dawn, when her hopes of a happily married future were dimmest. But tonight, when all her dreams had been realized and then some, every lonely evening was worth it.

Hugh frowned. "Why did they want to dance with you?"

She blushed. There was that forbidden topic again, money. "It was not for my charm or beauty," she said. "Although I never had much of either, so perhaps I should be grateful you don't seem to mind."

He didn't say anything for a moment. "Only those who know you can appreciate how much charm and beauty you've got."

Or are too kind to say otherwise, she thought, but did not say. Even so, his words brought a warm glow to her skin unrelated to the exertion of dancing. "But you didn't know me then," she pointed out. "You still asked me to dance, not once but twice."

"And that won your heart?" He asked it almost warily.

"Well." Eliza averted her eyes, knowing her face was red. "You also kissed me . . ."

Hugh said nothing. When she finally glanced up, wondering if she'd said something wrong, he was watching her with shadowed, almost brooding eyes. "I did kiss you. That was the moment I knew I would marry you."

Her lips parted in astonished delight.

His expression eased. A sensual smile curved his lips. "Subject to your agreement, of course. I was inexpressibly relieved when you said yes."

As if she would have said no. As if a girl like her might have turned down an earl like him, even if she hadn't been madly in love and scandalously attracted to him. "Did you ever doubt I would accept?"

His smile faded. "I don't want to take you for granted."

Her throat felt tight. She had always been the quiet girl at the side of the room, the one who giggled from nerves and never said anything witty. No other man had ever complimented her beauty or her charm, or even suggested she had any. But Hugh—oh, Hugh had caught her by surprise, taking the time to really look at her and see her heart, flattening her defenses before she had time to raise them. She could not have dreamed of a more perfect husband.

The waltz ended. Hugh's hands lingered on her. "Who else have you promised a dance to?" he murmured.

"Oh—Mr. Jennings, and Lord Edward Rivers, and . . . someone else," she said, flustered. "Why?"

"I feel very jealous tonight." He winked and finally released her, retaining her hand to walk from the floor with her by his side. "Would you like some champagne?" He led her to a quieter spot at the back of the room.

She gave an embarrassed laugh. "Do you know, I think I shall visit the ladies' retiring room first."

He grinned. "Of course. I'll fetch the champagne and find you when you return."

Chapter 26

ⓢ❧ⓢ

ELIZA MADE HER way through the crowded assembly rooms in search of the retiring room. She meant to apply a cool cloth to her forehead and let her rioting emotions calm down. If she had been raised as a lady of the *ton*, surely she would be able to feel this much and not let it make her knees weak and her heart race. Plain, shy Eliza Cross wanted to have a cup of tea in some quiet corner and marvel at what her life had become, but the Countess of Hastings needed to compose herself and glide back into the ballroom, ready for her husband's hot, passionate glances and still able to dance and converse with aplomb.

But the retiring room was as crowded as the ballroom. One young lady had torn her gown, and was sobbing in dismay as two maids fussed over it. In the back of the room, three matrons sat together chatting comfortably; one of them had her foot elevated on a hassock. Several other ladies were occupied with maids fixing their hair and blotting their brows, and there was almost as much noise as in the ballroom. Eliza got her own cool cloth and dabbed at her face. Her eyes were bright and her color was high, and her lips were set in a permanent happy curve. She smiled at her reflection in the mirror. She looked like what she was: a woman in love.

When she went back into the ballroom, it was even more crowded. Jostled from the left by a group of dandies, squeezing past a clutch of giggling young girls in white, she tried to find Hugh. There were so many tall, dark-haired men in black jackets and breeches, it was not easy to spot him. But there he was, all the way across the room, on the other side of the dancers. He was talking to a beaming Henrietta and a handsome young man who held her hand on his arm. The dowager countess stood beside her daughter, smiling graciously. It looked for all the world as though the young man was asking Hugh's permission to call on Henrietta. Eliza almost gasped aloud in delight at the thought.

She was halfway to his side when someone said her name. She turned to see a man she did not know, bowing low.

"I hope you'll grant me pardon for introducing myself, Lady Hastings," he said. "Sir Richard Nesbit, at your service. I wanted to offer my congratulations."

Eliza felt very self-conscious. "For what, sir?"

"On your marriage. I knew your husband's late father very well, and I've watched Hastings grow from a small boy." He winked at her, with a roguish smile.

"Oh." Eliza relaxed and even smiled back at

him. An old friend of the family. "How kind of you, Sir Richard. Thank you."

"Old Hastings—your father-in-law, as would have been—was a great man, a capital fellow. He'd be pleased as anything to see his son married so advantageously."

Eliza hesitated, suddenly uneasy. No one would have called her a splendid catch; she was not eligible or beautiful or any of the things that made girls advantageous matches . . . except for one thing . . . Remembering Georgiana's advice, she straightened her spine and replied formally, "I'm sure I don't understand, sir."

He laughed. "You do, you do. Your father was set upon it, wasn't he? He must be pleased to see his plans come to such fruition."

The smile was completely gone from her lips. Eliza stared at him, stony-faced, and said nothing.

Sir Richard was not deterred. He leaned closer. "You understand now—yes, you do! He made a great match for you, and I can't say I blame him. Hastings would have been the catch of the Season, if he hadn't been drowning in debt—almost one foot in the Fleet. I'll grant Edward Cross this—he never misses an opportunity. An old title, a decent young man, and all for a mere six percent premium." He shook his head, still grinning broadly.

"What do you mean?" Eliza heard her own voice, and it sounded alien and loud. "What are you accusing my father of?"

"Accusing!" Sir Richard snorted. "He did it! I know, I sold him an old debt myself. Never thought

I'd see a farthing of it, after young Hastings told me he hadn't a feather to fly with and wouldn't pay any but the most pressing of his father's notes. Well, of course I sold it to Cross! Everyone did. He bought up every promissory note and debt of honor Hastings owed. What other choice did the boy have then, but to wed the man's only daughter?" He chuckled again. "Cross bought him for you, and a fine bargain he made, eh? A countess!"

The music and the conversation around her blended into a dull roar. Eliza felt numb. She wanted to call Sir Richard a liar, she wanted to slap her hands over her ears and run away, she wanted to stop thinking that his words made so much sense. A handsome, eligible earl. A sudden business dealing with her father, when Papa rarely did business with noblemen directly. So many calls and visits when Papa was away. Papa's insistence that an earl could marry a girl like her if he wanted to.

In front of her, Sir Richard said something excusing himself. Still smiling like a cat who'd found the cream pot, he bowed and walked away. Eliza watched him go, frozen in shock and mounting horror.

The slightly shabby house, unfit for an earl's household. The lack of funds for new draperies. The way Hugh appeared at the theater, after Papa maneuvered to keep her from inviting Georgiana. The dowager's coolness to her—Henrietta's and Edith's disdain—even the way he seduced her so soon after proposing, ensuring she couldn't change her mind.

Eliza covered her mouth with one hand as every kiss, every touch, every seemingly besotted act flashed through her mind in new and sinister colors. Had her father bought him? Papa had teased and teased about finding a penniless nobleman to marry her. But she hadn't thought Hugh was penniless—it had lulled her into thinking he must actually care for her.

Had it all been a lie?

"Eliza!" Edith touched her arm. Her bright smile faded when Eliza jerked and almost recoiled from her hand. "Are you unwell?" the girl asked in concern.

"No, I . . ." Eliza pressed her hands to her temples. Could it be true? "What did you want, Edith?"

"Mama sent me to find you," said her sister-in-law. Some of her excitement returned. "Lord William Parker-Jones has asked permission to call upon Henrietta. Mama wants to present him to you."

Papa had always been a speculator. She'd had to tell him not to interfere in her marriage. He asked about grandchildren every time he came to visit—always when Hugh, as well as his mother and sisters, was away from the house. Was that coincidence? Hugh had hardly said one word about Papa since their wedding, despite being so involved in business with him before the wedding that he had to come to Greenwich several times.

Could it be true? Was everything about her marriage a lie?

"Eliza?" asked Edith in concern. "You look ghastly. Let me fetch Hugh."

"No!" She seized Edith's wrist. "No—I—I have a headache. Absolutely splitting, I'm afraid. Can—will you help me go home?"

"Oh no, let me fetch Hugh to take you," the girl began.

Eliza squeezed her wrist. "No, no—I can't wait." The other girl stared at her in alarm, her blue eyes as round as saucers. Eliza tried to smile. "I don't want to ruin everyone's evening," she said. "Not when Henrietta has such happy news. Please just . . . tell them I went home. I'm sure I'll be fine after a cup of tea and some rest."

"I really think—"

"Edith!" She squeezed again, harder. "Please help me. I want the carriage."

"Hugh will take you home," whispered the girl, now looking frightened.

Eliza did not want Hugh, not now. If she saw him now, she would say something she might regret later—or worse, something she regretted immediately. If she let Edith go, the girl would run to tell him. "Walk with me, please," she said to Edith. "Then you may go tell Hugh. I need to go home."

Edith slowly nodded. Eliza exhaled in relief, but when she took a step toward the door, she nearly fell. She had been standing so stiffly, her knees almost buckled when she tried to walk. With a startled exclamation, Edith threw her arm around Eliza's waist and supported her. "My goodness, Eliza, are you certain you can make it home?"

"There's nowhere to lie down here," Eliza said.

"The retiring room—"

"It's so crowded and noisy in there, it will make my head ache even worse." She fixed her eyes on the arched doorway, flanked by pilasters festooned with swags of ivy and silk flowers. Lady Montgomery had spared no expense tonight. Just like Hugh, once he had her dowry funds. Once Papa had paid all his debts.

Edith said nothing more until they reached the vestibule. Then she asked a servant to summon the Hastings carriage, and sent another to find Eliza's cloak.

"Stay with me," Eliza said, a fine tremor in her voice.

"I will," promised Edith, sounding worried. "I can send one of the footmen for a doctor—"

"I don't think that's necessary." She looked at Edith, who had hated her so much and been jilted because of her, and who now looked so concerned for her. Did Edith know? Eliza released the girl's arm and mustered a smile. "It's only a headache. I'm not used to balls, you know—I danced too much, and it's so loud. I just need to go home. You'll let Hugh know, won't you?"

A wide, relieved smile broke out on Edith's face. "Of course! I—I almost thought you didn't want me to tell him, for a moment. But that was silly, wasn't it? He'll be right behind you, you know, no matter what I tell him." She laughed sheepishly, shaking her head as if she'd been silly. "I could tell him you lost a shoe buckle and he'd follow you home. He's as devoted as a puppy."

A puppy. If Sir Richard was right, Hugh had been lying to her almost from the moment they met.

Eliza stepped into the carriage and sank into the seat. She waved at Edith, watching from the steps, and the girl waved back, smiling again. "Be well," Edith called as the driver set the horses in motion. "Finch, drive slowly," she added to the coachman.

Eliza let the swaying of the carriage rock her from side to side; she didn't want to think or feel at the moment. Perhaps it was all wrong. Perhaps Sir Richard was a liar, or had misunderstood what Papa intended in buying his note from Hugh's father. Perhaps Hugh didn't even know Papa had bought the debt. She'd never heard Hugh or any of his family mention Sir Richard, for all the man's claims to being an old friend. The shock of his charge had made her flee, but perhaps once she had some space, some time to think about it, a sensible explanation would come to her.

But he had planted a seed that had already sprouted a vile vine, thorny and malignant, and the only way to kill it was to dig it out, roots and all.

It took no time at all to return to St. James's Street. Wilkins was surprised to see her again, and alone, but she told him she had a headache. Mary hurried off to prepare a soothing cup of tea, and Eliza went to her room.

Willy jumped up and barked eagerly at her appearance. Angus must have gone to bed if Willy was already in his basket by her hearth. Eliza's heart softened at the sight of him; her dog was only allowed into her bedroom at night, spending the rest of the day out with Angus. She went down on her knees and Willy flung himself at her, licking her face wildly until she had to laugh.

"What should I believe, Willy?" she whispered, resting her face in his soft black-and-white fur. "Would Papa do such a thing?"

Willy sat back and regarded her quizzically, his tongue hanging out. He woofed at her. "You're right," she said softly, hating every word. "He would. But would Hugh cooperate with such a scheme?"

The dog licked her face again. He didn't know, either.

She thought of Hugh, her husband, who declared he wanted her to himself for a day and took her to Primrose Hill. Who made love to her and told her he loved her. Could that man have been lying to her? She closed her eyes and remembered their first waltz, when he had taken her out into the mist on Lady Thayne's terrace and kissed her so passionately, like a lover. He had wanted her then; she vividly recalled the feel of his aroused body against hers . . .

But wanting was not the same as loving. And he hadn't said he loved her, or even cared for her, until well after they were wed.

Perhaps he hadn't loved her when he proposed but had fallen in love with her since. Even if it began as an untruth, it was real now. Eliza wanted desperately to believe that her husband's avowals of love had not been lies, or at least not complete lies. She could pardon old lies, she thought wildly, as long as he'd meant it when he said he loved her tonight . . .

But if she believed Papa could have bought all of Hugh's debts and forced him to marry her, it was hard to believe Hugh would have forgiven that so easily and quickly.

As if in a trance, Eliza got to her feet and picked up a lamp. Willy followed her across the room, his tail wagging, and she didn't tell him to stay. She opened the door and went down the corridor, meeting Mary with a tray in her hands.

"I've brought your tea, my lady," said her startled maid. "Do you not want it in your room?"

"Hmm? Oh yes, in my room will be lovely, Mary." Eliza smiled absently. "I'm just going to get a book from His Lordship's study."

She had seen Hugh in his study at his desk. He kept the ledgers himself. If his debts had been as enormous as Sir Richard said they were, Hugh must have made payments on them, and they would be recorded in the ledgers. She would just look at them. If there were no debts, she would know Sir Richard had lied to her. There would be no need to confront Papa or Hugh about anything. She would be quietly resting in bed, sipping her tea, when her devoted husband came to check on her.

The study was dark and hushed, making her feel like a criminal breaking in with nefarious intent. She put the lamp down on the desk. Where were the ledgers? The bookcase seemed an obvious place; she scanned the shelves and found several ledgers. They were all neatly kept, and all for past years. Only one was in handwriting she recognized as Hugh's, and she set it on the desk.

It took a few minutes to decipher his notation. She had kept the household accounts at Greenwich, but the dowager countess still held the books here. Eliza was not accustomed to the scope of an earl's estate, but she began to make it out. There were payments to servants, bills from the modiste, the butcher, the farrier. Eliza flipped the pages, scanning as quickly as she could.

The first one made her blink; mortgage on Rosemere. It was a large amount. Henrietta had told her Rosemere was let to tenants, which was a great pity because they all loved Cornwall dearly. There was a mortgage on another property as well—Norcross Hall, the Hastings seat in Essex. Now that she knew what to look for, the debts began leaping out at her. Eliza's lips moved silently as she tried to add up the amounts paid and guess at the underlying debt. She gave up when the amount climbed over thirty thousand pounds.

Willy put his head in her lap and she stroked his head, staring blindly at the pages in front of her.

Well, plenty of estates were mortgaged. Georgiana said her brother was always writing to his bankers, negotiating new loans. Just because Hugh had debt didn't mean he was in trouble. The wealthiest peers had incomes of tens of thousands of pounds a year, more than sufficient to pay their mortgages. If that were true, though, the income must be recorded somewhere else.

"I need the current ledger," she whispered.

Willy cocked his head and she gave him a decisive nod. "Yes. If everything continued on after our wedding as it had before, then it means our marriage changed nothing."

She was making excuses for him and she hated herself for it.

The current ledger was not on the shelves with the other ones. Eliza returned to the big leather chair and opened a drawer of the desk. Nothing. Another drawer; still nothing. The third drawer held a familiar book, and she took it out with trembling hands. As she did so, a packet came with it, and fell to the floor.

She recognized her father's handwriting first. It was only the word *Hastings*, written in Papa's jagged scrawl on the outer wrapping, but it made her flinch. Slowly she unfolded the paper to see what her father had given Hugh. It might be a commendation to his boot maker, or a list of fine wines . . .

Paid in Full, read the top paper, a promissory note for two thousand pounds. *Paid in Full*, scrawled across a large bill from the carriage maker. *Paid*, on a summary of charges from the wine merchant. *Satisfied in Entirety*, across a deed for the property in Essex.

Eliza's hand was over her mouth. *Paid in Full*. *Paid in Full*. Every page of the packet, dozens of bills and loans and promissory notes, all marked paid. She let them slide through her fingers, a flurry of damning proof that her father had bought Hugh's debts just as Sir Richard Nesbit said. Feverishly she opened the current ledger, praying that there would be a notation indicating that Hugh was repaying her father, that perhaps Papa had done it as a token of kindness to his future son-in-law.

There was none. She did see clear annotations of some of her dowry funds, put into different accounts. Hugh tracked everything, down to the farthing. But there were no payments on any loan or mortgage since Hugh had come to call at Greenwich.

And Eliza knew, to her very bones, that Nesbit had told her the truth.

Chapter 27

HUGH WAS BEGINNING to wonder where Eliza had gone.

The ladies' retiring room, she'd said. With two sisters, Hugh knew that could lead to a long delay, so he was not surprised when she didn't return quickly. He greeted friends, refilled his glass of wine, and managed to avoid coming face-to-face with Lord Livingston, who was holding court in a far corner of the room.

Henrietta found him, with a tall young fellow at her side. Hugh knew William Parker-Jones, youngest son of the Marquess of Downes, but it still gave him a start to hear the fellow ask permission to call upon Henrietta. His sister glowed every time Lord William glanced her way, and Hugh realized his youngest sister was not a girl anymore.

"I see from Henrietta's expression I must say yes," he told the young man. "But I must also tell you that I am determined she shall make her debut and have a Season next year."

"Of course," said Lord William warmly. "I

never meant to prevent it." He stole a glance at Henrietta, pink-cheeked and beaming. "I might hope to steal a march on all those other fellows who will be sure to ask your permission next year, though."

Hugh chuckled. "You can do your best. Henrietta will decide more than I whether you succeed."

The dowager countess joined them, and Henrietta shared her happy news. Rose exclaimed in delight, and they talked for a while. Edith came by and was presented to her sister's new suitor, but slipped away when her mother murmured something to her. When Lord William left to go inform his own mother, Rose sent her regards to the marchioness.

"Henrietta, my darling, how lovely. He's a charming boy, of such good family." Rose squeezed her daughter's hand.

"Are you truly pleased, Mama? Do you approve?" Without waiting for an answer, she spun to Hugh. "Did you mean what you said, Hugh—that I shall have my choice?"

"Why wouldn't I?" he asked in pretend affront. "Do you intend to choose badly?"

She laughed, but sobered quickly. "No! It's only . . . a very novel thought, that gentlemen will be calling on me and courting me and trying to make love to me. It all looked so exciting and romantic when it was Edith, and I did almost die of envy, but now . . . You will tell me if you think I'm making a mistake, won't you?"

Like Benwick, she meant. "I will," he promised. "I want to see you happy."

She sighed, her smile returning. "Where is Eliza? I cannot wait to tell her."

"I don't know." Hugh raised his head and scanned the room. He didn't see her, and she'd been gone quite a while. Off across the room, he spied Lord Livingston in conversation with his son and Sir Richard Nesbit. The viscount was facing him, and when Hugh glanced his way, their eyes met. Livingston's lip curled, and he raised his glass in mocking salute. Hugh scowled and looked away.

"I sent Edith to fetch Eliza," said his mother. "I wanted to present Lord William to her. I wonder why she's taking so long."

Hugh frowned. He couldn't see Edith, either. Perhaps they were both in the retiring room, but that suggested Eliza was unwell. It must be half an hour since she'd left. "I'll find them," he told his mother and sister, and set off through the crowd.

He met Edith in the arched doorway of the room. "Oh, Hugh, there you are," she exclaimed in patent relief. "Eliza asked me to find you."

"What's wrong?" He was instantly concerned. She'd been fine when she left. "Where is she?"

"She went home in the carriage."

"What?"

Edith put up her hands at his sharp question. "I wanted to find you, but she insisted on going immediately. Finch will take her home safely, so I let her go."

"Why did she want to leave?" he demanded. By God, if Livingston had said something to her . . .

"She said she had a headache, that it was so loud in here and she had danced too much."

Hugh's frown deepened. That was possible, but seemed very unlike Eliza. "Did she seem very ill?"

Edith hesitated, then confessed, "Yes. Or perhaps not ill, but very odd. She had a distant look, and I don't think she paid attention to half of what I said to her. I believe she had something else on her mind. She looked almost dazed."

God damn it. Rage, hot and violent, shot through him. It must have been Livingston or Benwick, the spineless little toad. He thought of Livingston's malicious smirk. They were retaliating for Eliza's set-down to Benwick, or perhaps his mother's drawing room campaign to defend her. "I'm going home to make certain she's well."

Edith grinned. "I told her you would."

He took Edith back to their mother and told her he would send the carriage back for them. "Of course, dear," she said. "But Hugh . . ." She pulled him a step away from his sisters. "Be gentle," she admonished. "There may be a very good reason for her abrupt departure."

"I'm sure there is, Mother," he said. "Eliza's not rash or impulsive."

"No." She lifted one brow. "A *very* good reason. When a newly married lady suddenly takes ill . . ." She made a delicate gesture with one hand. "Be gentle," she said again, beginning to smile.

His jaw dropped. But of course—he should have thought of that. His tension subsided, re-

placed by a dazed wonder. Could Eliza be with
child? He would have preferred that she tell him
herself, but his mother had borne children and he
had not; surely she would know what she spoke
of, urging him to be gentle and understanding.
"I will be," he promised his mother, and headed
for the door again, this time plowing through the
crowd impatiently.

He didn't bother to wait for someone to see
if Finch had returned with the carriage. He left
instructions for his driver when he returned and
set off on foot. It wasn't far, and would be faster
to walk, with the street clogged by carriages. He
hoped Eliza had gone home for a happy reason;
a child! And so soon after their marriage. Perhaps it *had* been Livingston, but his steps sped
up as he imagined Eliza pregnant. Holding their
child in her arms, singing softly. A dark-haired
son. A little girl with wide green eyes and a shy
smile.

"Where is Lady Hastings?" he asked the butler as he walked through the front door, already
peeling off his coat and gloves.

Wilkins bowed. "She retired to her room, my
lord."

Hugh was halfway up the stairs. "Excellent."
Should he send for a doctor to examine her? He
ought to have asked his mother. He grinned, taking the final steps two at a time. He ought to ask
Eliza.

But she was not in the room. Mary, her maid,
was there, arranging a pot of tea and accoutre-

ments on the table near the fireplace. "Lady Hastings?" he asked, a touch impatiently. Surely she should be in bed.

"She said she wanted to fetch a book from your study, my lord," said the girl.

Hugh paused. His study? "Very good," he said, but his enthusiasm had suffered a sudden chill. Why would Eliza go there for a book? The library was small but had a fine selection of novels, thanks to his mother and sisters. There was nothing half so entertaining in his study.

But when he pushed open the study door, she was not choosing a book. She sat in the chair behind his desk, her head bowed. Willy popped out from behind the desk at his entrance and loped across the room for a greeting. Hugh rubbed the dog's ears without looking away from her. "Eliza?"

Her head came up. Her face was ghostly white, and he came forward in sudden alarm, only to stop short as she lurched to her feet. "I am such a fool," she said thickly, bracing her arms on the desk.

He frowned. "No. What do you mean?"

For answer she opened her hand and scattered a handful of crumpled papers on the desk. Hugh's stomach dropped as he realized what they were.

"He bought them all, didn't he?" she said, appearing mesmerized by the debt notes, the word *Paid* standing out on one like the imprint of a cloven hoof.

In spite of himself Hugh's temper stirred

again. He should have burned those notes, true; but to find them she had gone through his desk. Eliza wasn't the sort to do that on a whim. Someone had told her. Was this what Livingston had done? But no—how could Livingston have known? "Yes," he said, more harshly than he intended.

She nodded, a stiff, jerky motion. "At least fifty thousand pounds."

"Close to eighty."

She flinched. "I never was good at sums." She raised her eyes to his. They were flat, almost empty. "That's a lot of money."

He said nothing. Who the bloody hell had told her? He hadn't told a soul—not his mother, not his solicitor, not a single friend. The only other person who knew the whole story was her father. Why on earth would Cross tell her, though? Especially now, when they were married until death parted them, when he'd fallen in love with her, and when she might be carrying his heir?

Was that it? Cross had been particularly keen to have contact with his grandchild. He must have noticed Hugh was not eager for that to happen. Perhaps this was a plot to separate them—

Hugh closed his eyes for a moment. That wasn't it. He'd become so attached to the idea of a child, in just the time it took him to walk home, that he'd begun to believe it was true. But Eliza hadn't come home because pregnancy made her ill; there probably was no child. She'd left the ball because she wanted to search his desk.

His wife straightened her shoulders. Her mouth

pulled down at the sides and she looked miserable for a moment. Then she took a deep breath and faced him, her chin high and her eyes beginning to blaze. "Was it all a lie?"

His mouth twisted cynically. "Ask your father."

Her chest heaved. "Was there ever ore on your Cornish property?"

Hugh hesitated, but what was the point of lying now? She clearly knew, from the tone of her questions. The only one who could have told her everything was Cross, or someone Cross had told, and if her own father had broken the vow of silence he extorted from Hugh, there was no reason he shouldn't answer her. "Not that I know of."

"Did you really mean to allow him to dig it up on the chance there was?"

"No."

"Was it chance when we met at the theater, and the Thayne ball?"

"No."

She quivered as if struck. "Did you know my father would be away when you called in Greenwich?"

"Often. Yes."

Her chin went up and down, nodding faintly as he confirmed everything she probably already knew. "Would you have ever come to Greenwich if my father hadn't done this?" She waved at the debts.

Unexpectedly frustration and anger rolled over him again, as fresh as the first time he'd gone to Cross's house, tense with dread and anxiety about why the man had bought every debt he owed. When Cross had let him know that he had Hugh hooked like a trout—no matter how hard he wriggled, the barb was in deep and wouldn't be dislodged. "No," he said in a clipped tone.

A tear slid down her cheek. "Was everything a lie?"

"A lie? No." His gaze tracked down her figure, over her plump, soft breasts, her slender waist, the curve of her hips, back to her face, which had become so beautiful and so dear to him. "When I kissed you it was not a lie. When I made love to you, it was not a lie."

"But not because you cared for me, not then."

His hands were in fists. *No more lies.* "Not the way I do now."

"Now?" She snatched up the balled-up debts and threw them at him. "You expect I'll believe anything, don't you? You let me believe you cared for me—even loved me!"

"I never said it," he pointed out, "until I meant it."

"No," she said bitterly. "You never said it. You paid compliments to turn my head so I wouldn't realize the truth. You sent me bloody *flowers*, and like an idiot I fell for it. Your mother knew, didn't she? That's why she was so cool when I came to tea!" Her eyes widened. "You made her invite me, didn't you? Dazzle the awkward spinster so she'll fall desperately, stupidly in love."

Hugh flinched. That was exactly what he'd done. "I am sorry for that."

"I never expected a man would fall in love with

me and be swept away by passion," she said in a slightly calmer voice. "I should have known. It was too good to be real."

"But it is real," he said in a low voice. "Now."

"Now. *Now.*" She was crying, tears sliding down her cheeks. "Why should I believe that? Is Papa dangling some other enticement in front of you now?"

His temper broke. Hugh knew he deserved her wrath, but her father—her beloved papa—was the one who had caused the whole thing, and she'd said not one word against him. "You should ask him," he lashed out. "Ask your dear papa why he did it. Ask him what conditions he put upon the bargain he offered me—that I not tell you, that I court you properly, that I win your heart—conditions I had no way to counter, since he owned enough debt to ruin me and my family. And before you protest that he wouldn't have done such a thing," he added in a near-snarl, as she opened her mouth in outrage, "he said he'd set the bailiffs on me if I breathed a word of his plan to you. Do you envy my choice? Go to prison, or court a girl." They stared at each other, Eliza white-faced and infuriated and Hugh breathing violently. "I only agreed to it because you didn't know," he said, some of his fury spent. "You were kind and lovely, and I thought there was a chance . . ."

"A chance I would be gullible enough to fall for it?"

A chance he would come to care for her. God alone knew how well that chance had paid off.

He loved her to distraction. But now she was staring at him with revulsion, and a little piece of his heart died. As she'd said: it was too good to be real. "A chance we would be happy together," he said quietly. "Go ask your father." He turned on his heel and left.

Chapter 28

❧❧❧

Eliza stood gasping in shock as her husband walked away from her. He hadn't denied a thing. His footsteps sounded like shots as he walked away, until the distant slam of the door told her he'd left the house.

Willy nudged her hand and whined. Eliza started, and reached down to comfort her dog without thinking.

Dear God. It was all true. Papa had coerced Hugh to court her and marry her. Even if he did care for her now, it had all been a lie. She'd been duped, conned, swindled, made a perfect fool.

By her own father.

She didn't consciously start moving, but somehow she went up the stairs to her bedchamber, Willy at her heels, and rang for Mary. When the girl appeared, Eliza was sitting at her dressing table, pulling the pins from her hair. "Fetch my blue serge," she said.

"Now?" the maid blurted in astonishment. "I thought you were unwell, my lady . . ."

"I'm perfectly well." Aside from a brutal wound to her heart. "Bring the dress. I'm going out."

"But . . ." Mary's protest faded under a quelling look from Eliza. "Did the tea not please you?" she ventured.

Eliza hadn't touched it. "There's nothing wrong with the tea. You may bring it here." Mary scurried over with the tray and poured the cup. "Please just brush out my hair and pin it up as usual."

She could see her maid in the mirror. Mary was confused and upset as she ran the brush through Eliza's hair, taking down the soft twists and pinned-up tendrils that had looked so lovely earlier. "Don't be alarmed, Mary," she said, reaching for the tea. "I have to go somewhere, and wish to travel more comfortably."

"So late, madam?" Mary coiled her hair into the chignon she wore every day.

"I have to go at once," she softly replied. She couldn't sleep in her bed—Hugh's bed—without knowing exactly what her father had done. Had Hugh exaggerated? Had he told her everything, or was there worse to come?

Most of all, though, she wanted to know *why* her father would do such a thing to her. How many times had he told her it was just the two of them? How many times had he promised to protect her always, never to hurt her, even when her hurts were as trivial as a broken stem of the flowers she picked? Could he really have stolen her choice of husband, forced Hugh to deceive her, and set her up to look like the stupidest girl in Britain? Her heart hurt until she thought it might rupture.

Clothed in her sturdy blue dress, no longer in silk and jewels, she went down and sent the footman out to hire a hackney.

"My lady?" he asked uncertainly.

She forced a smile. "I must go tonight, Thomas. And you know Finch is still waiting on the ladies at the ball. He won't be home for hours."

There was one good thing about being a countess; the servants didn't dare argue with her. Thomas nodded and put on his cap to go get a carriage.

How desperately she wished Sophie or Georgiana were here. They had always been the leaders, always brave and bold. They would know what to do, and be decisive and clever about doing it. But Sophie was at Chiswick, rusticating in the country with her honestly devoted husband, and Georgiana was still at the Montgomery ball, no doubt dancing in Lord Sterling's arms at this moment, blissfully certain of his love. She had been that way herself, just hours ago. In anguish, she dashed off a note to Georgiana and told Wilkins to have it delivered first thing in the morning. Depending how things went, she might need a friend.

The carriage arrived. Thomas helped her in, and Eliza instructed the driver to take her to Greenwich. She meant to get the truth from her father.

HUGH STRODE INTO THE Vega Club still seething.

How quickly and cataclysmically one's life could change, he thought furiously. In the space of a few minutes, he had fallen from his wife's favor and perhaps lost her love as well. Damn Cross and his loose tongue. Just when Hugh had made peace with what he'd done, realized how fortunate he'd been, and surrendered his heart to her, Eliza threw it all back in his face. And even if he deserved it, the tide of despair was black and thick and made him want to punch someone.

He ordered a large brandy. Normally he did not drink much at Vega's, but tonight it was necessary. He downed it without savoring or even tasting it, moodily watching a spirited round at the hazard table. Hazard was a fool's game. He never played a game so devoid of skill and strategy.

He was, however, a crack hand at other games.

Eighty thousand pounds. Cross had bought him for that sum. Hugh swished the last of his brandy and thought of what it would take to win that much. He didn't need to—he hadn't needed to gamble since he began courting Eliza. His accounts were flush now, thanks to her dowry and the release of any obligation to pay old debts. He'd begun putting plans into effect to raise the income from his estates, which was still shockingly low for an earl. It would take time to rebuild his estate to true prosperity, but it would have been impossible without Eliza.

But if he could repay Cross . . .

It would ameliorate the guilt of what he'd done. It was the only thing he could do to demonstrate to Eliza that her father's money might have motivated him in the beginning, but no longer. He put down his glass and moved toward the tables with no limit, where people played for the highest stakes, and found a place playing loo. Loo was his best game, and with no limit, one could make a fortune at it.

Of course, one could also lose, but this time Hugh did not mean to lose.

He started well. Luck was on his side tonight, ironically, and he racked up five thousand pounds in short order. At some point Robert Fairfield slid into the chair next to him. "Back at it, Hastings?" he asked as the cards were dealt again. "You've not been here in weeks."

Because he'd been trying to win Eliza. Hugh collected his cards. "I was busy."

Fairfield laughed. "Of course! Now you've got your bride settled, and can return to your old haunts."

He was only here because he couldn't be with her. It would take a long time to forget the expression on her face, shocked and disgusted and deeply hurt. Hugh tossed some markers into the pot for his ante. "You should only sit there if you came prepared to lose badly, Fairfield."

His friend roared with laughter and tossed in his own ante. "We'll see, we'll see!"

Hugh won almost three thousand pounds from him before his old schoolmate pushed back his chair. "You weren't joking with me," said Fairfield under his breath. "Absolutely vicious, Hastings."

"I look forward to playing with you again." Fairfield put up his hands in surrender and walked off, still laughing. Hugh studied his markers. Up nearly ten thousand. Normally he would consider it an evening well spent and go home. But it was only a fraction of what he needed.

"Fancy seeing you here again, Hastings," said a sly voice.

He looked up to see Robert Grenville taking Fairfield's seat. It took all his equanimity not to stand up and walk away. The last time he'd played with Grenville had been the disastrous night when he let thirteen thousand pounds slip through his fingers.

The same night, now that he thought about it, that Edward Cross had first approached him.

It did not inspire a warm or welcoming feeling in his chest. "Grenville," he said in barely civil greeting.

The other man laughed. "Come, you can't hold it against me. Our last game, I mean," he said as Hugh glanced sharply at him. Grenville leaned close and lowered his voice. "All's fair at Vega's tables, aye?"

Hugh had never thought anything else, and yet there was something about the man's tone that put him on guard. "Not everything, Grenville," he said with unusual hauteur. "A gentleman would know." He held up a hand, stopping the dealer from giving him cards. "Not this hand."

Grenville's face darkened. He took his cards and threw a handful of markers into the center of the table. "Lost your stomach for risk?"

"No," said Hugh evenly. "For the company."

Now the man openly scowled, although it disappeared soon. "No matter." He played, tossing the queen of spades onto the table and winning the trick. "For the right inducement, you'll sit at a table with anyone, just like the rest of us. Isn't that right?"

"No." Hugh lounged in his chair, spinning his brandy glass between his fingers. He hadn't drunk anything beyond the one glass when he'd stormed into the club, vibrating with anger and anguish over the confrontation with Eliza. He never drank when gambling. Now he watched Grenville, trying to decide if he hated the man because he'd won that night many weeks ago, or because he was an arrogant ass.

"No?" Grenville wore a queer little smile. "Perhaps not. Not since you've got your heiress and can afford to be fastidious again."

"Do not mention my wife," Hugh said, very quietly. His dislike of Grenville veered close to hatred when the man said her name.

Grenville threw down another card and won the round. "When I've known her all her life? I'll speak of her if I please, Lord Hastings."

His glass came to a stop. Hugh breathed through his nose. "All her life?"

"That's right." Grenville's smile turned smug and vindictive. "Such a sweet little girl she was. And grown into a very pleasant lady. Fit to be a countess." He laughed, but no one else did. "Her father always said so."

He could hear his own heartbeat, hard against his ribs. Grenville and Cross were friends. Of course. He'd never put it together. Cross had said something about never playing against Grenville, and Hugh had believed that meant he didn't care for the man—which was all wrong.

"You've known her all her life?" He tried to keep his tone even and only mildly curious. "I didn't know you were such a friend of the family."

Grenville faced him, no longer laughing or cynical. "I am," he said in subtle menace. "Cross and I go back for ages."

"I didn't know," murmured Hugh, as if taken aback by the coincidence. "Perhaps you could advise me. He and I have not hit it off."

"Advice?" Grenville looked him over with faint contempt. "Remember that he always plays to win. He never stops until he gets what he wants. Spare yourself the frustration and accommodate him."

Expressionless, Hugh said nothing. He sat forward in his chair and scraped up his collection of markers. It was clearly time to leave, with his nine thousand eight hundred pounds of blood money. Tomorrow he'd be back, alert to avoid Grenville, and he would play again. Just the thought of throwing the money in Cross's face had a motivating and soothing effect on his mind.

The play at the table was growing animated. The chap across from Hugh, Lord Talbot, exclaimed in disgust as he played. Grenville laughed, the sound menacing to Hugh's ears. Another man called for more wine, just like George Alderton had done many weeks ago, and told the servant to pour it for everyone at the table. A slim taciturn fellow named Southbridge made an unusually large opening bid, eliciting a curse from several players.

There was something off that Hugh couldn't put his finger on; he took his time gathering his winnings, watching the play. The hand ended, with Talbot having to pay the pot, which he did with an angry oath. It was an ordinary table of loo, with high stakes and crushing losses, until the cards were dealt again. The deal passed to Southbridge, and if Hugh hadn't been right next to Grenville he would have missed it: Southbridge gave him an extra card. And Grenville kept it, hiding it in his sleeve with such smooth ease Hugh realized he'd been expecting it.

He raised one hand, and a servant stepped up. "Fetch Dashwood," he murmured almost silently, naming the club owner. "Deal me in," he told Southbridge when the hand ended.

"Recovered your nerve?" asked Grenville with a smirk.

Hugh grinned lazily. "I have. I've never seen a poorer lot of players. It's foolish of me not to win some of your money." Everyone laughed as Southbridge dealt him cards, and play began. At some point Hugh saw, from the corner of his eye, Mr. Dashwood step up beside him, as silent as a ghost. Dashwood never interrupted play. He would stand there for half an hour, waiting until his patron chose to speak to him. Perfect.

During every hand, Hugh deliberately needled Grenville. It was not his usual habit, but tonight it came without effort. Grenville was not easily rattled, but Hugh took vengeful satisfaction in every annoyed glance and tightening of his mouth. And finally, in the last round of the hand, Grenville slipped. He shuffled his cards and reached for his wine, and his sleeve gaped for a moment.

"I say, Grenville," said Hugh, "it looks as though you've got a spare card in your cuff."

The other man froze for a bare second. "How dare you," he said with indignant offense. "It sounds as though you're calling me a cheat."

"I just remarked that you've got a card up your sleeve." Hugh raised one brow. "I suppose it's the extra one Southbridge dealt you."

Grenville inhaled loudly. Southbridge, who had as much charm as an owl, blinked. "I say, sir! That's too far."

Reclining in his chair, Hugh motioned at Grenville. "Look in his cuff. I can see the edge of it."

"That's a serious allegation, Lord Hastings," said Mr. Dashwood.

Hugh let his remaining cards fall to the table. "And if I'm wrong, you may banish me from your club." He glanced up at the owner. "But if I'm correct . . ."

Nicholas Dashwood was watching Robert Grenville, who sat in tense rage. "Would you turn out your cuffs, sir?"

Grenville's head went back. "If I decline?"

"I can also banish you from my club." Dashwood said it mildly, but there was steel in his tone.

Grenville rose. He gave his jacket a jerk, and withdrew the card from his sleeve. Lord Talbot swore in amazement under his breath. South-bridge's head sank on his shoulders.

"Don't bother," said Grenville coolly to Mr. Dashwood. He spun the card at Hugh. "I've had enough." He turned and strode out the door.

"Sir David," said Dashwood to Southbridge. "Did you deal him that card?"

The man shot a black look at Hugh. "I must have, without realizing my error."

Dashwood made a quiet noise in his throat, disbelieving. "See that you don't accidentally deal incorrectly again, sir."

Two spots of color burned in Southbridge's narrow face. "No."

With one more speaking look, Dashwood strolled away. His message had been heard; Southbridge would be watched closely from now on, and expelled at the slightest slip. Even worse, word would spread that he had cheated and got off. Almost in one motion, all the other players at the table except Hugh pushed back their chairs and left.

Southbridge leaned forward, spite shining in his eyes. "Fine work, Hastings."

"Spoiling a fixed game?" Hugh swept up his markers. "I take pride in it."

"Idiot," said Southbridge in contempt. "If any-one should have kept his mouth shut, it ought to be you."

Hugh just raised one brow in contempt.

Southbridge got to his feet. He smoothed one hand over his slicked-back hair. "You never saw

Grenville do it to you, I wager. Losing can leave a man open to other opportunities which far outstrip a paltry loss at the tables."

Hugh's hands slowed to a stop as the meaning sank in. Right. He might have guessed. "As you say," he said evenly, carefully, "it did work out to my benefit. I suppose Cross intended it that way."

Southbridge snorted. "It was more than you deserved. Ned Cross was a bigger fool than I thought when he chose you." He scooped up his markers and walked away.

He sat motionless as a statue. It was the final stroke, the only thing wanting in this miserable deception. Cross had set him up from the beginning, telling Grenville—and Alderton?—to ensure Hugh lost. What had the man said to him that first night? *Not every man knows how to face losing.* But Hugh did. Hugh kept his temper and lost honorably, even graciously, never thinking he'd been cheated, and in response Cross bought up all his debts and boxed him into a trap.

His chest hurt. Eliza couldn't have known this. He knew his wife, and she would never, ever approve of cheating, let alone cheating someone just to see how he handled a crushing loss.

And how the devil could Cross do such a thing? Sudden fury filled him. How dare that man think so little of his daughter that he felt it was necessary to break and trap and coerce a man to court her? Any sensible fellow would fall in love with her if only he spent a few days in her company. Cross could have filled his home with guests, taken a damn house in the middle of London and

let her find her own stride, even simply let her go
live with Lady Georgiana, where she would have
met any number of eligible men at her dazzling
friend's side. At least a few of them would have
been intelligent enough to discern Eliza's worth—
not in pounds sterling but in heart, in sense, in
joy, even in beauty, quiet and understated. The
urge to call Cross out burned in his chest.

And he'd told her to go ask her father. Hugh's
heart sank as he realized his mistake. He'd sent
her to the person who had caused all her pain,
but also the person least likely to tell her the
truth about what he'd done. The person who
openly admitted he was not a friend to Hugh,
who promised that if Hugh proved a poor husband, there was nothing he wouldn't do to settle
accounts.

He'd sent her right to the person who could
ruin his marriage and turn his wife against him
forever.

He strode through the salon. The early light of
dawn was just filtering through the windows in
the entrance hall. Forbes, the club manager, fell in
step with him. "I apologize for the difficulty you
had tonight, my lord—"

"Yes." He dumped his markers into the startled
manager's hands. "Credit these to my account. I
have to go to Greenwich."

Chapter 29

Eliza reached her father's house in Greenwich resolved to be calm and reasonable. There must be an explanation for everything.

It wasn't that she doubted Hugh. Why would he say those things to her if they weren't true? If put to the point of a knife, she would say that he did love her, now, just as he said. The hurt of hearing what he had done before, though, was too deep and too sharp to ignore. She had to know why and how and what her father had intended.

Papa. She gulped back a sob. How could he have done this to her?

The butler gaped at her in astonishment when he opened the door. "Miss Cross," he exclaimed. "I beg your pardon—Lady Hastings." He bowed.

"Never mind, Roberts." She let him take her cloak. "Is my father home?"

"No, ma'am, but he did say he would not be late."

It was already late. Eliza nodded. "I'll wait."

"Of course." He rushed to follow her to the

morning room, hastily lighting the lamps. "I shall tell him of your presence the moment he arrives."

"Thank you, Roberts." She smiled at the dear man, who had been butler here since she was a child.

"Shall I send for tea?"

Eliza knew the cook and kitchen maids would have gone to bed by now. "No, please don't wake Cook. I shall be fine."

"As you wish, ma'am." He bowed out, closing the door.

Eliza let out her breath. It felt strange to be here again, where she had once been so at home. In just a few weeks her sense of home had shifted, from her father's large elegant mansion to Hugh's house in St. James's Square, smaller and darker and desperately in need of renovation.

What choice did I have? echoed his voice in her mind. *Go to prison or court the girl.* He'd been forced to it, but he'd done it so gentlemanly. She remembered the soft brush of his hand against hers; the way he looked at her when he said he wanted to kiss her. He had waited for her encouragement at every turn. She wondered wildly what he would have done if she'd ever said no, turned him away and discouraged his attention.

A tear leaked from her eye. Hugh would have accepted it. She couldn't believe anything else, not after the way he tried so hard to shield his sister from heartbreak. Even more, the way he had tried to keep things from her. He had every reason to hate her father; a petty man would have told her everything the day after they were married, when there was nothing she could have done but despise both of them. Hugh, though . . . Hugh was kind and decent and passionate and he did fall in love with her. And she believed him.

A crunch of wheels on gravel sounded outside. She swiped at her eyes, not wanting to face her father as a teary-eyed mess. Within minutes the door burst open and Papa strode in, still wearing his greatcoat and hat with a deep scowl on his face.

"Eliza. What's wrong?" he demanded. "Why are you here?"

She backed away from the hands he reached out to lay on her shoulders. "I'm not ill," she said. "I discovered what you did."

"What?" Still frowning in concern, he took hold of her chin. "You look pale."

"I know," she repeated. "I know what you did."

His face went frighteningly still. She had never seen him look that way. "What did Hastings tell you?" he asked in a soft ominous voice.

No. It was not right to start with Hugh. She raised her chin. "Is it true you bought all of Hugh's debts so he would have no choice but to marry me?"

"Rubbish," said her father with scorn. "Who told you such a thing?"

"But I found the promissory notes," she replied. "I know you did it."

Papa paused, his expression inscrutable. "I did buy some of Hastings's debts. As speculation, nothing more."

"When?" She saw him hesitate again. "When

did you buy them, Papa? Before he came to call upon you here that first time? If you won't tell me, I shall call on every one of his creditors and ask them."

His fingers drummed against his thigh. "Before."

"Why?"

He sighed. "I took a chance, Lilibeth. He seemed a good fellow, and I thought, if he got to know you and you got to know him, you might take a liking to him."

"And what about his choice?" she exclaimed.

Papa threw up one hand, looking irked. "He had a choice! I never said he *must* marry you—never," he repeated firmly. "We . . . negotiated terms. If you turned him down, that would be that. In fact, he bargained for a sum of money in the event his suit was rejected. Hardly an innocent victim, if you ask me."

"What did he ask?" Eliza's heart felt hard and heavy, as if it would tear loose inside her chest.

"He wanted compensation if you turned him down. Ten thousand pounds, he demanded. Hefty compensation for a few calls, don't you think?"

Eliza couldn't breathe for a moment, and then realized why Hugh had wanted that. *Edith.* Mr. Benwick had been courting Edith and Hugh had needed a dowry for her, and quickly. Her knees almost gave out as she understood what her husband had done, not for himself but for his family. "It was no more than you deserved," she retorted to her father.

He sighed impatiently. "Of course! I expected it—I respected it. But don't let him tell you I forced him to everything."

She shook her head. "Papa. You know better. You bought all his debts and threatened to put the bailiffs on him. You coerced him, regardless of his feelings or interest. What if he'd been courting another lady?"

"I made certain he was not."

She stared at her parent, once more at a loss for words. "*Papa.*"

He scowled again, the irate expression he got when someone refused to recognize the logic of his position. "All I wanted was for you to have a look at someone. For someone—some highborn, decent fellow—to take a close look at you. I knew he'd see your worth, just as I thought you might take a fancy to him. You turned away all the chaps who came to call when you had your Season—"

"Because they only wanted your money!" she cried, aghast. "Most of them couldn't even remember my name!"

He waved it off. "And Hastings did. You told me just a few days ago that he made you happy. *Very* happy, you told me," he added as she gaped at him. "You might not approve of my methods, but I was right." He shrugged. "I think my speculation paid off handsomely."

Eliza could only stare in dumbfounded shock. "You told him he must court me properly," she whispered. "That he must win my heart, and never ever tell me that you'd manipulated him into doing it."

Her father's mouth twisted but he said nothing.

"What about my choice?" She clapped one fist to her breast. "What about my feelings?"

"You love him."

"But when I fell in love with him, he was only acting, on your orders." She put up one hand to stop his reply. "It was an arranged marriage, only I didn't know it. How could you do that to me?"

"Lilibeth," he said, "I wanted you to be happy. If left to yourself, you would have spent your entire life here, fussing over the rosebushes and coddling stray dogs. You needed something to pry you loose."

He might be right. Eliza had never wanted to face another London Season. But while she might be able to forgive her father for manipulating her into meeting a gentleman, it was much harder to forgive him on Hugh's behalf. Even deep in debt, Hugh had been an eligible match—blindingly handsome, charming and decent, in the prime of life and possessed of an old and illustrious title. He could have courted and married any number of heiresses or wealthy women in London.

"Perhaps," she said, choosing her words carefully, "you were right about me. I didn't know it disturbed you so terribly that I wasn't married. I took all your teasing about that as . . . well, as teasing. But you had no right, none at all, Papa, to do that to Hugh."

"He didn't come out too badly," muttered her father.

Eliza put her hands over her ears. "I don't want to hear another word! You lied to me, Papa. You tricked me and said nothing as I fell in love with a man who was only calling on me because you made him. Do you have any idea how stupid I feel? How mortified I felt when Richard Nesbit, a complete stranger, told me that you *bought* my husband for me?"

"Nesbit!" Her father's expression turned furious.

"He said he sold you some debt himself," she said, her voice trembling.

"That bloody scoundrel. He ought to know to keep his mouth closed. I'll deal with him, see if I don't," he vowed vengefully.

And Eliza gave up. He didn't see anything wrong with what he'd done. She had fallen in love with Hugh and Hugh had eventually fallen in love with her, so that made everything acceptable in his eyes. Even if they hadn't cared for each other, she would still be a married woman, a countess, and perhaps that's really all he wanted. There was a sharp pain in her chest, as if a deep fissure had split across her heart. "Good-bye, Papa," she said quietly. She walked by him and out the door.

"Lilibeth," he called, following. "Wait a moment. Eliza!"

She kept walking.

"Elizabeth," he said firmly. "Listen to me."

"I did," she retorted. "What you said offended me."

"But I meant well," he cajoled. "I only wanted to be a good father. Your mother would be appalled if I did nothing. What else was I to do?"

Eliza shook her head and walked on. The hack

she'd hired in London was still waiting, the driver drowsing on the box.

Her father strode past her and slapped one hand against the carriage door. "You're not going off in this," he said tersely. "What was Hastings thinking to let you take a ramshackle hired hack?"

Her breath shuddered in her lungs. "*I* chose it."

He grunted. "You'll let William take you home in the morning." He fished a guinea from his pocket and tossed it to the driver. "Go on, man."

Eliza wanted to scream at him. At least Hugh didn't overrule her every word. At least Hugh listened to what she said and respected her feelings. He, at least, had been honest with her when confronted.

"Come back inside," said her father, persuasive again. "Stay the night in your old room. In the morning you can shout at me some more, like your mother would have done, and I promise to take my scolding quietly."

She didn't want to, but she needed time to think. Without a word she went back into the house. Her father seemed to sense it was best not to speak, so he let her go in peace.

Back in her childhood room, Eliza paced restlessly. Who could advise her? Because she hadn't the slightest idea what to do. Even if her friends were here, what help would they be? Never had she wished more for her mother to be here still.

She sat on the bed and her eyes fell on the sampler she'd sewn at the age of ten. Her stitches had been so carefully placed. *This above all: to thine own self be true, And it must follow, as the night the day,*

Thou canst not then be false to any man. It had spoken to her young soul, and she'd chosen it over any number of Bible verses, with the help of the kind and patient headmistress at school.

She inhaled in discovery. Of course.

After a restless night's sleep, she rose at dawn and slipped quietly from the house. She did not want to shout at her father some more. She didn't want to speak to him at all right now. In the stable she roused William and asked him to prepare the traveling chaise. Within half an hour they were off, the house behind her quiet and still.

Chapter 30

By the time Hugh reached Greenwich, it was midmorning.

Eliza had not been at home in St. James's Square, quenching his hope of catching her. Mary, her maid, had been drowsing in the chair by the hearth, and when he woke her she could only stammer that her mistress had gone out the night before without saying where. She'd sent Thomas to hire a hackney carriage and left. Mary had fallen asleep waiting for her to return.

Hugh was not surprised she had gone to Greenwich. He'd told her to go, after all. He was unsettled that she had not come back yet. He gulped down a cup of coffee while his horse was brought around, and set out at once.

All the way down the river he thought about what he would say. Her father had coerced and lied to them both, but that was in the past. The present, and the future, did not need to be tainted by that. The sight of her shocked face, the tears in her eyes, had ripped aside the excuse he'd been hiding behind. Cross had required his vow of secrecy, but Hugh had known all along the truth might cost him dearly. And his response to that knowledge had been to double down on keeping the secret at all costs.

And as for who told her . . . It didn't really matter. He should have expected it to happen eventually and taken steps to inoculate himself. It had been in his power all along to tell her the truth, gently and calmly, and like a coward he had shied away from it. And now he was reaping the coward's bitter reward.

But when he arrived at Cross's Greenwich mansion, Eliza was not there, either.

"She left early this morning," Edward Cross said. He didn't look up at Hugh, only sat at the breakfast table, staring out the window and cradling a coffee cup in his hand.

"Where did she go?" Hugh demanded

Cross heaved a sigh. "I don't know." Finally he raised his moody gaze to meet Hugh's furious one. "Blasted Richard Nesbit told her about the debts."

Hugh's jaw clenched. That was what had pleased Livingston last night—he'd bet his last farthing the viscount had put Nesbit up to it, in retaliation for exposing Reggie Benwick's avarice. "Bugger him," he said rudely. "I don't care who told her, I only care to find her and see for myself that she's well."

"She was furious last night." Cross heaved himself out of his chair. "Called me a liar and a deceiver, and accused me of coercing you into loving her." He gave Hugh a belligerent look. "I never did that. Courting, yes, marriage, perhaps, but not of loving her. Don't you dare say I did!"

"No," Hugh bit out. "I fell in love with her because of Eliza herself. That's the only reason I never told her, you know. If she hadn't been who she is, I would have told her the day after the wedding and left you to her mercy."

Cross grunted. "And that was what she wanted! When she was a girl, she'd say to me, *Papa, I want someone to love me*. When she had her Season, she lamented that none of the young fellows seemed the sort to love someone. Too mad for gambling and carriage racing and drinking at their club! Well, she was right about them—a useless lot, most of the *ton*—so I decided to winnow the field. Find someone capable of love. Someone decent and honorable."

"Someone deeply in debt," Hugh couldn't help adding in a growl.

Cross waved one hand. "Leverage, nothing more. All I wanted was for you to take a look at her. If you did, I was sure you'd see how lovely and warm and wonderful my girl is . . ." He shrugged.

"Did you never think," Hugh began, "that if you had cultivated a different sort of acquaintance, or encouraged her to receive gentlemen who shared her interests—?"

"No." Cross slanted a defiant look at him. "I wanted a proper gentleman for her. She said all the fellows who came around were only after her dowry, so why shouldn't I make use of that?"

"I was never after her dowry," said Hugh between his teeth.

"I know. And that made you acceptable." Cross turned away, to stare out the window again. "It's the way things are, Hastings. Those without money want it; those with money want to get something of value in return."

"Is that why you told Robert Grenville to cheat at cards that night I played with him?"

Cross wheeled around. "What? How dare you. Of all the scurrilous—"

"Sir David Southbridge told me," bit out Hugh. "When he was caught scheming to help Grenville cheat again last night."

Cross looked startled. "That little—" He flung out one arm violently. "Both of them are capable of it, I suppose. But I never told him to do that. Never. I'm a businessman, not a cheat."

Hugh had heard enough. He turned and left without a word, although his fury died away as he rode back to London. He didn't care about Cross anymore. Where had Eliza gone? In desperation, he went to Lady Georgiana's house, where he found a disconcerting uproar. It seemed Lady Georgiana had snuck out after breakfast without leaving word. Her chaperone, the Countess of Sidlow, was apoplectic.

"That foolish, headstrong girl," she said, pacing the room. "I thought she'd gone to one of her friends in town, up in arms about something or other and wanting to put me out, but they all disclaim it. I don't know what I'll do now—that girl will be the death of me! I told Wakefield time and again that he needed to exert some control over her, and now you see, sir, this is his reward!" She shook her head in a fury. "And Lord Sterling will only put up with so many of her antics before he breaks the betrothal, and *then* where will she be? Oh, what a fool I was to agree to Wakefield's terms!"

Hugh thought the woman's concern should be for her charge, not her employer or herself, but he had a feeling Georgiana might have gone to Eliza—wherever she was. He murmured something vaguely reassuring and, at a loss for the moment, went home.

Mary, the maid, remembered under questioning that, yes, Eliza had written a note before she left. Wilkins added that he had sent it as directed, first thing that morning, to Lady Georgiana Lucas. Hugh was not surprised. It did not tell him where they'd gone, but at least she had a friend with her. In fact, he'd wager the Duchess of Ware was with them, as well.

He slumped in his study chair, letting his head fall back. He hadn't slept all night, had ridden to Greenwich and back, and was exhausted physically and emotionally. His eyes felt dry and unfocused. If his wife wanted to leave him, should he chase her down, or let her go? After the way they'd argued the night before, perhaps she never wanted to see him again.

"Hugh?"

He forced open his eyes. His mother stood in the study doorway, worried. His sisters peered around her. "May we come in, dear?"

He waved one hand, and she came in. She tried to close the door behind her, but Edith and Henrietta protested loudly. "Let them come," he said wearily. *No more lies.* Not to anyone.

"Is Eliza well?" asked his mother.

"Where is she?" Edith burst out. Her eyes were red. "I never should have let her leave alone last night, never! I am so sorry, Hugh!"

"I don't know where she is." He looked down at his hands. "I don't know if she'll come back."

Rose gasped. Henrietta's eyes were about to fall from her head. "What do you mean? Why wouldn't she?"

It took effort to lift his head. The three of them were so anxious, so concerned for Eliza—they who had objected violently to her from the start. All it took was Eliza's quiet charm, her open-hearted warmth, her determined desire to be friendly, and all three of them had fallen in love with her—just as he had done. "When I began courting Eliza, you all wondered why. Not the sort of girl you pictured for me," he said, looking at his mother. "Not the family connection you wanted," he added to his sisters. "Not even the girl I pictured for myself, in all honesty. But I had little choice in the matter, because I was almost bankrupt and Eliza is an heiress."

His mother's mouth fell open. "What? No—no, that can't be true. Your father—"

"Father left me little but debts and mortgages and delinquent loans. He spent his capital. He turned off most of the tenant farmers and converted profitable farmland into park and gardens." He glanced at each sister in turn. "He wagered and gave away and spent everything, including all the funds that should have been dowries for Edith and Henrietta."

Edith gasped. Rose looked like she might faint, both hands clutched to her throat. "I don't understand! He always promised me he would provide for us—for the girls, for you, for the estate, for me . . ."

"He lied." Hugh lifted one shoulder. "To everyone. I should have asked questions, but I never dreamt it could be so bad." He sighed as his mother stumbled into a chair, her face white. "Eliza's father wanted her to wed a gentleman. He decided I was a likely candidate, so he bought all the mortgages and debts of honor and unpaid bills . . . every scrap of paper Father ever signed pledging payment to anyone. I now owed Mr. Cross a fortune, and he made it clear to me that if I were to marry his daughter, all those debts would be forgiven. If I didn't marry her, well, he might have to call the bailiffs on me."

"That's blackmail!" burst out Henrietta.

Hugh stabbed one finger in the air as affirmation. He was beginning to feel a bit drunk from lack of sleep. "So you see, I really did have to court her. But she . . ." He sighed, remembering how Eliza's eyes had lit up when he called on her, how delighted she'd been even as she blushed in astonishment. "She was not what I expected. She was gentle, kind, sensible . . . She cut flowers from her own garden for her maid's sister's wedding. She's as unlike her father as anyone could be. And so even in the face of unified opposition, I married her." He paused. "I fell in love with her."

"But then . . . what happened?" whispered Edith. "I'm sorry, Hugh, for how I behaved toward her—toward you—"

He waved his hand. "I know, Edith. Someone told her at the ball last night. A dear old friend of Father's, actually. Sir Richard Nesbit."

"Nesbit!" His mother lurched out of her chair, furious. "That scoundrel! He was never your father's friend, such a putrid little mushroom of a man, *how dare he*!"

"He's vile," agreed Hugh.

"He . . . he's also a friend of Lord Livingston," said Edith, her voice quavering. "Mr. Benwick told me."

Hugh merely nodded at this confirmation of what he'd already guessed. "I don't know where Eliza's gone. I suspect she's with her friends, Lady Georgiana, and probably the Duchess of Ware as well. She sent a note to Lady Georgiana before she left last night."

"Is she coming back?" Henrietta cried. "What are you going to do, Hugh?"

He rubbed his eyes. They felt gritty. "I don't know." He was too tired and heartsick to think right now.

"Oh, but you must go after her," his mother exclaimed. "If you love her, you must."

"I don't know where she's gone," he pointed out again. "And I don't know if she wants me still." An image of his wife's face, white with shocked horror and humiliation, flashed through his mind. "What if she no longer loves me?"

"No!"

"Of course she does!"

"You mustn't think that, Hugh!"

He propped his elbows on the desk and rubbed his eyes again. "She knows I lied to her, all those times I called on her, courting her. Could you forgive someone that?" He looked at Edith. "It's not far off what Benwick did to you."

She flushed angrily. "It's not nearly the same."

Hugh hung his head. He had hurt Eliza deeply, which was exactly the same.

For a moment all was silent. Fuzzily Hugh wondered if he had been any better than Reggie Benwick. When he jilted Edith, everyone had agreed he no longer deserved her, and now his sister despised the man she had once believed she loved. And Eliza had thought her exactly right to do so . . .

His mother's hand landed on the nape of his neck, cool and gentle. "Chin up," she said softly. "Face forward." Just what his father used to say. Hugh raised his head. Rose was pale but her expression was determined. "Eliza loves you, dear. It is clear in every word she says, every glance she sends your way. You must give her a chance to forgive you. You must go after her."

"I know. But where?" He inhaled a deep breath. "I suppose I'll start in Chiswick—she might have gone to her friend the Duchess of Ware, or told the duchess where she meant to go."

Someone made a small noise. "Yes, Henrietta?" Rose asked.

"I . . . I might know where," said his sister in a tiny voice.

Hugh was on his feet before she finished speaking, no longer weary. "Where? How do you know, Henrietta?"

She shrank in her chair. "I am not certain—please don't think I knew all this time and simply didn't say—"

"Where?" he barked.

"She spoke very fondly of her school. She said the headmistress was the closest person she had to a mother, and at a time like this—"

"Her school?" Yes—he remembered now, from their picnic . . .

Henrietta nodded. "Mrs. Upton's Academy, in Hertfordshire."

Chapter 31

ELIZA HADN'T KNOWN how she would be received, but Mrs. Upton welcomed her as kindly as she had done over a decade ago, when Eliza walked through the doors of the academy at the age of eight, small for her age, plain, nervous, and very shy. As the years passed, other girls would sometimes whisper that Eliza was only there because her father agreed to make a large donation to the school, that she would never be a real lady. But Mrs. Upton had never treated her any differently than the daughters of dukes and viscounts; in fact, Eliza's determination to become ladylike seemed to endear her to the headmistress, who frequently took time to help Eliza outside of class.

Now the older woman brought her into the spare but elegant office and poured her a cup of tea. She apologized for being obliged to see to her students and teachers, but invited Eliza to make herself comfortable. Eliza was happy to be left alone. She drank her tea and decided to go for a walk, strolling the grounds of the school where she had spent so many years.

It was fortunate the academy wasn't far from Greenwich. Not only had it meant Eliza was able to go home for every holiday, she'd been able to invite her friends. Orphaned Sophie had come every time, and Georgiana had been there almost as often, escaping her dour older brother's home. But here, Eliza had been almost as happy as at home. The lessons were demanding, the teachers strict but kind, and she'd felt such purpose, striving to become a respectable lady like her mother and a source of pride to her father.

Eliza stopped at the fence of the paddock, watching girls half her age carefully guide their horses around the ring, riding habits beautifully arranged, under the keen eye of the etiquette teacher and a pair of grooms. Mrs. Upton believed a lady should be accomplished and able to demonstrate her accomplishments while looking elegant at the same time. The paddock had been built the year Eliza arrived. She rested her hands on the top rail of the fence and wondered if her father had paid for it. He'd wanted so much for her to be a lady. He had insisted she come to this school, which educated and finished aristocratic girls, the daughters of peers and noblemen and diplomats. Yes, she thought, he would have paid anything to secure her admission here.

It made her chest hurt to think of how many things her father must have manipulated in her life. She had loved Mrs. Upton's Academy, so she could forgive him for that, but Hugh—How could her beloved papa have thought it was acceptable to buy her a husband? Her hand curled into a fist as she realized that was the deception that hurt the most. Hugh . . . what choice had he had?

She sighed and walked on, past the gardens where she had first learned how to tend roses and discovered her love of flowers. She knew how fiercely Hugh cared for his mother and sisters. Her father had offered him the means to save them all, and he took it.

But not blindly or callously. *I only did it because I thought there was a chance we would be happy,* he'd said.

Eliza thought of the day they'd spent on Primrose Hill, where he told her he loved her. She wanted so desperately to believe it. But was that true? Was it possible? Could he love her after the way he'd been manipulated? She had fallen for him wildly, passionately . . . but not, she finally admitted, honestly. Her love had sprouted in shallow soil, fed with girlish dreams. She had noticed he never expressed any love for her, but she never asked, almost as if she knew why he didn't.

He had told her he'd been truthful about that much, that he'd never professed to love her when he did not. No—he said he'd not professed it *until* he meant it. Or did he simply want to believe it, too, now that they were wed until death did them part?

After lingering in the garden for quite some time, she returned to the main house. Mrs. Upton met her, cordial and patient, and they returned to the headmistress's office.

She said only that she did not know what to do; that she was at a loss, and needed a place to think. Mrs. Upton didn't press her—to pry would be rude. They talked of other things, trivial things, which had the soothing benefit of distracting Eliza. Gradually, subtly, Mrs. Upton's questions led Eliza into talking of London. Soon she was describing the society events she now attended, which led to mentions of her new family, and finally to her marriage.

"What has made you unhappy, my dear?" asked Mrs. Upton at last. "I assume it was something quite serious for you to come to Kings Langley."

Eliza stirred her tea. How to put it? "Yes, ma'am," she murmured.

"Was it perhaps something your father did?"

She jerked at the perceptive question. "How—how did you know?"

Mrs. Upton made a soft *tsk*. "I always feared Mr. Cross would push you too hard. He was absolutely set upon you becoming a lady. I remember he asked that you be assigned to share a room with the most eligible girl here." She smiled at Eliza's aghast look. "I refused to promise any such thing. It was more important that you be exposed to young ladies who would be good influences but also good friends. I know the world of the *ton* is not always a kind one, but you had such a kind heart. A vain, proud girl would have crushed your spirit." She sipped her own tea. "Your father, though, disagreed with me. He's a very persistent man."

"Yes." Eliza frowned at this evidence that her father had been scheming to manipulate her since she was a child. "You were right to oppose him. Thank you."

The headmistress smiled. "I insisted that I decide the rules of my own academy. I always believed that if I once gave way to a parent's demands, I would eventually be buffeted on all sides by demands from every one of them until I couldn't please any."

Certainly her father would have done that. "How do you stand up to a parent?" she asked. "They must insist on certain things—they are paying the bill, after all . . ."

"But I retain the power to refuse them," Mrs. Upton replied. "And I have." She smiled. "But more frequently I try to hold my ground without denying a girl I wish to admit. I have quite a soft spot for young ladies who have lost their mothers. It is hard enough to be a woman in this world; to do so without a mother is a great pity."

Yes, Eliza knew. She had often wondered how different her father would be if her mother were still alive. "My father interfered in my marriage." She didn't know how else to say it. "I fear it may be an unforgivable action."

"That is grave indeed," concurred Mrs. Upton. "I hope it was not to prevent an abuse by Lord Hastings."

"No! Hastings would *never* do anything like that," Eliza declared.

"But it has caused a rift with him," murmured the older woman perceptively. "Otherwise you would not be here, I think."

"I don't know what to do," Eliza admitted.

"And I cannot tell you," said Mrs. Upton gently. "If I taught you anything in your time here, you know that."

She did. Mrs. Upton wanted her young ladies to be self-assured and capable. It would have been lovely to be handed a solution, but Eliza knew she would have to find that herself. "But what would a lady do?"

Mrs. Upton smiled. "A lady conducts herself with grace and courage. However, every lady is also a woman, with passions and hopes and feelings. Only the woman can decide what her heart wants." She made a delicate motion with one hand. "And then the lady will pursue that, gracefully and courageously."

A knock at the door interrupted, and Mrs. Upton went to answer it. Eliza sipped her tea and thought as the headmistress engaged in a quiet conversation. She knew what her heart wanted—but how could she pursue it? How could she repair her marriage, founded on such a terrible deception, with both grace and courage?

"Lady Hastings," said Mrs. Upton, breaking into her thoughts, "you have visitors. Shall I show them in?"

Eliza froze. "Who is it?"

"I daresay they'll be welcome," said the headmistress with a smile. "You always trusted their advice when you were younger, even when Miss Graham led you into misadventure."

Sophie. Her friends had known where she would go. Her throat tight, Eliza nodded, and a moment later Sophie rushed into the room, Georgiana close on her heels. They flew into each other's arms without a word, and Mrs. Upton quietly slipped out, closing the door behind her.

"I should have guessed you would find me," said Eliza, trying to hide the sudden tears that had sprung into her eyes.

"We would have been here sooner if you'd mentioned it in your letter," said Georgiana. She took out a handkerchief and gave it to Eliza.

Eliza gave a watery laugh, mopping her cheeks. "I didn't even know I would come here until this morning! I've only been here a few hours."

"A few hours we might have been here to support you," said Georgiana pertly.

Eliza laughed again, weaker this time. "I'm astonished you're here at all. Did Lady Sidlow come with you?"

"Bother her," said Georgiana, but with a guilty flush. "I knew she wouldn't approve, so I didn't tell her."

"You ran away?"

"I went right to Sophie." Georgiana shook her head at Eliza's horrified expression. "I've been perfectly well chaperoned ever since."

"Oh no." Eliza looked at Sophie in apology. "And you were rusticating with His Grace—"

"His Grace is downstairs with the coach," Sophie told her. "Enough about us. What happened to you?"

That was Sophie—cut to the key point. Eliza's spirits dropped again, after the sudden delight at her friends' appearance. But . . . how was she to explain? It was too humiliating, too awful, too heartbreaking.

"What did Hastings do?" demanded Georgiana. "Why on earth would you leave him?"

"My father bribed him to court me," Eliza heard herself say. "He pretended to admire me. He made me love him. But he—he didn't feel anything for me."

Georgiana gaped, but Sophie was frowning. "This requires far more explanation. And tea." Ever the practical one, she rang for more tea, and soon they were settled around the tea table. Gradually Eliza managed to get out the whole story. Georgiana's exclamations of outrage and shock spurred her on, as did Sophie's direct questions.

"That's intolerable!" Georgiana flung herself out of her chair when she reached the end.

Sophie shushed her, gaze fixed on Eliza. "Do you love Hastings?"

Eliza flushed in misery. "I do. Desperately." Even after discovering the lies.

"You want to have a happy marriage with him."

"Yes." She'd never wanted anything else.

"Then you must trust him," said Sophie gently. "At least until he proves he's unworthy. Isn't that what you told me?"

"That was different!" Eliza was uncomfortably shocked to hear her own words turned back on her. Before Sophie married her duke, she'd kept many closely guarded secrets from him, uncertain of his affection. Eliza had been sure Ware loved her—who could not fall in love with Sophie, so beautiful and clever and daring?—

but Sophie hadn't been as confident. Eliza had assured her that if she only trusted him with the truth, the duke would love her even more. "The duke was madly in love with you—"

"You thought so," Sophie pointed out, "and I hoped so. But I didn't know until I confided the whole, ugly truth. I thought he might exclaim in disgust and walk out the door without a word, never wanting to see me again."

Eliza sat with her mouth open. That sounded almost like what she'd done to Hugh.

"Sophie, he pretended to love her when he did not!" interjected Georgiana. "Surely that deserves some punishment."

"Did he pretend?" Sophie was watching Eliza. "He told her he never said he loved her until he truly did."

Georgiana waved one hand. "He let her believe!"

I believed it because I wanted it to be true, Eliza thought with a pang.

"The way you let Lady Sidlow believe you're sending Nadine out to buy the gossip papers instead of the latest Minerva Press novel?" Sophie and Georgiana were still arguing.

"She also buys the gossip papers," Georgiana retorted. "I know how to sneak, Sophie. But no one is harmed by a few novels, while Hastings—"

"He didn't break my heart," said Eliza softly. "Hugh is not to blame for that."

That silenced her friends. Sophie and Georgiana exchanged somber glances. They knew she meant her father, who had been almost like a father to both of them.

But Hugh hadn't lied to her. He had held his tongue because he knew the truth would hurt her, but he hadn't deliberately set out to deceive her. Her father had. Hugh felt he had no choice but to call on her—and he only married her because he thought they could be happy together. That suggested that if he'd not thought so, he wouldn't have gone through with proposing and marrying her.

Perhaps she should have thought things through before she stormed out on him.

Even as she began to fear she'd made a terrible mistake, there was a knock on the door, just before Mrs. Upton came in. "I beg your pardon, my ladies, Your Grace, but you have another visitor. Lord Hastings is below, pleading to see you."

Her heart leapt and swelled with longing, and Eliza nodded before she could think better of it.

She could tell from the echo of his footsteps on the uncarpeted stairs that he ran up them. Mrs. Upton had left the door open, and he lurched into the doorway, catching himself with both hands on the frame. "Eliza," he said, his voice throbbing with relief. "Thank God."

"Have you come to grovel, sir?" asked Georgiana coolly.

Eliza flushed. Hugh's eyes never left her. "Yes." His voice was rough, edged with exhaustion.

"Well," began Georgiana, but Sophie cut her off. "Come with me to see how Ware is getting on."

She took hold of Georgiana's arm and pulled her out of the room.

Hugh stepped over the threshold and closed the door. He looked frightful, unshaven and with dark shadows under his eyes. She recognized the clothes he had worn the evening before. "Eliza. Are you . . . Are you well?"

She wanted to run to him and kiss him, comfort him and fuss over him, even after all that had happened. "Yes." She cleared her throat. "You look dreadful."

A faint smile crossed his face. He glanced down at himself. "I should have taken time to shave. Edith said so, but I could not wait."

It pricked her heart. "How did you know to come here?" she asked instead.

"Henrietta." His smile grew a little wider, a little rueful at her start of surprise. "You spoke so fondly of the place to her, and it made me recall our picnic, when you told me about it. You were not at your father's house in Greenwich, so it was worth trying."

"You went to Greenwich?" She tried to ask calmly, but her voice shook. What had Papa told him? What had he said to Papa?

"This morning." He rubbed one hand over his jaw. "Your father and I will never be friendly."

Her stomach knotted.

Hugh looked at her with yearning in his eyes. "He loves you—so much that he has no morals or compunction when it comes to doing what he thinks will make you happy."

Papa had not apologized. "He was wrong," she whispered. "What he did was terrible."

Hugh nodded. "I am well aware. But he said something that almost made me want to forgive him." Eliza tensed. "He said he only wanted me to look at you. That if I knew you, I would see what a treasure you are." He paused. "In that, he was absolutely correct. And while I hate his methods, I cannot hate him for introducing you to me. For my actions after that . . . I take full responsibility. I was wrong to deceive you, no matter what he demanded from me. I was wrong to court you with such calculation." He raised his hands and let them fall. "But I am not sorry I married you."

She wanted to run to him so badly her toes curled inside her shoes from the effort of not moving. "You have my dowry, you know," she said, striving for cold sense and logic. "No one can take it away. You don't have to say anything you don't mean."

His jaw hardened and his eyes flashed dangerously. "Your father coerced me with eighty thousand pounds. I intend to pay him back, every damn farthing of his bloody bribery. He can leave the rest of his fortune to the Foundling Hospital for all I care. I didn't come after you today for money. I *did* fall in love with you, in spite of your father and his schemes, and I don't want to lose you because I was too stupid not to have fallen in love with you the first moment you landed at my feet, wet and dirty from Willy's bath."

Her heart pounded in hope and anxiety. "Is that true?"

"Every word," he said in a low voice. "There is nothing but truth between us now, forever."

Of their own volition her feet started walking. Hugh took two steps and caught her in his arms, clasping her to him. Eliza clung to him, burying her face in his neck, breathing deep of his familiar scent. Had it only been a day? The hours had stretched until it seemed an eternity since they'd gone to the Montgomery ball.

He took a paper from his pocket and pressed it into her hand. "Keep this," he said raggedly. "Keep it until I have repaid all the debts your father bought and held over my head. Then you may give it back to me or rip it up and leave. But please . . . Give me a chance to prove myself to you."

Her heart lodged in her throat as she recognized a copy of their marriage lines.

He tipped up her chin until her gaze met his. "I want you for you, my love. If you no longer want me—"

"I do," she said, blinking back tears.

"Keep this," he repeated, folding his hand over hers, still clutching the record of their marriage. "Until you are sure."

Eliza thought she would always be sure, but she nodded. He rested his forehead against hers and exhaled. "Thank you," he whispered.

She gathered him to her, sliding her hands into his hair, smiling at the way it curled around her fingers. Perhaps he was right. What her father did was inexcusable, but not unforgivable—some day. If Papa could be right about both of them—that Eliza would have hidden at home forever with her garden and her dogs, that Hugh would fall for her if only he got to know her—perhaps she could forgive him.

Not now, when her heart still ached from discovery, but some day. Perhaps.

"I'm glad you came after me," she whispered. His head had come to rest on her shoulder, and she turned her face and pressed a kiss to his cheek. "Thank you."

Hugh's shoulders shook with silent laughter. "If I had been remotely hesitant in doing so, I would have been pursued from London by my furious family. They want you to come back, too—I daresay more than they want me back, after I confessed what I'd done."

She blushed. "No, of course they want you . . ."

"Eliza." He cupped her cheek. "I never told them how badly off my father left us. I thought I was protecting them, but really, I was only lying to them. You, on the other hand, never did. You were your kind, thoughtful, loving, considerate self, and—like me—once they knew you, they loved you." He paused. "Well, not at all the same way that I love you, nor even as much, I'd wager, but they were adamant that I should do everything in my power to persuade you to come home."

The wedding record crinkled between them.

"You've already said everything you needed to say to persuade me," she told him.

His lips curved. "May I say it again?"

She nodded.

"I love you. I love you, I love you, I love you."

By the last time, her lips were forming the words in time with his. Hugh grinned, his dimple showing. "My lady. My beloved wife."

"My beloved lord husband." She went up on her toes and pressed her lips to his. "Take us home."

Epilogue

Fourteen months later
Rosemere House
Cornwall

SUNLIGHT CREPT THROUGH the draperies, stealing up the side of the bed and finally across her face. Eliza wrinkled her nose as the beam roused her from sleep.

"Shh," came Hugh's voice in her ear. His hand came to rest on her hip before stroking slowly up her side. "I was dreaming of a beautiful woman in my bed, and here I find one. My own sleeping beauty."

She smiled without opening her eyes.

"My voluptuous sleeping beauty." He cupped her breast with a low growl of approval.

"I'm not sleeping," she whispered.

"Even better." He kissed the nape of her neck. "I might persuade you to let me have my way with you."

She laughed and twisted in his arms to face him. "I hope you will."

His hands paused; his expression sharpened. "Yes?"

Eliza nodded. It had been a long time since he made love to her properly—too long. Hugh moaned, rolling over her and covering her face with kisses until she laughed again.

A sudden noise made them both freeze. Willy, in his basket by the hearth, raised his head. Eliza looked in concern toward the darkest corner of the room, but Hugh turned her face back to him. "Don't make a sound," he breathed. "Not one sound, Eliza."

"Hugh! No—we can't—oh my—" He put one hand over her mouth to stop her protest. His other hand had got under her nightdress and moved between her legs. She shook her head frantically, even as she spread her legs for him, but Hugh only gave her a wicked smile, and Eliza's eyes rolled back in her head as he touched her in earnest.

He made love to her, hungrily but gently, and in complete silence. Every time Eliza moaned, his mouth was on hers, quieting her when she would have cried out in passion. He made her shake and writhe and rock her hips against his in pleading until he was inside her, hard and just as desperate as she was.

Almost the instant they stopped moving, though, finding ecstasy tight in each other's arms, the fretful sound came from the corner again. Within minutes it turned into a thin wail.

"He's awake," she said between gasps for breath.

"So am I." Her husband moved above her one

more time, his face fierce with satisfaction. "By God—I think I saw the heavenly host."

She raised one brow and touched his dimple. "I didn't realize you were left so unsatisfied these past two months."

Hugh grinned. His hair stood up in rumpled curls around his face, giving him a wild, rakish look. "Unsatisfied? I never said that. But there are levels of satisfaction . . ." She laughed, and he kissed her again.

The thin wail became a steady cry.

Hugh got up from the bed and crossed the room, returning with their six-week-old son in his arms. Eliza sat up against the pillows and reached for the baby, her heart almost bursting with love for both of them. Willy jumped onto the bed and sat protectively beside her, as he always did when she fed Simon, and Eliza silently amended her thought. She adored all three of them.

Later, when the nurse had taken the baby and Willy was outside running in the expansive gardens with Angus, Eliza washed and dressed. She looked through her dressing table drawers for her favorite hair combs as Mary brushed out her hair and pinned it up, and in the process she found a paper, folded and forgotten inside her jewel case.

"You may go, Mary," she told her maid, holding the paper close to her chest. Mary curtsied and left, and Eliza went to the door of the dressing room, where Hugh was finishing dressing. "Hugh," she said. "Come here."

"Whenever you want me, darling." He pushed a pin through his cravat and came to her.

They had been married a year and a half now, and she still found it hard to believe at times. Not only was he even more handsome now, with his hair grown out a bit and some color in his skin from the Cornish sun, but the way he looked at her had only grown more heated and devoted. Even when she was so round with child she could barely waddle across the room, he told her she was beautiful. Once, in the middle of an inexplicable crying fit, she said he must be either blind or in love, and he had only laughed and said it was the latter—madly, deeply in love with his wife.

Eliza had thought she was happy on her wedding day, but this was something else entirely. Not just starry-eyed in love, but certain beyond all doubt that there was no other man in the world for her, and that she was everything he wanted, as well.

Without a word she held out the paper. Puzzled, he unfolded it, and then his startled gaze shot to hers.

"You told me to keep it," she reminded him. "Until I was certain of you." She clasped her hands behind her back to hide their sudden trembling. "I've been certain for a long time, you know."

Slowly Hugh refolded the creased copy of their marriage lines he had given her so many months ago in Mrs. Upton's parlor. "Then why now?"

She smiled, a little guiltily. "Because I know you've been repaying Papa behind my back all this time."

His mouth quirked. She'd been opposed to that plan, saying her father owed it to both of them, and he had pretended to give in to her wishes. "Then you know I intend to repay every farthing of my father's debts."

"Yes. I've been writing to Papa." She paused. It had taken months for her temper to cool enough to write to her father. The first few letters had been brief and spare; her father was a stubborn man, and she hadn't expected him to admit fault readily.

But eventually, gradually, he had. He confessed that he had been wrong, and that he missed her. He told her he was no longer speaking to Robert Grenville and David Southbridge, whom he now realized were untrustworthy and shifty fellows. He acquired a dog, although he insisted it was only temporary. Eliza sensed her father's heart had changed, and when she told him she was expecting a child, his joy had been palpable but humble. He never asked to come see her or the baby, although his hope was clear in every letter.

And he told her Hugh was sending him payments every quarter. At first he had complained of it, and then he simply noted that Hugh was a persistent fellow, and seemed to know his father's debts down to the ha'penny. Eliza had told him to give the money to the Foundling Hospital if he didn't want it, and he had grumbled about that as well, but a fortnight later Eliza received a grateful letter from the director of the Hospital. Her father had donated the money in her name.

Her husband looked at her for a long moment. "You've invited him to visit, haven't you?"

"No," she said. "I would never do that without

speaking to you. But . . . I want to invite him. I want him to see Simon."

He reached for her hand. "Good."

Eliza jolted. "Good? You—you approve?"

"It means you've forgiven him." His smile was rueful. "As I knew you would. Your heart is too kind not to. Of course you should invite him, when you are ready to see him."

"Do you approve?" she asked hesitantly. "Papa was very unfair to you."

Hugh kissed her hand, his lips lingering on her pulse. "Unfair! I got the better of him in the end, for I have you, and now our own little Simon. If he comes to visit I shall probably feel obliged to thank him for it. So it is not my decision to make, but yours. What sort of husband do you think I am?"

"The best," she said. A lump formed in her throat as she smiled into his beloved face. "The only one for me."

"I'm very glad to hear it," he said, pulling her to him. "For I'll never let you go."

Next month, don't miss these exciting
new love stories only from
Avon Books

The Lady Is Daring by Megan Frampton
It was easy for society to overlook the bookish
Lady Ida Howlett. But little did they know that
behind a calm exterior beats the heart of an
adventuress, one who, determined to discover her
runaway sister's whereabouts, steals a carriage
and sets off on a daring mission. Then she
discovers she's not alone! Bennett, Lord Carson,
is inside, and he refuses to leave.

A Notorious Vow by Joanna Shupe
With the fate of her disgraced family resting on her
shoulders, Lady Christina Barclay has arrived in
New York City from London to quickly secure a
wealthy husband. But when her parents settle on an
intolerable suitor, Christina turns to her reclusive
neighbor, a darkly handsome and utterly compelling
inventor, for help.

The Forever Christmas Tree by Sandra Hill
He's got bad-boy looks and a Bah Humbug attitude,
so when the local paper asks the villagers to vote on
the "Biggest Local Grinch" as a fund-raising project,
Ethan Rutledge isn't surprised to hear he's made the
ballot. He might own the local Christmas Tree Farm,
but the holiday hasn't been welcome in his home
since Wendy Patterson left him heartbroken twelve
years ago. But now Wendy's back…

Discover great authors, exclusive offers,
and more at hc.com.

REL 0918